BEYOND *the* HIGHER GROUND

A NOVEL

THOMAS A. BRIGGER

PAGE PUBLISHING, INC.
Conneaut Lake, PA

First originally published by Page Publishing 2019

ISBN 978-1-64544-967-6 (pbk)
ISBN 978-1-64544-968-3 (digital)

Printed in the United States of America

For Ellen

April 2017

S*he's gone, Tuck.*

The words had surfaced as always, heavy and severe, as he awoke to the commotion of landing. Mason suppressed the past once again as he struggled into the aisle and exited the plane, moving quickly to the car rental counter, to the rental lot and out of the airport.

Springtime growth surrounded the highway ahead with budding trees and wildflowers flowing into the magnificence of the Blue Ridge range, conforming to what Google had displayed before he left Trenton. But it was not quite as expected as he drove on from the airport, passing deteriorating mountain burgs that seemed frozen in time that was not their best time and aging businesses that were long past whatever time they flourished in. Homes appeared sporadically, many that were no more than ramshackle structures on pitted lanes, where spent vehicles rusted among the emerging weed growth and the hollow stares of residents emanated from side yards and broken porches. There was a conflict here, a vague dissonance that seemed to underlie the rustic countryside and the isolated and sometimes abandoned industrial plants. The disconnect seemed oddly appropriate, as his charge for being here gradually became secondary to his curiosity, despite Leo's curt description of this part of Wells County,

Virginia, as a desolate lost cause, offering little more than cheap labor in submission to a legacy of desperation, that desperation founded as coal mines were closing and perpetuated by the diminishing offer of employment that the plants held, not in hope but merely as a thin and vulnerable means to survival. Driving on, Mason already sensed that there was more to this place than even Leo was aware of.

The GPS announced the exit to Two Stump Road in a quarter mile, and Mason approached the narrow ramp slowly as it took him onto a poorly maintained pavement that dissolved into a heavily wooded area, then rising to a sharp curve and an unmarked intersection that the GPS proclaimed to be Mills Hollow Road, turn right. The GPS then marked his destination on the right in about one-half mile, but it did not appear as announced. He made a U-turn and drove slowly back, searching in vain for the address in his hand but seeing no structure except a small house on the other side of the road where two men were sitting on a front porch. Regretting his desperation, Mason turned his rental car into the graveled driveway, feeling as if he was about to experience something foreign and bizarre as he got out of the car and walked slowly toward the house. Even without speaking, the two men on the porch before him tacitly confirmed his expectations.

One of the men was young, tall, and broad shouldered with blond hair nesting a filthy cap in thick tufts, wearing jeans thinning at the knees and a faded shirt that was sparse and frayed at the collar. He was muscular and robust in his prime but strangely inanimate, his pale blue eyes shallow and without dimension, as if painted in the soft inset of his face. The other was considerably older, thin, and oddly proportioned, his tiny head burdened by thick glasses and nesting in a cradle of knotty arms as he leaned backward in his chair against the faded wood siding of the house. Mason regarded both men carefully as he walked through the yard, the two of them sitting there with neither motion nor apparent cause as he approached, simply staring at him in the same transparent wonderment that infants display from the arms of tending mothers.

He stopped at the porch steps, a forbidding assembly, cupped and split more from neglect than use—bare wood and traces of gray paint that led to the faded deck in no better state of repair than the straight-backed chairs that the porch sitters occupied. The house was a pathetic clapboard single story with dust-laden windows and mossy black roof, colorless and trivial amid the untrimmed confinement of the tiny yard, about which random bits of debris and old tools lay in various stages of deterioration among the sparse grass and weeds. Behind and to one side of the house was a small shed, dilapidated and unpainted as it seemed to be leaning into itself, the onetime door flat amid the weeds that grew around it, and the wasted hulk of a pickup truck that still had some of its dull white finish showing obstinately through rusted dents and creases. Mason hesitated, feeling vulnerable in the presence of an unyielding culture that, until now, he could only imagine from hearsay and still regarded as something foreign, yet nonetheless imperatively rooted in some undefined commonality with himself. Unable to conceal his uneasiness, he spoke *foolishly*, he thought, his words spilling out haphazardly.

"Good morning. I'm looking for 62 Mills Hollow." Mason waited politely for the response that came only in the form of a slight movement of the older man.

"I've been up and down here. This is Mills Hollow Road, isn't it?" he paused, glancing over his shoulder toward the road and then back toward the two on the porch, who remained silent and unaffected. Mason continued, "I must be close," pause again, no response. "Your mail box is 59 and my GPS says that I have arrived, so I figure I'm missing something."

He waited, having nothing more to say, standing there before the two, the younger one staring at something on the ground beyond Mason's left leg and the older one cocking his head slowly, as if Mason's words were just now reaching his ears, dribbling in from the cool mountain air and reassembling into some form of translated coherence. He (the older one) leaned forward, the front legs of his chair clicking distinctively on the porch deck as he dropped his arms to his lap, his eyes swelling like fishbowls through thick lenses, which gave him a grotesque, almost menacing countenance as his mouth formed to speak, pursing and opening well in advance of any sound.

"That would be Newley's place," he said slowly in a voice dry and worn as the wood about the house and porch. "It's over there."

He nodded beyond Mason, who turned instinctively in the direction of the nod toward a narrow driveway entrance across the road, almost completely obscured by growth and a large locust tree that was severely gashed well into its trunk. "Ain't got no mailbox," the man continued. "Kid whacked it off night afore last when he missed the bend. Durn near killed hisself. Ain't got no sense nohow, that boy. Always bustin' 'round that bend like he takin' a turn at Bristol. I told Jeff"—he turned to the younger man, who still seemed mesmerized by something on the ground—"din't I, Jeff"—the younger man lifted his head as if awakened from sleep but kept his eyes blankly on the lawn—"I told Jeff that boy's going to git hisself killed and there be a blessin' if he don't kill someone else whilst he's at it." He leaned back again, crossing his arms behind his head as before, and he looked away from Mason, his chin lifting slightly as if he were attempting to hear some barely discernible whispering in the breeze that hushed gently about the house and yard.

Mason hesitated again, somewhat taken aback by the abruptness of the conversation. He stood there, awkward and exposed, unsure of the expected protocol. The silence of the moment was unsettling. "Thank you," he said, turning his head toward the entrance across the road. He looked back at the men on the porch, regarding them with a slight raise of his hand and turned to leave. As he walked away, he heard the chair legs click again on the porch deck behind him and the older man's voice, dry and raspy as before, but a little shriller now.

"If ya come to see Newlys, they ain't there."

Mason stopped and turned, again facing the house. The older man continued, now sitting erect in his chair, "Ansel died last fall. Ol' lady gone too. Died in her bed 's what I heerd. So if ya come alookin' fer 'em, they ain't there." He leaned forward again, elbows propped on tiny denim-clad legs, his head tensed as if he were arguing a point in debate. He eyed Mason severely through the distorted depth of his glasses. Mason started to speak, feeling unexpectedly challenged, but the little man went on, his voice rising sharply in the breeze. "Ain't nobody been there since. Nobody livin' there, that is. 'Cep th' feller what owns it now, and he been havin' some folks in and out, what with fixin' it up an' all. But he don't live there. Just comes and goes and them folks he got just comes and goes and don't stay and ain't nobody really livin' there. Not since Ansel and the ol' lady died. So if you ain't one of them fellers what comes and goes and ya come to see Newleys, they ain't there."

The man paused, still leaning forward, his round little mouth poised open, not gaping but stiff-lipped and dark, like a portal from which whatever knowledge he possessed might tumble forth. Mason, now more amused than anything else, looked at him with a vague fascination, as one regards conversation in a foreign language. He hesitated, somewhat in politeness but more so from a sense of diversion and the expectation of more, but the man did not continue, sitting there as if frozen in his position, blinking through the bottled lenses. The wind picked up a little, and Mason could hear the faint drone of a truck on the highway as it shifted and accelerated about the dips and rises in the walled valley beyond, other sounds discretely and subtly emerging in the constancy of the breeze: birds, a shuffling sound in the trees behind the house, a dog barking in the distance.

Then the older man spoke again, with the same abruptness as before, as if he had been silenced and reenergized by some mechanical switch, the little mouth moving in advance of words like a puppet out of sync with its holder. "Be a pity, though. Nurse found 'em when she come to tend the ol' lady. Found Ansel there in the front yard, dead as a rock and been there for days, and the ol' lady dead in her bed. Be a pity, don't it? Ansel and the ol' lady dead and nobody knowin', not even me an' Jeff, here, nobody knowin' but that they be gettin' along and doin' what they done and that nurse hadn't been there, so a different one come later and found them both dead." He shook his head, moving it independently of his body, which remained stiffly positioned in the chair. "Be a pity, don't it?"

Mason stood patiently as the man spoke, still amused by the unsolicited bit of local gossip, conflicted by the self-generated urgency of his appointment, and an emerging desire to encourage more of the man's hearsay, having developed in his rather transitory adult life a keen and sometimes compulsive interest in the colloquial history of his surroundings. Nevertheless, he had a full schedule and realized his need to move on. Still attempting to extract himself politely, he acknowledged the information, carefully avoiding any encouragement to continue. "That's a shame," he responded. "Actually, I didn't know them. I'm here to meet a Mr. Wellman about renting the house—"

"Ain't there," the older man interrupted, with such abruptness that Mason instinctively took a half-step back, a movement that he immediately regretted as an obvious loss of control in strange company. He desperately attempted to regain his composure and extricate himself from the man's prattling.

"I…beg your pardon."

"Ain't there yet. Not Cletus Wellman, not nobody. Ain't nobody been there all day. Been somebody there we'd a seen 'em. And we ain't seein' nuthin' yet, are we, Jeff?" He turned to his younger companion, who still had not moved or changed his gaze or acknowledged Mason before him on the lawn but sat there, lumpish and dumb, his dull countenance slightly affected by the inclusion. The older man continued, "Reckon if Cletus set to meetcha, he'd be along presently. Reckon you set there awaitin' fer 'im, he'd be along." He lifted his chin, twisting his neck as he spoke. "You can set here iffen you want."

Mason smiled at the proposition of remaining and overcame the temptation to accept the offer, turning his head slightly. "Thanks, but I think I'll go on over and have a look around." He turned to walk away but stopped in favor of an obligatory sense of courtesy, turning back toward the two on the porch. "In case we end up as neighbors, I'm Tucker Mason." He considered stepping forward to offer a handshake but decided not to, sensing an invasive element in his presence that would make such a gesture somewhat violating and pretentious. There was another excruciating lack of response from the porch and the awkwardness of his position on the lawn suddenly seemed unbearable. But the little man spoke again before Mason could walk away.

"Cecil Beckman." His tone was more in the form of an address than an introduction. "Dis here's Jeff." He leaned back in the chair and crossed his arms on his chest, his chin lowered. Observing the obvious disconnect, Mason waved his hand awkwardly, mumbling, "Pleased to meet you," and walked away, desperately attempting to conceal his relief to escape as he opened the door of the idling car. As he backed the car out of the driveway, he glanced at the porch and its two occupants who sat with the same rigid disassociation as when he had found them, motionless and unaffected, like background props on an empty stage.

Gravel and dried mud crunched under the wheels of the car as Mason turned slowly into the drive across the road. To the left were the scarred locust tree and the path of stripped vegetation and churned earth where the kid had taken out the mailbox and apparently rolled his car into the ditch that ran parallel to the road. The remains of the mailbox itself were partially visible under a crushed bush in the bank of the ditch—trashed and fragmented bits of gray metal pressed into the earth like shredded paper. The drive was rutted and unpaved, twisting severely and banked into the slope of Mills Hollow Road, which dropped abruptly and curled down a steep hill into a darkly wooded vale, with a few apparently abandoned structures that either hid behind the trees or, like Cecil Beckman's, sat obtusely near the road. Mason proceeded carefully, wishing he had his Jeep instead of the rented Buick, which bounced and slid about the narrow cut that neither terminated nor continued but simply faded into a sparsely graveled lot in the yard around Ansel Newley's former residence.

The house appeared suddenly, emerging in a clearing of the dense woods amid an acre or more of recently trimmed lawn, a moderately sized single-story structure of white frame and matching trim with a disproportionate covered front porch that ran the full width. The house and porch were freshly painted and showed evidence of minor repairs. A small outbuilding, larger than a storage shed or garage but too small to be called a barn, was situated to the right and in front of the house partially enclosing the lot. The yard itself was randomly interspersed with budding forsythia and various shrubs, mostly unattended and showing the wooded heaviness of old plantings, in base kinship with the forest beyond that encircled the place with a kind of walled confinement. Mason opened the car door and got out, casually looking around as he strolled up to the porch, where he sat on a white iron chair that had not been recently painted but showed evidence of harsh cleaning and still bore scrub marks on its flat surfaces.

The place in general held a primitive sense of revival, and the layers of white paint and new rails on the porch and cheap new hardware on the front door were a kind of temporary rescue from the ruinous state of so many of the houses (Cecil Beckman's included) that Mason had passed driving in from the airport that morning. The restoration was not extensive, being more of a rude conformance to the home that it once was—someone named Ansel Newley's home that he shared with his wife and where he probably raised children and had the fleeting pleasures of life sifting through its very boards until that moment, as chronicled by Cecil Beckman, when Ansel and his wife passed on, and the walls were painted to obscure whatever thriving they contained and promulgated for how many years—walls covered like Ansel in his grave, his corpse covered with earth, and his legacy with white paint. It was the sense of renewal that attracted Mason to the place, the neat cleansing of mortality and fitness for his presence, the memories that he did not share now to be obscured and scrubbed clean as the chair he was sitting on.

If Leo was right, Mason thought, this was probably as good as it would get. Leo, sitting back in his chair in the Trenton office, rubbing his hand through the sparse patch of red hair on his freckled forehead, had said that he would be best to find a place to rent and stay out of the motels because there wouldn't be much to do, and the motels are hardly habitable for more than a night or two. "Besides, it's cheaper in the long run," Leo had said. "You're going to live there for more than a year, Tuck, and you won't find anything like what you had in Denver, so I'd recommend that you rent yourself a house somewhere near the site. You shouldn't have any trouble finding one, but you may have to work at finding a decent one. In all honesty, we didn't see much when we were down there." "We," referring to Leo himself and whoever from Estimating had been to Wells County to check out the site and bid the prison project and then again to finalize the contract details in a crowded meeting room at the airport, when Mike Beal was there, and it was to be his job. But Mike had to beg out shortly after the project commenced, his wife drawing the line at eighteen months in Southwestern Virginia. He sat there in the conference room in Trenton, offering, "Sure, Tuck can handle it," and everyone knowing full well that, despite his successes, Mason had no prison-building experience but also knowing that the alternative could land duty building a prison in Wells County, Virginia, that could be regarded as a kind of sentence in itself and, in Mike's case, a means to divorce. So they all endorsed Mason's capability to build the prison, though Tom Doenitz was skeptical, looking to Leo across the table with obvious concern without so much as a sideways glance at Mason or even peripheral notice of his presence, and Leo, ever confident in his intrinsic necessity to his employer, sitting back, nodding slightly, almost defiantly, the challenge being laid upon not one of his own, not Mason nor any other subordinated project manager in the employment of Doenitz Building Company whom Leo had either trained or retrained but on Leo himself. The decision was made then between Leo and Tom, having little to do with Mason's capability or experience (or lack of it) or mere breathing presence in the room to accept the job while the others quietly bated, their eyes trained to the table. Mason was then handed forth, the decision being made with no more affectation than Tom Doenitz's brief glare at Leo and Leo claiming unspoken once again the rights to competency, all in a moment, all in the instant of an agenda check-off in a weekly meeting of the project team. But despite his trepidation about the assignment or his quiet resentment of Leo's arrogant pandering of his services, despite the droll, unfitting circumstance of Wells County and the overwhelming unbuilt prison, Mason felt a welcoming sense of renewal, sitting there on that porch in the now warming morning breeze.

A renewal was appropriate; renewal in the sense of this house, which was not really renewal but a covering of white paint over old boards that, beneath the white coating, were no better than the waste of Cecil Beckman's rotting abode, perhaps not really renewal but a covering of the past, obscuring the loss like the change of scenery might obscure Katherine. And Katherine, not forgotten but also covered over, still there under the whitewash, hidden and revealed only in the fleeting interjections of his thoughts. Mason would call it a renewal, a reassembling of pieces to an image that might resemble its former presence but reformed for its current purpose: the wreck of Ansel Newley's home and the painful, heartbreaking loss of Katherine covered over and trimmed neatly for a beginning away from all things past. Appropriate, Mason thought, sitting there in that old iron chair, with its layers of worn enamel scrubbed clean, the place being fitted well and secluded, not in Denver, not in Maryland or Ohio or any other place he had lived, appropriate for renewal in the freshness of spring, so he could breathe out the lingering past and live to whatever end there was beyond Wells County, Virginia, and its Low Creek Maximum Security Prison, the prison itself being representative of newness and initiation. He leaned back, comfortable perhaps for the first time since he had left Denver, warmly regarding this place as a suitable home for the time being (home being such a relative issue in his life) so much so that the gray Suburban creeping around the bend and into the lot already seemed a violation of his privacy.

Cletus Wellman climbed out of his car slowly in a series of short mechanical movements that revealed some painful process in his exit, which was further accentuated by the tentative stiffness of his form as he walked, carefully measuring each step as he proceeded toward the porch. He was a small colorless man with a rather clerical presence and pervading fastidiousness that affected his uneasy motion. His thinning hair was brushed neatly back over a pale scalp, and he had a plainness about the face and wash-and-wear white shirt and ill-fitting trousers and hairless arms that dangled in sparse definition from his short sleeves like appendages on a toy that could be removed and interchanged. He could easily be taken for a back-office subordinate, except for the incongruous sense of purpose that he bore as he rigidly and painstakingly placed one foot in front of the other as one would walk barefoot over rough ground. Mason watched him casually, questioning in his mind whether the man would actually make it to the porch or seize up altogether and fall over like a statue off its base, brittle and teetering as it toppled to the grass. Eventually arriving at the porch, he reached out his right hand toward Mason, the other steadying his meticulous ascent of the porch steps.

"Mr. Mason," he breathed, gasping slightly, "Cletus Wellman." Mason instinctively took the man's hand and shook it. "Apologies for making you wait, sir. You been here long?"

"No. Just a few minutes."

"Well, sorry anyway." He was fumbling with a large ring of keys that he had held close to his body as he approached the porch. "I been running behind today, and to beat it all, I got it in the back." He looked up at Mason from the keys. "Spasms. Get 'em ever so often." He grabbed one of the keys, holding it between his thumb and forefinger as the others dropped noisily on the ring below it. "Come on in, and I'll show you around."

As he worked the key into the front door, Wellman looked back at Mason, pausing as he spoke, "Wife says you come to build the prison." Mason had spoken with Mrs. Wellman when he called the number on a scrap piece of paper that Casey had passed to him in Trenton the week before. "How long you figure you'd stay?" Wellman continued. The door opened with a slight creak.

"About a year and a half, if the schedule holds."

"Like the other guy from your company, McAfee, isn't it?"

"Yeah, Casey McAfee. He told me you rented him a house near Kingsport."

"Yep, rented several places out to prison builders." Wellman still had his hand on the door knob. "Year and a half. Is that a long time to build a prison?"

"Not really. It's a big facility, fourteen hundred cells. Actually, it's—"

"No matter," Wellman interrupted as he entered the house. "Don't know much about prisons and don't need to start learning now."

Mason listened distantly as Wellman took him quickly from room to room and showed him about the sparse inside of the house with an urgency that would normally have been annoying had Mason not already made his decision about the house by its exterior, considering its position and location more important than the new floor in the kitchen or the proximate convenience of the three tiny bedrooms and renovated single bath, all of which had been meticulously cleaned and recently painted. He followed Wellman as he stepped outside from the back door onto a small but intricately built wooden deck, then into the yard, where Wellman pointed to the new Cavitette that was buried near the tree line. Wellman had talked continuously as he moved about the rooms, describing them as if he were reading from a script, Mason nodding and commenting politely but not too much so as to initiate further conversation or contemplative delay that would keep Wellman there any longer than necessary by the courtesy due. The tour ended at the structure adjacent to the house that Wellman referred to as the shop. "I lost the key to it, but if you think you might want to use it, I can get a new key made. Oh, by the way, we had a security system installed because of some break-ins while we were doing the renovations. Figured it was someone looking to steal tools or such. Nothing was stolen, but we left the system in place and will continue to pay for the service. That can give you some peace of mind although I don't think you would have much to worry about on this mountain." He looked up at Mason. "So what do you think?"

Mason looked back at the house and then at Wellman, sensing that Wellman's urgency was borne of the pain in his back and was not his usual business demeanor. He had no intention of keeping the man any longer than necessary in his discomfort, quickly addressing the rent issues that Wellman, with beads of sweat now appearing on his forehead, rattled at eight hundred and no lawn service, you pay your own utilities, and Mason requesting a written quote for approval of the home office, indicating an e-mail address on his business card. Then Wellman proceeded back to his car in painful short steps that Mason closely matched as he accompanied the man across the lot. "It's a nice place," he said, "close to the prison site and the highway. Seems like it's in fairly good shape."

"Took a lot of fix up. Only had one owner, though, the man who built it originally."

"Really." Mason remembered his conversation with Cecil Beckman. "I understand he died here last year."

Wellman hesitated slightly, turning his head toward Mason with a strange, inquisitive look. Mason continued, realizing Wellman's apparent surprise at his knowledge of such information. "I spoke with a man across the road, and he told me that the former owner had died last year."

Wellman opened the car door, carefully pulling it past his body as he smiled painfully at Mason. "Oh, you met Cecil. Like an old washwoman, isn't he?" He gripped the door and began to slide back first onto the seat.

Mason shrugged. "I don't know. He seemed okay. Appears to know a lot about what's going on around here."

"Talks a lot. Hard to know when you can believe him." Wellman grabbed his pants as he drew his legs into the car. "He's harmless though. Give him a beer, and he'll pass bull to you all night if you can stand it. Crazy old bird."

"What about the owner?" Mason's curiosity seemed impulsive even to himself.

Wellman looked at Mason, briefly studying his face before answering. "Died right here in the middle of the lot. Poor guy." He started the car and now appeared to be quite agitated. "Call me as soon as you get your approval. I need you to fill out an application too so we know who it is we got living here. I'll send one to you. Pleasure meeting you, Mr. Mason, but I got another appointment. You're welcome to stay if you want to look around awhile." The door thumped shut, and the Suburban backed up slowly, turning in the lot and rocking about the rutted driveway as it disappeared around the bend. Mason looked at his watch and realized that he was late for a meeting at the prison site. As he got into the rental car, he looked around once more, satisfied with the place and his attitude in general, taking in the quaintness and simplicity of the house and lot and the thick wall of Appalachian forest that surrounded it with oak and hickory and heavy brush. The brush, however, was slightly disturbing for reasons not immediate but revealing afterward as he drove forward—a movement and fading glimpse of color occurring to him after its passing, his eye catching and losing something in the foliage that faded and disappeared as he drove on, and he realized only as he pulled out onto the road and saw Cecil Beckman sitting alone on his porch that it was Jeff, standing partially behind an oak tree and watching from the cover of a thicket near the drive.

B right's Mountain was indistinguishable from its neighboring peaks to anyone except the local residents of Wells County before the state of Virginia designated it as the site for a maximum security prison. The selection of this site had been mildly debated, some considering this location as a concessionary response to the objections of wealthier districts while others viewed the construction of a prison towering over the area as a continuance of the gradual degradation of Appalachian heritage. But to the residents of nearby Low Creek and its immediate neighbors, any facility that might offer a means to a government paycheck for some of the one quarter of its population who were unemployed or underemployed was welcome. So the site was approved with little need for active campaigning in the legislature, and Bright's Mountain was prepared to receive its holdings by having its crest removed and top leveled, and its scarred revelation could now be identified easily from aircraft at thirty thousand feet and passersby on the four-lane highway that traversed this corner of Southwestern Virginia.

Preparation of the prison building site was accomplished by drilling into the peak and setting off explosives deep underground, which caused the steeply sloping hillside to crumble in vertical sections that fell in thick plumes of dust, leaving piles of rock and dirt that were then shoved over the side of the mountain until a sizable notch was carved out with a rigidly flat surface for the building pads and an imposing shear wall of rock constituting its eastern boundary. The remaining exposures of the site were defined by a panoramic view of the Low Creek Valley and surrounding mountains, which seemed more suited for a tourist attraction than the benefit of what the Virginia Department of Corrections considered the worst of its incarcerated population.

Mason approached the site with the usual apprehension that accompanies new assignments, driving slowly on the dirt and gravel access road that twisted a half mile uphill from Mills Hollow Road, cautiously considering not the construction itself but the untamed condition that seemed to envelop it, the construction vulnerable and foreign in this endless swell of earth known as Appalachia to outsiders but as universe to those who claimed no ownership except by heritage of location and who submitted to it naturally. The road turned into the north side of the site and faded into a myriad of rutted and fading tracks, spreading like a river delta into the sea of dirt and activity about the building pads. The site had no order beyond its expectation, as the inherent symmetry of the intended buildings was not yet fully achieved and was now restricted to the emerging pads and the Doenitz office trailer, the latter being situated at the termination of the road in a controlling position over anyone entering the area, as well as making a suitable check-in station for the subcontractors who would queue their respective trailers alongside it, eventually creating a neat row of similar structures with wooden porches that would line up symmetrically like urban row houses overlooking the valley and facing the eventual prison structure. The trailer gave Mason an encouraging sense of stability as he parked in front of it, noting its double-wide familiarity and the requisite "Doenitz Building Company" sign and logo and Casey beside it, emerging from the ubiquitous backdrop of dust and rock in the glare of the late morning sun.

Casey McAfee had been assigned as superintendent earlier but now could be Leo's hedge against the risk of his untested project manager. Mike Beal had said, "Sure, Tuck can handle it," and all agreed, but Leo was well aware of the capabilities of his subordinates, and despite Mason's experience in building large structures, he had never built a prison. Leo's confidence in Mason was borne of his own ability to develop competency, and that ability, sacrosanct in the company and imperative to the provision of his employment, was far too vital for the hazard of Mason's unsupported presence. So Casey could balance the default, and Leo's brilliance would be sustained, and Mason's exposure redeemed. Mason knew Casey well, having initially been delivered by Leo to his tutelage in Maryland after two years in the home office in Trenton; the journeyman sojourn to the field that was mandatory for all aspiring Doenitz project managers, where Casey or other veterans like him would reveal the actuality of the business, taking trainees in the father-like fashion that Leo had promulgated in the home office, such that if Leo was indeed the Father of Form then Casey was the Father of Function, giving substance to the instruction gained. "Like boot camp in the army," Leo had called it, referring to Mason's seven months in subordination to the man whom he would eventually rise above by design in the company hierarchy. Mason's respect for Casey preceded his position, and he was both relieved and anxious as Casey greeted him.

After a brief walk-down of the site, Casey led Mason to the trailer, which was the usual Doenitz specification with dusty cheap wood paneling and worn vinyl tile floor that bore muddy streaks made undoubtedly by some begrudging laborer's mop in preparation for Mason's visit. The offices were as yet unfurnished except for one in the rear, which Mason would eventually claim as his own, where there were two battered steel folding chairs and an old steel desk upon which Casey unrolled blueprints and discussed the intricacies of the project with Mason, describing details in his caustic firmness of voice that resounded years of communicating in the chaotic environment of his work. Mason listened earnestly as Casey spoke, offering his acknowledgment with forced concentration, though the spectacular view through a rear window of the mountains beyond occasionally stole his attention, causing Casey to look up over the rim of his half glasses with a riveting glare and "are you with me, Tuck?" and Mason, embarrassed, would return to the matter at hand like a chastened schoolboy.

It was half past noon when Casey finally leaned back in his chair, holding his glasses with one hand and slapping the table with the other. "Damn," he said, his voice reverberating against the thin walls of the trailer, "it's past lunch time already. C'mon, let's go eat." He stood up and excused himself into the tiny restroom, still talking to Mason through the door. "Where are you staying tonight, Tuck?"

"I'm not. Leo wants me in Trenton tomorrow to meet with the architect. I'll be back next week for good, though."

Casey came out of the restroom, wiping his hands with a paper towel. "I guess that's okay." He opened the door, peering out at the site and rubbing his chin with his thumb. "Pads are in good shape." He motioned for Mason to follow him as he walked out. "Mike did a good job on the preconstruction stuff, but I'll need you here next week, boss. Make sure that fat ass Leo doesn't hang on to you any longer than that."

"I'll be here," Mason answered as he followed.

When they exited the trailer, Mason noticed that the left front tire on his rental car was flat. Casey motioned to a laborer who was spreading gravel nearby and instructed him to change it, his voice transcendent over the sound of earth-moving equipment and the continuous crumbling of the mountaintop. The laborer caught the keys from Mason and was opening the trunk of the rental as they climbed into Casey's pickup and drove down the severely curving access road toward Low Creek. The stringency of Casey's disposition seemed to soften as they drove away from the site, and he seemed to become more personable as they progressed down the hill, mellowing gradually as if his demeanor at the site was reserved solely for the rigors that toughened experienced builders to the mien of their environment. It was a quality that Mason admired greatly in Casey; the inherent ability to match his intensity to the necessity of circumstance and leave the rigid demands of his responsibilities at the jobsite, giving him a depth of character rarely demonstrated by his peers. As they approached the second turn Casey asked Mason, "Did you get ahold of Cletus?"

Mason answered, "Yeah. I met him this morning. He's got a nice little place for me just down the road."

Casey downshifted as the road became steeper. He looked hard at Mason, though still without the severity of his jobsite persona. "What the hell do you want to live there for?" He rubbed his hand across the short thickness of hair on his scalp. "Look, Cletus has some apartments in Kingsport near my place. A lot of the subs are moving in there too. Shoot, Tuck, you don't want to live out here all by yourself."

Mason withheld his annoyance at the comment, and he started to say that it was Leo's recommendation but caught himself. "I know. Mrs. Wellman told me about the apartments when I called. But that's forty minutes either way. I'd rather be a little closer to work."

The pickup lurched a bit as Casey shifted and turned onto Two Stump Road and the highway in the direction of the Low Creek business district. He shook his head slightly. "Well, suit yourself, boss. I don't know why Cletus showed you that place anyway. Just the same, it seems to me like you'll be awful lonesome out here."

The word "lonesome" seemed to have an unusual brutality, unusual because despite the fact that so much of Mason's life had been spent alone, he had seldom considered the impact of loneliness until recently. His mind wandered off with it as Casey turned a corner into the Low Creek business district.

"Here it is, Tuck, beautiful downtown Low Creek," Casey said as the heart of Low Creek commerce and government emerged around him, four blocks of worn-out buildings in frame and old brick, none more than three-stories high, some empty, some partially in use for whatever minor business they housed amid crumbling streets and sidewalks that were noticeably unattended, plain houses with neatly trimmed yards, a church with rust streaks running down its yellowing white steeple, flanked by a bank and gas station; a quaint, regressive assembly that seemed to exist for no reason other than its precedent need in the relative prosperity of times past. Mason stared through the window of Casey's truck, still contemplating loneliness as Katherine entered his thoughts, her essence dissolving as he helplessly longed for her presence, the buildings fading into a soft blur as his attention turned inward.

"C'mon, Tuck."

Mason blinked as he realized that the pickup had stopped, and Casey was climbing out. He got himself out and Casey was saying something about the food here as he walked ahead through a dusty storefront with a painted sign that said HARLEY'S RESTAURANT. Mason followed sheepishly, embarrassed by his obvious daydreaming, into a plain but impeccably clean dining room with a buffet line set up along two exterior walls and a dozen or so tables in the center. The tables were occupied mostly by construction workers from the prison and the local regulars, all regarding each other in colloquial rituals and noisy conversation among themselves so that the place had the atmosphere more of a family gathering than a restaurant. Mason and Casey took their food from the line and sat down at a table near the front, where a waitress approached them with two plastic water glasses and paper napkins as Casey bantered with others in the room. The waitress was thin, easily in her late seventies or more, her white dress hanging in haphazard pleats that scarcely concealed the frailty of her body, gray hair pulled back to reveal the ravages of time and exposure about her face and blue-framed glasses that seemed oppressive on the thin ridge of her nose. Casey took her hand and pulled her to him. He winked at Mason as he spoke. "Ya still love me, darlin'?"

The waitress laughed with a low cackling sound that was perhaps the vestige of a giggle from some time ago, the tight creases of her face drawing together as she stiffly tossed her head back. She placed her hand on Casey's shoulder, looking down at him through her thick glasses. "You's my man" came slowly from the thin line of her lips in a static monotone that bespoke her years.

He released her hand, and she blushed as she smoothed her apron. "Verna Lee, this is Tucker," Casey said as he arranged his plate on the table. "Now you treat him good because he's going to be my boss from now on."

Verna Lee touched Mason's arm. "Nice to meetcha, Mr. Tucker. We'll take good care o' ya. You settin' up in Kingsport like my man here?"

"No, ma'am, I'm staying near the prison in Wells County."

She lifted Mason's glass and wiped the table beneath it with a damp cloth. "Where 'bouts?"

"On Mills Hollow Road."

Verna Lee stopped, holding the cloth away from her as she spoke. "Ain't many houses there to take from. Y'ain't movin' to Newley's house, are ya?"

"Yes, ma'am. Well, I haven't rented it yet, but I intend to. Do you know the house?"

She wrapped the cloth around her hand and held the ends tightly, so the thin and mottled skin turned white around mildly arthritic knuckles. A sudden darkness seemed to come about her face as the smile left it entirely. Her already-weakened voice was even lower and somewhat strained when she spoke again, and Mason had to lean slightly toward her to hear beyond the noise in the room. "I knowed Thelma and Ansel just real good, honey," she paused briefly, looking at Mason with a restrained sadness in her eyes, which were red-rimmed and translucent behind the lenses, and then continued in the same feeble tone. "Whatch ya wantin' to live there for?" Briefly forcing the smile back to reveal the gaps among her damaged teeth, she touched Casey. "Y'oughta move in to Kingsport like my feller here." Casey looked up from his pulled pork and beans, and Verna Lee patted him on the shoulder, looking away from Mason but not necessarily at Casey. "You best tell your boss that that mountain ain't no place for folks what don't come from here." She turned to walk away, disregarding Mason entirely as she shook her head, her voice trailing behind her. "Ain't no place 't all. You boys be good now, y'hear?"

Mason looked at Casey. "Did I say something wrong?"

"They're a strange bunch, Tuck, but good people," Casey answered as he broke a piece of bread. "I guess it'll take some time to get to know them. This corn bread is outstanding."

Mason watched Verna Lee disappear through a metal-clad doorway into the kitchen. "I don't know. She seemed kind of pissed off, didn't she?"

"She's old. Who the hell's Thelma and Andrew?"

"Ansel. They were the people who used to live in the house I'm renting."

"Cletus tell you that?"

"No. I heard it from one of the neighbors out there. An old guy across the street gave me the whole low-down. Actually, I don't think this place is nearly as bad as Leo made it out to be."

Casey peered over his half-glasses and shrugged. He wiped his mouth with his napkin, seeming uncomfortable and apprehensive, as if he were struggling to remember a rehearsed line. Looking at Mason, he spoke in the slow, obligatory tone of a visitor at the funeral for someone he didn't know. "Tuck, ah, about your wife. I'm real sorry..."

Katherine's face passed in Mason's mind, and he felt her presence briefly, as if a door had opened to reveal her and quickly closed, her appearance fading behind it. After what seemed a long time, he answered quietly, "Thanks, Casey."

"Well," Casey said, raising his hands above the table, "we all felt real bad, you know. I was in Puerto Rico on Tommy Doenitz's goddamn hotel job and couldn't make it to the funeral. We sent flowers." He was obviously trying to find a way out of the awkwardness caused by the reference. "It's gotta be tough, Tuck. Maybe the change here will do you some good."

"Sure," Mason said as he tried in vain to regain his composure. He could feel a tightening in his throat as he spoke. The ensuing silence was unbearable. Casey's face grew serious, and he was obviously searching for some redemption as he sat back in his chair.

"You ought to consider staying in Kingsport with us, Tuck. Just think about it."

"I'll think about it." Mason looked across the room, avoiding Casey's eyes and harboring a growing resentment for the man's persistence about his living accommodations.

They finished lunch, and as they returned to the jobsite, Mason noticed with some amusement how Casey's manner seemed to gradually harden again as they neared the top of the mountain. Casey checked his watch as they entered the office trailer. "What time's your flight, Tuck?"

Mason pulled an itinerary from his shirt pocket. "Five seventeen."

Casey took his hard hat from the table and began to roll up the plans that they had been working with before lunch. "You probably ought to get on then. Sometimes there's traffic in Kingsport, and you need time to get rid of that rental car. You know how to get back to the airport, okay?"

"Same way I came in, I guess." Mason realized that Casey was anxious to have him out of his way. He began to pack his backpack as

Casey stepped out of the trailer, the thin door slamming shut behind him. Mason followed a few minutes later and found Casey with the laborer who had been assigned to replace the flat tire on the rental. They were standing near the open trunk of the car, which looked strangely incapacitated with the narrow temporary spare mounted on the left front wheel. The laborer was pointing at something inside the trunk, talking in the animated fashion of someone trying to prove a point as Casey stood in obvious disagreement, shaking his head and grinning under the brim of his hard hat with his hands on his hips. Mason approached them and looked into the trunk, where the flat tire lay with the short stub of a pencil stuck into a small hole in the sidewall.

Casey turned to Mason. "Cabby thinks someone shot your tire, Tuck." He looked at Cabby and turned back to Mason, still grinning in what appeared to Mason as condescension toward the laborer. "You didn't piss off one of the locals on your way up here, did you?"

Mason, feeling an obligation to dignify Cabby's sincerity, addressed him directly. "What makes you think that, Cabby?"

Cabby pointed at the inserted pencil stub but addressed Casey with his reply. "Ain't no way I never seen a tire get flat wid a hole like 'at in the side. Hit'sa bullet hole, boss, shor's hell."

Casey backed Cabby away with his hand and slammed the trunk deck, looking at Mason with his eyes rolling upward. Cabby protested as he was dismissed but stepped away immediately when a piercing glare from Casey signaled the unequivocal termination of the conversation. He walked away muttering, "Ain't no goddamn rebar" and disappeared into the activity on the building pads. Casey stepped around to the driver's side of the car, opening the door. He spoke with his face close to Mason as Mason obligingly entered the car. "Excavators cut and bent up some rebar for markers when they built the access road. You probably hit one just right, and it popped up and stuck your tire. Damn Cabby watches too much television." He stood back and gave a short wave with his hand. "Have a good trip, Tuck. Tell Leo you got to be here next week."

The car door was closed before Mason could speak, and he felt a bit compromised as Casey walked away in the direction of the building pads, the dust swirling about him and another piece of the mountain crumbling in a heap beyond him as he faded from Mason's view. Mason drove slowly down the access road, casually scanning the compacted dirt and gravel for pieces of rebar or anything else that might have caused his tire to go flat, but he saw nothing, taking little concern for Cabby's theory or, for that matter, any cause for the puncture because flat tires on construction sites were as common as the debris that caused them and were usually accepted as a minor hazard of the business. He turned right onto Two Stump Road and proceeded to the highway, suppressing an urge to pass it and continue on Mills Hollow Road and have another look at the house there, admitting to himself that his decision not to go had nothing to do with a lack of time but was more of a self-consciousness before Cecil Beckman's porch vigil and Jeff's apparent interest from the woods.

The highway was sparsely occupied by local traffic and the occasional eighteen wheelers that strained and downshifted on the rises and dips as the road rolled and twisted through the valley, parallel to a creek called Bents Run. The stream flowed well below the elevation of the pavement, making it visible only occasionally to passing vehicles as it carved its way through the valley, which in some places was so narrow as to only allow space for the highway and creek and wide enough in others to accommodate a random hamlet or the incongruous symmetry of an industrial plant. The mountains that defined the valley rose sheer and forbidding at the narrow passages, creating an imposing walled presence above the road and then opening gradually into less severe slopes where the houses of varying size and condition appeared subtly, scant and haphazard among the trees and rocks and spring foliage that lent a natural fullness to the place. There was a strange presence about the homes, a profound sense of containment that pervaded the occupied residences and abandoned structures. Mason drove forward with the same feeling of conflict that he had experienced driving in from the airport that morning, wondering to himself why he felt drawn to Wells County while still sensing some trepidation, that perhaps leaving Denver was never quite a reality until he actually arrived elsewhere and his establishment here, however temporary, might give release to the former, as one foot stepping forward signals release of the other following, moving on and the painful loss behind—Katherine behind him now and just the shadowing memories creeping into his thoughts, hovering like apparitions in a dense fog. He drove on absently, the scenery passing as if he might be standing still, driving more by instinct than purpose as his thoughts wandered, and he caught himself in the reverie with the same private embarrassment that he had experienced with Casey earlier, noting with concern his tendency to daydream of late as something imposing and superseding his distraction caused adrenaline to rise at the moment of its sighting in the rearview mirror. Green and rusty gray, it filled the mirror before hitting the rear bumper of the rental car with a muffled crunching sound. Mason rebounded from the headrest and accelerated enough at a bend in the road to catch in the mirror the profile of an old and battered flatbed truck with wooden side gates. It was gaining on him again as a semi ahead struggled on a rise, so close that Mason had to brake hard and then accelerate to pass, though not enough as the flatbed hit again, this time from such an angle as to cause the rental to spin, barely missing the rear of the semi as it skidded sideways briefly, Mason righting it too late as it slid to the shoulder at the crest of the hill and the steep incline that took the car in its momentum; trees, grass, rocks, and water appearing in rapid succession amid the thump and crush of steel and glass, recurring and diminishing in harsh impact as motion suspended with the senses, and all was dissipated into a shattering prevalence of darkness.

III

Katherine passed like a shadow in the mist that collected about him, close but beyond his reach, passing quickly so that it was more the trailing draft of her presence that he noticed as it dispersed near him like a single breath. He spoke wistfully into the mist, *So this is how it is.*

And there was Denver, when he had stumbled senseless and unfeeling about the process due, the occurrence of life and death being as one without the reality—the reality being in his possession then but packaged and set aside to remain sealed and unaffected as he numbly plodded about. But it had not been real yet. The denial was immediate and unbroken as he put the cell phone back into his pocket and proceeded as if drawn forward without motivation, his car moving by its own intent and purpose as it accelerated and stopped and accelerated again and released him to the hospital parking lot where he again was drawn, his feet not his own but borrowed for the denial as they carried him and he possessing neither resistance nor inducement but acquiescing to the moment that was not real— not yet, not even when he saw Jack's face, broken and grave in the helplessness of a father's loss, and Helen, pathetic and small as she quivered in the singular pain of severance that only mothers know, her head buried in Jack's chest and Jack looking up with his father's eyes and his father's pain and the want of strength that will curse a father forever in his grief, the words not real to Mason until he had heard them echoing in countless nights and screaming at one sunrise after another until the reality would quiet them with its own subtle and encompassing truth, the words not just words but the manifestation of the hopeless ruin in that father's face, *She's gone, Tuck.*

And it was not yet real. Not in the sober faces of those who then moved graceless and desperate about a room and collected in the doorways, standing in small groups, whispering and nodding in the dim hush as they each in turn segregated to regard Jack and Helen and even himself with a restrained formality that scarcely concealed their bewilderment of the inevitable truth—that truth evidenced by the dark casket amid the flowered softness in a corner of the room, but it was not real, not for anyone there because it was only time and this place that gave it cause and time had its limits, and they would leave this place, relieved and redeemed as they breathed the fresh evening air, alive again and the place behind them in its stifling and menacing admonition of the truth they would not have, not them nor Jack nor Helen nor himself, not then, not yet. He saw them shift about, titled by Helen's low commentary as they approached as relatives and friends and neighbors and those who knew Jack and Katherine's friends from school, and then it was his turn when Leo arrived, Leo's weighty, sympathetic presence preceding the small group of laborers who shuffled in through the door, moving in such close cadence that they stumbled among themselves, ribald and austere in their borrowed suits and blazers, neckties askew and loose beneath unbuttoned collars on thick necks that turned and stretched like sunning reptiles as they stood pathetic and sad before the casket. He saw them and loved them for their dutiful presence, and he loved Helen at that moment for she was moved in the way that Katherine would have been moved, and she went to them as Katherine would have gone to them, shaking each rough and gentle hand and smiling as only she and Katherine could when it was not real, and they could leave it behind them, all of them anesthetized by the occasion as they then stood again, now in the dewy grass with the sun bright on their shoulders amid the languid apathy of trees and polished stones and innocent of the reality that was and would be as they turned away, their heads bowed, unmindful of the loss that was lowered and covered with earth and revered solemnly behind them as they slowly walked to their cars. And he was left alone, unfeeling and provisional, still drawn beyond the reality, the denial leaving him weightless and gullible in the unknowing comfort of the autumn breeze.

So it was. Not the reality but the callused rebuttal of the truth, knowing but refusing to own that which is no less than a birthright; full payment was yet due as he lay alone and woke alone and remained for days and nights suspended in time, the time slipping about him like water flowing, cleansing gradually the feigned innocence of denial until he sat up as if pulled, and he could feel her presence in the bed, and her scent was everywhere he touched but not her; she was not there. And it was there, suddenly bursting its seal like a dam bursting from a single fissure in its wall, and it was all around him in a smothering inundation as he ran into the night, exploded into the night, and it left him totally and justly with himself as he expelled the denial in the shuddering, gasping trade of innocence and echoed that stark, eternal revelation of man's consequential retribution for living, Jack's voice cold and unrequited statement about him in the rock stillness of that night, *She's gone, Tuck.*

So this is how it is, he spoke into the fog, *this is how it is*. The numbness having ceased and the reality now resident so that the father's words would fade into their eternal reverberation of the universe, never ceasing but adding to that distant wailing of the inevitable blight of man's being, and there was only Katherine now, in the face of a woman at the airport, a voice in a crowd, the delicate turn of a hand or toss of hair or posture or walk or any brief reminder of what was once her so that a thousand women would all possess some part of those attributes that, if assembled, could be Katherine but not Katherine as they surrounded him, taunting him to believe and in Katherine herself, soft and ethereal as she brushed him with her interminable presence. He spoke, suspended in the fog like a balloon drifting aimlessly in a cloud, unseen and unheard, perhaps not even speaking but merely assembling the thought and resolving to himself, that resolution hollow and without substance so he would need to repeat it over and over again, *so this is how it is, so this is how it is.*

31

Voices emerged nearby, not suddenly but augmenting gradually in the obstinacy of his consciousness, rising indistinguishable at first as one and then separating into two until he recognized Leo's deep drone and Casey's impatient staccato as the two parried somewhere in the grayness. He could hear their solemn tones, speaking to one another nearby in some indefinable proximity wherein the speakers were oblivious to his presence. He struggled for their notice against the unsettling restraint of something familiar yet disturbing in the fog; another voice, solitary and distant, separate from the others as if behind an unseen partition, speaking indiscernibly in constant tenor, subtly revealing its owner by inflection alone as Mason vainly strained to hear, and he could tell by inflection alone that it was Katherine, her words spilling about him indiscriminately with no more meaning than the incidence of her presence elsewhere in the dream. He resisted as the others pulled him from her, extracted him from her imminence in the mist to the actuality of her loss, and she was gone when he awakened.

He saw Casey first, sitting back, fingers laced behind the leathered neck and elbows pressing forward as if in some sort of restraint. As Casey spoke his lips seemed to move out of sync with his words. "Hey, Dopey, you come to join the living for a while?"

Mason blinked instinctively, and the room seemed to move about him as his eyelids dropped and raised heavily like trap doors. The room seemed changed from the night before, when he had lain there, painfully disoriented in the darkness, the pale yellow light in the hallway flowing about the night-shift nurses who slid quietly past the door. Sunlight now trickled from a window that he had not noticed before, and the room seemed to grow as he slowly came around, conscious and aware but still unsteady from the sleeping and dulled by the drugs that numbed his pain. He turned toward Leo who was leaning toward him on the bed. Leo's voice was full and mellow, and it seemed to fill the room as he spoke. "How're you doin' there, buddy. You feeling all right?"

Mason twisted against the brace that held his left arm and shoulder snugly to his side. There was a tightness in his throat as he attempted to speak, and he immediately withdrew the effort, his attention drawing fully to the cup of water that Leo held out to him. The water was cool on his lips, but he found it difficult to swallow, taking small sips as the cup tipped slightly in Leo's patient hand. Eventually, he found his free arm and sluggishly waved the cup away as Leo receded a bit, and Casey reappeared in a corner near the window, which was now streaming with sunlight. Mason tried again to speak, this time succeeding weakly as his breath escaped around his words. "Damn, how long have I been sleeping?"

Leo shrugged, his face bunching in ample folds. "I don't know. Casey just picked me up at the airport. We've only been here about twenty minutes or so. I expect you've been sleeping for some time."

A nurse appeared suddenly beside the bed and said something to Mason as she took his wrist, timing his pulse with her watch as Leo retreated clumsily and stood against the wall where Casey was still leaning back in his chair, the two of them silent and awkward as the nurse busied herself with Mason's chart and adjusted his bed. She was a small woman, not particularly friendly but displaying a rather detached sense of caring as she took his blood pressure and propped the pillow behind him. "Dr. Klees will be in shortly," she said as she smoothed his sheet and collected some things from the tray beside him. "I'll have some breakfast brought up if you feel like eating yet." She disappeared before Mason could respond.

Casey's voice broke the ensuing silence. "Tell you what, Tuck. Why don't we go get some coffee while you get yourself together?" He was standing now, stiff and nervously shifting from one foot to the other, and Mason could see that he was extremely uncomfortable with the environment of the hospital.

Leo leaned over the bed again. "Anything we can get you, buddy?" His enormous hand was clamped around Mason's free arm. "We'll be back after the doctor sees you." He turned and followed Casey and Mason could hear them talking quietly to each other as they left.

Mason dropped back to the pillow as the events of the previous day and night began to collect in his recollection like photographs spread out of sequence: the cold lighting in the X-ray room, pale and sterile above the voice *turn this way and hold—can you do that?...* He had lain on a bed, and the curtain was pulled back. *I'm Dr. Klees... It's badly dislocated, and there is a small linear fracture along the collarbone...but there appears to be no permanent damage... that knee will be sore for a while...just the same. I want to keep you overnight to make sure.*

He had lain sideways in the car for what seemed a long time; it was strangely silent, almost serene, and he was heavy, so heavy that his body felt as if it would collapse from its own weight piled against the door...darkness and shards of light emerging...voices... *Hang in there, fella, don't try to move. We're gonna gitcha out. Just stay quiet, and we'll cutcha loose...* The sky was blue above him as they moved him, blue and so incredibly close that he might reach up and touch it... the sirens seemed distant and intermittent...

"Good morning, Mr. Mason." Dr. Klees stood by the bed with a clipboard held flat against his chest. He was a young man, possibly younger than Mason, tall and thin, his white coat hanging stiffly from his shoulders as he spoke. "How are you feeling today?"

"Like I was in a car wreck." Mason's throat seemed strained when he spoke.

Dr. Klees pursed his lips a bit and looked at the clipboard. "I see you're still a little hoarse. You should probably try to get up and move around a little. Take it easy, though, you've had a lot of pain medication. Dr. Mayhew will be in later to look at your shoulder and knee. If everything's okay, there should be no reason you can't go home today."

"I was headed to New Jersey," Mason said, his voice a little stronger now but still difficult.

"Is that home? Turn your head." Dr. Klees pressed his fingers against the soft tissue of Mason's throat. "Does that hurt?"

"Yeah, a little. For the time being, it's home."

The doctor pulled a cell phone from his pocket and read it as he spoke. "I'm not real keen on you traveling right away. You're banged up pretty good, and you will be in a fair amount of pain." He looked up from the phone. "The concussion wasn't severe, but any blow to the head is serious. I'd like to see a CAT scan before you do much of anything." He placed the phone back into his pocket. "Is there anyone here whom you can stay with for a few days?"

Casey had reentered the room as the doctor was talking, and he stood by the window as he spoke. "We got him covered, doc." He turned toward Mason, the discomfort of his presence still obvious in his face, and his voice was loud and forced. "Tuck, you're going to bunk up with me for a few days. Leo says you got nothing to go home to in Trenton except a one-bedroom apartment in some half-assed complex. Hell, I've got plenty of space, and besides, I can keep you up to speed on the job while you're healing."

Mason was not pleased with the thought of spending time in someone else's home, and he suddenly felt helpless and vulnerable, an exposure that was particularly distasteful in front of Casey. He struggled to sit up, pushing against the bed with his free arm. "I need to get back to Trenton. All my stuff is there, and I need my car," Mason said, pressing desperately for his independence.

"You'll get there in time, Tuck." Casey was now facing the window with his hands on his hips, his voice beginning to carry the harshness that it maintained at the jobsite. "Meantime, you just hang out at my place till you can travel, and then you can get your stuff." He continued to stare at something outside the window. "We got it all set up, so you just get yourself right, okay?"

Dr. Klees wrote something on his clipboard. "That being the case, you can go any time you're ready, provided Dr. Mayhew doesn't have any problem with it. I'll leave some information with your discharge package. I'm going to give you something for pain, and I want to make an appointment with my office the day after tomorrow. We can also schedule a CAT scan and some other tests." He shook Mason's hand and left the room, his stiff white coat swinging on his thin frame as he walked out.

Mason wanted to argue with Casey, but he had no valid rebuttal, feeling somewhat compromised by the situation. The pain in his shoulder was returning severely, and he suddenly felt extremely exhausted. He pushed himself up a little more on the bed with his free arm. "Where's Leo?" he asked.

Casey tossed his head toward the door. "On the phone."

"I wish he hadn't come."

"Oh, you know Mother Leo." Casey turned from the window and faced Mason, his voice a little quieter as he began to pace about. "You want to get dressed, Tuck? I don't think that's going to be an easy task, all trussed up like you are, but I'll help you if you want." He opened the narrow cabinet on the wall near the door. "Your clothes are in here."

"I probably ought to wait for the orthopedic guy to come," Mason said, the resignation in his voice apparent even to himself. He held up the end of the hospital gown and flicked it back.

Leo stuck his head through the door and motioned to Casey who rolled his eyes at Mason and followed Leo into the hall. Mason lay his head back on the pillow, feeling spent and distressed, and dozed off briefly before the nurse returned with a tray containing his breakfast. He nibbled at the food and drank some orange juice, eventually pushing the tray to the side as he dozed off again. The orthopedic specialist who had treated him the night before, Dr. Mayhew, visited him and examined his shoulder and knee, discussing his injuries as if they were body damage to a car. The movement of the examination was painful, and Mason was sore and troubled as he lay alone in the hospital room for what seemed a long time, dozing and waking intermittently as the pain medicine that the nurse had given him after Dr. Mayhew left took effect. Casey and Leo did not return.

Eventually, an orderly arrived and helped him dress, carefully and patiently loosening the binding of his left arm and slipping his shirt over the wounded shoulder then bunching the pants over his ankles and up his legs in the same fashion, following with shoes and socks and the light jacket sleeved only on the free arm. The orderly then produced a wheelchair from the hall and held his good arm as he sat heavily in the leather strap seat with his left leg propped in front. They proceeded down the hall, past other rooms with their bedridden occupants to an elevator and then to the cashier's desk near the hospital lobby where a woman helped him with his paperwork and discharge instructions. Casey was waiting at the hospital entrance next to his pickup truck, where Leo sat in the cab holding his eternal cell phone to his ear, his large shoulder pressed against the window. Mason was wondering how in the world he was going ever fit on the seat next to Leo's immense frame when a woman climbed out of a late model Cadillac that had pulled up behind the truck. She was blond and attractive in blue jeans and a crisp white blouse that was seductively unbuttoned at the top. Mason watched her curiously as she waved to Casey.

Casey and the orderly helped Mason into the Cadillac, carefully avoiding pressure to his left side, and then Casey leaned through the open door as the woman climbed back in on the driver's side. "Tuck, Mrs. Wellman is going to take you to my place and get you set up while I run Fat Boy up to the site," Casey said. He grinned, tapping Mason with the back of his hand. "See what you've done here? You get some time off, and I get stuck with Leo in my face." He nodded toward the woman. "Thanks, Sally. I owe you one. I'll catch you later, Tuck." He slammed the door and walked quickly toward the pickup but stopped midway and returned to the car, tapping on the window, which Mason opened with his free hand.

"By the way, Tuck," Casey said, "a state trooper was hanging around the emergency room last night looking to get a statement from you, but you were too far out of it. That truck that ran you off the road was stolen. It belongs to a guy we had delivering straw bales to the site for silt checks. He was down in the swale by the access road when whoever ran up on you stole his truck in broad daylight. Figure that. Anyway, whoever hit you took off, on foot I guess, and left the truck half sunk in Bents Creek about a hundred yards from your rental car. So the police and that poor guy who owns the truck would like to find him."

Mason wanted to know more about the accident, but the pain and discomfort of his condition limited him to a shallow nod of his head as he looked pathetically up at Casey.

"Anyway," Casey continued, "I expect the police will still want to talk to you. Sally, take this boy home and put him to bed. We'll be back a little later if I don't throw Big-Ass off the mountain."

They drove slowly through the hospital parking lot, and Sally introduced herself, and he acknowledged her politely but said little, feeling somewhat exhausted and distracted by pain and embarrassed by a disturbing sense of helplessness. Sally, however, continued, talking constantly as they proceeded out of the parking lot and onto the main highway, Casey's pickup truck turning in the opposite direction with Leo still jammed against the door, his cell phone tight against his cheek.

Sally was an amiable woman, loquacious and engaging, with soft brown compassionate eyes and a natural easiness that Mason found comforting despite the awkwardness of his situation. She rambled on about her two sons, one a banker in Lexington and the other graduating from the University of Tennessee, and that she lived in Kingsport and managed the Holiday Inn Express there, which Cletus owned with some partners, and helped Cletus with some of his investment properties. Mason realized that she was apparently married to the same Cletus Wellman whom he had met the previous day and was the same woman he had talked to on the phone when he had called to inquire about the rental properties. He found it rather difficult and even amusing to place this woman in the company of that diminutive man with the bad back, but he had seen stranger matches in the past and dismissed it without further consideration.

Sally continued, her voice melodious and flowing, "Cletus has a lot of property, you know. He's got apartment buildings and houses all around but mostly in Kingsport and Johnson City. He's also in a partnership with some men in an industrial park and some office buildings near the airport and, of course, the Bright's Mountain property. He also has a Chevy dealership on the highway just outside of Low Creek. That's his home base, though. Sellin' cars is still his first love."

"Sounds like a busy man," Mason offered for no other reason than politeness.

"Oh, Cletus is always busy. Twenty-four hours a day. Walks around with a cell phone stuck to his head. Kinda like your boss I met this morning. Mr. Holcomb?"

"You met Leo?"

"Well, kinda. He shook my hand while he was on the phone. He's a lot like Cletus."

"What about you?" Despite his distractions, Mason was now enjoying the conversation, the content being incidental to Sally's almost childlike colloquialism and the strangely appealing sound of her voice.

She turned toward him and smiled. "What about me?"

"You sound pretty busy yourself."

Sally giggled. "Honey, you make sure you talk like that in front of Cletus, will ya."

"Well, I would think the hotel alone would take up a lot of time."

"Oh, it does. I spend most of my time there, matter of fact." Then, touching his leg lightly with her finger tips, she said in a lower voice, "But I got plenty of help, sugar, so I usually can get away when I need to. So if you're trying to make a point that this is taking me away from my work, it ain't the case."

Kingsport, Tennessee, appeared gradually before them, an orderly metropolis integrating modern architecture with the preservation of Southern charm and dominated by the enormous Eastman Chemical facility that occupied the west side of the road for several miles. The town itself was typical of many of the Southern and Midwestern towns that Mason had visited, with a neatly arranged public square lined by oak trees and benches and a bronze monument in the center, town hall and a high school and then a downtown section with department stores and specialty shops along the wide sidewalks and diagonal on-street parking spaces and converted gas streetlamps, restaurants with handwritten specials displayed in the windows, then houses, neatly arranged in brick and siding and painted wood trim—well-kept homes with small front lawns close to the street and narrow walks leading to porch stoops and painted front doors. Walmart and a state police facility were at the far end of the populated area. Sally turned off the main drag onto a narrow two-lane road that led up a steep hill, at the top of which stood a rather new two-story colonial house with an enormous front lawn that was defined by a white rail fence and a long drive lined by shade trees. The house was clearly the largest in the area, and it seemed a little out of place among the smaller and older Kingsport residences.

"That's where me and Cletus live," she said, pointing at the house but keeping her eyes on the road, which twisted on the top of the hill and then proceeded into a residential area consisting of a small apartment complex and about twenty single homes and duplexes.

Sally pulled into a blacktop driveway in front of one of the duplexes. "This here's Casey's place," she said as she pulled on the emergency brake. "Marty lives next door. Do you know Marty?"

Mason shook his head slightly, the pain in his shoulder prohibiting much movement. "No, ma'am, I don't think I do."

"Well, he does something at that prison you boys are building. I'm sure you'll be meetin' him soon." She got out of the car and walked around to Mason's side, gently helping him out. "We got a bunch of you boys here," she continued as she slowly walked Mason to the front door, stopping to point across the street. "Over there's four in that other duplex and then across the street's three more in that little house there with the blue shutters. Then there's a bunch more in the apartments. Ol' Cletus was sure glad to see you guys come to town. Durn nearly rented out everything he's got."

The drive from the hospital had caused Mason's knee to stiffen, and his shoulder was throbbing incessantly. He was extremely fatigued and found it embarrassingly difficult to maintain his composure. Sally walked him through the front door of the duplex and helped him to a green recliner in the small living room. "You set here a second, dear, while I get your bed ready. Oh, by the way, I got your pain pills here in my purse. Casey gave 'em to me at the hospital. You need to take these?" She held a small brown bottle that she had extracted from her purse and squinted at the label before putting on a pair of reading glasses that she fished from a side pocket of the purse. "It says here that you are supposed to take these every four hours for pain." She looked over the top of her glasses at Mason. "Honey, by the looks o' you, I'd say you was about due." She left the room and returned with two of the pills and a glass of water. Mason took the pills and handed the glass back to her, and she disappeared into the kitchen. "You want something to eat, Tucker?" she called from the kitchen. "I can fix you something if you're hungry."

"No, ma'am. Thank you. I'm really not hungry at all."

"You gotta quit callin' me ma'am, sweetie. I ain't your mama."

Mason smiled. "Okay, Sally. Listen, I'll be fine here. I really appreciate your help, but there's no need to—"

"Oh, hush, you," Sally interrupted as she walked from the kitchen to another part of the house. "I'll go in good time. Casey's got this place done just like a man would. Ain't never seen a man yet who knew how to set a home. It just ain't in 'em." Mason could hear her move about as she spoke. "I expect you'll be needin' to eat something eventually, Tucker. To get your strength back. God knows what Casey's gonna have around here to feed you."

A drawer opened and shut somewhere in another room, and Sally returned to the living room. Her hair had loosened a bit in the front and fell over one eye, causing her to seem a little disheveled as she brushed it back. She helped him out of the chair, her hands gently wrapped around his free arm, and he could feel her close to him as she walked him into a bedroom, a tiny space with an iron twin bed frame that was pulled down to reveal clean white sheets and two sparse pillows propped against the wall. The only other furniture in the room was an old nightstand next to the bed and a dresser with severe scratches on one side. The single window was covered by steel blinds that were separated and broken in places. Mason removed his shoes with Sally's help and climbed onto the bed. Sally stood looking at him with her hands on her hips. "You sure don't look in much comfort there, honey, but it'll have to do ya for now," she said. "I don't know why they don't just let you stay at that hospital for another day or two." She turned to the window and held the frayed cord for the blinds in her hand. "I don't think I can do you much good with this window either. If I could, I'd catch you some fresh air. Cletus needs to get this fixed, and I'm gonna tell him so."

"You've done plenty, Sally," Mason said as he adjusted his position on the bed. "Really, I'm quite comfortable here."

Sally left the room briefly and returned with her purse and a torn envelope that had a Holiday Inn Express imprint in the corner. She sat down on the edge of the bed and shuffled through the purse until she found a pen and then wrote some numbers on the envelope. "This here's where you can reach me if you need anything.

That's the motel I run. I'd give you my cell phone number, but I let the battery run down. Now you don't get bashful, y'hear. Anything you need." She dropped the pen back into the purse and leaned forward, her brown eyes quiet and appealing as she looked at Mason and smiled. "Tucker, I know you ain't feelin' too good about all this. You're a friend of Casey's, and he's a friend of mine, and we all help our friends around here. Just like that." Her voice was soft and had a genuine, irresistible sweetness about it as she touched him lightly on the chest. "Casey says you was run off the road. That's a fine howdy for folks comin' to visit, ain't it now?" she said as she stood up, still close enough for Mason to sense her warmth and femininity and the trace of perfume about her hair. "I ain't far away, so you just call. I got some work that needs tendin', or I'd stick around a bit. Anyway, I expect Casey will be back before too long."

Mason thanked her weakly as she walked out. The pain in his shoulder was less intense but still there as he lay rigid and uncomfortable in the old bed frame that he figured Casey picked up at some garage sale so he could have an extra flop if needed for someone visiting the prison site. He looked at the broken window blind, the light fading behind it as the afternoon expired, the entire day seeming like another dream that he would awaken from to find himself in the relative comfort of the hospital, anonymous amid the hallways and patient rooms and beds and the unending process of healing. He fell asleep quickly, sleeping soundly for an interminable amount of time in the stillness of the room, without dreaming, without Katherine, without thought as his mind simply took its respite.

It was nearly dark when Casey and Leo returned. Mason felt considerably better when he awoke, though his shoulder continued to hurt, and he was suddenly hungry. Casey made a simple dinner served with cold beer. They ate at a small table in the kitchen, discussing the prison project in detail, Leo and Casey dominating the conversation, and Mason respectively acquiescing in favor of the food, speaking only when addressed and listening attentively to the discussion. After dinner, Mason and Leo moved to the living room while Casey cleaned up the dishes, Mason following Casey's direction to the recliner, and Leo to the sofa which took his fullness as he sat. The conversation continued over coffee and then beer again, remaining largely with the prison but occasionally diverting to anecdotes about others in the company and mild barbs between Leo and Casey. They were interrupted by a knock at the front door, which opened immediately before Casey could get to it, and Sally walked in, carrying two large shopping bags.

"It's just me, boys. Get decent now. There's a lady in the house," Sally said as she set one bag on the floor and took the other into the kitchen.

Casey seemed unfazed by her entrance. "Get yourself a beer, kid, and sit down a while."

"Thank you, dear," she called from the kitchen. "I got some things for the patient." She came into the living room with a bottle of beer in her hand and sat on the arm of the sofa next to Leo, tucking her bare feet into the cushion. "I brought you some clothes, sweetie, since you didn't have a bag with you," she said to Mason as she waved off Leo's offer of space on the sofa next to him. She pointed to the bags on the floor. "I figured you're about the same size as my boy at college, so I brought you some of his stuff. I also stopped at Walmart and got you some socks and underwear. I had to guess at your size, but I bet I'm close. I raised two boys, ya know, so I'm pretty good at sizing men's shorts."

Mason was embarrassed by her efforts and insisted on reimbursing her for the items she bought, but she refused with a rather staged glare. "Don't be silly, you. It's just socks and underwear from the Walmart. The socks was on sale anyway," she said, rolling her eyes at Casey and then back to Tucker. "You ain't beholden, dear."

"Just let me pay for the socks and underwear, and I'll feel a lot better," Mason persisted.

"No, sir," she returned in the same exaggerated tone. "Now you just behave and drink your beer." She leaned forward, speaking in a lower tone but still teasing. "But if it'll make you feel better, I'll holler next time I need panties and socks."

Sally winked at Casey and looked back at Mason. "I got you a razor too. We don't want that sweet face to get all bristly now, do we?"

Mason could do nothing more than accept Sally's consideration as gracefully as possible. She stayed for a short time longer, drinking her beer and talking constantly as she teased Casey and Mason and regarded Leo with a relative sense of distance. "Well, boys, I'd like to stay and shoot the bull with you some more, but I gotta get home before Cletus thinks I run off." She left as abruptly as she entered, calling over her shoulder as she walked out the door, "I'll come check on you tomorrow, sweetie. It's been a pleasure, Mr. Holcomb." The door closed loudly behind her.

After a few minutes, Leo stood up and said, "Well, I'm ready to hit the sack." He looked at Casey as he gathered his briefcase and some rolled plans that he had brought back from the jobsite. "Can I get a cab or something?"

Casey laughed. "Damn, Leo, this ain't New York, for crissake." He looked at Mason and shook his head.

Leo smiled, unaffected as he looked down at Casey who was sitting on one of the kitchen chairs with his feet hooked into a rung below him. "Then you can haul me back to the motel."

They left after Casey helped Mason remove his arm from the sleeve in the brace. Mason took some more of his pain medicine, washed down with the last of the beer he had been nursing all evening, and climbed onto his bed. The bedroom was totally dark now as he closed his eyes, trying desperately to put the last two days into some sort of order and perspective as Katherine crossed his thoughts like a distant star in the darkness. He struggled to recall the details as he lay there, painful and worn on the bed frame, revisiting in his mind the flatbed truck appearing in his rearview mirror and his first sense of awareness when he came to in the overturned car and the hospital and Sally driving him to Casey's duplex. But there was something still not surfacing as he reviewed the sequence of events, something that kept bringing him back to the rental car, wrecked and sideways in Bents Creek, the paramedics talking through the space where the windshield had been—*Hang on there, fella, don't try to move.* No, before that. Something else that seemed padded and obscure in his memory, occurring in the first emergence of his senses amid the glass and the deflated air bag and the heaviness of his body as he lay crumpled against the car door, something there, indifferent and subtle beyond immediate recollection but potently critical and foreboding in the murky semiconscious moment when he awakened. He lay on the bed with his eyes open in the darkness, pressing his memory in a futile query of its deepest recesses as he drifted off to sleep, almost sleeping when the lost remembrance found him coldly and suddenly so that he sat up in the darkness with its overwhelming revelation: there was another—before the sirens and the voices, there was another, breathing heavily and bearded, sideways where the windshield had been... *You...kin you hear me? You don't come back, y'hear. You don't never come back here agin...*

The Jeep bounced from a pothole on the ramp to the Pennsylvania Turnpike, causing its load to shift, and Mason adjusted the rearview mirror to make sure nothing had come loose from where it had been packed by the two laborers that Leo had sent over. It had only taken them a half hour to load the few possessions that he had with him in the little one-room furnished apartment that he had rented when he had arrived from Denver last fall. The laborers had arrived at seven thirty, and by eight fifteen, the assistant manager from the complex had made her inspection. The apartment was still as he had left it three weeks ago to spend a single day in Virginia—a small, dimly lit confinement that he was glad to leave behind now in favor of the house he had rented from Cletus Wellman on Bright's Mountain. He had climbed stiffly behind the wheel of his Jeep, steering mostly with his right hand as the left arm was still quite useless beneath the healing shoulder. The radio was turned on so low he could barely hear it, and he drove quietly, Trenton quickly disappearing behind him as the dew steamed from the rooftops, and the road shined silvery ahead in the morning sun that was rising behind him. There was a dull aching in his shoulder, and the knee was still stiff, the bruise now just a faint yellowing of the skin where it was yet sensitive to touch, but he felt good otherwise. He drove on, absently regarding the Philadelphia suburbs, thoughtless and unfeeling at first as he proceeded without much concern for the eight-hour trip ahead, the hum of the road and the indiscernible sound of the radio distantly lulling him into a kind of peaceful state that he found somewhat comforting though brief as he rolled into the Pennsylvania countryside.

The past three weeks gradually began to enter his thoughts, isolated in his mind like a chronological footnote, the time extracted and served as if in parallel to the expected progression of his charge in Virginia. The events were now before him, sequenced in order for his review in an unappealing reflection that would serve no purpose except to violate his resolve, a futile obstruction to the hopefulness that he had so desperately been trying to attain. He turned the radio up and tried to dispel his recollection, but it was there nonetheless, unavoidable and poignant as he again recalled the flatbed truck in his mirror, the hospital, Casey's rented duplex, and Sally. Wonderful, comic, brilliantly annoying Sally. He could write off the entire ordeal as one of those unexpected inconveniences of life that, all in all, could have been much worse—much worse had it not been for Sally, and he began to realize that it was her pressing on his mind, the circumstance of her presence simply a vehicle for her entry, the wrecked rental car and injuries, and the time spent merely a base for her incidence. It was all there before him as he proceeded along the turnpike in the late April morning, obstinately governing his thoughts, not in the sense of things that had occurred but in the context of Sally, and it was Sally who seemed to guide him through the recollection and Sally who determined the sequence and Sally who persisted in his mind like a revelation.

She always appeared suddenly and left with such abruptness that her presence seemed to remain like an echo of her commotion, talking incessantly in her sweet, melodious way as she drove him to the doctor's office and the physical therapist or made his bed in the morning or had coffee with him, walking in uninvited but imminently welcome, never hurried but always in motion, she and Mason talking sometimes for an hour or more in Casey's kitchen, patient and colloquial as she chatted about her sons or the Holiday Inn or (to Mason's amusement) told stories of her childhood on Cade's Mountain. He found, to his own private embarrassment, that he missed her when he started going to the site with Casey on the mornings that he did not have to go to the therapist. On a Friday night, she sat and drank beer with them when he and Casey and some of the others from the prison site collected in Casey's living room telling stories, and she told her stories and addressed everyone there in her inimitable way that made you feel a special closeness to her. "Now, Marty," she said to Cavalone, standing behind him and massaging his shoulders, "let's not be judgmental. My mama always said if you don't have nothin' good to say about someone, you're best to say nothin' at all. Honey, in your case, that might mean a lot of quiet time." She kept working Marty's shoulders as she spoke. "How's that feel, darlin'? You know, the other night, Cletus came home crabbin' about his partners in the industrial park, and I did the same thing for him. It shut him up for several hours. Short of a hot bath it was the most relaxin' thing I could have done for myself." Mason smiled as he recalled it, all of them laughing in Casey's living room. Even Cavalone. That was Sally and Mason regretted the fact that he would see less of her now that he was getting back on track.

He had forgotten how much he enjoyed the presence of a woman. Since Katherine's passing, his engagement with the opposite sex had been limited to the perfunctory incidence of everyday life, perhaps largely by circumstance, but he admitted to himself, there was probably more to it—the latent, encompassing fear that what was taken once could be taken again, that the pain and the emptiness and the ever-present sense of loss could be repeated, that the anguish and heaviness of doubt could double in its intensity and crush the fragile spark of reconstitution that he clung to so tenuously. The risk was too great, the resolve too feeble, and Katherine's death still apparent like an open wound that had only begun to heal, scarring in thin layers as he cautiously moved on. But Sally provided a safe bridge; easily ten years his senior and contentedly married, she innocently rekindled the feminine experience without the abysmal hazard of a relationship that could evolve into the kind of singularity that he and Katherine shared, only to be shattered and dismembered by the insidious notice of fate. Sally was for everyone, Cletus's wife and confidant of the masses, capable of restoring the primordial senses with her touch and her smile and infinite female candor, yet so unavailable for the sweet and lethal consummation that Mason could admire her as one admires a painting, privately owning only that which the eye will accept and the mind will perceive in the image of the beholder but without the ardent passion of the painter, thereby leaving all the better for the experience, unaffected and sheltered by the insular void of dimension. He could love her, he told himself, as they all loved her, and she could love him as she loved them all, and there was no risk at the moment, for it would always end as it began. He would keep it that way and never reach beyond the laughter and never look beyond the softness of her eyes or probe beyond the humor of her stories or ask beyond the conversation that was offered, and Sally would remain, safely, for everyone.

The turnpike opened ahead of him into the Allegheny Mountains, which rose suddenly green and misty all around him, budding full and verdant in their spring growth, early growth that peaks vibrantly one or two days a year before the brilliant flowering of yellow and pink and blue and silvery white would disperse in random dustings like the delicate brush strokes of an impressionist landscape. He drove on, his mind floating about the prison schedules and paperwork and subcontract budgets, Sally's life on Cade's Mountain, Katherine in her distance, raise and lower the shoulder a half inch at a time, the house in Denver, the house on Bright's Mountain, Cecil Beckman and Ansel Newley, Casey's rented duplex, Verna Lee's strange admonition—suddenly his mind was flooding like a torrent and overflowing, drawing his senses inward as his attention snapped away from the overloading of issues at hand like the breaking of an electrical circuit, dismissing all except the unresolved questioning from the state police investigator, randomly focused in Mason's thoughts as he drove in the brightness of the late morning sun.

The investigator was Randel John Dean, a tall, excruciatingly thin man with long bony hands that hung from the sleeves of his coat like bundles of dry sticks, sitting in Casey's living room, his dog-eared notebook teetering on a pointed knee, craning his chin upward as he spoke, his voice high pitched and tinny. "Semitruck driver pulled over about three hundred yards ahead of you, maybe some distance more, over the hill because he couldn't stop so well on the grade. Said he ran back as soon as he pulled over and got to the car first. Said no one else was there, and you appeared unconscious when he got there. I kinda wonder, Mr. Mason"—he ran the back of his fingers down the side of his neck, sliding them through the ample gap of his shirt collar—"if maybe you got a little confused about who was there. I kinda wonder if maybe the paramedics was there when you came to, and you just didn't catch it all the way it was. You figure that could be the case, Mr. Mason?'

"No," Mason said, feeling the warmth of his anger rising in his cheeks. "I don't think that could be the case. Whoever was driving that flatbed ran me off the road on purpose. I *know* that's what happened."

The investigator sucked his cheeks and made a clicking sound as he studied his notes. He looked at Mason with watery gray eyes that seemed to roll about as if they were too small for their sockets and spoke slowly, his voice like gravel on a metal roof, "Could be, sir, could be. But I'm investigating an accident here with nothing to go on but two vehicles in the creek and your statement. I mean, no offense to you when I say there isn't much to go on, Mr. Mason. It's just that I'm having a tough time figuring out what happened so I can put it in my report. As far as who stole the truck, that's the sheriff's jurisdiction. I just handle what happens on the highway. Like I said, sir, I'm only here because we couldn't get a statement from you at the scene." He looked at his notes and then back at Mason. "My guess is that some boys from Low Creek was curious about that prison you been building and found that truck a-settin' there and decided to take it for a run. Suppose maybe they came up on you a little too fast on the highway, and both vehicles went off the road, and they got scared and run off in the woods. At least, that's what I figure could have happened."

Mason leaned forward in Casey's green recliner and pulled at the brace on his shoulder. He bristled at Randal John Dean. "Then what about the guy I saw?"

Dean closed his notebook and stood to leave, his wrinkled suit hanging loosely from his frame and the pants bunched about his worn shoes. "The semi driver said he didn't see anything except your car and that stake bed in the creek, and there wasn't no one around, except, of course, you, trapped in the car and hurt like you were." He tucked the notebook under his arm. "I got the description like you said it, Mr. Mason. I'm sure the sheriff will look into it."

Scrawny bastard, Mason thought as the faceless beard and voice resounded in his memory... *You don't never come back here agin...*

The fuel gauge was almost on empty as he pulled into a service plaza. He refueled, slowly and cautiously stepping from the Jeep on the stiff knee, carefully stretching his shoulder in the breeze as he managed the pump with his right hand and then visited the restroom before reentering the turnpike. Katherine was somewhere distant in his mind as he approached the ramp to southbound Interstate 81, and he felt a shiver of longing as he looked down the continuing stretch of the turnpike on which he had last driven five years ago when he first went to Denver. Five years. It seemed like a hundred years, and it seemed like yesterday, the memory pulling at him as he drove on, drawing him back in a kind of pained reverie that was full upon him now, engrossing him in its extracts as he embraced its vitality and cursed its disastrous termination.

* * *

"We have a joint venture partner in Denver, you know Patrelli Brothers," Leo had said, sitting in the conference room in Trenton with his sleeves rolled up and his immense forearms resting on the table. "I want you to do the PM liaison and manage the partnership. You handle that for me, Tuck, and if things work out, you can build the business there and make yourself a nice little income." The business card slid across the table two weeks later. "See Jack Murray when you get there. He's managing the work for Patrelli."

"Get yourself situated, Tuck," Jack said, leading him to his office. "We're going to get together later with the project people and bring you up to speed. Also, if you don't have any plans, my wife and I would like to have you over to dinner tonight. Nothing fancy. We just imagine what it's like to be new in town and thought you might like a home-cooked meal with some plain folk. Kinda our way of saying welcome to Denver."

Helen opened a beer and handed it to him on the patio, where he and Jack sat discussing business, and then they talked awhile about Denver, and he felt unusually comfortable in their presence, chatting lightly as strangers do, the shadowed mountains beyond them like a mural that gently enclosed the patio and house and Denver itself. He felt a welcoming sense of presence like a homecoming of sorts—a peculiar belonging to the place he had only known for a day and could love for a lifetime.

"Where are you from, Tuck?" Jack asked as Helen reentered the house to check on dinner.

Mason paused briefly, the pause perhaps noticeable only to himself. "Ohio, originally," he said, looking away into the fading sunset behind the mountains in the distance. "How about you Jack? Always been here?"

"Damn near," Jack answered, his gaze following Mason's into the mountains. "I was born in Nebraska, but I've been here most of my life."

They stood silently for a moment, facing the high mountains west of Jack's patio. "They're almost mesmerizing, aren't they? As long as I've lived here, going on forty years now, I still find them rather awesome. Sometimes I come out here and just stare at them. They're magnificent." He turned toward Mason. "I've never been to Ohio. What's it like there?"

"It's got its good points, I guess," Mason returned, half turning toward Jack but still looking at the mountains. "Nothing like this, of course. There's nothing in Ohio like this."

"Nor in Nebraska," Jack said. "But I still love Nebraska. Family there and all. We visit them at least once a year. You have family still in Ohio, Tuck?"

The question always annoyed Mason, though he was not sure why. "Some," he said with restraint. "My father and his wife, stepsisters," he offered further to satisfy what he expected to be the next question, wishing the subject could be terminated but knowing that this was never enough; people always seemed to want to know more, always kept pressing the questions. But Jack simply nodded politely and looked back toward the mountains.

At dinner, Helen and Jack conversed easily, allowing Mason to govern the conversation as they discussed the lighter issues, and Mason and Jack swapped stories about the construction business. "Just one daughter," Helen answered to Jack's question. "She's away studying art in Europe on a fellowship…" And the conversation turned to colleges and then the rising cost of education, and Helen told a story about her former college roommate, a woman named June Crosby, who had run unsuccessfully for Congress a year ago and was campaigning for tax relief on college tuition. Mason actually enjoyed the evening, surprising himself with his sociability, considering the fact that he rarely accepted such invitations and normally was uncomfortable even in small groups. But Jack and Helen were different, unassuming and cordial, yet demonstrating a natural respect for privacy that gradually won Mason's confidence, and he, perhaps for the first time in his life, began to develop a sense of trust that carried beyond that evening and into the office and other times at the house at Jack's repeated invitation.

He was on the patio again, and it was warmer now in the early summer when Jack turned, his face quietly open and smiling. "This is our daughter Katherine, Tuck." And now the dimension and texture of life such as he had never known unfolded before him like a bloom as she smiled and took his hand, rather coolly he would remind her later, and he fumbled through dinner as she spoke, her voice clear like Jack's, and her features firm and defined like Helen's. They talked into the night, and she said, "It was certainly nice to meet you, Tucker," but not "will I see you again?" or even so innocent as "I'll see you later," and he was both enamored and crushed as he left and even more so two days later at the office when Jack announced that he was leaving early to take his daughter to the airport.

"Where is she going?" Mason asked, desperately attempting to appear unaffected.

Jack snapped his briefcase and stood up. "Paris," he said. "She still has another four months until she's finished."

Mason nodded and failed again to remain distant. "Wish her well for me, okay?" He felt cheated by the callousness of the moment, cruelly shattering the fragile fantasy of hope that he had harbored since the instant he met her on her father's patio. He tried to reason with himself, rationalizing his male tendency to find attraction so suddenly and desire so passionately that he would awaken at night and covet the touch of her long brown hair or smooth skin of her cheek or the sound of her voice. He thought of her constantly in the following months, always anticipating Jack's mention of her and shrewdly steering Helen in conversation that would lead to Katherine, even occasionally asking in subtle discourse how she was getting along, as if the mere mention of her name might somehow bring her closer, somehow allow him to touch her by proxy of her parents. It had never happened before, not like this, not so passionately, so overwhelmingly suffocating him from one brief encounter. There had been others, sweet and tumultuous affairs based on sex and companionship, always brief and usually ending in the awkward recognition of that hollow void of sustenance that he could never seem to comprehend but longed for nonetheless; the fabled consummation that transcended flesh and circumstance and gave endurance to those few and fortunate couples, perhaps whom he had not known and only marginally believed to exist, who lived in absolute and natural commitment as they attended one another in selfless contribution to the wholeness of their being. He tried desperately to reason with himself; he had only met her once and then only in staged pleasantry to satisfy the request of her parents, perhaps relieved to see him leave and turn her thoughts to some continental gadabout who waited longingly in a Paris flat for her to return to his bed, disregarding the occasion of some friend of her father's and maybe laughing about having to endure another clumsy construction guy fumbling through dinner and barely speaking in sentences. But she was still there nonetheless, distracting him with her image smiling politely across the table in Jack and Helen's dining room, and he had pined for her with adolescent fervor, having no more than a few hours of compromised memory to hold in her stead, helpless and pathetic until Jack's offhanded invitation to stop over after work. "Katherine's back home, you know. She asked about you, and, of course, Helen never misses an opportunity to feed you. I don't know, Tuck. The women in my house seem to have some kind of attraction to you. Maybe I should be concerned." The joking missing its point as Mason felt the rush of apprehension and screaming sensation of hope as he showered and fussed over which shirt he should wear and drove to Jack's house nervously, pondering the significance of the opportunity and the tremendously imminent potential for disappointment.

"I couldn't wait to see you," Katherine would tell him later, and they were as old friends in the presence of her parents, awkwardly regarding each other distantly at first but acquiescing to their mutual weaknesses as she walked him to his car, and they talked for a long time in the clarity and chill of the autumn night, then as the anxious and willing inquisitors of the base attraction as they warmly shared the following Saturday evening in a small Italian restaurant that Mason had selected only after visiting it earlier in the week to sample its fare and consider the appropriateness of its seating arrangement, then as lovers, passionately requited in their every waking moment, spending their time together wholly dedicated to the wonderful experience of life and loving, finding a closeness that led to a oneness of being that Mason could never before imagine, and they recognized together in the following spring their desire for the fulfillment of a lifetime. Mason was fly-fishing with Jack when he told him, Jack standing there, knee-deep in the water and grinning as he closed his creel and looked at Mason with his understated candor, beaming in the cool morning sunlight with the satisfaction that fathers rarely know. "Well, you damn well *better* marry her, Mason. You'll break a lot of hearts if you don't."

* * *

Mason stopped at a service plaza near Roanoke and got out of the car, painfully stretching his shoulder and measuring the stiffness in his leg as he walked around the perimeter of the parking lot to its easternmost boundary. There was a Wendy's restaurant at the opposite end of the plaza, maybe four hundred yards. Enough distance, he thought, to walk off the stiffness and increase the circulation. Slowly extending and flexing his left leg in an exaggerated fashion, he made his way to the restaurant and got in line among the travel-worn tourists and truckers and impatient business types, who waited abjectly as a young cashier shouted orders to the kitchen crew. He took his lunch to go, walking back to the Jeep where he could eat alone on the open tailgate, and he sat there quietly, taking in the fresh late-morning air and the misty rise of the Blue Ridge mountains in the distance. There was still a slight chill in the air that offset the warmth of the sun as he stared at the horizon, quiet and introspect, the abstraction of his thoughts preempting his sandwich and water. He finished and drove away with the emergence of Sally's voice in the background, as it had been the day before, when she was to drive him to the airport but arrived two hours early, "Come on now, sweetie. Gitcher stuff here. I got somethin' I want to show ya."

Sally had driven him eastward on the highway and then up a two-lane road that rose steeply at times and was carved severely into the side of a relatively high ridge. She got out of the car and climbed up on an enormous flat rock, away from the side of the road and facing a narrow valley where a river flowed violently through its rocky basin and disappeared beyond a hulking, square-topped ridge. She stood there, unusually quiet and pensive as the breeze blew her hair across her face and fluttered her windbreaker, her body still and erect as if she were waiting for something. Mason hobbled gingerly around the front of the car and worked his way to her side and said, "Sally, what the hell are we doing here?" But she only smiled at him and turned her gaze back to the valley beyond, still smiling, not with her usual girlish wide-eyed expression but with a complexity of experience and longing and serenity that he had not seen before in the three weeks that he had known her. Sally seemed uncharacteristically peaceful, yet fully submissive to the massive environment that seemed to envelop her in its vastness. Mason stood silently beside her and shuffled his weight from the injured leg, bewildered by the sudden change in Sally's demeanor.

Eventually she spoke, her voice soft and clear amid the quiet rush of the breeze. "I was born over there," she said, pointing to the nearest rise on the ridge beyond the valley, a blunt mass of trees and rock that was separated from the rest of the ridge by a shallow gap that notched the point where it continued westward.

"That's Cade's Mountain?" Mason asked. Sally looked at him and smiled again, stroking her hair from her face as the breeze continued and nodding her head in the direction of the valley below.

"There was a trail, the old folks called it a trace, that ran down the side of the mountain to a little town called Rustle just beyond that bend in the river. We would walk down there, and Daddy would get us candy from the store there, and we would sit by the river and watch folks come and go while Daddy went about his business. One time in the early spring, the river ran full and muddy over its banks. It don't now 'cause it's been dammed upstream, and the river was right there in front of the store, and we, my sisters and me, we was scared 'cause it so swollen and forbiddin' and swirled about so full of tree trunks and other things that floated half out of the water, and it come so close to the road that it splashed on the broken pavement and filled the potholes with foam and slimy mud. Folks was makin' a day of it, movin' their vehicles and collectin' at the high ground to watch. I remember Mr. Satch, who owned the store where we got our candy, standin' in his doorway with a look on his face that made me sad for him, just standin' there watching that river work its way up to his store and not a thing he could do about it until it got there and gave its due. May Jean started crying and said that the river was coming to get us, but Daddy told us that the river don't have no desire but to move on and find its way to the flat land and the ocean. Daddy said the river had no mind of its own and didn't know whether something was in its way or not, but people have their own mind and make their own decisions and sometimes those decisions meant that they stayed too close to a river that got all swelled up from the snow melt and rain. He told us that *his* decision was to let the river be and let it do what it was going to do, and I can remember walking up that muddy trail with my candy in my hand and hearing that river behind us, and I asked him why anyone would want to live near a river that could rise so quick and wash your house away. He stopped and looked back, and I thought at first that he didn't hear me, but then he kinda sighed and looked down at me with a strange kinda sad look in his eyes and said, *'Cause it don't matter, Sally. 'Cause it's in us all to take odds with the world, and we don't do no better if we back off from the river just to fall off a cliff somewhere else. It just don't matter. If it ain't the river, it'll be something else.'* That's just what he said. I remember it well, but it was a long time before I really knew what he meant."

A semi labored on the steep road behind them, shifting hard, and Mason could hear the strain of its gears as it neared the top of the hill. Sally looked toward the mountain. "The road on the other side was the main highway around here before they built the interstate. After Daddy was gone, Mama had a little stand where she sold vegetables from the truck garden behind our house. Me and my sisters would work the stand with her. I used to love to talk with the folks who would stop to buy their vegetables. I would help them pick out the best ones and put them in bags all wrapped up nice and sometimes I'd get some change or a dollar for totin' bags of produce out to someone's car. I was always so fascinated, talkin' with people from different places who always seemed happy to spend some time with me there. Always made me feel kinda special. Mama didn't like it, me carryin' on with strangers and all. She said a girl my age shouldn't try so hard to get herself noticed 'cause there was a lot of strange people in the world, and young girls—I was maybe fifteen at the time—was fair pickin' for men with bad desires. 'Course, my sisters weren't like me. Emma had a sharp tongue and never liked workin' the stand. May Jean just stayed close to Mama, ya know. She was the youngest. I liked it, though, workin' that little stand with Mama and havin' them people talk about where they'd been what they'd been doin', layin' out the beans and onions and cucumbers so neat and pretty in the baskets and settin' in the shade when business slowed on hot days, watchin' the heat rise from the road, ya know how it gets all wavy like everythin's meltin'. I used to set and imagine that the whole world could melt into the road and flow away like that river over there. Every mornin' we would load up Granddaddy's old pick'm-up, and Mama would drive us down to the stand with me and Mama in the seat and May Jean and Emma back with the bushel baskets aholdin' on for dear life when the truck hit a bump, and I can still remember like it was yesterday, the smell of earth and livin' things and the cars that would line up to buy our vegetables. It was a good time."

She looked at Mason, her eyes narrowing slightly as she held her hair to keep it from blowing in her face. "Good times is when there ain't no bad to deal with, ain't it, Tucker? Daddy always said all things are relative, that one person's good life ain't worth spit to another, and the only thing that separates us from animals is the fact that we can figure for ourselves what is and ain't worth dealin' with."

They stood quietly for a moment, and Mason looked away, rubbing the shoulder where the brace had been removed two days earlier. He looked at his watch. There was still plenty of time to catch his plane. Then Sally spoke again, her voice even softer now, and Mason had to strain to hear it over the sound of the breeze and traffic behind them. Her eyes caught his as he looked up, and she held his gaze briefly against his will. "Casey told me about how you lost your wife, Tucker. I just want ya to know that I'm real sorry about it. Folks will always tell you that you can't change what's already happened even though it hurts so bad that sometimes you can't do nothin' else but set about and wish to have things go back to the way they was. But there ain't no goin' back. I know that, Tucker. I know that just like you do."

It was early evening when he turned off the interstate onto the four-lane highway that led to Bright's Mountain. There was some traffic in Kingsport, but the highway was fairly clear as he made his way to Mills Hollow Road. Cecil Beckman was on his porch as expected, though Jeff was nowhere to be seen, which made Mason a bit uncomfortable, considering the incidence of Jeff hiding in the brush when he first met with Cletus Wellman. Mason waved as he passed, and Cecil acknowledged him with a subtle nod, just as he did when Mason and Sally drove out to the house to meet the moving van several days before. They had come to receive the used furniture that he had bought from a dilapidated warehouse behind Cletus's used car dealership in Bristol. Sally had taken him there and helped him pick out a sofa and chairs, a bedroom set, kitchen table, lamps, and other items that Cletus had somehow accumulated and offered for sale to his tenants, all managed by an attendant named Joebob, a short, cantankerous man with braces on his legs, who led them through the dimly lit inventory and haggled with Sally over the cost of the order and who should pay for delivery. Sally prevailed over Joebob's objections and extracted what Mason thought was a fair price for the furniture, including the agreement to pay for delivery if Joebob would throw in two large wicker chairs. He bought curtains, a mattress, and other items as suggested by Sally from JC Penny in Kingsport and a riding lawn mower from a man in Gate City who had advertised in an online offer site.

It wasn't the perfect setup, considering what he had become accustomed to. The intolerable cache of furniture and appliances sitting in storage near Denver had crossed his mind briefly, but he dismissed it immediately, considering its representative burden to be more than he was willing to contend with at this time. Helen had argued with him, begged him to keep it, at least some of it. "Katherine loved the leather couch. Can't you hang onto it? Store it somewhere? Tuck, I'm sure she would have wanted you to. I'm sure she wouldn't have wanted it sold off like this. My god, dear, you're going to need furniture anyway. It just seems so cold to sell it."

He had then stood quietly in the living room while the packers from Brown-Wiley Moving and Storage shrink-wrapped the leather couch that Jack and Helen had given them as a wedding gift and chairs they had bought with Katherine's first paycheck as a down payment, the dining room set that they had to wait to afford, the bedroom set that had belonged to her aunt Tilly, the kitchen table that came from her parent's basement, the Monet print, the replica of Rodin's *Thinker* that he referred to as the naked guy, her easel, the wicker wastebasket from the bathroom, and countless other items, each with its own identity, each with its own contribution to the substance of their existence. The packers were Miguel and Bess, Miguel barely able to speak English as he diligently wrapped the photographs from the table in the hallway and placed them in a box cushioned with paper. Bess was a portly woman who smiled constantly and coached Miguel patiently from the kitchen, where she wrapped each dish and glass separately and placed them in a box with the china clock that Katherine had bought in Paris and the shiny lacquered papier-mâché vegetables from the counter. Mason said nothing more than was absolutely necessary in response to Bess's questions as he watched each item as it was tagged with a small red sticker before it faded into the wrapping paper and disappeared into its designated labeled box. When the boxes were filled, they were taped shut and shoved aside, and the movers carried the boxes and furniture out to the truck, removing his life with Katherine one piece at a time until the place was empty, leaving him alone and devastated in the empty room with the pink inventory slip in his hand and the echoing bare walls and path-marked carpet, untrodden and deep where the furniture had been like a lingering shadow of that existence that had been within those walls, fading beyond those possessions that were no less than the fulcrum of two lives in balance as one, each providing the pivotal support of the other like children on a seesaw until one leaves the teeterboard, sending the other crashing to the ground in the harsh and painful realization of the loss. He had considered it, the neat stacks of wrapped articles in dark storage like artifacts in a tomb, placed in acquiescence to Helen's desperate and futile grasping at the diminishing legacy of her daughter. It would be no less than a desecration, he thought, no less than the exhumation of Katherine herself. He had answered Sally's question with only a slight hesitation, "No, I'll need to get some furniture."

Mason noticed that the mailbox had been replaced as he entered the driveway. Sally's Cadillac was in the lot when he approached the house, and she was on the front porch, attempting a conversation on her cell phone. "Whatcha say, sugar? Come again. I ain't gettin' such good reception out here. Honey, I'll have to call you back. I can't understand a thing you're sayin'." She arose from one of the wicker chairs and walked down the porch steps, holding the phone away from her like it was some foreign object she had found in the yard. "Durn cell service is next to nothin' out here. You're right on time, sweetie. How was your trip back? You doin' okay?"

"I'm doing well, Sally, thank you," Mason answered as he stepped from the car and stretched, wincing slightly at the pain that had been plaguing his shoulder for the past hour.

"You're kinda hurtin' is what I think," she returned as she touched his arm and peered into the back of the Jeep. "This thing's full up all right, but I gotta say you ain't got much to your name.

Well, I guess the way you guys move about, you ain't got much time to accumulate a lot o' stuff."

There was a noise inside the house, and Mason instinctively looked in the direction of the front door, where, to his surprise and consternation, Jeff appeared, carrying a plastic bucket full of tools and a frayed extension cord. Sally seemed to notice Mason's concern and smiled at him as she motioned to Jeff and said, "Come here, sweetie, are you all done in there?" Jeff was stopped at the door, looking down as if he had forgotten something important.

Sally's voice was a little higher than before, and she spoke slowly with a staged inflection that she might have used when speaking to a child. "Now, come on, darlin', let's not get bashful. I need you to unload Tucker's car on account o' he's got 'im a sore shoulder and can't do it hisself. You know Tucker, don'tcha? He's your neighbor now, honey, so come on down here and help us out."

Jeff kept looking down as he shuffled forward, his enormous and worn shoes clumping heavily on the steps, and his head wagging from side to side as he walked.

"Put the bucket down, honey," Sally said. Jeff stopped and looked up in her direction but not necessarily at her. "It's okay," she continued, "I'll keep an eye on it for you. The cord too. Now come on down here and help out so Tucker can move in."

Jeff pulled each item from the car and held it up to Mason, always avoiding Mason's eyes as he did so and moving slowly to each location as directed, sometimes stopping midway as if he had forgotten where he was headed. "Kind of a strange character," Mason commented as Jeff disappeared into the house with a computer desk that he carried as if it weighed nothing.

"Oh, he's a little slow, but just as sweet as can be once you get him to warm up to you. Strong as an ox and good with tools too. I just got him to fix the air-conditioner in the bedroom. Durn Cletus and his cheap help. That thing either musta fell right out of the window or whoever Cletus paid to put it in there never got it done. Anyways, I found it hangin' half out and got Jeff to come over and put it in right. It's gonna get hot soon, and you're gonna want it." She looked at Mason. "He's a good boy. Really."

"Well, I'm sure he's okay if you say so," Mason said. "The day I met Cletus out here, he was hiding in the bushes by the driveway. Kind of gave me the creeps."

Sally smiled, her eyes turned up in a kind of benign resignation, as if Mason's concern was simply some trivial observation by a meddlesome neighbor that had to be explained repeatedly. "Oh, he does that sometimes. It's curiosity. Just gets nosy, I guess. He done a lot of that when Cletus was havin' the place fixed up. Don't mean nothin' by it. Never does any harm. He just likes to watch is all. He ain't real good at making up to people, but he likes to be around folks when they'll have him. He don't know how to do that, so he watches careful from a distance." She looked at Mason, and he knew that she could see the doubt on his face. Her voice then lowered a bit as she spoke, not directly at Mason but into the breeze, as if she were convincing herself as well. "Did ya ever notice how children like to hide and watch when something's goin' on that they ain't sure about? That's what he does 'cause he ain't much more than a child inside. It ain't like he's retarded 'cause in some respects, he's real smart. It's more like some of him grew up just fine, and the rest of him never came around. It's good for both him and Cecil that—"

She stopped as Jeff lumbered from the house and looked inside the Jeep. He turned to Sally and then to Mason, still avoiding eye contact with Mason and said to neither of them in particular, his voice heavy and dull as he spoke, "Hit's empty. Thar ain't no more."

Mason hesitated, realizing that this was the first time he had heard the man speak. "That's fine, Jeff," he said. "I really appreciate the help—"

Sally interrupted, touching Jeff as she spoke, "That's good, sweetie. You're all done." She stuffed some bills in his pocket. "Make sure Cecil takes care of this for you, or you might lose it. Your beer's in the refrigerator. Get it and go on home now and let Tucker get settled. You give my best to Cecil now, ya hear?" Jeff turned slowly and shuffled toward the house without any regard to either Mason or Sally.

"I put some food in the refrigerator for you," she said to Mason as she opened her car door. "It ain't much, but it'll get you by until you

63

can do your grocery shoppin' this weekend." She turned toward Jeff, who was making his way down the porch steps with a twelve-pack. "Don't forget your bucket, Sweetie. And your cord," she called. Jeff stopped and picked up the items, looking straight ahead as he walked on down the drive. Sally turned back to Mason as he approached her. "I gotta run, but you call if you need anything. You gonna be okay, honey?"

Mason held Sally's door as she got into the car. "Sally," he said as she fussed with her key ring, "I don't know how to thank you for all you've done."

"Oh, you. Just pay your rent on time so Cletus can make his fortune." She started the car. "You don't be a stranger, Tucker Mason, y'hear? I gotta go. I'm way behind. Oh, I almost forgot. I got a new lock put on the shop there. Casey got one of his boys to pick up your lawn mower and had him put it in there for you. You gotta get the key back from Casey."

She pulled the car door closed and drove down the drive, waving to Jeff, who was still lumbering on with his beer and bucket of tools, the extension cord wrapped over his shoulder and his head wagging from side to side as he disappeared beyond the trees. Sally's defense of Jeff was not convincing, and Mason could feel a sense of furtiveness about the man, more so in his absence, the suspicion being considerably more prevalent with imagination as Mason wondered whether Jeff had continued home or might, perhaps, be again hiding in the brush.

Mason stood briefly in the lot, carefully regarding the house and the shop and the clearing in which they were situated, the tree line that was already darkening as the sun dissolved beyond the foliage, the lawn that swelled gently behind the house into the fullness of the woods, and the flat suspension of colorless sky that stretched above the highest branches. There was an order of things here, a natural synthesis of the buildings and the forested enclave of their location that seemed to encompass him in the soft fold of its dimensions. He struggled to consider his arrival as the initiation of a positive event in his life, as he felt when he first sat on the porch that day when he first met Cletus Wellman, but failed, instead feeling suddenly isolated, suspended in the singularity of the place, immersed in the chill of the air and the sweetness of fresh growth and the incredible silence that accompanied the waning daylight as Katherine drifted through his thoughts like the faint notice of rain in the wind. And the sadness returned, the old sadness that he seemed to have known forever, the imminent desolation that had always been there, resident and obtuse in the gravity of his soul, holding him now and taking him into himself as he sat for a long time on the old iron chair on the porch, alone in the impermeable darkness of the Appalachian night.

asey could see it. He could translate the blue lines on paper into the rigid utility of a prison, clearly envisioning the flat walls and angles and the perspective textures, the cells and catwalks, the open areas, the collective pods, the commissary, the warehouse, the dining areas, the connecting walkways, the guard towers, the silvery fence and razor wire that would enclose the compound. He could stand on the pads and describe in intricate detail the elevations and door locations and the relative positions of the gun posts, the tolerances of the cell placements, the logistical difficulties of the exercise yards, the critical positioning of the light towers. For Casey, the actual construction was simply a replication of the model he had already built in his mind, each component a replacement of the corresponding piece in his creation that merely gave substance and color and texture to what for him was already there. From experience, he could hear the iron slam of the cell doors being tested and the echoing footsteps of guards in training on the catwalks, and he could see the cold simplicity of the light fixtures in the common areas that reflected in muted gray tones from the enameled walls and the shadows cast in the cells from tiny openings that were not really windows but eye-level portals of daylight, through which prisoners could glimpse at no more than the walls of another pod as their world shrank into the universe of concrete and steel and capsular passages. Although he had built prisons before, Casey's perception was not just from the similar experience but the accumulation of time spent in the service of his calling, the dirt-taste years of concrete and wood and iron and glass and asphalt and plastics joined surfaces and finishes and walls that rose from the ground in defiance of the natural order they violated and the intricate devices that warmed and cooled and lighted and flowed in man's exceptive departure from nature. It was here that Casey could claim ownership. He knew nothing of the resulting use of the structures he built, for that beginning was an end for him, the success of his labor was revealed in its termination, and his legacy remained in the structures themselves, leaving the occurrence of their use to whoever cared to claim it. "We build buildings," he had told Mason. "That's the beauty of it. What happens afterwards is someone else's issue. We move on to the next building while those who accept our work remain in whatever stuck-in-the-mud process it is that takes their life away a little at a time until they can see nothing more than the walls of their office or their position on the assembly line or, what the hell, this damn prison. It's all the same as I see it. I'm telling you, Tuck, I wouldn't have it any other way. It's a damn good life as far as I'm concerned."

A damn good life, Mason mused to himself as he drove up the side of Bright's Mountain, the description having a different meaning for him though of no less consequence than Casey's stone-clad world of assemblies. His development in the business and success in Denver were born not of the buildings themselves but the abstract product of his training, manifested not in the gritty muster of labor and materials but in the consortium of schedules and documents and eternal sessions in meeting rooms that transcribed intent into substance. His fulfillment was not on the sunbaked building pad but contained within the doublewide trailer, the metal-clad composite extension of the Doenitz Building Company, with his office in the rear and the large conference room where they had butted several folding tables together and the open areas with workstations for the schedulers and trade managers and where the process of construction was condensed into updated computer programs that would translate the Low Creek Maximum Security Prison into the base elements of enterprise. He could not see the unbuilt prison, his format for measurement being in pixels on a dusty flat screen and marks on a plan and the careful recording of time and cost and adherence for which he had squandered his time in Maryland despite Casey's careful instruction, that assignment spent like a child tottering after his father in a workplace visit well beyond the comprehension of the child, who, wide eyed and impatient, followed the instruction to the satisfaction of the father in hope of an early return to his playthings. There was a comfort here, in the makeshift environment of the trailer, a familiarity with counterfeit processes of construction that would serve as an apt diversion to the heaviness of his thoughts. He entered the trailer on the first day after his return to Wells County as one entering another world, or perhaps returning, in welcome respite from the implosive loneliness that waited like a sensing predator beyond the gates of the prison site.

The routine established quickly. He had awakened on that first day as the pale light was just beginning to filter through the trees and the color of morning was muted in the lingering grayness of night, strange and disoriented in the little house, its confinements a bit overbearing as he put on the coffee and stepped onto the front porch and then into the yard, feeling the grass cold and wet beneath his bare feet as he stretched his healing left leg and moved about in a pronounced stroll, heel-ball-toe in measured progression, gradually increasing his speed until the knee was hot but no longer throbbing. The following day, he put on his running shoes and extended his journey to the perimeter of the yard once and then twice, then graduating in the ensuing mornings to the driveway and up Mills Hollow Road, each day extending the distance and velocity until he was running, slowly at first, the shoulder straining painfully against the motion as it reestablished its concert with the rest of the body. He left the house early, sometimes meeting Casey at Harley's or some roadside stop on the highway for breakfast and other days going directly to the site, casually having his juice and granola bars on the small wooden landing outside the entrance of the trailer as the surrounding mountains undulated in their eternal haze before him. With the exception of his weekly visit to the physical therapist, he generally stayed at the site until everyone else had left, the security guard locking the gate behind him as the mountains were transforming into yellowing shadows that flowed into the valleys as he descended to Mills Hollow Road and his little rented house, neat and secure within its clearing as if it were viewed through a tiny hole in the barrier of its wooded perimeter.

He made acceptable progress during the first week, selecting his staff from the stack of memos and résumés that Leo had sent the previous week, including a scheduler named Ralph Watson, who had worked with him briefly in Denver, a new hire for the mechanical-electrical work, an intern from Virginia Tech and Tom Bailey, whose time remaining toward retirement was measured by descending numbers on a calendar as he obligingly accepted the duties of QC and safety coordinator. An ad in the local papers for the administrator position had produced an enormous number of résumés, which he and Sally had sifted through on Casey's kitchen table two weeks earlier, settling on five finalists whom he interviewed, again with Sally's help, at a borrowed room in the Low Creek courthouse. He settled on a young woman named Jamie who lived in Norton and had considerable experience as a construction secretary despite her apparent youth. Jamie's husband was a day hand on a casual labor crew at the Carstar plant on the other side of Oak City, and her three children were left in the care of her mother while she worked. She was a small woman, with tiny features giving a rather childlike impression that was supported by her milk-white complexion and narrow eyeglasses, and it was only after Sally's prompting that Mason was able to look past her physical presence and hire her on the merits of her capabilities. By the end of that week, the office was in order, and he was able to divert his time to the business at hand and the incredible flow of e-mail and Casey's eternal list of resource needs. "Well, boss, it's a shame you got off to such a bad start here, but I gotta admit, you're catching up just fine," Casey said as he leaned back from his breakfast in a smoky rest stop on the highway called Haber's that smelled of greasy food and old wood flooring amid working folk on their way to whatever paid and those who would be working if the opportunity presented itself. "You got your pencils counted and seats for your people and the computer's plugged in, most of the subs are on board, and the footers are done on two cell pods. I'd say we're ready to get serious about this goddamn prison, wouldn't you?"

On Saturday morning, Mason drove into Low Creek and had breakfast at Harley's, leisurely reading the news on his tablet over coffee in the presence of the usual Saturday crowd, a ritualistic collection of locals, mostly older men who regarded Mason with a kind of walleyed curiosity as they openly gawked over their conversations and fried eggs and sausage from the buffet, their coffee cups gripped like mallets in calloused hands as they talked among themselves with thick voices that seemed to roll about the dining room like distant thunder. Mason had taken his tray to a table near the front window where the light was best for reading and he could gaze occasionally at the slow movement of the town as it revived its languid motion of pickup trucks and old cars and people occasionally strolling on the sidewalks, not aimlessly but not with any obvious purpose either, moving and greeting in a sort of rigid proposition that Mason found perplexing, considering his notional expectation of a laid-back society of country folk and his observation of what appeared to be a sense of latent anxiety. He could see the streetlight changing at the intersection of Main Street and Park Avenue, often without a vehicle to release by its regimen, and he could hear the singular undercurrent of the sparse community of Low Creek, distant and regressive beyond the occasional ding of the pump at the town's only gas station. Verna Lee poured his coffee slowly and regarded him with the same distance that she had shown him early in the week when he and Casey had their lunch there and she bantered with Casey as usual but kept subtle deference for Mason, a careful, inoffensive space that he considered masterful in its insinuation. She smiled coolly but pleasantly at him, her rotting teeth showing behind the thinness of her lips, and she was turning to move away when he spoke to her, his words rolling without process as if they were placed on his lips by someone else, surprising even himself with the intervention as he stopped her midstride. "I moved in, Verna Lee. I believe I told you I'm staying at the Newley place."

Verna Lee turned, her eyes at first glaring and harsh beneath her glasses and then mellowing quickly, the coffeepot gripped tightly in her hand. She said quietly, "Well, I guess we's neighbors then, Mr. Tucker," and paused only briefly but without the fluidity of someone younger who might have been successful at the graceful termination. Her movements seemed bound by the tightness and rigor of age that held her for the split second of impediment and gave Mason his entry again, and he, still astonished by his own impetuousness, spoke as if programmed to an objective.

"Neighbors. Is that so?"

She paused as if contemplating, her eyes reflecting a despondency that Mason at first took as disapproval, but he quickly realized the sense of strained resignation, as if she were too weary to resist that which she so obviously wished to avoid. "I live in the holler, just below where Newleys lived," she said.

There was a tautness between them, a conflict that bewildered Mason and obviously troubled Verna Lee, so intense and so stringent that it seemed to bind them into a strange sense of commonality. She hesitated again, perhaps frustrated by the slowing of the response that was no more than her age would allow, and Mason continued.

"Verna Lee," he said softly, almost plaintively, casually touching the coffee mug to his lips but not sipping its contents, "why shouldn't I stay there?" He stopped there, wishing even as the words flowed to call them back, to let her continue with her coffeepot to the other tables and leave him to his newspapers. She stood motionless, the second or two of her hesitation seeming to both of them like an eternity against the creaking strain of their opposition, her eyes appearing filmy and heavy behind her glasses as the room and the town and the entire universe began to compress into the space between them. His anticipation of her response was excruciating, and he was becoming deeply regretful of what he now considered an intrusion.

"It ain't that," she said. "It ain't that a'tall. We're very pleased to have ya, Mr. Tucker. That's a fact, sir." Her head was tucked away from him as she spoke, and she moved away, her frailty overtaking her resolve as she walked across the room with the measured steps of infirmity that decried the consequence of her age. Mason sipped his coffee and watched her as she approached a table where several old men sat. They joked with her as she filled their mugs and then one of them leaned forward and spoke quietly to her as he glanced at Mason and quickly returned his eyes back to Verna Lee, who was craning over the table to him as she answered him, close to his ear with her hand on his shoulder. He nodded, raising his head with a mechanical motion as she stole another look in Mason's direction and rejoined his conversation with the others at the table. Mason accepted his own unfamiliar spectacle in the company of the others in the room and turned to look out the window.

Across the street was a hardware store on the first floor of a small brick building with nothing more than a battered green wooden door and a small display window, where some tools and other items were leaning against a yellow cardboard backdrop and a rusted metal sign advertising tool sharpening hung from two wires. The words CLAPPER'S HARDWARE were barely visible on the brick above the display, several feet below another sign that was centered between the two windows on the second floor, reading H. MERRIMAN, DENTIST. Mason recognized the single vehicle parked in front as the truck he had seen behind Cecil Beckman's house, unmistakable with its missing tailgate and rusted door panels and the old two-by-eight board that served as a front bumper. He watched as Cecil eventually emerged from the store while Jeff held the door, and it was then that he first realized Cecil's affliction: Cecil's legs were severely crippled and moving erratically between a pair of old wooden crutches. Jeff opened the passenger side door of the truck and literally placed Cecil on the seat while the crutches were placed beneath the seat. Jeff then climbed in on the driver's side, and Mason mused to himself about the possibility of the man actually having a license. A third man came out of the store and leaned his elbows on the passenger side door of the truck, apparently continuing a conversation with Cecil through the open window. Jeff did not start the engine but sat with both hands on the wheel, facing forward as if he were driving. After a few more minutes, the man on the sidewalk stepped back and slapped his hand on the roof of the truck, which Jeff started and drove into a U-turn, passing in front of the restaurant so Mason could see Cecil, who was still talking, emphasizing his point with his hands as Jeff gripped the steering wheel and stared straight ahead. Mason smiled at the ludicrous association of the two, still feeling a sense of misgiving about Jeff despite Sally's ineffective downplaying of his mannerisms.

Verna Lee's presence surprised him as he turned from the window. She was standing at his table again, setting down the coffeepot as her hands twisted together in the wrap of her apron, silent in the abated stillness of old people. Her eyes were fixed on him now with a firmness overtaking the undercurrent tiredness that seemed to prevail in the dimensions of her age-worn face. She appeared extremely small and fragile, shrinking in thinly wrinkled skin over the tiny rack of her skeleton. Her mouth moved slowly as she spoke, as if repressed by the weight of her words, which struggled forth feebly. "Mr. Tucker," she said in a dry voice that seemed on the verge of cracking, "I don't mean to make you feel unwelcome in Low Creek. It ain't that a'tall. You folks what come to build things here are our guests as I see it. It surely ain't my notion to put you outa sorts. Understand?" Mason nodded slowly, puzzled and wordless in her unexpected presence. She continued, still holding him almost mesmerized in her gaze, which seemed to intensify as she spoke, "If you want to live on that mountain, that's your business, and you can do that 'cause it ain't no more than a mountain to you and a place to build your prison and stay on whilst you're buildin' it. You can leave on when you're done, knowin' nothin' about the place and like as not won't be affected. I hope so. I truly do."

She stood quietly before him, grave and austere as she twisted the apron around her hands. Mason wished she would go away and considered the availability of other restaurants in the area. At that moment, he had little desire to return to Harley's. His voice seemed distant and compromised, as if someone else were speaking, respondent to her gravity. "Just what is it that I don't know?"

Verna Lee smiled, her face conforming to the display of broken teeth in a pinched upturn of the wrinkles on her forehead and about her mouth. The severity of her mood seemed to soften into a weary capitulation. "More than I can tell you when I'm workin', honey," she continued. "Maybe it's best you don't know. But I could tell you things. I expect I know as much about that place as anyone, havin' been there as long as I have an' seein' what I seen an' hearin' what I heard."

"And suppose I wanted to know," Mason said. "Would you tell me?"

"I expect I would, honey. If you was to come visit me, I expect I would." She touched his shoulder. "How's your coffee?"

"It's fine, thank you," Mason said instinctively as she patted his shoulder and turned away, shuffling her white Keds as she retrieved her coffeepot and circulated about the room with the regulars.

He paid his check and left, both amused and annoyed by the people of Low Creek that he had met so far, remembering Casey's words on the first day he had arrived there, now more than a month ago: "They're a strange bunch, Tuck, but good people."

The sign at the entrance for the access road for the prison appeared larger than usual as he drove up the hill on Two Stump Road that rose from Low Creek to the highway. He debated with himself as to whether or not he should pass it up entirely and go on about his plans for the day, conceding to the force of habit that he had developed in Denver to spend an hour or two on Saturday mornings in his office to clean up unattended issues from the previous week. There was some activity at the site: excavators taking advantage of dry weather, a plumbing crew on overtime to catch up with the schedule, the explosives crew loading their equipment now that the mountain had been sufficiently cut away to accommodate the structures. Several vehicles were parked in front of the office trailer as he pulled up to it, including one he recognized as the Ford Escape belonging to Marty Cavalone, the site-work coordinator who, in subordination to Casey, was responsible for getting the building pads ready for construction. Cavalone was not one of the regular Doenitz personnel, having been hired on contract by Leo for this particular project because of his extensive experience in deep-cut earth removal. At first, Mason had considered his dour-faced brooding and cynicism as a potential management problem. However, in the past week, he had learned to appreciate the man's capabilities and dedication to his work, as well as discover an exquisitely dry sense of humor and deadpan honesty beneath the coarse exterior.

Cavalone was seated at the head of the group of tables in the conference area, conducting a meeting with some of the subcontractors to address schedule issues for which Mason had requested resolutions by the following Monday. Mason went into his office and began sorting through cost variance reports, his concentration distracted by the bizarre conversation with Verna Lee. He eventually gave up his effort and returned to the conference area as the meeting there was breaking up, breezing lightly with the subcontractors as Cavalone excused them with his usual profanities. Mason turned his attention to the large aerial photographs of the site that were hanging on the wall opposite his office. The photographs were there in keeping with a Doenitz custom of having aerials taken at various stages of large projects and mounted throughout the home and remote offices. Mason, however, had always considered them as marginally useful and seldom paid much attention to them. Cavalone reentered the trailer and tapped the center of the photograph that Mason was looking at. "Prison's right there, boss," he said with his usual sarcasm.

Mason shook his head and turned toward Cavalone. "No shit, smart-ass."

Cavalone was packing his ancient leather briefcase as he spoke, "So what are you looking for anyway?"

"You know that old waitress at Harley's? The one Casey's always horsing around with?"

"Yeah, what about her?"

"She seems to have a real burr up her butt about my living accommodations. Apparently, she lives in the same neighborhood. She got all worked up when I told her I'd moved in, and then she gave me some kind of mumbo jumbo about the things she knows but couldn't tell me. Really strange stuff. Anyway, I'm just trying to get my bearings here."

Cavalone picked up an area map from the conference table and asked Mason to show him where he lived. Mason pointed to the spot on the map, and Cavalone held the map to the wall adjacent to the photograph, tracing with his finger from the map to the photograph. "Right there's your place." He looked at Mason, noting the confusion on his face. Again, with his finger, he outlined a large, irregular area. "Here, this is all Bright's Mountain. Your place is right here, boss, just below where we are standing right now." He stood back a bit and ran his finger down to the west side of the mountain and southward along the valley below. "I can see how you would get confused, though," he continued. "See how Two Stump Road turns sharply in either direction from the highway ramp?" He pointed to a dark depression that curled around the northwest slope. "This is actually Mills Hollow Road. You just can't see it through the trees. It runs up the side of the mountain and then downward into this hollow, right below your place." He was pointing at a dark, almost black area at the north base of the mountain.

"She said she lives in 'the holler.' That must be it," Mason said, tapping the spot with his pen.

"Okay," Cavalone said as he folded the map and returned it to his briefcase, "so you live on Bright's Mountain, and you got a wacky old lady for a neighbor. Any other revelations we can dig up for you today, boss? Or is this enough for one day?"

"That's plenty, Marty, thanks." Mason was still looking at the photograph without noticing the sarcasm.

Cavalone closed the briefcase and started toward the door. "Well, in that case, I'm outa here. Casey and I are going up to Bristol to see the museum. You're welcome to come along if you want."

Mason turned toward him, his pen still on the dark spot on the photograph. "No thanks. I have a lot of things I want to get accomplished today. I'll see you Monday."

Cavalone pulled the door closed behind him as Mason returned to the photograph, feeling mildly astonished by the discovery and a little unsettled by Verna Lee's strange behavior.

The highway was almost empty as he entered it, having stopped by the house to make a list of things he would need: groceries, cleaning materials, magazines, a power strip for the computer, a gasoline can, oil for the lawn mower, and other items that he listed as he checked around the house. On the previous night, he had finally gotten around to opening the shop door using the key that Casey had left on his desk in the trailer. He had found the lawn mower parked in the center of a worn wood floor that was severely damaged and split in places, with bolt holes where machinery had apparently been mounted for a long time, the outlines of the bases still visible where the wood was smooth and still bearing its original coat of dull varnish. The place had a musty smell of disuse and age, dark except for a single bulb and two small windows that were so accumulated with dirt that the daylight barely penetrated through the smudged panes. Along the wall were several workbenches, some that were braced with stanchions to support machinery and others with shelves and clamp marks, all empty and abandoned amid sawdust swept and pocketed in the corners and hard caked around the rusting bench legs and windowsills. Mason had considered the usefulness of the place and left it, locking the door behind him, feeling an uneasy sense of curiosity that would remain like a placard above the door whenever he passed it, and he wondered about it now as he drove onto the highway and into Kingsport, amusing himself with the obvious effect that Verna Lee's ramblings seem to have on his imagination.

There was a refreshing sense of civility in Kingsport, relative to the ascetic indifference of Low Creek. The Saturday traffic was rhythmic and progressive downtown and around the square as people moved deliberately about their business. Mason accomplished his mission at Walmart and Kroger's, gradually loading the Jeep with necessities and finally stopping at "Flowers by Ruthann," a well-appointed storefront in a restored old building near the edge of the business district. The shop was busy, and he waited patiently amid the sweet floral essence and soft music from some unknown origin while a middle-aged woman and a young girl waited on customers efficiently yet with a natural attentiveness that forestalled any impatience on those who were waiting for service. The woman fussed with the arrangement that Mason had selected while he copied Sally's address onto a small card and wrote a note of thanks for all she had done for him. He passed the card across the counter, and the woman noted the address, looking up at him with a strange inquisitiveness that made him wonder if he had written something unintelligible. She fastened the card into the arrangement and smiled, rather curtly, he thought, and she said, "I'll have this delivered first thing on Monday."

"Is there any way I can have it delivered today?" Mason asked.

"I could, but there wouldn't be anyone there to receive it. Sally and Cletus are in Knoxville at their son's graduation," she said, smiling now. "Won't be back till late tomorrow night, so we'd be best to wait till Monday, don't ya think?" She was a short amiable woman with a soft round face and clear blue eyes that emanated a sense of assuming frankness.

"You know Sally?" Mason asked.

"Oh sure. My husband works for Cletus, and me and Sally have been friends for years." She looked at the floral arrangement on the counter, which was the largest from her refrigerated display case. "Quite a nice thing, sending her these flowers."

Mason could tell she was fishing, and there was no reason not to satisfy her curiosity. "She's been very kind to me. I'm from out of town, and she has given me a lot of help. I just wanted her to know how much it's appreciated."

The woman smiled again as she returned his credit card. "Well, I'm sure she'll love it," she said, a slight trace of what seemed to be doubt showing through the smile. "You take care now," she concluded as she moved the flowers to a back counter and addressed another customer. He left with the realization that, with few exceptions, most of the people he had contact with since his arrival seemed to give him an uncomfortable feeling of suspicion as if he were visiting unexpectedly in a foreign country. Without really convincing himself, he passed it off as a product of his own awkwardness in social situations coupled with the unrequited memory of being run off the road when he first arrived. Regardless of the circumstances, he had had enough for one day and was glad to be headed home.

It was late afternoon when he got back to the rented house. He made an early dinner and spent the rest of the evening cleaning and arranging, the work bringing to recollection the time he and his mother moved into the house in Youngstown when he was ten years old. He could recall her voice, unusually full and cheerful from the kitchen as he unloaded his things from the boxes that had been placed in his bedroom: "This time it's just you and me, Tucker. This will be our home for good. This is where you'll grow up, and when you leave and get married and have a family of your own, I'll be right here for my grandchildren because I'm just not leaving this house. This is our home now and always will be. So what do you think of that?"

So what do you think of that? he said aloud, shoving the kitchen chair he had moved to sweep under the table so hard that the table skidded a few inches with a clunk as he recalled the possessions stacked haphazardly on a small strip of grass between the sidewalk and street, his mother standing in the yard, alone and pathetic with that blank look on her face and saying nothing as the men awkwardly carried things past her, the people across the street watching discretely, walking slowly but not stopping and whispering to one another as they disapprovingly shook their heads and disappeared into their houses. He could see them peering past their curtains as his mother spoke quietly on the sidewalk with the sheriff's deputy and then handed the little ring of keys to Mr. Bagliocci, who was neither vindictive nor sympathetic as he pocketed the keys and walked to his car, glancing casually at the evicted furniture and unboxed items stacked like trash for pickup before he drove away, without looking back, slowly to the end of the street and then out of sight. They said nothing as they sat on the front step in the heat, the sun brutal and unending as they waited, and he wanted to know what they were waiting for, but he did not ask, would not ask, did not speak to her or look at her, nor did she attempt to engage him, knowing that the revelations and apologies of that morning were the limit of the boy's capacity, the two of them waiting in the heat as the cars drove by slowly, their occupants mouthing in bug-eyed derision behind closed windows as they passed. He saw the U-Haul as it made the turn and moved toward them, and he knew it was for them, and his mother did not ask him to help as she and the two men loaded things, the tall man walking to her first, and she kissed him and said, "This is Tucker. Tucker, this is Steve," and Steve's hand stayed extended before him even as he turned away. Then Steve and the other man finished loading the truck and were gone, and they sat in the sun again, waiting as the heat from the sidewalk rose to their faces, and the sweat dripped from his nose to little splotches that dried on the concrete until Steve returned in a car with cold Cokes, and they sat again, his mother and Steve now on the step and he on the hot grass by the sidewalk until his grandparents arrived. His grandfather helped him take his things from the little pile that had not been loaded on the truck, and they put them into the trunk of the car. Then his mother hugged him and breathed another promise, and he could feel the wetness where her hair stuck to her face in tears and sweat and the familiar mother scent and the invasive minted gin smell that seemed as if it were from somewhere nearby and was not hers. He turned away, and he felt it hard in his stomach as he sat there in Grandpa's air-conditioned car, the leather seats cool on his legs as she talked to her father, and Grandma smiled from the front seat and said nothing as they drove away. He watched through the window as the house grew smaller and smaller and then disappeared as if it had shifted into oblivion with the other houses, and then the streets passed and got smaller and disappeared as well.

VI

He awoke early on Sunday and made breakfast at home. The sun was filtering through the tree line behind the house as he finished cleaning the dishes and put on his running shoes and shorts. He stretched carefully on the front porch, testing the knee and shoulder before jogging down the driveway and over the hill on Mills Hollow Road, the knee warming up well as he ran eastward on Two Stump. It felt good to be running again, running now seeming to be the only consistency in his life—perhaps, at least in his perception, the only gratifying experience that had not changed or disappeared. He had a passion about it, beginning in high school with the first day on the cross-country team that he had joined reluctantly at the urging of the freshman adviser, the act itself having more meaning than the competition offered as the disappointments and confusion of his life fell behind him, freeing him in a sense so that it was only after his legs wore out and his lungs burned like hot coals that he wanted to cry out, not from the pain but the overwhelming suffocation of reality that caught up with him as he collapsed with the other first-day contenders who wheezed and gasped on the dry September grass. He continued to run throughout that first season, and the treasured memories of the following three seasons (he placed third in the state in his senior year), through the South Carolina heat in college, on busy roads in New Jersey, along the Chesapeake Bay and snowy Rocky Mountain trails, usually alone except for the seven sanctioned marathons and when Katherine ran beside him in the park near their house. Katherine was slow at first but willing, and he paced impatiently with her until she gained adequate strength to stay with him for several miles, and he could see her now, stretching as the early morning sun reflected from the pale smooth skin of her legs and her shadowed face childlike beneath her cap and her long brown ponytail bouncing rhythmically across her shoulders. He could see her now, waiting for him in the crowd as he turned the bend in the MS marathon in Denver, her face before him sweet and lovely and her voice rising clear and unabashed above the others, calling, "I love you, Tucker Mason," as he caught her eyes and felt her smile, and it ran like an electrical charge through his body.

Two Stump Road turned sharply past the highway ramp to a long steep decline that he preferred to avoid, minding the tenderness in his knee as he turned back toward the house. The sun was warm and fully above him now as he slowed on the Mills Hollow hill, passing Cecil Beckman, who was already seated on his chair on the front porch, and Jeff, who was loading something into the pickup truck. Cecil nodded solemnly to Mason's waving hand as Jeff looked up from his work with an empty stare, his massive frame rigid and hulking in the weeds beside the house. Mason was walking by the time he reached his driveway, slightly limping as his knee gave in to its weakness. He stretched carefully on the front porch and walked into the house, returning to the porch with a towel and the pitcher of cold water that he kept in the refrigerator. The iron chair seemed a bit uninviting, so he pulled one of the wicker chairs that he had bought from Joebob to the center of the porch and sat down heavily to remove his shoes. He was drinking from the pitcher and nearly dropped it as he looked up and saw the little girl quietly staring at him from the yard between the house and the shop.

He had little experience with children but guessed her age somewhere around seven though perhaps small for her age. She was dressed in bright blue shorts and a white T-shirt that was too large for her small frame, her blond hair brushed neatly about her shoulders and giving her an innocent appearance as she stood there, perfectly still, her dark eyes like tiny stones above high cheekbones, and a small mouth that was partially open and fixed round as if she were startled. It took him a few moments to regain enough composure to speak, fumbling for words, partially from his inexperience in communicating with children but more so from her unexpected presence in his yard so early on a Sunday morning, or at any time, for that matter.

"Well, hello. Who are you?" he asked awkwardly, not exactly sure how to address her. She did not respond and remained still and quiet, and Mason was reminded of his first encounter with Cecil Beckman and Jeff. He tried again, hoping to seem less intimidating. "Are you here with someone?" Still no response. "Well, my name's Tucker. My friends call me Tuck. What do your friends call you?" He looked around, finding it difficult to believe that a child her age would be in his yard unattended but saw no one. "Do you live around here? I think maybe you're my neighbor. Are you my neighbor?" Leaning forward slowly, he put his elbows on the porch rail and rested his chin on his forearms, speaking as softly as he could, realizing now that she was clearly frightened. "Well, it's certainly nice of you to visit me. I have some work to do now but maybe you can come back sometime, and we can have another little chat. Okay? And maybe when you come back, you can bring your name with you and maybe your mom or dad."

He felt a sense of desperation, not knowing what to do about a strange child standing in his yard, when she stepped forward, raising one foot and placing it flat beneath her and following with the other, then standing still again as before as her mouth rose at the corners into a kind of pinched smile that revealed the childlike symmetry of her teeth, and she drew in a short breath, her voice surprisingly deep and strained, and she was obviously struggling to form her words, her eyes firmly set on his, "She said you need to go now," rolled from the little round mouth. "She said he's coming back, and you have to go now. Sh-she said I should tell you that."

Taken aback, not only from what seemed like a warning but the strange sound of its delivery, Mason said nothing at first as the girl returned to the same countenance that she had held before speaking. With some difficulty, he responded, fumbling for words, "Who said? What are you talking about?" But the girl was stepping back as he spoke, reversing with a flat-footed retreat as she turned, holding her stare briefly before she began to run, slowly at first and then with surprising agility as she bolted around the corner of the shop.

"Wait!" he called as she disappeared, and he stood up to find that his knee had stiffened sufficiently to impede his movement, causing him to limp down the steps, and he was further hampered as his bare feet came into contact with the gravel in the lot. He loosened quickly as he ran around the shop and caught sight of the girl just before she ran and ducked into a thicket at the perimeter of the lawn. The grass was still cool to the bottoms of his feet as he trotted across the yard, admonishing himself that he was probably wasting time chasing her but moving nevertheless to the small gap in the brush where she had scampered in like a mouse slipping through a crack in a baseboard. He stepped partially into the gap, expecting to find a clearing or path, but he found only a forbidding heaviness of blackberry bushes that blocked his movement with thorns that were like barbed wire discarded in a heap. Stepping back into the lawn, he looked around the thicket and poked his head into the opening again, refusing to disbelieve what he knew he had seen, his foot finding a loose thorn in the grass. The thorn fell away as he jerked the foot upward, and he returned quickly to the porch, slipping the shoes unlaced onto his feet and ran back to the thicket, this time entering the opening fully, and he found himself inside a dark hollow area defined by thick shrubbery and the blackberry bushes and covered almost entirely by the bows of an ancient pine tree that grew beside them. At first, he could see nowhere for the girl to have gone, and he stood there, bewildered and annoyed, his thoughts ranging from curiosity to anger to concern for the safety of the child in the unforgiving brush. Then as he was about to retreat back into the yard, he noticed a small open patch in the shaded area beneath one of the pine boughs.

Knowing little about wooded areas, Mason had assumed that the mass of trees, shrubs, thickets, and weeds that defined the edge of the yard was the prevailing texture of the woods behind it, not realizing until now that the thickness of growth could only exist where the sun had enough access to permit it. As he leaned beneath the pine bough, almost down on his hands and knees, he saw the forest beyond it, open and wooded beneath a tall canopy of branches through which random shafts of sunlight shone upon the tree trunks and foliage. He stepped forward from beneath the pine bough and stood up, briefly absorbed by the vibrancy of the place but immediately feeling a sense of urgency and vulnerability as he moved carefully among the trees, not expecting to see the girl but hoping to find a path that she would have taken in her retreat from his yard. Her childish admonition could be nothing more than playful consequence of a dare, and he considered the possibility of a half dozen other children giggling from behind the trees as he stumbled foolishly, stepping on his shoelaces as he fell forward and rammed his still-tender shoulder into a low branch. He tied the shoes and ran on, rubbing the shoulder as the frustration of Wells County began to affect him with the recollection of the bearded face in his broken windshield and Verna Lee's senseless prattle and the dubious inference of the florist in Kingsport and now this pain-in-the-ass kid whose parents were going to hear from him when he caught up with her.

The ground was now continually dropping beneath his feet, sometimes so severely that he had to steady himself by grabbing the smaller tree trunks, leaning toward the ground at times so he could smell the dirt and rotting leaves below him. He stopped, realizing that the little girl must have scurried off in a different direction and tried to get his bearings, picturing in his mind the map and aerial photograph that he had studied with Cavalone the previous day. The ground rose ahead of him a short distance and then seemed to level out slightly before dropping again into a dark flat area where the sun only broke through occasionally, dappling the uppermost leaves and leaving the forest floor dark and mossy. Mason had given up on finding the little girl but was drawn to this place by curiosity and continued forward, soon finding himself among the closeness of the trees and dead wood that smelled of mold and decay and the damp-ness that seemed to permeate the air. It was substantially cooler here, and he felt a chill in the stillness that penetrated his sweat-soaked shirt and caused him to shiver slightly. He stood quietly among the lushness of the ferns and ivy that grew in clumps about the deadfall, noticing a dense proximity of trees enclosing a small clearing about twenty yards ahead. As he neared the clearing, he noticed two narrow trails leading into it, or more likely one trail that traversed it, and he felt an unwarranted sense of foreboding that he attributed to his imagination as he stood there, considering the two dark entrances as one choosing between two doors, hearing nothing at first but the light rush of breeze through the treetops and the birds that chirped invisibly among the branches. He moved cautiously to his right where the trail was hard packed beneath a scattering of growth and leaves, indicating, perhaps, that its frequency of use was mostly in the past as it gradually restored its keeping with the forest. The path ran fairly straight at first, like a corridor through the brush and timber, and then became twisted, descending steeply in places and sometimes obscured to the point of disappearing altogether where the leaves and fallen branches were as thick as on the adjoining ground. Mason walked for some distance and began to tire of the trail and the woods and his pursuit of the little girl. But he pressed on, realizing now that he had covered some distance since he first left his yard and was not entirely sure of his relative position and reasoning that the trail would logically have to lead somewhere, probably back to Two Stump Road, where he could get his bearings and walk home. He was feeling quite foolish at this point and pictured himself climbing out of the woods in his wet shirt and running shorts to the amusement of one of the locals passing by in a pickup truck.

He kept moving along the path until it opened into another clearing that was larger than the first. His knee had begun throbbing and was quite weak now, so he stopped and climbed up to sit on the rotting trunk of an enormous tree that had fallen across one end of the clearing. At the other end of the clearing, he could see the path that had led him there, as well as its apparent continuation about thirty yards to the left that seemed to run parallel to the slope as it disappeared among the trees. It was only after he jumped down from his seat on the fallen tree that he noticed the third path, which was completely blocked at its entrance by the tree and appeared to be largely overgrown from disuse to the point that it was hard to distinguish its direction after a few feet from the clearing. As best as he could determine, this path seemed to lead more in the direction of his house, so he climbed back over the dead tree, pushing his way through the brush and saplings that obscured the path and, favoring the knee, moved carefully forward for a few hundred yards, stopping as a deep hollow opened before him suddenly at a bend in the trail. The ground fell so steeply just a few feet in front of him that he imagined he would have fallen down the slope had he been moving as fast as he had been earlier. He stood quietly, attempting again to get his bearings and realizing that he was indeed lost somewhere on the west slope of Bright's Mountain, a fact that both amused and embarrassed him as he looked around at the vastness and impermeable depth of the place, noticing now that the undercurrent of natural sounds that had pervaded the woods seemed to have dissipated to an eerie silence that held him suspended as if holding his breath. He was running now, his feet thumping on the path as he limped along the ridge, descending and then rising, so he was again climbing and pulling himself along until he reached a level clearing and stumbled into the brightness of the late-morning sun.

Mason looked back toward the path, bewildered by the incredible sense of panic that had gripped him as he ran. He leaned forward and caught his breath as he rubbed his knee, debating whether or not to reenter the path. Right now, he just wanted to get home and put some ice on his knee and shoulder and forget that he ever had seen the little girl in his yard and to commit to himself that he would never again set foot in that godforsaken woods. He stretched and turned away from the woods, seeing only the eyes at first, dark blue and intense as they drew his focus inward to them as if to impart their terror. He stood frozen for a moment as the fixation held him captivated until he was able to comprehend a woman's face in the periphery of the eyes, soft and pale with high cheekbones and narrow lips held tight and pressed above a trembling chin, her long reddish hair neatly draped over thin shoulders, which barely held the open shirt that hung from them, revealing a designer T-shirt beneath the denim with some indistinguishable printing across the front. As the periphery opened further, Mason noticed the small house behind her, and then he saw the ancient double-barreled shotgun, held waist high in trembling hands that gripped the stock so tightly that the knuckles showed white against the dark wood and steel.

"You can't be here," the woman said, her voice low and strangely timorous as her eyes held firmly on his. "You need to move elsewhere."

Mason stood quiet and speechless before her, carefully regarding her form as he tried to compose himself. She was thin and pale, sickly, perhaps, though there was a subdued vibrancy about her, a pulsing volatility that made the presence of the shotgun even more threatening. He spoke carefully to her, constantly watching her hands on the gun, "I'm sorry. I didn't mean to intrude. My name's Tucker Mason. I just recently moved here. I got lost in the woods and—"

"You have to go," she interrupted. "Now go on and make your plans to move out." The slight movement that she made with the shotgun drew Mason's attention to it, and he noticed the severely rusted barrel and trigger guard, the corrosion so advanced that he seriously doubted that the gun could be fired. She held it away from her body, her hands wrapped awkwardly around the stock, and it was apparent that its feel was foreign and disturbing to her. He briefly considered the possibility of taking it from her. Disarming her so easily seemed a bit belligerent, considering the fact that he had been chasing a child through the woods and was a total stranger with no justification for being on someone's secluded property. He chose the obvious alternative, which was to extract himself as quickly as possible, although returning to the woods was not an option.

"Okay, ma'am," Mason said, turning his palms up and returning to the captivation of her hollow stare. "I'm really sorry to disturb you. I was just lost and had no intention to bother anyone." As he was speaking, she looked quickly and furtively over her shoulder toward the house, and he realized that the terror in her eyes was not for him but for something else in that direction, though he could see nothing threatening as he stole a look at the house for himself. He moved sideways, still facing her as he stepped in the direction of the house, surmising that the road must be just to the other side of it.

"Not that way," she shouted, shaking her head violently. "Back the way you came."

Mason looked back at the opening in the brush where he had come out of the woods and considered the alternative. "I...ah... need to get to the road," he stammered as he continued to move away from the woman, his eyes alternating between the shotgun and her face, which was contorting tightly as tears streamed and dripped from the soft protrusions of her cheekbones. She did not move to face him as he circled behind her but stood there sobbing uncontrollably.

"Please," he heard her say in a nearly inaudible voice as he backed away from her and began to run, turning clear of the house, the weeds in the long-neglected lawn whipping about his legs as he ran. He broke into a full sprint, imagining the shotgun pointed at his back when he saw the driveway, weed-choked gravel access followed through another heavily wooded area for several hundred yards and then across a rotting wooden bridge before it terminated at near a willow copse that hid the road from his immediate vision.

He slowed to a walk when he got to the road, mainly due to the stiffness in his knee, feeling hollow and weak, though he did not dare stop or even look back until he was a clear distance from the driveway. The road was not familiar, though he was fairly sure it was Two Stump for the simple reason that he was not aware of any other roads in the area. Guessing that he was headed north by the position of the sun, he continued along the road to a sharp bend that overlooked a steep gorge before continuing downward where, in the distance ahead, he could see what appeared to be where Mill Hollow road spilled away into the hollow below. He stopped, leaning on a large rock at the bend and looked behind him, his mind racing as he rubbed his knee and twisted the shoulder slowly. Breathing deeply, bewildered and maybe angry about the experience of the past hour— was it that long?—he found an emerging revulsion for Wells County, Virginia, and Cletus Wellman's goddamn house in this goddamn goofy-assed nest of hillbillies, and Leo could take that goddamn prison and stick it for all he cared. He walked forward furiously, his heels hitting heavily on the pavement despite the discomfort in his knee, his anger directed as much at himself as anything else, fatigued and thirsty in the late-morning sun.

Cecil Beckman's sudden and imminent presence on his front porch had a strange effect on Mason as he descended on Mills Hollow Road, the relative familiarity giving a rather tacit sense of comfort despite the suspicion he had acquired of anyone who lived in or near Wells County. Mason, disgusted and desperately thirsty, intended at first to ignore the man, having had quite enough of the aberrant creatures he apparently had for neighbors. However, his natural inquisitiveness seemed to prevail as he turned into Cecil's driveway, thinking that, perhaps, there could be some explanation, some redeeming resolution for Low Creek that Cecil, weird as he was, could offer. Mason approached the porch, stopping at the steps, as he had done several weeks ago. Surprisingly, it was Cecil who spoke first.

"Been runnin' again, are ya? Never could figger why a body would run widdout somethin' a-chasing him. 'Course, it ain't no business of mine nohow. Ain't no more bother than me a-settin here, I guess. 'Cept I probably ain't as tired as you. Whatcha do to yerself there? Ya take a spill or somethin'?"

Mason looked instinctively down at himself, realizing only then the dark stain on his shirt where he had run his shoulder into the tree branch earlier and the scratches on his legs, some of which were bleeding in tiny streaks down the shin. "Yeah, I…took a spill," he answered, having no desire to explain anything further.

Cecil scratched his head, staring at Mason without expression. "Somethin' I could do fer ya?" he asked.

Mason was unprepared to answer. "Uh, no, thank you. I just thought I'd stop and say good morning." He was really feeling foolish now, wishing he had never entered the yard, and he was extremely tired.

"Well," Cecil said as he leaned back in his chair, tilting it against the wood siding, "Good mornin'." He remained leaning back, looking straight ahead as if Mason wasn't there. Mason, however, was determined to remain for some reason he was unable to define as he stood there, sweating and bruised, feeling rather absurd in his running shorts and soiled shirt and shoes over bare feet and blood drying on his legs. He struggled for something to say that would engage Cecil into some kind of conversation.

"Where's Jeff?" he asked.

"Ain't here."

"Is he your son?"

Cecil turned slightly toward him, remaining in his tilted position. "Nope."

"Your grandson?"

"Nope."

"Well, I saw him here earlier. Anyway, I just was wondering if he was related to you."

"Ain't."

Mason could see that there was probably little hope in gaining any information from the man but decided to try once more to engage him. "There aren't many people living around here. At least not compared to what I'm used to." He immediately wished he could recall the words, thinking that Cecil might find the comment condescending. But Cecil simply stared ahead and answered, "Yup."

Mason continued, willing to make one last attempt before giving up. "There's a house about a half mile in that direction." He pointed toward the direction he came from. "Sits back from the road a bit, kind of in the woods. You know the one I'm talking about?"

Cecil turned his head toward Mason and glared through his thick glasses. "Yeah, I know it."

"Can you tell me who lives there?"

"Ain't nobody lives there."

"Well, I think someone does live there. I saw someone there this morning. Maybe they just moved in."

"Ain't nobody lives there."

Obviously, Mason was getting nowhere. As he started to turn away and excuse himself, he remembered his conversation with Cletus several weeks ago: "Give him a beer, and he'll pass bull to you all night..."

"Well," Mason said, "I guess I should go. Just wanted to say hi." He turned to walk away but stopped and looked back at Cecil. "Hey, maybe you might want to have a beer sometime."

Cecil leaned forward, his chair legs tapping the floor of the porch. He adjusted his glasses and looked at Mason with what appeared to be a sort of childish smile. "Ya gotcha some beer?'

"Sure. Got plenty in my refrigerator."

Cecil leaned even further over his knees. "Well," he said, revealing the gaps of missing teeth, "I reckon iffen you got beer and need someone to help ya drink it, ya mights just as well bring it over."

Mason turned again and was walking out of the yard as he spoke, "I'll do that. Maybe tonight. That okay with you?

"Yup."

Once in his house, Mason showered and treated the scratches on his legs. He retrieved the ice packs that he had kept in the freezer and placed them on the knee and shoulder as he sat on the porch in one wicker chair with his feet on the other. Leaning his head back, he felt the physical and mental exhaustion that the day's events had caused, and he dozed off into a shallow sleep for an hour or so, waking with a start that caused both ice packs to fall to the porch floor. Though he could not remember dreaming, a gripping panic had quickened his pulse and caused his heart to thump in his chest as he sat up in the chair, blinking as he adjusted his eyesight to the daylight in the yard. He remained seated for a moment, composing himself in the shade of the porch, silently analyzing his unfounded alarm upon waking, finally concluding that he had experienced one of those obscure nightmares that fade from detailed recollection, leaving only the residual fear of its implications. It must have been quite a dream, though, he thought to himself, and he was almost glad to have forgotten its terrors, considering the possibility that his mind had reached its limit of weird things today and, obligingly, obliterated the memory. Nevertheless, the fear was still there as he struggled to regain some equanimity, gazing into the lot at nothing in particular, something then catching his attention suddenly, though at first he did not know what it was exactly; something askew that he noticed after the fact in the same way that one would notice details of a car only after it has passed on the road, his focus returning to the shop and the door that was partially opened.

He slipped on his moccasins and got up slowly from the chair, stepping carefully down the steps into the gravel lot. He approached the shop but did not walk directly to the door, choosing to examine the area around it first, his mind clamoring to determine whether he could have possibly opened the door himself. Not possible, he concluded, as he peered around the side of the shop opposite the house, seeing nothing unusual in the yard beyond. He crossed back past the door, keeping a distance from it as he checked between the house and the other side of the shop, seeing nothing but the annoying reminder of his ridiculous pursuit of the little girl across the yard that morning. Positioning himself to the hinged side of the door, he reached forward and pressed it fully open, following it slowly as he adjusted his eyes to the darkness inside.

It would be no surprise, he thought to himself as he flicked on the light, to find another one of these whacked-out hill-jacks standing in there, goofy-eyed like some kind of mountain zombie. But to his relief, no one was there, and the shop appeared unchanged from the way he had left it the day before. He stood in the middle of it, carefully inspecting the lawn mower and garden tools, the benches, the floor. The windows were still locked, and the door should have been, because he could clearly remember locking and testing it the day before, then hooking the key to his key chain before leaving. It was the key chain that troubled him now, as he ran into the house to his bedroom, finding it in exactly the position he had left it on his dresser. He was suddenly chilled by the possibility that someone could have entered the house and taken the keys and then reentered to replace them. But that would be impossible with the alarm on. Holding the keys tightly, he walked through the kitchen and checked the back door, finding its dead bolt securely in place. He then returned to the shop and inspected it once more. Still seeing nothing out of place, he slammed the door and locked it, vowing to call Sally first thing in the morning and have the lock changed.

Mason stood in the lot, unnerved by the prospect of someone actually entering the shop while he slept on the porch and angry about the day in general. Weakly convincing himself that he had been mistaken about locking the door, he walked into the house and slammed the front door shut behind him, throwing the dead bolt hard into its slide. He turned on the television, thankful for the small satellite dish mounted on the back porch and watched a news program while he ate a sandwich and pulled the burrs from the laces on his running shoes.

Jeff was sitting on the porch steps when Mason arrived that evening. He raised his head slightly as Mason acknowledged him but kept his eyes straight ahead, staring into the yard. Cecil was in his usual place in his chair on the porch, and he beckoned Mason to sit in the chair next to him, which, Mason realized, was reserved for him, leaving Jeff to the steps. Bringing beer to Cecil's house obviously carried privileges. Mason handed Cecil a can of beer from the six-pack he carried and reached one down to Jeff, who took it into his massive hand without looking back, silently cracking the tab and drinking half of the contents in one gulp.

Cecil took a long drink and held the can out in front of him. He said to Mason, "Right neighborly o' ya to come visit, Mr.—what's yer name again?"

"Tucker. Tucker Mason. Most people call me Tuck."

"Right nice o' ya, Tuck." Cecil took another drink as Jeff belched noisily. They sat drinking quietly for a while, saying nothing as Jeff finished off his beer and crushed the can in his hand. Mason handed another down to him. Then Cecil said, "So ya come to build that prison and then ya head off. Is that it?"

"Yeah. That's what I'm doing."

"An' whilst you're here, you figger to find out about us mountain folk. Is that it?"

"I'd like to know some things."

Cecil eyed Mason as he rubbed the heavy gray stubble on his chin. "Well, you ain't the first nosy sombitch come around wantin' to know stuff, and you probably ain't the last." He reached into the six-pack and popped open another beer, then leaning his chair back until his head rested against the siding of the house, asked, "So what is it you're so desperate to know?"

T he walls of the prison were now appearing in stark, singular assemblies on the building pads, the heavy precast end panels of cell blocks 3 and 4 set in place with a crane in three days while the masonry crew had begun the commissary envelope, their scaffolds rising with the courses of concrete block that ran from the corners to the center of the east and south walls. Two of the prefabricated cells had arrived and sat prominently on the ground near the entrance where Casey had ordered them fitted up as prototypes before releasing the rest of the cells from the fabricator in Louisville. Mason watched briefly from his office as a flatbed with two more end panels completed the excruciating two hours it took to climb up the access road in low gear, a logistical problem that Casey had resolved by pacing deliveries so that eight trucks arrived per day, making the climb in pairs spaced a hundred yards apart to allow other vehicles adequate room for passing. The panels were then off-loaded immediately near their erection points as Casey chastened truckers to pull their empty rigs off the site to provide space for the next delivery.

Jamie moved efficiently around the conference area outside Mason's office, quietly arranging materials for the weekly Friday scheduling meeting as Mason pulled his papers together and grabbed a yellow legal pad, which he carried to his usual position at the near end of the cluster of tables. He could hear the footsteps of the subcontractors and his own staff as they clumped heavily on the wooded stairs that led to the trailer, and he was glad for their presence, the necessity of his time and concentration taking him from the distractions of the past several weeks and giving him some respite from the bizarre occurrences at the house he had rented and the equally bizarre, yet admittedly intriguing, commentary from Cecil Beckman, whose fragmented vignettes had not really answered any questions and, if anything, made the circumstances more perplexing.

Mason had at first tried to make light of it to himself, crediting coincidence and his own absentmindedness for the circumstances of that Sunday three weeks ago that led him to Cecil's porch, where Cecil prattled on between gulps of beer, wiping his mouth with his forearm and stopping his rambling discourse only long enough for Jeff to lift him from his seat and, in one movement, swing him gently over the porch rail to the ground where he wobbled on twisted legs as he urinated in the weeds beside the house. Cecil had at least one story for each of Mason's questions, usually getting sidetracked into another story that reminded him of another event and, of course, another story so that Mason would often have to repeat the original question in frustration. But Mason listened nonetheless, the stories eventually constituting a vague relevance to a rather staggered history of the area that both fascinated and disturbed him enough to induce him to return several times, possibly out of loneliness as much as curiosity, each time carrying beer like some kind of ritualistic offering for Cecil's continuing saga, the intensity of which always increased as the beer was consumed. Cecil talked incessantly, often getting animated as he squirmed about his hard wooden chair, following Mason through the thick lenses of his glasses when Mason would suddenly rise from the oppressive chair that Jeff always dutifully vacated for him to stretch his legs and relieve his posterior. Jeff always sat heavily on the porch steps, solemnly drinking and belching and occasionally raising his head toward Cecil to validate some point in a story without taking his staring eyes from the yard before him. Yet, despite the discomfort of the chair and the mosquitoes and Cecil's sometimes infantile demeanor, not to mention Jeff's oafishness piled on the porch steps and the fact that he still did not know who was so clearly offended by his presence in Wells County, Mason actually found himself enjoying these visits.

The reality, however, still was always with him as he returned home, and he was always aware of the peculiarity of his situation: the shop door was open again as he walked up the driveway from Cecil Beckman's on that Sunday night and ajar enough to reveal the absolute darkness within that seemed to obscure not only the interior of the shop but the source of all the strange things that would occur over the next few weeks. Mason and Sally played some phone tag, finally connecting the following evening, and she thanked him for the flowers and talked some about her son's graduation before Mason told her about the shop door. The locksmith from Kingsport arrived the next day, handing Mason the keys ("this one's for the latch and this one's for the deadbolt, just like Mrs. Wellman told me"). Sally showed up that night.

"Just the same," she said, slipping her bare feet beneath her as she sat on one of the wicker chairs on the front porch. "I hate to think that one of Casey's laborers would have reproduced that key when they delivered the lawn mower. I honestly don't think it was them." She leaned toward him, touching his arm as she continued. "Now don't shoot me, darlin'. I'm just tryin' to help. But the locksmith said maybe that lock wasn't workin' right. Ya know what I mean? Like maybe it wasn't catchin'. That's why I had 'em put the double locks on. I use that locksmith 'cause that's who Cletus has his account with, and I certainly ain't sayin' they're the best, but they ain't gone wrong on us yet. Anyway, I feel a lot better about thinkin' that way, don't you?"

Mason smiled at her subtle humor. "You mean thinking that way instead of thinking someone was in the shop?"

Sally's eyes held him in their sincerity. "Well, I don't know who would go in there or why. Do you? Really now, Tucker, do you have any idea? If there was someone in there, why didn't they steal somethin'?"

"Cecil across the road says there are ghosts up here," Mason said quietly, embarrassed for the reference.

"Oh pooh. Cecil'd say anything to make a good story."

"So you're saying that there are no ghosts?" Mason returned, failing to achieve sincerity in his voice.

Sally looked briefly at the floor and then back at him, her tone growing noticeably quieter. "There's been tales about ghosts on Bright's Mountain for's long as I can remember, sweetie. Mountain folk are partial to ghost stories, so it ain't hard to get a good one rollin'."

"So you think Cecil's making it all up?"

"Oh, he's probably just puttin' spice to some old story he heard when he was a boy. I can't much deny that I done the same thing myself a few times. I still don't think it was a ghost or anything else what opened that door." Sally pointed toward the shop. "I think we solved that mystery and put it up for good."

Mason stood and leaned over the porch rail. "Okay, Sally. I'll go with you on the shop door. But what about the other stuff?"

She turned back to him, though he continued to stare off into the distance, where the sun was setting beyond the tree line. "What other stuff?" she asked.

He told her about the little girl in his yard and the woman who had chased him at gunpoint and Verna Lee's ambiguous agitation by his presence on Bright's Mountain. Sally listened politely as he spoke, showing neither disbelief nor corroboration of his story but simply nodding in quiet reception. Her eyes fixed on him as she sat unmoving in the wicker chair. When he finished, she smiled and said, "Sweetie, I'm awful sorry you're bein' affected like this. Truth is, I don't have a clue as to who you saw in your yard or who's so protective of Correl's house up there. There really aren't many people livin' on this side of the mountain anymore."

"Correl's house?" Mason said. "Is that who lives there?" Members of the Correl family had figured prominently in Cecil Beckman's stories, though Cecil had always evaded questions about the family, much to Mason's frustration.

Sally held her wrist in front of her, squinting as she attempted in vain to see the face of her watch in the waning daylight. "Like I said, there ain't nobody livin' there. Correl's the ones what built it. They're all gone for some time now. Been a number of people lived there. Even my mama. But as far as I know, it's empty now."

"Your mother lived there?"

She squinted at the watch again and answered quietly, "For a time, she did. After I was gone." She didn't seem to want to elaborate.

There was a brief silence, and Mason continued, "So what's with the old waitress from Harley's?" He was relieved to see the smile return to Sally's face.

"Oh, Verna Lee ought to know better. I expect she's just gettin' a little strange in her old age."

Sally pulled her feet from underneath her and put them on the floor, leaning forward over her knees. "Listen, sugar," she said, her eyes warm and sympathetic, "if you ain't comfortable up here, then why don't we consider movin' you to Kingsport. Cletus has bought another two-family, and he's fixin' it up real good. You figure that might work out for you?"

Mason sat back in his chair and stared at the tree line in the waning sunlight. He hesitated for a moment, contemplating the air of capitulation that seemed to accompany her offer. "I don't know, Sally," he said, his eyes still fixed on the trees, "I kind of like it here. Besides, I hate the thought of moving again."

"Well, the offer's there if you change your mind," Sally said as she stood up, stretching backward with her hands on her hips as she stepped into her sandals. "I gotta go now, sweetie, but I'll be checkin' on you." There was a sense of genuine concern about her that Mason found comforting. He wanted her to stay, and the feeling embarrassed him privately.

"Thanks for coming out, Sally," he said as he watched her form moving gracefully in the twilight shadows to her car. She smiled and waved to him, and he sat alone on the porch, watching her car as it pulled out of the driveway and disappeared beyond the trees, her tail lights flickering through the leaves and fading with the sound of the car as it found the road and drove away.

"Tucker," Jamie said, taking him from his thoughts with a slight start. Her childlike voice was always clear and refreshing amid the crassness of the jobsite. "I put the summary schedules on your table for you, but I can get you the detail if you want it. I just didn't think you'd be wanting to mess with all that stuff in your meeting." The door opened as Cavalone entered, talking over his shoulder to one of the subcontractors who was following him. The rest of the meeting attendees followed closely behind, their shoes clumping noisily on the floor of the trailer. Casey entered last, slamming the door behind him. Mason thanked Jamie, and she dismissed herself, politely acknowledging the others as she disappeared into her cubicle.

The meeting ended shortly before noon. Casey and Cavalone persuaded Mason to have lunch with them at Harley's, and they sat at Casey's usual table while Verna Lee teased with them as she filled their plastic water glasses. Since the Saturday morning when she had seemed so disturbed by his presence, Verna Lee had changed her demeanor around Mason, treating him with the same familiarity as the others, though with a subtle sense of respectful commonality, as if they shared some great, unspoken secret. She touched him on the shoulder as she moved around the table. "How's the boss today? Is these boys behavin' themselves?" she said as she shuffled on, not necessarily waiting for an answer.

After lunch, the afternoon was spent mostly on the building pads attending to the usual issues of construction with Casey, the dust swirling in the breeze and settling on Mason's skin as he perspired in the heat of early summer sun. It was almost four o'clock when he finally got back into the trailer and began to process his paperwork and e-mails as the work on the site began to wind down. At five thirty, Jamie walked into his office and asked him if she would be needed anymore.

"No, Jamie, have a good weekend," he told her, and she turned, her clothing loose and fluttering on the sparseness of her form as she locked the filing cabinets and left, carefully closing the door behind her.

Work on the site had ceased by now, and Casey appeared briefly in the trailer to finish up some business before leaving, calling his goodbye over his shoulder to Mason as he left, the door slamming hard behind him. Mason watched him through the window as he watched the security guard lock the entry gate and drove his truck down the access road. Alone in the trailer, Mason sat in front of his computer and stared through the window at the valley below as the first shadows of evening were cast across the mountains. Incidents of the last three weeks emerged again in his mind, disturbing things that had occurred with such innocuous subtlety that he hesitated to even acknowledge them to himself although their collateral effect on him was causing a rather portentous sense of insecurity and, strangely, an almost obsessive curiosity. He sat back from his desk as they arose in his consciousness: the wicker chairs upside down on the porch when he got home from work, the twisted vines hanging from the front doorknob, the way the crickets and locusts would suddenly stop their chorus in the trees at night. He was mowing the lawn on a Sunday when the gasoline can unexplainably exploded where he had left it on the opposite side of the house, sending a plume of flames into the air and leaving a large burn spot in the grass. After his run on several mornings, he found objects on the porch: an old shoe, a spent bullet casing, small, shiny stones that did not match anything in the gravel lot, a pile of tiny wood slivers, broken glass, and other trivial items, always placed neatly in front of the door at exactly the same location. Loud thumps would occur at the front door late at night, and long scratches appeared on his car one morning. What sounded like an air horn would break the silence in early morning hours. He returned from the jobsite on a Friday afternoon and found one pane of the bedroom window broken although the window remained locked. It was after he had called the sheriff's office that he realized the hole in the headboard of his bed. He dug the lead fragments of a bullet from the wall in the adjoining bathroom with a pocket knife.

Deputy Gabriel Setty slid his thumb across the hole in the headboard and opened his palm to reveal the bullet fragments that Mason had handed to him. "Ain't much left of it," he said, staring at the tiny blob of lead in his hand. "High caliber. Probably a lot of hunting rifles around here what could claim it."

Mason tried to maintain his composure, though he was still shaking slightly from the realization that someone had actually shot a gun into his house. The deputy checked the path of the bullet thoroughly with a kind of abstracted curiosity, sliding a pencil through the holes and peering through the window at the wall of trees across the lawn. He moved through the kitchen and out the back door into the lawn, drawing a line in the air from the window to the tree line. Making notes in a small spiral notebook, he returned to the house and stared out the window, making a clicking sound with his tongue. He then walked outside again, and Mason followed.

"So what do you think?" Mason asked, getting restless with the deputy's apparently pointless investigation.

The deputy raised his chin in the air and sniffed. He was young, well under thirty, slightly overweight and cumbersome in his ill-fitting uniform and the heavy equipment belt around his waist. His face had a soft, vulnerable look with a slight reddening on his cheeks that made him appear even younger than his years, and Mason imagined he had had to deal with baby-face jokes most of his life. Mason seriously doubted the man's capability.

"What I think, Mr. Mason, is that somebody was doin' some target shootin' off somewhere in the woods and your house caught a stray bullet. Folks just don't realize how far a bullet can travel. Could have been a mile or more away."

Mason shook his head. "Are you telling me that someone could shoot from a mile off, miss all the trees along the way and hit my house by accident?" He could feel the anger rising in his throat, thinking back to his interview with the state accident investigator in Casey's living room. "Come on, Deputy, for crissake, that's about as far-fetched as you can get."

Deputy Setty turned toward Mason, blinking his eyes as his lower lip and chin quivered. He stood silent and motionless for a moment, apparently searching for words to reply to Mason's implied challenge of his forensic capability. "I could pretty well figure the trajectory of the bullet by the angle of the entry hole in the wall and the path it took," he said finally, his voice taking on an authoritative tone despite his obvious insecurity. "It actually came down over the trees there. More'n likely it came from the ridge over on the other side of the four-lane. Like I said, these things can travel surprising long distances." He looked toward the tops of the trees across the yard. "I'll tell you what, though. I'll take a ride over there and see if anyone's been shootin' a rifle at birds or somethin'. Folks can get irresponsible with a gun sometimes."

Mason was bristling at the deputy's incompetence. "You know what I think, Deputy? I think someone shot out my window on purpose. I think someone has a burr up his ass about me living here for some reason and is trying to scare me away. There have been a lot of strange things going on around here lately, and quite frankly, I'm getting damn sick of it. So if you are going to check around, I would hope you would do it around here first."

The deputy wrote something in his notebook, exhibiting a strange calmness that apparently came from the fact that Mason's loss of control defaulted to his favor. He looked at Mason with a renewed sense of self-confidence. "What kind of strange things, Mr. Mason?" he asked with a developing sense of arrogance.

The question was unsettling to Mason. Suddenly, relating the string of incidents that had occurred prior to this one seemed like foolish paranoia as he briefly described the things that had occurred. Deputy Setty listened politely, jotting in his notebook as Mason spoke. After Mason finished, the deputy stuffed the notebook into his back pocket and started walking to his patrol car.

"I'll check out the Correl place, Mr. Mason. Who knows, there might be someone squattin' over there and doing something they ain't supposed to. Just the same, I wouldn't just walk out of the woods uninvited onto someone's property. Folks around here get pretty protective. You know what I mean?" He opened the door of his patrol car, an aging but well-kept Ford Bronco, and jerked his thumb toward the driveway. "As far as the other things, well there's a nutcase lives across the road. He's harmless, I'm sure, but I'll have a word with his keeper and make sure he's being properly supervised."

"It's not him," Mason returned immediately, shaking his head. He had considered Jeff's propensity for eavesdropping but dismissed any other suspicions when he got to know the man, as much as that was possible, and realized that this was far beyond Jeff's capability. "I know them," he said. "It's not Jeff."

The deputy smiled slightly as he removed his hat and got into his car. He closed the door and opened the window. "Mr. Mason," he said, almost pompously, "some folks have a hard time adjustin' to life in these mountains. I grew up here, so I don't know one way or the other. I guess I'd be the same way iffen I had to move to a big city, ya know? You take care now, Mr. Mason, and I'll follow up and check around to make sure nobody's tryin' to git ya. If I find out who was shootin' a gun in the air, I'll make sure they pay up for that window too. You call if you have any more trouble." He backed up and pulled out of the driveway before Mason could respond.

"Idiot deputy," Mason spat as he kicked at the gravel in the lot. He moved the bed to another wall in his bedroom and slept on the couch in the living room that night, waking and dreaming sporadically until dawn...

Mason shut down his computer and left the trailer, locking the door behind him as the evening filled into the hills in looming shadows from the setting sun. It was still warm, and the humidity increased as he drove to the lower elevation down the access road to Two Stump where he made the left turn toward Low Creek. There were a dozen or so vehicles in front of Harley's as he pulled into the lot, mostly the older cars and pickups that prevailed among the locals. Mason went through the buffet line, took hearty portions of fried chicken and mashed potatoes and sat at the usual small table near the window that he liked when he was there alone. Verna Lee had worked the lunch shift, so a young waitress named Dawn brought him a water glass and napkin. She was a heavy girl, friendly and always smiling despite the obvious discomfort of her uniform, which was about two sizes too small, and she joked with Mason briefly about coming here twice in one day before she moved awkwardly to the other tables in the room.

He finished his dinner and left the restaurant, realizing that he had left his cell phone in the car while he was eating. Sally had called him earlier and offered again to relocate him to the two-family that Cletus had recently purchased. "It's still good, sweetie," Sally had said, "but Cletus says they still ain't done with fixin' it up. He says it'll be a week or maybe two. In the meantime, why don't you stay here at the Inn where I can keep an eye on ya?" Mason had declined the offer, preferring not to appear desperate. He knew that the call currently indicated on his voice mail was Sally attempting to change his mind, which would frustrate him since in truth he really wanted some of Sally's reassuring company. Nevertheless, he had other plans for the evening.

Dusk was approaching as he drove out, his mind racing from one fragmented thought to another as Katherine slid quietly into his consciousness, and he could hear her voice softly by his side.

* * *

"When I was in France," she was saying, "the headmaster at the school where I was teaching took several of us for a weekend at this ancient villa near the coast. It was a beautiful place, almost like a castle, with stone palisades and tiered gardens and an enormous hall with all sorts of relics and old paintings everywhere." She was lying on her stomach as she spoke, with her chin resting on a pillow, and Mason could see her silhouette in the moonlight as he gently stroked the softness of her back. She continued, "But I never saw a scarier place once it got dark. It seemed like shadows were moving everywhere, and there was this constant creaking sound in my room and other distant, indescribable sounds, you know like things that go *bump* in the night. I just remember lying there in the dark recalling every ghost story I had ever heard and probably making up some I hadn't heard. Anyway, I was so terrified that I finally got out of bed and forced myself to look out the window just to prove to myself that there was nothing to be afraid of. And do you know what I saw?"

"What did you see?" Mason complied as he ran his fingers through the length of her hair and along the bare skin on her shoulders.

"Well, nothing actually. But I have to admit that it was one of the most exhilarating feelings I ever had, standing there as terrified as I was and looking into that courtyard. As strange as it sounds, I believe I was actually disappointed when nothing was there." She laughed, and Mason leaned forward to kiss her...

* * *

The road twisted severely ahead, and he had to brake several times on the steep hill as he turned onto a narrow graveled lane that was barely wide enough to pass more than one vehicle, with trees on either side that rose densely above and joined to form a sort of canopy over Mason's Jeep. He could barely see a darkened barn in a small clearing to one side of the road and another small structure that might have been a house sitting close to the road at a sharp turn. If there were other buildings, it was too dark to see them beyond the headlights, and the road became narrower still and in worse condition, until it seemed to terminate at a house, standing straight ahead with a single lamp in a front window and the violet glow of an insect light on the covered porch. There did not appear to be any sort of driveway, so he pulled up close to an old Buick that was parked to one side of the yard and got out of the Jeep. Tree frogs chanted in the distance as he approached, and the insect light blinded him somewhat as it hummed incessantly and snapped a mosquito in midflight. Mason knocked on the door, and a voice called softly to him, not from the house but from the far end of the porch, in the darkness beyond the insect light.

"Over here, honey," Verna Lee said. "I knew you'd be a-comin' sooner or later."

VIII

The air was thick with the pungency of summer growth and the aging wood of the porch, the boards of which creaked under his feet as Mason felt his way along the loose railing. He could see Verna Lee's form in the dusk shadows, silhouetted by the insect light that flickered dimly on her lenses and briefly revealed the brittleness of her extended hand as she directed him to an aluminum lawn chair in the corner opposite her. There was barely enough webbing in the chair to hold his weight as he leaned back gingerly, sensing her proximity and the frailty of her age as her hand receded slowly into the shadows. He sat motionless for a moment, feeling a disquieting sense of immersion that seemed to pull him like a weight to the chair, and he was strangely claustrophobic as if walled in by the emerging dusk beyond the porch rail.

"Ain't a fittin' night," said Verna Lee, her voice lacking its usual infirmity as it drifted in the darkness. "Skeeters like to eat you alive, they do. Gets too hot in the house till it cools down outside and then the air just gets damp and heavy. Breeds sickness and bad for the joints. Hot an' humid days is what we got. Early this year and gonna be like that till the leaves fall. An' rain. I expect we'll see a lot o' rain this year."

Mason made some sort of acknowledgment, having no real interest in small talk at this time, his focus narrowing to matters at hand as he listened impatiently.

"Don't get much company except family here these days," she continued. 'That's why I like to work in town. Right kind o' Avril to have me. He's the man what owns Harley's now. You know there's a lot o' younger gals available." She paused and leaned back in her chair, so the light reflected from her temple and revealed the gray-and-white hair pulled back to a tight knot. "Course, I'm gettin' old an' tired these days an' probably won't work much longer. I got some pension from my husband, rest his soul, so I reckon I'll be settlin' in soon and let someone else have the job. Just the same, it's gettin' lonely in this ol' holler. Ain't nobody lives here but me now with my grandson gone an' all."

"Your grandson lives here with you?"

"Used to. Stayed here 'cause he didn't get along with his daddy. My daughter died o' cancer three years ago. After that, the boy and his daddy just fought. Movin' him in here was helpful to me though."

"Why did he leave?"

"Not by his druthers. Wrecked his car up the road. Got hurt so bad they had to operate on him and laid him up for a time."

"That's a shame. Where is he now?"

"Back with his daddy. Jake, that's his daddy, Jake and me don't get along, much less talk, so I can't really say if the boy's doin' good or not. Just the same, it's gettin' kinda hard to put up here these days."

"Maybe you should move to town," Mason said involuntarily, wishing to dispense with the conversation and get to his issues.

Verna Lee laughed, and he could see her face briefly as she lay her head back into the light. "Honey, I was in this house a long time before you was even born. Reckon it's best I just stay put. I'm as much a part o' this holler as the trees is an' I'm durn near older'n most. Be fittin' if I just' get buried here too, but they tell me that ain't allowed no more." She adjusted her glasses and leaned forward as she continued, "'Course, you didn't come here to chitchat, did you? You come here 'cause you been in that house Ansel Newley built when he was too stubborn not to. And you been seein' things that don't make no sense and ya figger on leavin' it, 'cept you can't help wonderin' about it. So here you set and you ain't sure about wantin' to know, and you ain't even sure why ya come here, are ya, Mr. Tucker?" There was a strangeness about her voice, a forcefulness that was neither friendly nor aggressive, nor did her tone carry the implied mockery of her words. She spoke as if she were addressing no one in particular, Mason's presence seemed more like a representation of a larger audience somewhere in the woods beyond the porch rail.

"'Course," she continued, "don't think I ain't glad to have ya, honey. It's just that it ain't pleasin' to know that it ain't me what drew you here. You wouldn't be here iffen it weren't for the things what happened up there, and you bein' so hell-bent to know what you ain't sure you want to know. Even now you ain't sure iffen ya want to stay or leave. But you ain't leavin', are you, Mr. Tucker? I figger you'd set there all night awaitin' for me to give you some great revelation 'cause it's been eatin' at ya and gettin' worse, and Cecil ain't givin' no more'n yer gonna git on some corner in Low Creek." She moved forward in her chair, and Mason could see the blue veins above her temple as she spoke, her voice softening now, "That's how it is, ain't it, Mr. Tucker?"

A strange sound in the distance caused Mason to start a little in his chair, and he looked off into the darkness, partially distracted from Verna Lee's discourse.

"Hoot owl," she said, her smile flashing briefly in the light. "Come fall you'll hear a lot more of 'em up there.

"Up there?" Mason asked.

"Up there where you been hangin' yer hat."

He turned away from the light and let his eyes adjust to the darkness. A hazy moon had emerged from the clouds and reflected dimly from what appeared to be a shallow stream about forty feet from the house. The house itself apparently sat in a small semicircular clearing with the forest rising dark and impenetrable behind it like the walls of a fortress, the ghostlike fringe of the treetops looming ominously below a scattering of clouds. He thought about her, an old woman living in such abject isolation, and how lonely she must be here. There was a sudden heaviness about him, a smothering pall of sadness that held him inert and helpless as his own loneliness seemed to swell from within, and he felt desperately vulnerable. He struggled against it, knowing well the futility of escape from the nemesis that plagued him, and he wondered if she could feel it, if she shared the vast emptiness of being that could overtake his consciousness and consume him with such devastating consequence that he might cry out as he had so long ago, his childlike voice fading and dissipating unheard in the darkness. It was not this place, forbidding as it was, that brought it on. It was her, in this place, no less severely fixed in the waste of her being than he was himself, and he knew then how she felt, how she lived.

The owl hooted again somewhere in the woods, but he ignored it as he began to ponder the absurdity of his situation. There was no need for this. He had come to build a prison. So what happened? Why the obsession with Bright's Mountain? This was not his home. He was here to do a job and move on. *A damn good life…* If the locals had a problem with his presence, he should just step aside and get the job done. This pathetic old woman was none of his concern, and she was already bringing him down. And for what?

Mason turned back toward Verna Lee in her shadowy corner of the porch. "Well, I guess you're right," he said. "There have been strange things happening. And Cecil tells some great stories, but he has no explanation for the goings-on around my house. And yes, I'm not sure whether I really even want to know what's going on or just pack up and move out and let you and Cecil and this weird, godforsaken mountain to yourselves." He stood up and felt for the porch rail to guide his exit. "But I *am* leaving." The insect light was full in his eyes now, and he could no longer see her beyond its obtrusive glow. "You're right, Verna Lee," he continued. "I didn't come here to be neighborly, and I apologize for the intrusion. I should have better manners. I hope my coming here hasn't inconvenienced you." He worked his way past the insect light to the porch steps. "You have a good evening, ma'am. Hopefully, it will cool down enough to go inside soon."

Verna Lee's voice was sarcastic and menacing as it seemed to float in the darkness as if separated from its originator. "Good night, Mr. Tucker. Come back anytime now, y'hear?"

The night seemed to close around Verna Lee's house as Mason walked to his car, the insect light and the lamp in the front window diminishing as if swallowed by the darkness in his rearview mirror as he drove slowly down the narrow road. A sliver of moonlight trickled through the trees above him, glimmering dimly on the dampness that had collected on the hood of his Jeep. He was restless in the confinement of the car, affected by something foreign to his senses that seemed to stir about him like the distraction of voices in a crowd, like the breath-stealing press of humanity in such close proximity that he would wait in embarrassment to take another elevator or suffer unbearably on a sold-out flight, his essence turning inward as the world seemed to fall away beneath him while he tumbled freely like a leaf dropping from the fullness of a tree to its inevitable assimilation with the earth below. There was more to it than this, he thought. Something else, heavy and portentous in the darkness behind him that held him there; he only realized after he turned around how slowly he had been driving.

And it was there later, when his mind rushed like a torrent, the rooms of his house casting shadows in the yellow light of the bedroom lamp while he packed some clothes and a shaving kit into a small grip and set the alarm and left, intending to move on to the Holiday Inn in Kingsport, his own breathing being the only sound beyond the click of the lock on the front door, and he was driving again, the trees passing in a grotesque procession of shadows along the periphery of the headlights as he made his way to the highway, his car turning as if by its own decision on Mills Hollow Road.

Verna Lee eyed him cautiously when she answered the door.

"What happened up there?" he asked.

"I knew you heard me."

The insect light was off, and the porch rails were silvery wisps in the moonlight as the spring on the screen door pinged, and he was in her kitchen, sitting on an old chair with chrome chipping on the legs and thin stuffing compressed beneath cracked vinyl, listening by the light of a single white fixture on the ceiling as she leaned across the smooth wood of the table, her hands folded beyond the age-worn sinew of her arms, propped on her elbows so her tiny shoulders hunched upward almost to her neck. She spoke slowly, emotionally, respectfully exacting her words as if she were lecturing, a sense of quiet enjoyment prevailing in her discourse.

"There ain't nothin' in this world what can't be explained," she said, "I'm sure about that. I'm an ol' woman what's seen a lot o' things overtime, and overtime I mostly figured out what's what. And I still believe that if I set my mind to it I could understand just what happened up there."

Mason leaned back in his chair and looked at the open window across the room, and he could hear the sounds of night beyond the flat blackness of the screen and the low hum of an electric fan that oscillated on the counter. He tilted his head toward Verna Lee. "What happened in the house?"

"No more than what everyone knew about."

"Is it haunted?" He pressed to reveal his skepticism.

She laughed. "Some folks say the whole mountain is haunted. Fact is, I don't believe in that stuff anymore'n you do. I reckon, in a way, you and me is about the same in that regard, ain't we? All I'm sayin' is that you and I know of things what we can't explain. Confoundin', ain't it?"

"I haven't told you anything."

"So you turned your car around so you could come back and spend a little social time with a ol' woman you barely know. That's right neighborly of you, Mr. Tucker. Would you like some tea?"

Mason smiled at her cynicism. He began to realize the alacrity of her humor that transcended her years and found himself actually enjoying her company, not like he enjoyed Cecil, who could drink beer and spin a good story, but for the latent sophistication that Verna Lee seemed to be sharing with him. This was not her Harley's Restaurant demeanor, and he felt as if he had just been initiated into a rather select society. "Some things have happened," he said. "Strange things that don't seem to make any sense."

"And it disturbs you when I say you shouldn't be a-livin' there."

"You never really said exactly that."

She worked the arthritic knuckles of her right hand, the resulting pain flashing only briefly across her face as she looked down at the table and then back to Mason. "Well, I'm a-tellin' ya."

"Are you telling me why?"

"Nope. And it ain't because I don't intend to. It's 'cause I got work in the morning, and an ol' woman workin' needs her sleep." She leaned forward across the table and eyed Mason severely. "But I'm a-tellin' you that things happened up there that shouldn't have, and bein' the only sane person left on this side o' Bright's Mountain, it's my place to tell you that it may not be a safe place for you."

"You're teasing me."

"Call it what you want, I'm goin' to bed."

"What happened to Ansel?"

"He died."

"How?

"You come back some time at a respectable hour, and I'll tell you what I wish I never knew. Better still that you don't though. Be better if you just move on to Kingsport and forget about that place." She stood up, slowly but with surprising capability for her age. "Mr. Tucker, you need to find yourself somewhere else to live."

"I intend to," he said softly.

Verna Lee smiled, as if she had won a minor victory and sat down again and leaned back in her chair as she studied him silently. "That's better," she said. "We need to be honest with each other if we're goin' to find the truth here."

"So tell me the truth."

She leaned forward as before, her eyes still fixed on his. "The truth for me is only what I know," she said.

Mason suppressed a smile. "Do you think the mountain is evil?"

Verna Lee shook her head. "Nope, I don't. That don't mean there ain't evil here though."

"I don't understand."

"Things ain't evil, Mr. Tucker. Folks are. If there's evil on this mountain, it's here because it was brought here."

"By Correl's?"

She got a rather surprised look on her face and smiled slightly. "I'd say by Correl's," she said, her eyes dropping slowly to the table.

The breeze from the fan on the counter passed gently across his face as Mason studied her in the pale kitchen light. Verna Lee sat quietly, leaning heavily on the table as the fatigue of age and emotion began to overtake her, despite her obvious desire to continue. He also wished to continue but realized that she was spent and needed to rest. "Suppose I come back, and you can fill me in on the evil Correls," he said quietly, rising from the table as he spoke.

He took her arm as she stood up and led her to the front room. When they got to the door, Verna Lee looked up at him in the light of the lamp in the window. "Tell me one thing 'fore you go, Mr. Tucker. What made you come here?"

"Nothing in particular," he said as he flicked the latch on the screen door.

She glared sharply at him. "Don't play coy with me."

The room suddenly seemed extremely small, shadowed in the dim light of the lamp. The shop door came to his recollection, and he could see the printing in large red letters as he had that morning, indiscernible at first as he trotted up the driveway from his run and then clearly visible, the words GO AWAY painted there, crude and uneven, the paint heavy in some places and barely covering in others so that it looked as if it had been there for a long time and not applied in the past hour while he was running. He had stood there briefly, attempting feebly to dismiss it as a childish prank but knowing even then that this was enough, and he had decided to leave it even before he kicked the small, stained package that was lying on the front porch and sent it flopping half opened through the rails and into the yard. He entered the house with neither urgency nor deliberation and showered with no more consideration than the day ahead. And he drove to the jobsite with the same feeling, not in anger or fear but with the quiet satisfaction that the decision allows once it is made, a calm resolution that trivialized not only the painted admonition on the door but the rest of Wells County as well. All things fell in order as the day progressed mechanically, and he went through the motions of his business, still calm and resolute, having no more than the desire to know and peaceably discharge (though he simply called it curiosity) that which perhaps had been no more than an inconvenience until now—until this woman had somehow drawn him into a weird kind of mutual obsession that was both exhilarating and frightening, not so much in its objective but in the raw sense of revelation that he seemed to be experiencing about himself.

"Someone painted a warning on the door of Ansel's shop while I was running this morning," Mason said as he walked through the opened screen door, which slammed shut behind him.

"Well, that's interestin'. I got no idea who woulda done it though. Might be best if you paid it some heed," Verna Lee said flatly as Mason proceeded into the yard. "Good night, Mr. Tucker."

"Do you know what I like best about it, Tuck?" Katherine said as she appeared in front of him, partially obscuring the house from his view. "It's ours. That's what I like. Just the fact that it's our house to share and raise a family in and grow old and silly in. It gets its identity from us, you know." She turned toward the house and pointed at it. "That's the Mason's house. You know, Tuck and Katherine."

She turned back to him, and he could see the contentment in her eyes and her perfect smile as she opened her arms to him, rising before him and gracefully beckoning him to the softness of her presence. He felt a rush of longing and desire, and he tried to move toward her but was hopelessly immobile as she drifted backward and faded, the house also drifting into the granular aspect of an old photograph. Katherine was still speaking, but he could not understand her words; her voice was muted by the wind that seemed to come from all directions now. He remained helplessly fixed in his position, imprisoned by the hard cast of his own body that rigidly held him from her, calling to her as she continued to fade into the dissipating texture of the house...

Katherine! Mason's voice echoed in the darkness as he awakened and lay staring at the tiny green light of the smoke detector overhead. He sat on the side of the bed and rubbed his face with his hands, slowly regaining his sensibility and presence in the Holiday

Inn Express, Kingsport, Tennessee. Sometime during the night, he had undressed and climbed under the covers, but he had no recollection of doing so. The curtains were still pulled open, and he could see the first light of morning through the window as he collected his thoughts and recounted the bizarre night before, wondering if that too had only been another bad dream. He dressed quickly and stepped outside, tasting the fresh morning air with an unfounded sense of relief, and he watched the sun rise from an open stairway where he sat for a long time before returning to his room.

Sally arrived while he was still having breakfast in the lobby dining area. "Well, I see you changed your mind after all," she said as she poured herself some coffee and sat at his table.

Mason closed his tablet and looked at her across the table. He felt a twinge of embarrassment for his attraction to her as he studied the softness of her face, which was remarkably youthful despite the gentle creasing that emerged subtly about her eyes and mouth. Her presence was fresh and feminine and welcome, and he would have been content to sit there quietly with her all morning. He quickly pulled his senses and struggled for something to say. "There was more vandalism," he eventually mumbled as he reached awkwardly for his coffee cup.

"Oh, mercy. Sweetie, I'm so sorry about all this. What happened now?" She leaned toward him and Mason caught the faint scent of her perfume as she spoke.

"Nothing disastrous," he returned. "Just some paint on the shop door. Anyway, I figured it was time to let whoever wants me out of that house have their way. I came here to build a prison. It doesn't matter much where I'm staying. It just isn't worth putting up with all this crap."

Sally sighed. "Sweetie, I feel so bad about this. I know it don't help much, but I told Cletus he ain't gettin' no rent till you get settled."

"It's not your fault, Sally. You can't help it if there's some family up there who wants to scare me off the mountain."

She raised her eyebrows. "Some family? Why do you say that?"

Mason smiled, feeling a sense of shrewdness by his deduction. "I've been warned by a woman and a child who were sent by a man. Seems like a family to me."

"There ain't no families livin' on Bright's Mountain that I know of, sugar. In fact, like I told you before, there ain't much of anybody up there since the state of Virginia bought most of the land. Only folks I know of livin' around there is Cecil and Jeff and Verna Lee Capron down in the holler from where you…was livin'." She touched his hand softly. "Honey, I don't know what's been going on up there, and I don't think I wanna know. That durn Cletus and his slick deals anyway. He oughta be shot for renting that house out in the first place. It ain't like he needs the money, what with the state paying him just for keeping it."

"What do you mean?"

Sally hesitated, pensively folding the small sweetener packet which she had emptied into her coffee cup before she spoke. "Well, ya know Cletus fancies himself as quite a businessman. 'Course, you gotta give him that, considerin' he's done better'n most around here. Anyway, when they first started talkin' about buildin' the prison up there, he about drove himself crazy tryin' to figure out just how he could profit by it. Then he drove over to where they built another prison just like the one you're buildin' here, and he talked to some folks what had made money dealin' with the state of Virginia. Next thing I know, he was up there on Bright's Mountain buyin' up everything he could get his hands on, which wasn't too hard, considering most of those homes have been abandoned for years. He eventually got some partners, and they have some deal with the state to develop the property, but I ain't too sure how it works. All I know is that he gets taxpayer money for keepin' it. Of course, it was a good thing for Ansel Newley, considering he and his wife were planning on leavin' anyway, her health being as it was. Same for Cecil Beckman."

"You mean Cletus owns Cecil's place too?"

"Honey, Cletus owns most everything on Mills Hollow Road from your place to where Mills Hollow Road turns off into the hollow where Verna Lee lives. He'd own that too if she'd sell it to him, but I can assure you that won't happen. God knows he tried every which way he could to get her to sell, but she just brushed him off like flies off a horsetail."

Mason stood up and took the coffeepot from the hot plate across the room and refilled both cups. "So what you're saying is that Cletus owns the Correl house as well."

Sally looked up at him and smiled. "I guess I shoulda told ya that. Bought it last fall. Anyway, that's how I knew nobody was living there. Cletus said the place was too run-down to rent out."

"Then what about the woman I saw there?"

"Squatters, most likely."

"The deputy sheriff said he was going to check it out when I told him about what I saw."

"You mean Gabe Setty? I don't know what Sheriff Miller sees in that boy. No, he didn't check it out, but he called Cletus about it, and Cletus said he would go up there himself as soon as he got the chance. 'Course, that usually means ol' Sally's gonna to get the job eventually. It don't matter though. I need to see the damage what was done at your place last night anyway, so why don't we both go on up there and take a look-see for ourselves. We need to call the sheriff again, but this time, I'll make sure Rafe Miller gets out there himself instead o' that halfwit deputy. He normally wouldn't, but Rafe's an old friend, so I think I can get him to come out."

The desk clerk occupied Sally with some business, and Sally called the sheriff's office while Mason went to his room and returned with his car keys and a spiral notebook that he had brought with him the night before. As they drove to Bright's Mountain in Mason's Jeep, Mason grilled Sally with questions about the Correl family and Cecil Beckman and Verna Lee Capron and Cletus's reasons for buying up the property on the west side of the mountain until Sally finally threw her hands up, saying, "Lord in heaven, darlin', what's with the interrogation? I thought you said you didn't give a care about what happens up there."

Mason felt his face flush. He sighed deeply as he watched the continual change in scenery pass by on the highway. "Sorry," he said quietly. "Just curious, I guess."

They exited on Two Stump Road, turning first into the partially hidden drive that led to the rundown little house that someone named Correl had built at some point in time, leaving it with some kind of history that seemed to be revealing itself in small pieces. The rotting little bridge groaned and creaked under the weight of the Jeep's front wheels, so much that Mason backed off, and they got out and walked the distance to the house, reversing the path he had taken several weeks ago when he had so brazenly escaped from the strange woman and her rusted shotgun.

The house was indeed rundown. Mason had never really got a good look at it, having been somewhat distracted as he ran through the yard the last time he was there. Everything, from the roof, which was caving in in several places, to the shattered windows and broken porch rails gave evidence of years of disuse and abandonment. It was a plain clapboard, evidently well-built originally, though it was now in such a state of deterioration that any attempt at renovating it even to the barest essentials of habitation would be a major, if not impossible, undertaking. They walked carefully through the weed-choked yard, peering in windows and doors, Mason eventually entering the front door after bridging the gaps in the porch deck with some old boards that he found stacked nearby.

The inside of the house had the musty odor of disuse with large chunks of plaster littered about the warped hardwood floor and old lath showing through on walls like the skeletal remains of life gradually returning to its base origins. Sunlight streamed through the broken windowpanes and diffused into the shadows, giving the place an almost surrealistic appearance. Sally walked around with what Mason considered a strange interest as she stood in each room, carefully studying its features as if she were attempting to recollect something relevant to her own past. Mason watched her as she touched the counter in the kitchen and stared almost wistfully out the window. "You've been here before?" he asked, feeling as if he was violating some sacred meditation.

She turned to him and smiled briefly, a sense of sadness seeming to overtake her as she leaned against the filthy porcelain sink. "No, I haven't."

Her gaze slowly turned toward the window. "I took up and left when I was eighteen. It seemed like everybody was in a hurry to leave Cade's Mountain back then, and I was no exception. Mama was left all by herself, what with me and Emma gone and May Jean dead and buried. She got so lonely, I guess. Anyone who'd give her the time of day was better than the alternative, so she took up with Ez Correl, who was getting older and, I guess, welcomed some companionship. Mama didn't tell us about it until after she had moved in and was livin' here. I never saw much of Mama after that. She said Ez wouldn't let us come visit and said Ez wouldn't let her come visit us. I was livin' in Knoxville at the time, but I think it was just as much her not wantin' us to see what she had become as it was Ez's meanness. She died here before she ever got to enjoy her grandchildren."

Sally's eyes filled with tears as she turned again to the window. "I guess this is as close to Mama as I've been in a long time. I'm sorry, Tuck. Let me be a minute, and I'll be fine. I just didn't expect it to affect me this way." Mason reached over and touched her shoulder, softly brushing her hair from her face as he turned and walked out the back door.

There were several ruined outbuildings in the backyard including the charred remains of what appeared to have been a small barn. Mason made some notes in the notebook and walked around for a while until Sally finally came out. "You didn't know you'd have to put up with ol' crybaby today, did ya," she said in her usual tone.

"It's okay, Sally."

She touched him on the cheek as she walked by. "You're so sweet." She stopped a few feet from the burned-out barn. "Correls was big moonshiners years ago. I bet one o' these buildings was where they kept their still. You think so?"

Mason smiled, relieved to have her back to her usual self. "I can't say. I really don't know much about moonshining."

"Me neither."

Sally crossed her arms and appeared to shudder slightly. "Sweetie," she said, moving closer still, almost touching Mason, "I really would like to get out of here. You seen enough yet?"

When they got back to the car, Sally tapped the spiral notebook. "You're taking notes. For someone who claims he doesn't care, you sure seem to be awfully curious in your disinterest." Mason looked sideways at her, and she quickly withdrew her hand. "Oops. I wasn't trying to be nosy or anything."

"It's okay," Mason said, amused by her reaction. "It's more than just notes. I've been writing down things I've heard from Cecil and Verna Lee and…you. Kind of a journal. I don't know. I guess I'm just fascinated with some of the stories and with this part of the country in general. I've always been like that, interested in the places I've lived in, but I have to admit, I'm a little more diligent here, considering the things that have gone on. Go ahead, you can look at it."

She took the notebook carefully from the dashboard and opened it. "My lord, darlin', you got to be the most meticulous notetaker I ever saw."

Mason glanced sideways at her and returned his eyes to the road ahead as they approached his driveway.

Sheriff Rafael Miller walked out from behind the shop as they were getting out of the car. He was a lean man in his midfifties, appearing a bit disheveled because of the slack fit of his clothing, his face weathered and lined with the brooding sincerity of experience. There were two cars in the lot, a typical police squad car with "Wells County Sheriff" in bold letters on the side and the Ford Bronco that Mason recognized as Deputy Setty's. The deputy appeared briefly as he walked around the back of the house while Mason and Sally got out of the Jeep and met the sheriff in the lot. Sally introduced Mason, and they walked over to the shop to inspect the writing on the door. Sheriff Miller stood quietly for a while, looking intensely at the door and then at the house and yard before turning back to Mason.

"You say someone's been harassing you since you moved in, Mr. Mason?" the sheriff asked, carefully eyeing Mason as he spoke.

"Yeah," Mason answered, feeling somewhat annoyed by the question. "I explained everything to the deputy last week."

The sheriff put his hands on his hips and looked back at the house again where the deputy had reappeared and was on his knees now inspecting something in the side yard. "Yep," he said, shuffling his foot in the sparse gravel of the lot and looking again at the deputy in the side yard, "I know that. But I wonder if you'd mind telling me again, just to make sure I got it all."

Mason looked at Sally and shook his head. She smiled and said softly, "Go ahead, darlin'. He's just doin' his job." Then she said to the sheriff, "Rafe, why don't we all just set on the porch and let Tucker tell you everythin' what's been happening here—"

She was interrupted by Deputy Setty who seemed somewhat excited as he called the sheriff to see what he had found near the house. Sheriff Miller threw an apologetic glance toward Sally and answered the deputy, "What is it Gabe?"

"Something I think you ought to see, sheriff," the deputy answered, a sense of alarm trailing in his voice. He was holding something in his rubber-gloved hand, away from his body as if it were contaminated in some way. Mason followed the sheriff and Sally across the lot toward Deputy Setty, and as they came closer, he recognized the object in the deputy's quivering hand as the small paper bag that he had kicked into the lawn the day before. Setty opened the bag and held it up to the sheriff, close to his face so that the sheriff had to pull his head back a bit to see inside.

"Shit sake, Gabe," Sheriff Miller gasped as he pushed the bag away and stepped back suddenly, stumbling into Sally so hard that she almost fell over. "Jesus God," he continued as he grabbed Sally, "you got more sense than to stick something like that into a man's face. What the hell's in there, anyway?"

Setty's boyish face was flushed. "It's a heart. I couldn't figure what it was at first till I got a good look at it in the light. But it's a heart for sure. A goddamn heart in a paper bag." He was still holding the bag away from his body, and his hand was trembling so hard the bag shook like a leaf in the wind.

They all stood there, motionless and silent, except for the deputy whose trembling and heavy breathing was the only movement besides the gentle breeze in the trees beyond. Miller looked over his shoulder at Mason and then at Sally and said nothing as he walked to his car, leaving them standing there dumbfounded and staring at the bag as if it were suspended in the air and the deputy didn't exist. The sheriff returned with two plastic bags, one of which he held open as the deputy gingerly dumped the purplish lump from the paper bag into it. He held it up at arm's length and studied it as Setty folded the paper bag and put it into the other container. "My guess it's from a deer," the sheriff said as he handed the bag to Setty. "I've done enough hunting to know one. Just the same, we'll get it checked out." He looked at Mason, squinting in the sunlight through his glasses. "What say we sit down here and you tell me just what the hell's goin' on, Mr. Mason," he said, keeping his eyes on Mason as he spoke.

Shafts of sunlight were beginning to filter through the lattice trim above the porch as Sheriff Miller sat on one of the wicker chairs with his forearms resting on his knees. He eyed Mason keenly, occasionally dropping his gaze to the floor between his feet or his deputy in the yard, listening politely to Mason's terse description of events that had occurred over the past month, Mason making no secret of his growing impatience with the whole situation. When he finished, the sheriff pulled a folded piece of yellow writing paper from his shirt pocket and scribbled some notes and sat quietly for a moment, contemplating the shop door and the yard beyond. He rubbed his chin and looked furtively at Mason and then at Sally who finally broke the awkward silence.

"So what do you figure, Rafe?" she asked without the acerbic tone that Mason would have carried with the question.

Miller looked back at the shop and back at Sally. "I don't know, Sally," he said slowly, turning his gaze to Mason. "It really isn't making much sense. Just the same, it's a curious situation, isn't it?" He sucked his lip and hesitated before speaking again, addressing Mason specifically. "Mr. Mason, can you think of any reason for all this?" His voice seemed almost apologetic.

Mason bristled but was compensated by the apparent sincerity in the man's tone of voice. "I wish I could. At first, I thought it was some local activist who had something against the prison. But I don't know now. This seems to be personal with me."

The deputy called something to the sheriff who nodded in his general direction but kept his eyes on Mason as Deputy Setty got into his car and drove away. "Well," the sheriff said as he rose stiffly from the chair, "it isn't that I don't believe you, Mr. Mason, even though your story is a bit of a handful—you have to admit that. I just really don't know what to make of it and, frankly, don't know what to do for you. I'd like to take a day or two and mull it over if you don't mind." He started down the porch steps. "In the meantime, I'd suggest you keep a careful eye on things around here till we figure out just what's going on. Sally, good to see you as always. Say hey to Cletus for me, will ya?"

"You know I will. Thanks, Rafe," Sally said.

The sheriff opened his car door and stopped. "By the way, Sally, I just found out that Thane Correl was out of prison. Did you know that?"

"No, I didn't know that," Sally answered with a slightly caustic air. "Don't really care neither," she added.

"Well, I just thought you might be interested to know. Paroled to Kentucky last fall, so I doubt we see any of him around here. Just thought you'd like to know, that's all." Sheriff Miller climbed into his car and proceeded slowly down the drive and onto Mills Hollow Road.

Mason shook his head and looked at Sally. "There's that name again."

Sally smiled. "Correls again. Thane might just be the worst of the bunch. I'm sure Cecil has some good stories about him. He was a wild one. Hasn't been around here for years, in prison, and all. But he *was* a bad one. Anyway, he was the last of the Correls to be around here to my knowledge."

It was midafternoon when Mason finished packing some things to take back to the motel while Sally made some phone calls. Mason's iPhone rang, and he asked her to answer it as he hauled his suitcase and a box of computer items out to the Jeep. Sally came out to the porch and announced the caller. "Sweetie, there's a woman on the phone who says she's your sister." Then more quietly as he passed her on the porch, she added, "I didn't know you had a sister." Mason disregarded her as he entered the house and answered the telephone.

"Oh, Tucker, thank God," the woman's voice on the other end said as he answered. "We had no idea where to find you. We tried all day yesterday and finally got this number from Jack Murray."

Mason stood quietly for a moment, as if stunned by the sound of her voice. "What is it, Sherry?" he finally managed to respond weakly.

"It...it's Dad. He had a massive heart attack on Wednesday. Tuck, we tried to contact you but didn't have any idea how. We really did try."

"Is he okay?"

There was a dull silence on the phone followed by Sherry's long sigh and response in a quivering voice. "He...he passed away yesterday, Tuck."

X

Cameron James Mason. That was it. Just a name and nothing more that came to mind as Mason leaned back in his seat and struggled for some memory, good or bad, of his father. Cameron James Mason. Not so much a name but more like an icon in the upper left corner of the check that arrived so rudely on the first of each month during those years when the cleansing began—sophomore year, or was it the summer before, when the first check came to his dorm in the mail, and the separation of father and son was transacted, purchased in installments that gained in principle remuneration like a mortgage, a reparation for the past that, perhaps, should not have been. Cameron James Mason. He could think of nothing more as the plane landed in Cleveland and the faceless shadow of what might have been a father emerged dimly from the tarmac below, fading and without dimension, its distance paid for and the account settled when the final check had arrived and the parting was effected with such subtlety that the son felt not the loss but the emptiness of never having, not the separation but the singularity of the disconnect, so complete that Mason now felt strangely imposed as if he had been summoned to the funeral of a stranger.

He rented a car at the airport and drove thoughtlessly toward Solon, the landmarks he passed having the strange familiarity of places in a dream, foreign yet habitual places that seemed like echoes of some distant life that may not have been except for the dream.

A creeping sense of foreboding began to overtake him as he turned off the highway—the deep saddening heaviness of loss that was his only association with this place since his deliverance; that loss being death, for it was no more than death that brought him here, and his presence represented a kind of death in itself. Fitting, it seemed, that there would be no reason to return except to witness the decimation of yet one more vestige of the forgotten past, one more funeral, one more break in the conjoining nexus of his childhood: First his mother, and the welling of emotion, not as much for her loss as the abject prohibition of her aspirations that carried her yearning beyond him, and it was only then, at her death, that he could realize the tragedy of her existence. Then his grandmother, two years later, kindly and helpless to the end, unrequited in the rescue of a daughter whose failure was, in fact, prescribed beyond the weight of a mother's guilt. He returned only seven months later for his grandfather and witnessed sadly the emanation of life from the man who had loved so deeply but could not bear his losses as he lay sallow and dulled in his bed, regarding Mason's hastened arrival with the last of his comforting warmth before he released his soul and thereby released Mason from yet another tendril in the darkness behind him. *Death*, Mason thought as he drove. Death, bringing him here and releasing him again in some kind of macabre continuum of repetition that would have him return to the same airport and the same roads and the same places to witness the same event with the same people, less one more each time, perhaps until there were no more to witness.

This is like a bad movie, he thought as he turned the car onto Route 29 and accelerated past the eternal billboard that now seemed so ironically inappropriate; the image of someone who might have been his father, bizarre and grotesque now in its single dimension above the words "Cam Mason Chevrolet—*Depend on It*" passing like floating debris as he submerged into the river of his dreaming that carried in its unworldly current the litany of events that were otherwise buried in this place but floated to the surface for his review upon each death.

He drove on as always, passing the exit and continuing eastward on 29 as it proceeded—descended—into the forsaken industrial area that seemed to deteriorate more with each trip, with each death; rusted steel and stained concrete in vine-covered obscurity, roads cracked and pitted as the car rocked over railroad tracks and even the trees were stifled and dull amid the emerging ruin of what had never really succeeded to begin with, heat rising from the pavement like toxic fumes that would strangle those who knew better, those who knew that there was another world, another place and time, and this place and this time could fade and dissipate into the lumpish dust that collected on roofs and in the corners of abandonment. There was a parking spot directly across the street behind an old Dodge pickup with rusted fenders and one wheel missing as it stood precariously on a jack stand like some storybook pirate on his peg leg. The house was still there, brittle and old now, grotesque in flaking green paint along the pitted porch rail and the broken screen on the front door fluttering loosely in the warm breeze. The open space beyond it was dark and forbidding like an open tomb, and he remembered it, the screen door creaking and slamming behind him as he ran onto the porch, its painted floor splintered beneath his feet, sitting there in the warmth of his mother's lap, her voice resonating from within as he leaned to her breast, the cars passing, his father holding the baby stiffly, the bareness of the backyard as it rose sharply to the trees and pressed upward to the tracks, the gentle rumbling and clatter of steel as each car passed in the obscurity of the trees. A young woman appeared in the doorway, hesitating there as she lit a cigarette and then stepping carefully down to the bottom stair, where she sat and smoked, her blond hair falling wildly about her shoulders and sticking to her face in the pervasive heat. Mason watched her for a while before he pulled forward slowly past the truck in front of him and then accelerated quickly, the woman watching him casually as he drove down the street and around the block and back onto 29 and the Beresford exit and the inevitable burden of reality, another billboard taunting him at the exit, the words "DEPEND ON IT" remaining in his consciousness like a hovering shadow.

Depend on it! And nothing else came to mind as he stood before the casket in the glory of the flowers and the impossible crush of humanity about the room, numbly regarding the perplexity of old acquaintances and suspicious faithful who whispered and nodded to the prodigal who had returned too late for forgiveness. The room seemed to move about him as he stood alone, except for the occasional brief inquisition of the son by those brazen enough to acknowledge the true possibility of his existence. The woman who Marianne pointed in his direction after a furtive inquiry in the hallway extended her trembling hand, her eyes meeting his as she spoke, "I worked for Mr. Mason for twelve years and never realized he had a son. I mean, I knew the girls...we all knew the girls." She turned to the casket and touched an enormous spray of orchids, turning slowly back to Mason as her gaze intensified with the tears that rolled slowly down her cheeks. "He...your father was such a wonderful man, you know." The woman turned again to the casket and crossed herself before dissolving into the crowd.

I'm sure they all knew the girls, Mason mused to himself as Marianne moved an elderly gentleman in his direction, the words 'my stepson, Tucker' giving him an unwarranted chill as Marianne coolly completed the introduction and Mason exchanged some trivialities with the old man, who turned abruptly and walked away mumbling and nodding into the crowd. Mason looked in the direction of the casket, feeling distant and invisible, as if he were observing the scene through a window as he watched the people who approached and lovingly regarded the remains of Cameron James Mason and solemnly consoled one another before floating into the adjacent parlor to collect in tight little groups. The crowd was still filtering in when he awkwardly paid his regards to Marianne and his stepsisters and left, with no further acknowledgement to the enormous group of new and old strangers who had come to witness the passing of someone named Cam Mason who, for all he knew, may have only existed on weathered billboards and cheesy commercials, sharing nothing more than a name with the distant memory of his father.

Sherry walked him to his car and they said nothing at first as they proceeded slowly through the sweltering evening air. "Tuck," she finally said, touching the suit jacket that he had removed and carried on his arm, "I...I know this is difficult for you. I know that you and Dad, well...."

"That he stopped being my father and then changed his mind?" Mason bristled, wishing immediately that he had not said it. Sherry was the only member of Cameron James Mason's second family that he felt any kinship to. She was the youngest and the only offspring of Cameron and Marianne, sometimes suffering in that enviable position from the presence of Marianne's two other daughters from a previous marriage. It was Sherry who had appointed herself as emissary of Mason's estranged family, eternally hopeful of reconciliation as she apologetically attended as proxy for her father at his graduation from Clemson and his wedding, invited to the latter only at Katherine's insistence. "They're still your family, Tuck," Katherine had said as she shoved the list back at him across the kitchen table. "Maybe this is your opportunity to bury whatever has happened in the past and start over. How do you know they won't come?" Mason remembered the strange feeling he had when he picked Sherry up at the airport, how he imagined her obstinacy with her parents protesting her traveling alone but failing even then to turn the determination that Mason so deeply admired. He liked Sherry and, despite his preference to the contrary, harbored a latent sibling bond with her.

"Hey, I'm sorry," he said now as she stopped, the look on Sherry's face somewhere between pain and understanding.

"It's ok, Tuck," Sherry said softly. She looked away, into the busy street in front of the funeral home and at the setting sun that reflected from the adjacent buildings. "I guess," she continued slowly, "there's a lot of history that I don't know about—maybe that I don't want to know about. I only knew a wonderful father and a generous man who was loved by everyone who came in contact with him." She looked back at Mason, her eyes sad and desperate. "I don't know anything about Dad's life before us. I guess I never really wanted to know. But people change, Tuck. Whatever he was before, whatever happened that hurt you both so much, I...I just can't believe that it was so bad that you can't forgive him now. For your own sake, Tuck."

Mason unlocked the car door and opened it. He stood rigidly as she threw her arms around his neck and hugged him, and he could feel the dampness of her tears against his cheek. "He's gone, Tuck," she breathed into his ear, "please..." Sherry sobbed heavily, and he held her there for a long time before she eventually pulled away from him and kissed him on the cheek. "I'll see you tomorrow," she said quietly as she turned and walked quickly back to the funeral home.

It was almost dark when Mason checked in at the same Quality Inn that he had stayed in before, always refusing offers from Sherry to stay at the house when he was in town. After eating only part of his dinner at the Denny's across the street, he lay on the bed, holding the TV remote in his hand as he drifted into the old obscurity that flowed about him and gradually took him as he slid from the dim light of the hotel room.

And he lay quietly in his bed, keeping perfectly still in the darkness, his eyes fixed on the yellow light that lined the door and flooded the space beyond it. He could hear them in the kitchen downstairs, their voices rising and falling in random scales that echoed through the hall as they shouted, indiscernible except for their inflection and his mother's occasional shrill rebukes. He closed his eyes tightly and pressed his fingers on his ears, falling backward now…and it was dark, strangely dark and dampness old and heavy hung in the air. Randy looked up at him, his eyes cold and dark amid the terror of his face, like small round holes in the pale reflected light, pleading silently with his arms outstretched, pleading desperately as his face grew large and pale until it was like a moon with two perfectly round holes for eyes and his mouth open wide…

Mason opened his eyes and stared briefly at the remote in his hand. He stood up quickly and turned on the television. Two newscasters were alternately reading from a teleprompter. He propped the pillows behind him and sat back on the bed, listening half-heartedly as the news team rambled on in their dull staccato, a woman with perfectly coiffed blond hair and a younger man who sat stiffly and never moved his upper lip when he spoke. The program continued through several commercials and a sports report. The weather tease was "rain in the forecast," and Mason waited through another series of commercials to see if his father's burial would be appropriately punctuated by rain and cloudy skies. His distractions had him away from the commercials when a noisy piece for Cam Mason Chevrolet caught his attention. *Depend on it* was the last thing he heard as he clicked off the television and threw the remote across the room. He brushed his teeth sullenly and climbed into bed, thankful for the quiet solitude of the room, his thoughts random and scattered as he lay quietly in the darkness, remembering.

* * *

Katherine kissed his forehead and pulled her chair closer to him. "You were close to your grandparents, weren't you?" she said softly.

He looked at the mountains in the distance. "Yeah," he sighed. "Actually, they probably had as much time spent raising me than either of my parents. I lived with them for several years off and on."

"I thought you said you lived with your mother." He looked at her and could see no intent other than her usual caring inquisitiveness, though he knew that she resented his reticence about discussing his childhood as much as he hated talking about it.

He sat still for a moment, feeling heavy in the chair, secure on the deck, his deck, their deck, at their house, and it was their time as the old memories rose slowly in him, rising like a swell that splashed over the barriers of his denial and he spoke, at last, not just to Katherine but to the mountains and the breeze and the circumstance of his home—their home in Denver. The words spilled like poison from his mouth as his soul rejected the malfeasance of its secrets.

"My mother...she never got over what happened."

Katherine's eyes held him in their softness as she paused, patient and firm before him. She spoke quietly, "What, Tuck. What happened?"

"My brother..."

"You have a brother?"

"Had a brother. He died when I was seven."

Come on Randy. I'll take you next door. Come on!

"How did he die, Tuck?"

"They just couldn't handle it. I don't know. I guess they just couldn't accept it. When Dad left, I was almost glad to see him go. At least then they couldn't fight."

Maybe now it's over. Maybe now they won't blame each other, and it's over. It will be better when he comes back...

"Your parents separated after your brother died?"

"He left. Mom…we stayed for a while…but he didn't come back. We, Mom and me, we had to leave because she lost the house, and we moved into this little apartment in Akron. She worked nights, and it seemed like I was always alone. I was so scared there. Then we moved. We moved a lot then. Sometimes just the two of us and sometimes with others. It seemed like we were moving all the time."

"And your father. Where was your father?"

"I don't know. She never spoke of him. Or Randy. It was like they had never existed."

"Randy was your brother?"

"Yeah."

"Your father just disappeared?"

"Like he never existed. And Randy never existed."

"Oh, Tuck." Katherine was kneeling in front of him now, holding his hands in hers, her brown eyes never leaving his. "Go on. Talk to me. Please."

He looked away, toward the mountains in the distance, and felt the slight chill in the breeze as the dream flowed through him, filling him and bubbling forth as he spoke, "She wanted so badly for things to be better for us. She would get a new job…and lose it. Sometimes, I never really knew why—not then, anyway—she would send me to my grandparents to stay. Just for a few days, she would say. And I wouldn't see her for weeks at a time. She would visit and then leave. Grandpa would drive me to school, and I had my own room at their house. Then she would come and get me, and we would have a new place to live."

Katherine caressed his hand lightly, tracing the palm with her index finger, the soft strokes flowing like a current through his wrist, up his arm, and throughout his body. Her palm was warm as she pressed it to his, and he felt a strange sense of beckoning to that place he had so fervently desired and feared, the vulnerability restraining him slightly as he coalesced with the flow of time and matters, flowing now with her into the shadows of waning daylight that folded silently into the mountains. A light plane floated in the distance, and he watched it as it disappeared beyond the snowcapped peaks. He leaned forward and kissed her, feeling light in the chair now, almost buoyant in the safety of the deck and the house, their house.

"Sometimes..." he continued, "things were good. In Canton. We lived in Canton for a while, and I actually spent an entire year in the same school. Had some friends. There were some good times. Mom just wanted so badly to have a family again. That's all she wanted. It seemed so simple. But somewhere I guess when Randy died or when her husband left her, she lost whatever it is that holds a family. Like she lost the ability to sustain any kind of relationship at all. Even...even with me. There were men, and sometimes that was good. Most of them treated us well, but they never stayed around very long.

"Anyway, when I was in the seventh grade, I was staying at my grandparents then, he began to send her money. I don't know whether she found him, or he found her, but he started to send her money. I learned later that somewhere between then and the time he left, he had become successful. I guess he decided it might be a good idea to throw a little over the fence to the family that he left behind, or maybe a judge was involved. I don't know. She tore up the first few checks. Then I guess she realized that that didn't accomplish anything, so she started cashing them. She rented a place in Cleveland and got a good job, and I really thought things were finally going to get better. And they were for a while. But she lost the job and this time had to be hospitalized."

Katherine got up and pulled the other chair around to face him. "Deck's a little hard on the knees," she said and smiled at him as she sat and took his hands again. "Why was your mother hospitalized?" she asked, her eyes again constant before him.

He hesitated, the words forming too slowly as he raised his head slightly and felt the breeze on his face. "To dry out, I guess. I mean, I don't think there was anything else wrong with her. I don't know. Maybe my grandparents put her there. Anyway, my grandfather came into my room one night and said that I was going to have to move in with my father. My *father*. Grandpa said it like it was some kind of a sentence. For god's sake, I hadn't seen the man in seven years, and now I was supposed to live with him!"

135

"How was it?"

"How was what?" But he knew what she meant.

"Living with your father. I mean, it must have been a little weird after all those years."

He looked up at the sky, which was darkening in a slate-colored translucence above them. "Like I was a guest in their house. They were generally civil to me, my stepmother and her daughters. But I never felt comfortable there. They acted like I was some kind of stranger whom they had to tolerate. Always distant, you know, like I had some kind of disease. I didn't like it there. Except for Sherry, of course. She and I got along pretty well."

"And your father?"

"Avoided me when he could. And when he couldn't, it was like he was afraid of me or something. I never liked staying there. But he took care of me, sent me to a private high school, let me pick any college that I wanted. Once I started college, I almost never returned, taking summer jobs and internships around campus. He kept me funded, of course, probably to make sure I stayed away. Sent me monthly checks made out to Tucker S. Mason. There is no 'S' in my name. My middle initial is 'C' for Cameron, his name."

"What about your mother."

"She moved in with my grandparents. Mom…had a lot of trouble then. I'm not sure I know it all even now. Seems like no one ever wanted to tell me. She apparently recovered, but I never lived with her again." He shifted in his chair and leaned back, his eyes fixed on the emerging stars above. "You know," he continued slowly, "it may sound strange, but I think the best time I can remember with Mom is when she would come to visit me in college. She was sober then and would drive down on a Sunday and stay for two or three days. She loved the campus, loved to go for long walks. We would sit and talk for hours about my studies or running or just about anything, except the past. Those were probably our best times together."

He continued looking at the sky, but he could sense the tension in Katherine's hands. They sat quietly for a while. and he knew she would have to know more, that she would not withdraw now that she had penetrated so far. There was a heaviness in her voice when she finally spoke, clearing her throat softly at first as if she were about to read from a script. "Tuck," she said, her words now floating to him amid the old sounds of the past that were rising slowly in his head. "Tuck, what happened to your brother?" *And he could hear them, beyond the door, their voices harsh in the distance as the sound augmented in the darkness, pressing on as Randy pleaded, his arms outstretched beyond the glistening of moisture on the trees behind him, the trees black and ominous in the darkness, and it was all darkness except for the weak light about the yard that seemed to have no source and reflected dimly from the dampness...*

"Tuck," she persisted, almost whispering now, "how did Randy die?"

Wait here while I get help...

"Tuck, what happened to Randy?" *He's outside...* Mason closed his eyes against the shadows and light, his head dipping slowly until it touched Katherine's, her scent drawing him to her as she rubbed his hands where the tears dropped, his voice rasping from deep within as his lips parted in form, dry and quivering, the world imploding at this moment as his breath left him, and the words fell from him like icy drops of water to Katherine's waiting hands.

"I killed him."

XI

Rain drummed on the large umbrella that Mason had purchased from the sporting goods department at Walmart and dripped in steady flow from its rim as Sherry huddled close and clutched his lapel, her eyes swollen and red as she leaned into him. Beside them, Marianne stood stoically beneath an umbrella held by her brother while her other two daughters scarcely subdued their annoyance as they huddled against the downpour. Around them was a sea of umbrellas in various colors and sizes that floated in an undulating final tribute to Cameron James Mason. They had walked there in solemn procession in the driving rain from the small chapel at Gate of Heaven Cemetery where a middle-aged priest, known only as Father Jim, had spoken passionately of Cameron's miraculous recovery from alcoholism and indifference to become a crusading representative of Christ's rewards for those who would reach out to Him from the depths of even the most abject despair. The assembled faithful listened fervently as Father Jim described Cameron's incredible rise to prosperity and his untiring effort to share his good fortune with the community. As Father Jim continued with a litany of Cameron's largesse, Mason could only think of his mother, small and jaundiced in her bed as she passively resigned her life before him, her last words bearing upon him like a weight that would remain far beyond her expiration, "is Cam here?" She died in the grasp of her son and the helpless presence of her parents with a donation in her name to a foundation in Cleveland.

The rain subsided and ended as the final blessing was given, and the umbrellas folded, one by one, as those who had come to witness the final resting of Cameron James Mason solemnly passed the casket on its rails above the covered grave and marched in appropriate cadence to their cars. Sherry had pulled away from Mason to attend her mother, who stood catatonic before the casket until her daughters led her, pathetic and unfeeling, to her brother's car. Mason followed, keeping some distance from the crowd as he made his way to the car he had rented. The rain had been a brief but heavy shower, leaving in its wake the fetid closeness of the season, and he felt stifled and confined despite the rolling openness of the cemetery. There was no emotion, no resentment or outrage left in him, only the incessant memory of his mother, dying with the private and desperate hope that perhaps killed her as much as alcohol, having no more legacy than the death of one son and the bewilderment of another, having no more desire in life than the reconstitution of something that perhaps had never really existed, expiring like a distant puff of smoke in the universe, unknown and unaccomplished, homeless. Mason took off his coat and threw it into the back seat of his rental as he got in and started the engine, but he did not drive away, not yet. Steam was rising from the pavement and the clods of mud around the grave as the sun bore through the dissipating clouds, and the air-conditioning vents in the car blew cold against his perspiring face. He waited, numb and muddled in the deliberation of his life and the question of relevance as two sullen workers lowered Cameron James Mason into the earth.

Cameron James Mason. It was just a name, an empyreal fixture somewhere in the universe that somehow had touched him, ever so remotely, like a news report of events in a foreign country. Cameron James Mason. An icon for those who needed one, a secret hope for a woman who could only conceive of home as it had been, good or bad, and the walls that held a family. Two sons—one should not die. Put it aside. Move on. But one death begets another as the home crumbles, and there is the struggle to rebuild, but the fabric is weak and without substance, and there is no ending but the reality, and she resigns in the face of it. Because the home had components and one was gone and then another, she was without the quiet enjoyment of convention. She was weak, and the weak need a basis of convention. Mason watched as the backhoe was set in place, and Cameron James Mason was accepted into the universe with his legacy intact, his mortality signaled by the folding umbrellas as the unknowing masses balanced the loss to the legacy. Here again, another closure. He died in a sea of admiration. She died unknown except by those who held her by circumstance—Mason had stood with his grandparents on a cold November day and walked away, and his mother was interred as she lived, alone.

* * *

Katherine. They had been skiing all day, sitting by the fire, and the others were not there or were there and did not matter, and they talked, exhausted of the trivialities. "She just wanted to make a home for you, Tuck." Katherine leaned into him, and he could smell her hair and feel her softness against him. "I like to think that she's looking down right now and seeing that you have a home, that you have me, and that makes it right. I'm what she wanted for you, Tuck. You and me. We are home, and she knows it." He could see Katherine's eyes, captivating in their sincerity and naivete. They were home, on the deck, in the kitchen, in their bed. "The doctor had said let's give it another six months. There's no problem, just be patient. It's me and you now, Tuck. And then there *will* be children. This is our home now, Tuck. And there's no moving on now. You're home, Tuck. We're home..."

* * *

The street in front of his father's house was full of cars parked in tight sequence, so Mason parked on an adjacent cul-de-sac, walking slowly, deliberately toward the place that held him no less a stranger now than it did when he lived there. A young man in his early twenties wearing a white caterer's jacket greeted him at the door and offered to get him a drink, which Mason declined, preferring to avoid anything that might prolong his appearance. He made the rounds appropriately, speaking briefly but sincerely with Marianne and her daughters, Chris and Susan, carefully obliging them with his conversation as he gritted himself against the volatility of his emotions.

Father Jim cornered him in the kitchen. "So Marianne says you're in the construction business, Tucker. Build big buildings."

Mason hesitated, struggling for composure. "Yeah," he managed, immediately realizing the absence of respect in his tone. "Actually, Father, we build all kinds of buildings. The big ones are just more visible."

"Sounds like an interesting business, just the same," Father Jim returned as he fingered the label on his bottled water. He was a fair-skinned man with thinning red hair that was fading to gray at the temples, slightly overweight with a rather soft appearance, though his voice was clear and direct.

"It's got its good and bad points, just like any job. But I like it. It's a good life," Mason returned, assuming the priest wished as much as he for a termination.

But Father Jim remained in front of him, slightly awkward as he seemed to be calculating something before he spoke. "I understand that your wife passed away. Was it last fall? I'm very sorry, Tucker. Two deaths of loved ones so close together... Well, you know how close I am to this family, Tucker, and well, if there's anything I can do or maybe you just want to talk some time, you know I'm here, okay?"

No, Father, I don't know how close you are to this family. Why don't you tell me about it? Mason thought as he looked out the window at the perfectly manicured lawn and patio in the backyard. A small group had gathered on the patio, conversing casually as several small children played in the yard. The rain had stopped for some time now, but the grass was still wet, steaming in the late-morning sun.

"Thank you, Father," he finally answered as he turned back from the window and faced Father Jim. The priest smiled obligingly and excused himself with a consolatory pat on Mason's shoulder as Marianne entered the adjacent room. Mason suddenly felt stifled, the house suffocating him as it always had. He stepped outside onto the patio, avoiding eye contact with anyone as he walked to an unoccupied corner.

Realizing that he hadn't eaten since the night before, he took a sandwich from a caterer's tray and pulled a beer from a tub of ice that sweated precariously on the patio floor, and he rested quietly on a plastic chair in the dwindling shade. The group on the patio had diminished, and Mason realized that many of the guests were leaving. Sherry emerged from the kitchen, smiling at him as she approached some of the remaining guests on the other end of the patio. She was followed by Susan who stopped near Mason and lit a cigarette, releasing the smoke slowly through her parted lips as she turned toward him, regarding him as if she had just now noticed his presence.

"So, Tucker," Susan said as she sat heavily on a chair near his, "where're you living these days since Kathy died?" She was a tall woman, still fairly attractive despite the weight she had gained since he had last seen her.

Mason could feel the tension, the old awkwardness of her presence. "Virginia," he replied as struggled for neutrality in his delivery.

Susan took a long drag on the cigarette, smiling as she expelled the smoke through pursed lips. "Virginia, really. What part?"

"Southwestern, near the Kentucky and Tennessee borders."

"My lord," she returned, rolling her eyes in his direction, her gaze resting menacingly on him as she spoke, "that's like in the middle of nowhere. What on earth are you doing there?"

Mason wanted to get up and leave her with her cynicism but held to himself as he answered, avoiding any hesitation that might indicate the subordination that he imagined she was seeking, "Building a prison," he responded.

"A prison." She flicked her ash over the patio wall. "Well, I guess that's about as suitable a place as any for a prison. You like it there?"

Mason smiled. Still the same Susan—probing, seeking the weakness of her adversary as she pressed mercilessly for superiority. He recalled her, sitting at the dinner table on the first night in his father's house, chewing her food slowly and eyeing him as Marianne acknowledged his presence in her awkwardly staged voice. Susan had come to his room some time later, knocking on the open door before she entered and sat on the edge of his bed. "So I guess you're here to stay, aren't you, Tucker. Mother says Daddy had no choice but to take you because you have no place else to go. She said your mother is, ah…well, too sick to provide for you, so we have to take care of you. She said that I'm to treat you like my brother, that you are part of the family now." Susan ran her finger slowly along the headboard of the bed and looked around the room. "Tucker," she continued, "do you have any idea how hard this is for her? I mean, well, it's not like she doesn't have enough to worry about with her own kids, you know. And now you show up. Oh, don't get me wrong now. It's not that I really care. It's no skin off my nose, but just think of how this sets up for Mother, having to take in someone else's kid right when her own family is already demanding so much of her. It's not easy for her, Tucker. Just remember that." She stood up slowly and walked deliberately to the doorway, stopping briefly. "Oh, and one more thing, Tucker. You are *not* my brother."

He looked at her now across the table. Still the same Susan. "Yeah," he answered, feeling strangely complacent, as if he had some- how managed to neutralize her bitterness. "It's all right."

"Well," Susan returned as she studied the thin wisp of smoke rising from her cigarette, "I don't know what the hell you do there. But I guess that's your business. Anyway, it's good to see you turned out okay. It's just a shame that Daddy never got a chance to know about it." She stood up and flicked the cigarette into the yard as she reached down and lay her hand on Mason's shoulder. "Virginia. And then somewhere else, I guess." She laughed, her fingers dig- ging slightly as she continued. "I gotta admire you, Tucker. I really don't know how you do it, moving around all the time, never really being home. Especially after you seemed so settled in, where was it, Denver? Shame about what happened there. But you obviously picked up and got back into your old groove. Not everyone could do that, you know." She removed her hand slowly as she spoke. "Anyway, Tucker, thanks for coming. It means a lot to Mother, you know." Susan walked abruptly into the kitchen, letting the door slam behind her.

Sherry stepped away from the others on the patio and stood next to Mason, putting her hand on his shoulder. "So did the Snake Lady spread her poison as usual? How bad was it?"

"It's all right," Mason answered. "No worse than expected."

"She's been a little off her game since her divorce. What do you think?"

Mason took Sherry's hand and held it. "I'd say she's getting her old form back. Listen, I have to catch my plane." He stood up, still holding her hand. "Sherry," he said slowly, "I'm sorry about Dad... about the circumstances. I didn't mean to—"

"I know, Tuck," Sherry interrupted. She squeezed his hand and lowered her head a bit before she looked into his eyes, as if she were searching for some latent emotion. "Promise you'll stay in touch. Just an e-mail now and then, that's all. Okay?"

"Okay," he returned quietly, pressing himself for sincerity.

Mason paid his respects patiently to Marianne, carefully acknowledging family members as he made his way to the front room. Sherry hugged him at the door and placed a small scrap of paper with her e-mail address printed neatly on it into his hand as he stepped out. The early afternoon sun was full on the lawn as he walked across the yard and into the street, removing his suit coat as he made his way past the parked cars. A sense of urgency suddenly began to overtake him as he opened the car door, the suffocating heat rising from the enclosed car to meet him as he got in and started the engine. He drove away, slowly at first and then accelerating quickly as he made his way to the highway, appreciative of the distance between himself and that house and those people and the subtle mortality of Cameron James Mason.

Cameron James Mason. Still there as Mason sat at the clubroom bar at the airport, an hour ahead of his flight, gripping his drink as he stared through the window at the ground crews sweating in the midday sun, his thoughts sliding inward, regressing helplessly to this Ohio, this place of life and death and the thin, nebulous distinction between the two where Cameron James Mason died in such deliberation while others passed on with little more than the cessation of a heartbeat to signal the subtle passage, this place where one death begets another in such vacuous draft... *"Damn you, Cam," she said. "Damn you. Of all days." And the screen door slapped its frame as he dressed, and there was Randy's bed... Randy's coughing real bad, and she was on the porch. "Okay, honey, I'll be back. Go back to bed... Randy needs some cough medicine. I'll be right back..." "Damn you...bacterial infection closed his throat. Oh god, Tucker, why did you leave him... He's a little boy for god's sake, a little boy..." And he could hear them, beyond the door as he fell back on the bed...*

"How about you, are you ready?"

"Huh?" Mason turned from the window as the blond barmaid tapped his glass and repeated the question.

"No," he answered abruptly, adding a weak thank-you as he fumbled some bills from his wallet and laid them on the bar, stumbling over his backpack as he got down from the stool, and he was walking, almost running, through the concourse to the gate, the broken wheel on his carry-on clicking behind him as he boarded and found his seat. He settled in and felt exhausted as the plane taxied past the buildings and shadows along the runway... *"This time it's just you and me, Tucker. This will be our home for good..." "Tucker, this is Steve. Stay with Grandpa until I get us a new place..." "Why, Clemson? Construction management well okay." "You are not my brother. Does Daddy know you're not coming home..." "Oh god, Tucker...at least you could come home for Christmas, couldn't you...never realized he had a son...moving around all the time...we didn't know how to find you..."*

Sally raised her voice above the static in the cell phone. "Hi, sweetie, where are you? I can hardly hear you. What's all that racket?"

"I'm at the airport."

"Well, I guess that means you're coming back," Sally said. "Come on home, sweetie, we miss ya. Listen, I hope you don't mind staying at the Inn for a few nights. That durn Cletus said he'd have that two-family ready and—"

"Never mind, Sally," Mason interrupted, "I changed my mind. I'm staying at the house."

XII

Both sides of the long narrow driveway leading to the Wellman's house was lined with cars parked partially on the grass and encroaching the drive so that there was barely room for a single vehicle to pass between them. Mason found a spot at the end of the line on the right side, imagining, as he got out of his Jeep, the jockeying that would take place when folks began to go home. He had never cared much for parties, or any large social gatherings for that matter, having earned the nickname "Ghost" in college for his habit of disappearing rather suddenly from the group and reappearing later, subtly and unannounced. It was disturbing and frustrating, a constant struggle between the desire to belong and aversion to the circumstance. It had been different with Katherine. Although they seldom spoke about his shyness, she had a way of cajoling him into attendance but maintained a sense of understanding, keeping a reassuring presence for him while she so naturally mingled. Since her death, he had become almost reclusive, attending only business-related affairs awkwardly with predetermined excuses for his early departure as was his intent today. Anyone but Sally would have received his graciously conveyed regrets and carefully timed conflicts of travel that he had become so adept at crafting. But not Sally. "You and Casey and the boys will each get your own invite, but Casey said you'd probably try to squirm out, so I'm invitin' ya now so's ya can't." Not with Sally. So he had parked the Jeep and was now walking slowly between the two lines of cars with perspiration dripping slowly beneath his shirt, and the old anticipation, the old breathless feeling of the free fall, seemed to hover about him as he walked.

The Wellman's Fourth of July party had been announced by invitations handwritten by Sally, each with her personal note of encouragement, and Mason knew that he was not the only one disarmed by her proximity. The front yard was a full acre of fine turf, containing two large white canopies and a scattering of lawn chairs set in random small clusters. Beneath one canopy was a row of tables set up as a bar, behind which two young men in white coats mixed drinks and opened bottles of beer while another poured glasses of wine and delivered them on a small tray. The other canopy covered long lines of tables where dinner would be served.

Casey greeted him and instructed Cavalone to get a beer for the boss. "We were just talking about you, boss," Casey said as Cletus extended his hand and regarded him nervously. Casey continued, "I was just telling Cletus here that he ought to have his butt kicked for renting you that goddamn haunted house you're living in."

"Don't start on me about my living accommodations, Casey," Mason said, feeling an obligation to redeem Cletus who seemed embarrassed by the comment. Cletus appeared agitated, and Mason wondered whether it was due to Casey's indiscretion or just his normal demeanor, realizing that he had only met the man once before.

He addressed Cletus, purposely disregarding Casey. "How's your back? The last time we met you were in pretty bad shape," he said, doubting his acceptance.

Cletus looked at him without expression. "Better, thanks," he said. He nodded sideways toward one of the men standing next to him. "Doc here takes good care of me."

Cavalone returned and handed a bottle of beer to Mason as Cletus caught himself. "Shoot, look at me here. Some host." He introduced the two other men as Dr. Locke and Jimmy Cahn. Mason shook their hands as Cletus continued. "Mr. Mason here is in charge of building the prison." The two acknowledged Mason pleasantly.

"Actually, Casey does the building," Mason stated weakly, feeling a bit embarrassed. "I'm just the chief paper pusher."

Jimmy Cahn shook his head. He was a fairly tall man, thirtyish, and balding with a small paunch pressing his shirt and the sloping shoulders of one who had never been quite comfortable with his height. "Still seems a hell of a lot more exciting than selling cars for a living," he said, looking sideways at Cletus as he spoke.

"Careful now," Cletus admonished in a tone that could only be considered playful by those who knew him well. "Don't let him lead you on, Mr. Mason. Jimmy here is our sales manager at the dealership. And he doesn't complain at all on payday."

A woman approached the group and pulled Cletus aside. Cletus turned to the others and excused himself and Jimmy who obediently trotted behind him across the lawn. Casey and Cavalone had entered a conversation with some of the prison subcontractors nearby, leaving Mason alone with the doctor.

Dr. Locke was an amiable man, portly and quietly reserved in the propriety of his age, which Mason guessed to be easily late sixties. They chatted about the prison as they walked to the bar at Dr. Locke's suggestion, continuing in light conversation, pausing as the doctor ordered a double scotch neat from the bartender. He tipped the glass to his lips, looking at Mason with searching eyes that were remarkably clear and a subtle sense of sincerity. "Mr. Mason—" he began.

"Tuck, please," Mason interrupted.

"Okay, Tuck. You're the one who's staying at the Newley place, aren't you?"

Mason felt a twinge of regret for having come to the party, wondering anew what caused the locals to be so fascinated by his living arrangements. "Yeah, I'm the one," he answered, attempting to conceal his annoyance, but he could see the doctor was fully expecting some resistance, his eyes still fixed on Mason's, though without any obvious contempt.

"I guess a lot of people have been asking you about it, haven't they?" Dr. Locke continued sympathetically.

"About the house?" Mason replied as lightly as possible. "Well, it does seem to bring a lot of interest. But it's a nice place, and it sure beats staying in a hotel for eighteen months, so I really don't mind a little attention now and then."

"Sure," Dr. Locke returned immediately. "I don't blame you, Tuck. Don't blame you at all. It's a right nice little place for sure."

Sally appeared suddenly beside Dr. Locke, radiant in a white linen dress as she took his glass from his hand. "Well, doc, I see you met my li'l sweetie here. Ain't he the best?" She handed the glass to the bartender. "Jerry, take care of doc while I sneak Tucker off to some folks what Cletus wants him to meet. That okay with you, doc? I'll bring him straight back to you. Promise."

"By all means," Dr. Locke said as he took Sally's hand. "Let's not keep our gracious host waiting," he continued with a slight wink of familiarity. He raised his hand slightly to Mason. "Pleasure meeting you, Tuck. We'll talk again, I'm sure."

Sally held Mason's arm closely with both hands as they walked across the lawn, causing some embarrassment for Mason, not for the act itself but for the comfort he took from her presence. "Did everything go okay at the funeral?" she asked softly as they walked toward a small group of men near the other canopy. "You know we all felt real bad about your dad."

"It was okay. Thanks, Sally," he said without looking at her.

Cletus turned to them as they approached, and Sally disappeared as he introduced Mason to the others, a banker named O'Dell and two others who apparently had some business relationship with Cletus. One of the men immediately resumed his conversation, talking in a low voice until Cletus finally cut him off, apparently sensing Mason's awkwardness with the inclusion. They then talked randomly about the prison, and Mason quickly realized that Cletus wanted his presence for more than just the courtesies of being a good host. The prison was an important issue among the local business community, and Cletus was obviously scoring boasting points with his relationship with its managing director, which was the title he conferred with the introductions as he patted Mason on the back as if they had been friends for years. Despite his mild aversion to such unabashed exploitation, Mason obliged him, finding himself somewhat amused by the whole thing as he answered questions staged by Cletus about various aspects of the prison and Cletus's importance and close involvement with the construction personnel. Cletus was explaining how he had to "pull strings and put some business on the back burner" to find suitable accommodations for the crew when Sally returned, interrupting the conversation with her inimitable grace, and she took Mason away again in her close grasp.

"I want you to meet my babies," she said as they approached the house where two young men, in their early and midtwenties respectively, stepped away from the group there to be introduced by Sally as her sons, Zach and Martin. Both were amiable, talkative men conversing easily at Sally's prompting, and Mason actually found them enjoyable to be with, noting particularly in Zach, their mother's charm and many of her features. In a rather short time, Mason knew that Zach was a loan officer for a bank in Lexington, where he lived with his expectant wife, who was in the house now resting her swollen feet, and that Martin had been a defensive back for the University of Tennessee and had taken his first real job with the Eastman company in Kingsport. As they spoke, Mason could not help but notice the striking similarities between mother and sons, from Jack's brown eyes to Martin's thick blond hair and the way he moved his hands when he spoke. However, the prevalence of similarities to their mother contrasted sharply with the lack of any resemblance to Cletus, both men being tall and muscular with a common demeanor that was in such diametric opposition to their father that Mason had privately and regrettably questioned the lineage even before Zach had thrust his hand to him amid Sally's introduction with "Zach Hendy, Tucker. Glad to meet you."

The setting sun sent alternating shafts of pale light and shadows from the trees across the lawn, and lights were appearing from bollard fixtures along the driveway and near the house. The exposed bulbs strung about the cross braces of the canopies were coming on when Mason finally felt that he had spent sufficient time at the party to fulfill his social obligation. He had made the rounds appropriately, making a point to speak with each of the prison subcontractors and politely accommodating Cletus Wellman's introductions and was becoming desperately anxious to leave. "But you can't leave now, sugar," Sally said. "Ya gotta see the fireworks. They shoot 'em off down behind the high school so's everyone can see 'em from the square, but we got the best view from here 'cause of the hill. Ya gotta at least stay that long."

And he stayed that long, migrating in the emerging darkness with the crowd to a side yard where they collected to view the annual Kingsport fireworks display. He stood stiffly as the crowd gathered, taking large drinks from the beer that Casey had handed him and feeling the smothering closeness of those around him, their faces illuminated with the flashes above while he perspired and pleaded with himself to remain calm. The fireworks continued interminably, and the crowd intensified around him as more people drifted into the side yard, packing even tighter around him and filling the precious voids of space and brushing him absently with tilted heads, drinks in hands and voices murmuring in low swells in the airless night. And he was breathless, backing now, gasping quietly as he faded back, damp shirt and hair sticking to the back of his neck as it came about him with the same old free fall, grasping at the memory of previous therapy, Dr. Gutersen's voice distant and muffled in the thunderous show "We fear what we can't see or don't understand, Tucker. It's not the people around you or the walls that enclose you that you fear. It's something that they represent, something very real to you, something hidden deep inside you that only you can identify. When we find that something, we can start solving the problem..."

The sky flashed behind him as he rounded the corner of the house, and he was walking quickly now, his shirt sticking uncomfortably to his damp skin in the cool, humid summer night air, his chest tight about his pounding heart as his hands swung numbly at his sides, breathless, gasping in the stifling air that would not exhale, would not release him, and the lights were pale above, stringing orbs that swung in the breeze and remained when he shuttered his eyes from the strangling of circumstance, and it flowed through him, flowing hot like lava, hot and heavy flowing slowly as the old free fall consumed him once again in its rising swell, rising within deeply, and only feeling the cold metal as he leaned forward, the sweat dripping from his nose into the swirling vortex of space and light as it flowed slowly through, passing slowly and spending him in its wake. He took a deep breath and sat up in the folding chair that had somehow found itself beneath him, and he saw the canopy that had somehow placed itself above him, only then did he see the bar towel in the steady offering hand before him, his own hand rising without order to take it and press it to his face, drawing it slowly down over his chin and around the back of his neck.

"It's okay, Tuck. Just breathe," Dr. Locke said, and Mason could feel the doctor's light tap on his shoulder.

"I...I'm all right now. Thanks," he said, looking straight ahead and then turning slowly toward the doctor who was seated next to him. There was no escape from the embarrassment here as he painfully acknowledged the doctor with a weak smile, struggling in his exhaustion with the futility of his redemption and inability to develop a plausible explanation. He was expecting the usual bewilderment and concern, perhaps even a degree of emergency, but Dr. Locke remained unfazed, simply regarding him with a rather distant sense of compassion. The silence that followed was excruciating, but he was helpless to resolve it as he stared dumbly at the doctor. After what seemed to be a long time, Dr. Locke spoke, quietly and deliberately, but without the expected condescension, peering almost wistfully into the darkness beyond the canopy as he spoke.

"I get them myself, you know."

Mason blinked and tried hopelessly to dignify his presence by responding, but he could only utter what sounded like a grunt.

Dr. Locke turned back to him and smiled. "Panic attacks. Been happening for some time now. Actually started when my wife died. Comes and goes. Kinda makes things like this a bit difficult. I got some help for it, and it's much better now. Still happens now and then, but not quite as frequently and not nearly as intense." He pulled at Mason's sweat-laden shirt with his thumb and forefinger and let it drop, wiping his hand on his own shirt. "Looks like you had you a goody there, Tuck."

"Yeah. I guess I did."

"Well, you got yourself a real sympathizer here anyway. That's kind of rare, isn't it?"

"Yeah, I guess so," Mason said as he wiped his face again. "I had some help from a therapist in New Jersey, but they still occur every so often for me as well."

Mason ran the towel along the inside of his collar. His heart was still pounding in his chest, but he admitted to himself that the doctor's presence was indeed comforting. He stood up, dropping the towel to the chair as he breathed deeply, taking the air as if he were drinking it. "Thanks, Dr. Locke. I...well, I guess you know what I'm trying to say."

Dr. Locke smiled. "How about good night?"

Mason pulled at his wet shirt and let it drop against his skin. The sky beyond the canopy was lighting up as the fireworks display was ending in a loud finale, and he knew that the other guests would be returning from the side yard within a few minutes. "Yeah," he said to Dr. Locke who seemed oblivious to the fireworks, "I don't think I'm quite presentable right now."

"Understood," the doctor said, as he stood up. "Do you mind if I walk with you?"

They walked toward the driveway, saying nothing at first, the doctor pacing himself carefully with Mason, and it was obvious that he had consumed a fair amount of double scotches throughout the evening. As they approached Mason's Jeep, Dr. Locke spoke, carefully enunciating through his inebriation as he picked his way along the driveway. "You know, Tuck," he said, steadying himself against a car with his hand as he walked, "I have to admit that I was a bit surprised when I heard that Cletus had rented out old Ansel's place."

Mason stopped, suppressing the urge to reach out to the older man to keep him from falling. "Why's that?" he answered, once again feeling the same sensitivity that he had felt when Casey had first questioned him about his living accommodations.

Dr. Locke looked past him, blinking into the darkness with such intensity that Mason was tempted to look in the same direction. The doctor shook his head slightly. "Oh, nothing really. I guess maybe I'm just having a hard time dealing with getting older, I guess."

Mason said nothing, and Dr. Locke continued, "You see, Ansel and Thelma Newley were old friends of mine. Shoot, Thelma and I went all through school together. It's just hard, that's all."

The party had returned to the lawn, and there was considerable noise from beneath the canopies as Mason looked in that direction to avoid prolonging the conversation. However, the doctor remained annoyingly present, still blinking into the darkness as he steadied himself against the Jeep, and Mason knew that his only way out would be to see the conversation through to its natural conclusion. "I'm sure it's hard," he said, turning back to the doctor, who was still looking wistfully beyond him, "losing old friends like that. I really don't know much about them other than what Cletus and one of the neighbors told me, but I'm sure if they were your friends, it had to be hard."

Dr. Locke turned and faced Mason, a strange look of what could possibly have been surprise on his face. He stared at Mason briefly, numb faced in his inebriated state. Eventually he spoke, his voice clearer and perhaps a bit louder than before. He was looking down at the ground now, his foot grinding clumsily at the blacktop. "Still," he continued, "it's hard, with Ansel and Thelma going so sudden and all. Ansel was healthy, had the heart of a twenty-year-old. I know. I was his doctor for almost forty years. Thelma wasn't so lucky. Had a stroke but was rehabbing quite well. She and Ansel were planning to move to a retirement home in Norton." He shook his head. Cletus had them all fixed up to move. "Darn shame about what happened."

"Cletus?"

Dr. Locke stood motionless for a moment, his head bent slightly in the muted numbness of his inebriation. He then lifted his head slightly with a start as if he were awakening suddenly. "Yes. Cletus wanted Ansel's property, and Ansel was needing money, so Cletus bought the house and rented it back to Ansel. Ansel was paying rent for a while, but Sally just quit collecting it when Thelma got sick. I don't think Cletus had any argument for her though. He's really not such a bad sort, you know. Not that it would have done any good anyway."

"Well," Mason said after a brief silence, "it's a shame they're gone." He offered his hand to the doctor. "I really want to thank you for your help and understanding tonight, Dr. Locke," he said as he opened the door to the Jeep.

The doctor mumbled some sort of response, gripping Mason's hand as he fumbled in the pocket of his trousers and then produced a rather ragged business card. "Well, Tuck, I hope to see you again sometime. If there's anything I can ever do for you, please call me, will you?" He placed the card in Mason's hand. "Anything at all," he said as he turned slowly and began to walk away into the dim light of the bollards. "Good night, Tuck."

Someone had parked close to Mason's rear bumper, causing him to have to jockey a bit to get out of his parking space. There was not enough room to turn around between the two rows of cars in the driveway, so he had to drive toward the house where he could turn around in the broad apron near the garage. He hoped desperately not to bring any attention to himself as he pulled forward, the thought of being noticed disturbing to him yet second to something else, something that seemed to emerge unsettled from his conversation with Dr. Locke, slowly rising as he approached the doctor walking heavy-footed and unsteady along the row of cars, something that rose subtly but with such urgency that the window was open even before he could rectify his intent and his words seemed to spill out ahead of his judgment. "Dr. Locke," he said and the doctor stumbled a bit as he turned toward him, "how did Ansel Newley die?"

Dr. Locke looked briefly stupefied, blinking at Mason through the car window. "That's right. You're not from here," he said. "It was pretty big news around here. A big to-do with the local press and the town gossips over in Low Creek. Things like that just don't happen around here every day, you know."

"Things like what?"

"Like Ansel being killed."

"So how did he die?" Mason returned.

"Sheriff said it was murder. I suppose it was. All I know was that the coroner gave Ansel's cause of death as severe head trauma consistent with a blow from a blunt instrument. Thelma died by other means, but they didn't rule out murder for her either. There was a big investigation and all. Apparently, the visiting nurse that was helping Thelma was a suspect, but she disappeared, and they never found any trace of her. I guess that investigation is still ongoing, but I haven't seen much about it lately." Dr. Locke shook his head and began to walk unsteadily again. "Tragic," he said as he disappeared into the shadows beyond the driveway. "Tragic."

Mason carefully wended past the other cars in the driveway and pulled out on the road, driving slowly as Katherine touched the periphery of his thoughts. He was exhausted from his episode at the party and anxious to change out of his sweat-dampened clothes. The evening's events seemed to trail him as he recounted Cletus Wellman's shallow posturing and the two sons who were Sally's but uncoupled from the father who was never once seen in their presence throughout the evening and Dr. Locke and the banality of conversation, excepting, yes, now that bizarre resumption from someone now nameless and faceless in the subtle passing of names and handshakes but the voice now clearing from its obscurity with the others as it impatiently acknowledged the introduction and continued with such huddled persistence beyond its displeasure at Mason's intrusion.

* * *

"I'm telling you, Cletus, it was like I had seen a ghost. He came into the office after five thirty, so Linda Jane wasn't there, so he just walked into my office, and he just stood there, kind of staring at me with those devil eyes like his granddaddy and for a moment, just cause of the shock of seeing him there I guess, I thought it was…*him*. But I knew that couldn't be, but he's got him a beard just like the old man and God help me, I thought it was him like all those years ago."

Cletus shot a furtive glance at Mason and back at the speaker. "What did he want?"

"Well, I asked him just that, and at first, he just kind of stood there giving me that cold look like they could give you—you know what I mean—how he would look at you and say nothing like you weren't there, like he was looking right through you. Remember how old Ez could do that? Well, he just stood there like that, and I was kind of shocked at first, so we both just stood there and said nothing at first."

"So what did he want?"

"Well, I asked him that. I mean, he could see that I was leaving 'cause I was already out of my chair, and my laptop was closed on my desk 'cause I was just getting ready to go home to dinner. So I asked him if there was something I could do for him. And he just out and says he came to buy the Newley property."

"What did you tell him?"

"I told him we were closed for the day and to come back tomorrow, but he said he couldn't do that, and he wanted to talk right now. I told him that wasn't possible, and he would have to send a letter to the partnership, and he didn't like it. Just stood there with that cold look in his eyes, you know, that cold look like his granddaddy could give and how Ez would look right through you. That's how he looked at me, saying nothing, and I don't mind saying I was a little scared there for a moment. You know how they are. But I stood my ground and told him there was nothing I could do and wrote down the address for him and told him he'd have to go because we were closing up for the day."

"Did he leave?"

"Yeah. He gave me that damned, shit-faced devil look of theirs and finally walked out."

"Well, if he wants the Newley property, he can't have it," Cletus said, "The last thing we need is a drug dealer as a first resident. Just tell him no, and that's it."

* * *

Mason drove on in the darkness, passing the pale-yellow light in Cecil Beckman's front window as he pulled into his driveway, setting off the motion detectors that had been installed by Casey's order the day before, and the entire lawn around the house was illuminated beyond the single mercury lamp above the shop. He parked near the shop, away from the spot where Ansel Newley had died.

"Sheriff said it was murder," Dr. Locke had said.

Leo arrived for his periodic site visit the following morning. It was midafternoon before they really got into the review, Leo spending more time than usual walking the site with Casey, and there was the essential visit to Harley's for lunch. They worked late, Leo pressing to finish in order to catch a morning flight. Around eight thirty, Casey left the trailer to check with the security guard at the front gate. Mason locked up as Leo packed his briefcase, and the two of them walked slowly in the darkness, waiting for Casey's return. Leo laid his briefcase on the hood of Casey's truck, looking up at the stars that shone dimly through the summer haze. "Tuck," he said, shifting his weight clumsily in the way big men move in awkward moments, "I'm sorry to hear about your dad." And then looking squarely at Mason with the familiar fatherly manner that Mason felt was both his strength and weakness of character, he continued, "You okay, buddy? I mean, well you know what I mean. I just…"

"I'm fine, Leo. Thanks," Mason said quickly, holding Leo's coweyed gaze in the yellow light of the yard fixture between the trailers.

Leo shuffled again. "I know you are," he said apologetically. "You know I have to ask, and…"

"I'm okay, Leo. But thanks for asking, anyway."

They could hear the dirt crunching under Casey's boots as he approached out of the darkness. Leo took his briefcase from the hood of the truck and walked around to the passenger side. "You're doing a hell of a job here, Tuck," he said loud enough for Casey to hear, "but I'm still concerned about your finish schedules. See if you can get me some revisions by next week."

Casey opened the driver side door and rolled his eyes at Mason. "Revisions his fat ass," he hissed to Mason as he got in and closed the door. Mason followed them through the gate, which the security guard held open, and down the darkened access road toward Low Creek, following them to his turn at Two Stump as they proceeded down the highway toward Kingsport. He was exhausted from the long day, but his mind was on Leo for the moment.

* * *

Leo was waiting for him at the airport in Denver when Jack Murray had come to the empty house where he sat, had been sitting for some time, Jack saying nothing as he took him by the arm and led him to the car, Jack too stricken with his own grief to help, took him to the airport. Leo said, "Man loses his wife...shouldn't be alone...shouldn't travel alone." And the great bovine eyes rolled sadly as he dismissed Jack with one cumbersome hand extended as the other clamped Jack's shoulder, Leo taking the pain and suffering into himself so much so that Mason felt a sadness for him, for the chain-weight of compassion that drew him to his own like the father who carries the loss for the child. Leo, gathering the shards and fragments back to Trenton, said, "We have a spare room. You stay with me and Charlotte for a while."

"Just consider this your home," Charlotte said, but he couldn't and stayed only one day, and Leo said, "Okay, your call, if you're ready. But you're not going back to Denver. I want you here for a while, and then you can get back out in the field." He knew then Leo as the father, waiting patiently, passionately, as the child stands unsteadily alone, Leo knowing the retribution for mercy and allowing its subtle proxy as Mason immersed himself in the diversion of his work, slowly accepting the inevitable realization of the living. And there was Leo, again the rigid taskmaster, adequately satisfied in the silent redemption of his own as Mason, clinging to the thin modicum of life that had strained so precariously in the vacuum of his loss, moved on. Leo's concern earlier at the site was nothing less than that of the father he never had, and Mason wished privately that he would stay another day.

* * *

Cecil Beckman was sitting alone on his porch in his usual tilted-back position, his face shadowed by the pale-yellow lamp light in the front window of his house. He impassively accepted the can of beer that Mason offered from the six-pack that Casey had put in the refrigerator in the trailer and forgotten to serve. Cecil took a long drink from the can and spoke while Mason opened a can for himself and sat on the step.

"Workin' late, are ya?"

Mason stared straight ahead at the Jeep parked in Cecil's driveway. "My boss was in to inspect the site. Kept us late."

Cecil belched and sniffed in the shadow. "Thought you's movin' out."

Mason held the beer can tightly in both hands as he continued to stare straight ahead. "Changed my mind," he answered.

"Coulda fooled me. I thought right sure you was gone till you drove up the other night."

"Why?"

"Why what?"

"Why did you think I wasn't coming back?"

Cecil took another drink of beer and said nothing. Mason waited for an answer as the cicadas resumed their chant in the woods across the road. "No reason," Cecil finally said, his voice more subdued than usual. Mason turned toward him, wanting to press the issue, but Cecil continued, his head nodding toward road as he spoke. "Them lights come on about an hour ago. You got some kind o' artermatic switch or somethin'?"

Mason looked at the traces of light appearing through the trees across the road and stood up. "Shit," he said as he set his beer on the step.

"Now don't be gittin' yer tail in the wind. I sent Jeff over there. Reckon if somethin' was out o' place he'd a been over here blubberin' about it by now."

"How long has he been there?"

"Hour, maybe," Cecil returned, "Don't matter. He can't tell a minute from a month noways. You come here for somethin'. Set yerself and drink your beer. Jeff'll keep your house till you git there."

Mason looked again in the direction of his house as he slowly sat down and picked up the beer can. "It's a motion switch. Anything the size of a human being comes into the yard, and the lights come on."

"You mean like a deer?"

"Yeah. I guess a deer could set it off."

"Sounds like you're getting a little antsy about your well-bein' over there."

Mason disregarded the comment and continued to stare at the light shining dimly through the trees, frustrated by his reticence to go home. They sat quietly for a few minutes while the cicadas swelled in alternating crescendos. Cecil finally spoke, a strange, compassionate air trailing in his voice.

"What's on yer mind?"

Mason looked up at the half moon rising in the darkened sky. "The truth," he said, barely recognizing the sound of his own voice. He could hear Cecil shifting slightly in the chair behind him.

"Truth about what?"

"The truth about a lot of things. About what's really going on, has been going on, on this mountain. About Ansel Newley. About the Correls. Things like that."

Cecil slapped a mosquito on his arm. "Ansel's dead. Correls is all dead or livin' somewhere else. That's the truth."

A bner Beckman was the oldest of three children who were orphaned when their parents and four siblings died of influenza in the spring of 1918. Being too young to care for themselves, the remaining Beckman children were made wards of the state and stayed with distant relatives named McCabe until suitable foster homes could be found. To the best of his recollection, Abner's two younger sisters were picked up one Sunday morning and taken away, but he never knew where to and never heard of them again. Abner, on the other hand, being ten years old and more difficult to place, ended up staying with the McCabe's, who, despite hard times and four young children of their own, raised him as one of the family in their house on Bright's Mountain.

Mr. McCabe was a blacksmith by trade, but his small iron and metals shop in Low Creek suffered from the progressions of industry, and he struggled to survive. Abner was still in school when he started working in McCabe's shop, learning the trades and helping out with what little business was available. That was where he learned about tool sharpening, which was the only part of the business that actually seemed to be holding its own at the time, and he took a genuine interest in it, gradually gaining some notoriety for his mastery in Low Creek and the adjoining area. When Mr. McCabe took sick and died in 1929, the shop was barely breaking even, so Abner, desperate to feed the family that now depended on him, closed it and set out with a new enterprise in McCabe's aging Model T, traveling around the county with a wooden box of files and whetstones and the old stone wheel that he had unbolted from the shop floor, offering to sharpen just about anything that would hold an edge. Although he fared better than most of his peers, it was a tough way to make a living, and he often had to take his payment in trade, accepting a few eggs or a cut of meat for his services, times being as they were. Nevertheless, he persisted, soon becoming a well-recognized icon of the area, and the McCabe family was able to escape many of the more extreme hardships that plagued the residents of Wells County during the Depression years.

The natural-born McCabe children moved out one by one as they came of age, the boys going to the mines, and the only girl marrying a school teacher in Bristol, and Abner was eventually left alone to care for the ailing Mrs. McCabe, who loved him as one of her own. In early fall of 1934, two months before she succumbed to tuberculosis, she had Abner drive her into Low Creek to visit an attorney who managed the transaction for the sale of her house to Abner for the price of one dollar, a move that created a considerable amount of angst among her natural children upon her death. Nevertheless, Abner remained living in the house and continued with his business, which was growing steadily and providing enough income to keep him fed and reasonably comfortable at a time when anything beyond the base necessities of life were rarely known around Wells County, Virginia.

Two years later, Abner married the daughter of one of his customers, a young girl barely seventeen years old named Lissa. She was a small girl and somewhat sickly, but she proved to be a good wife and kept the house well while Abner expanded his sharpening business beyond Wells County, sometimes working well into the evenings to build a nest egg for the family that he and Lissa would inevitably be raising in the coming years. Lissa became pregnant, but she had a rough time with it, progressively getting weaker as her time drew near, and spending her last month in bed under orders from the doctor whom Abner had summoned from Low Creek. Her time finally came during a heavy snowstorm, and Abner knew that the midwife from Norton would never get there in such weather, so he sought help from the closest neighbor, Piney Correl. Piney was in poor health herself, but she was far too kindhearted to refuse, so Abner wrapped her in his coat and carried her through the blinding snow to his house, arriving just in time to deliver the child. It was a difficult birth, far too strenuous for Piney's weak heart, and she collapsed during the delivery, leaving Abner in desperation as he tried to stop Lissa's hemorrhaging with towels and bedsheets.

Lissa died during childbirth in the winter of 1938, and Piney Correl died with her, but the baby survived, and with the help of neighbors, Abner raised the child himself, naming the boy Cecil after Abner's paternal grandfather. Cecil favored his mother, being small and prone to sickness like she was, causing Abner to cut back on his services in order to care for him. World War II created additional hardship as the people of Wells County dealt with the commercial restrictions of war, and gasoline rationing severely curtailed Abner's ability to travel about the countryside. Exempt from the draft but barely surviving with a child to feed, he visited Harry Clapper, offering to share his profits in return for Harry using his hardware store as a collection point for the knives, axes, scythes, lawn mower blades, and other items that folks would normally set out for Abner to sharpen as he made his rounds. Harry was skeptical at first, but he agreed to Abner's proposition and placed a sign in his window advertising the service. The constants of enterprise prevailed as things still needed to be sharpened, and customers gradually began leaving their dulled blades at the store. Abner would pick them up twice a week to hone the edges in the front room of his house, which he had converted to a rudimentary shop, with a small bench and the worn-out stone wheel that had been mounted to the floor of the old Model T for the past thirteen years. By the time the war ended, Abner had similar agreements with a half dozen other shops in the county, and the business was flourishing enough to sustain him and his son, as well as to allow for suitable replacements for the Model T and McCabe's old tools.

When Cecil started school, his father's business was at the height of production. Abner was generally gone before dawn to pick up the day's work, leaving the boy to walk every day to the schoolhouse on

Two Stump Road, and he would be working in the front room when Cecil returned in the afternoon. Cecil helped on weekends and at night as he got older, learning the skills from his father and eventually becoming adept enough to allow Abner to expand the business even further. On school holidays and during the summer, the boy would go with his father on the pickup runs and sometimes, when business allowed, they would have lunch at a restaurant and take in some fishing in Bents Creek before returning to the house. It was a good time, in Cecil's recollection, the best of his life until the day he awoke paralyzed in his bed, lying there in terror until his father found him and took him to the hospital in Kingsport, wrapped in a blanket in the back of his pickup truck.

Cecil recovered from polio in the fall of 1952, but the paralysis in his legs remained. Time spent caring for the boy and the cost of treatment had put Abner into such debt that he had to expand his business again, working long hours for customers as far away as Johnson City and Bristol. Cecil returned to school, but being a poor student and severely crippled, it was a trial that he could only bear so much of, so he eventually convinced Abner to allow him to quit and work full time in the sharpening business. From then on, Cecil spent his days seated at the bench in the front room of the house on the chair that his father had modified to accommodate his paralyzed legs and the braces that kept them from breaking, honing keen edges while his father tended to customers in surrounding counties. They continued this way for many years, successful, as Cecil saw it.

Cecil did not recollect when things started to turn. His world had shrunk into the small front room of his father's house, and time seemed to flow independent of his position at the bench. He just knew that Abner gradually was around the house more than before, sometimes sitting for an hour or two in afternoons on the porch before joining Cecil in the front room, and sometimes Cecil also would have a few spare minutes to sit and rest his eyes a bit. They were eating supper one night when Abner finally acknowledged the competition that was eating into their monopoly—a machine shop in Norton, two brothers in Low Creek, three or four other Johnny-come-latelies who were out hustling work from his customers. There was still a good sense of loyalty, but Abner was getting older and set in his ways, and younger store managers were changing the way things were done. The business was indeed slowing down, but with some money stored away and a still steady flow of income, Abner saw no harm in slowing down with it. Cecil, in his midfifties now and knowing nothing other than Abner's example, followed his father's lead. Before long, Cecil was, once again, riding with his father as he traveled about on customer visits, which, over time, became gradually less frequent.

At the time of Abner's death, the only remaining customer for his tool sharpening service was Clapper's Hardware in Low Creek, which, despite changing hands several times over the years, still honored the agreement made with Abner over fifty years prior. Nevertheless, the twice-weekly trip to Clapper's was about all Abner's advancing age and poor health would allow, so the income dwindled to barely enough for the two men to exist on, and sometimes they would have to cut back to one meal a day in order to have enough left over to pay the light bill and buy gasoline for Abner's aging pickup truck. Cecil managed whatever sharpening work there was to be done, and Abner spent most of his time sitting on the porch, if the weather was good, or by the small window in the front room. With little business to be had and nothing else to do, Cecil, more often than not, sat there with him.

Abner died in bed a week before his eighty-seventh birthday. Cecil found him but, having no telephone and unable to drive, could do nothing about it except strap the braces onto his brittle legs and drag them behind the old crutches that he had used since childhood as he set out, leaving the house alone for the first time in his life. Unaccustomed as he was to any distance on the crutches, he fell into a ditch by the side of the road where he lay for hours until Verna Lee Capron found him. For some time, Verna Lee took care of him, stopping in on her way to and from her job at Harley's to bring him food and help around the house, as well as sending her son into Low Creek to pick up the sharpening work from Clapper's Hardware and run other errands. Cecil, however, was becoming desperately needy, without enough income to keep the lights on, and despite Verna Lee's assistance, he was concerned for his well-being. That was when

Verna Lee showed up one day with a woman who Cecil only knew as Carol, and things changed for the better. Carol was from the Virginia Department of Human Services.

Verna Lee continued to check in on Cecil, and her son still made the weekly trips to Clapper's to keep him working, but it was Carol who saw to it that he received a monthly check and took him to Low Creek to cash it, and it was Carol who sent people out to do minor repairs to the house and saw to it that Cecil got new braces for his legs, and it was Carol who sent the rehabilitation specialist to teach him how to get around the house without crutches and learn to take care of himself. Having been cared for by his father for his entire life, Cecil was embarking on a new existence, catching glimpses of the world on the small television that Carol gave him and the newspapers and old magazines that Verna Lee collected and left in a box next to his workbench. After a lifetime with nothing to look forward to except the next sunrise, Cecil was beginning to take an interest in the world outside his little house on Mills Hollow Road, remote and foreign as it was.

On one of her visits, Carol brought another man whose name Cecil does not recall. He asked Cecil a lot of questions and took notes on a clipboard as he walked around the house and yard. When Carol returned the next week, she told Cecil that things had changed and that she couldn't come to visit him anymore. She explained further that she was concerned about him having no one left to help but Verna Lee, who was getting older herself. Cecil recollected the feeling of hopelessness that he felt as Carol showed him the brochure for what Cecil referred to as an old folk's home, though Carol gave it a somewhat fancier name. "Of course," Carol said, "you will have to give them title to your house and part of your social security check, but that's all you will ever have to pay, and all of your needs will be taken care of for the rest of your life. Honestly, Cecil, I just don't know what else to do." Cecil resigned himself to leaving the only home he had ever known, and he was frightened by the thought of it. Carol left him with the papers and told him to think it over, promising to come back the following week to take him to visit the "old folks home."

As Cecil saw it, Cletus Wellman's visit several days later was no less than a miracle. Cecil was skeptical at first, suspicious of anyone who would come all the way from Kingsport to see him, considering that visitors had always been somewhat of a rarity, even when Abner was still living. There had been others in the past year, nosing around and asking questions that he could not answer. It all had to do with the prison that was going to be built, but that was none of Cecil's business, and he disregarded them with little consideration of their purpose. But Cletus Wellman was different, sitting easily on the porch and telling about his memories of Abner making regular visits to a hardware store next to the auto repair shop in Kingsport. They chatted for some time, and in the course of their conversation, Cecil explained how he was going to have to give up his house and move to an old folk's home. "That ain't right," Cletus said.

Cletus Wellman returned on each of the next two consecutive days, bringing his wife on the second day, who told Cecil that they had a proposition for him that would keep him in his own house and able to support himself. Cecil had no idea why these people had taken such an interest in him, but being somewhat helpless for an alternative, he listened to Sally with suspicious resignation as she explained that she knew of a young man who was useful but couldn't hold a steady job because he had trouble remembering things. Sally went on to say that the young man had a driver's license, and it might be worth the consideration of moving him in with Cecil, if Cecil would have him, so the two could help each other get along. She also said that Cletus wanted to buy his house but didn't need it right away, so he could sell it to Cletus and stay there until Cletus needed it, and when that time came, Cletus would give him another place to live on the mountain. Cecil isn't sure how everything transpired after that, but he does know that he signed some papers, and that Sally showed up one day with a big man wearing new clothes and carrying a suitcase who she introduced as Jefferson Davis Trapp. Cecil also knows that ever since then he receives a check for $241.44 every month and that Cletus told him that he would receive that check for the rest of his life. So with that check and his social security check and the check that came every month for Jefferson Davis Trapp, supplemented by the scarce income made from sharpening tools that Jeff, as he was called, picked up from Clapper's every week, Cecil was able to continue living independently in, what was by his standards, reasonable comfort.

That was what Mason knew about Cecil Beckman, told to him by Cecil himself, not in the chronological form that Mason spliced together in his notebook in the evenings after his visits to Cecil's porch, but in Cecil's inimitable piecemeal fashion as he rambled on about life as he saw it from his isolated knothole to the world. Having never been a part of that world, Cecil had no opinion, had no friends or enemies, no hopes or desires, no successes, no secrets. The truth to Cecil Beckman was the single dimension of life as seen from the porch of his house and the passenger seat of the monstrous old pickup truck and whatever he accumulated from Low Creek gossip. So when Mason stopped on his way home and asked Cecil for the truth about Ansel Newley's death and the Correl family, he received no more or less than the answer he expected: "Ansel's dead. Correls is all dead or livin' somewhere else. That's the truth."

Mason looked at the beer can in his hand and then back to Cecil, who was staring straight ahead into the darkness beyond his front yard. "How did Ansel die?" he asked.

Cecil turned toward Mason as the reflection from the bulb in the porch fixture reflected brightly from his lenses, his mouth moving ahead of his words. "Busted his head's what I heard."

"I heard he was murdered."

"Sheriff said he was. Deputies come here askin' all about it. I told 'em iffen someone was to go to Ansel's house and bust his head, like as not me an' Jeff woulda seen 'em. An' we ain't seen nothin', 'cept that nurse what come to help the ol' lady. Dint matter though. They kep' a-comin' an' askin' the same questions over an' over. Even made Jeff go with 'em to the sheriff's office a coupla times cuz the deputies thought Jeff mighta kilt Ansel and maybe the ol' lady too. Dint matter, though. They finally give up an' I never heard no more 'bout it. I just figger Ansel fell an' busted his head somehow."

"Is that all?"

"All I know. If I knowed anythin' else, I'da told ya, since it seems so important to ya."

Mason finished his beer and stood up. "Well, I was just curious." He started walking toward his car. "Thanks for having Jeff house sit for me. I'll send him back."

Cecil was again staring into the darkness. "Yup."

Jeff was sitting on the front steps when Mason got out of the car. He was studying something between his shoes and only looked up briefly when Mason approached him.

"Thanks, Jeff. You can go home now," Mason said. "I really appreciate your keeping an eye on things for me."

Jeff stood up, turning slowly toward Mason as he squinted in the harsh glare of the security lights. "They come on," he said, "widdout no switch. They shut off afore an' come on again when I stood up. Figger it's busted."

"Yeah, it might be. I'll have it checked."

"Want I should fix it?"

"No, Jeff. You've done enough. Go on home now. Cecil's waiting for you. Thanks again for watching my house."

Jeff said nothing more and lumbered down the driveway, shaking his head as he disappeared into the darkness beyond the lot.

Mason retrieved a flashlight from the house and inspected the exterior, checking each window and door carefully. He made a light dinner and ate slowly as he watched the news on television, too tired to give any more consideration to Ansel Newley or anything else about Wells County. The TV reception was unusually poor, fading in and out amid such static that he eventually turned it off and walked onto the front porch. The motion detectors that Casey had installed were directed toward the lot and driveway, which was the only apparent access to the house, so the porch was dark, except for the faded light emanating from the mercury fixture above the shop door.

He liked the darkness and sat carefully on the iron chair, mindful of the motion detectors and considering with some amusement Jeff's earlier observations. It was a humid night, full of subtle indescribable sounds.

The memory of Katherine's voice trailed him as he dozed off…
"You need to keep your sense of perspective, Tuck. You know sometimes we tend to dwell on things and make them worse than they are. I don't mean to diminish the importance or gravity of anything, but you can't change the past. It's just that—the past. The facts are that your parents were alcoholics, and you had a tough childhood because of it. Your brother suffocated from an infection that closed his throat. Did he die because your parents were negligent? Maybe. What I do know is that a seven-year-old boy cannot be held accountable for much of anything, much less diagnosing and treating a pediatric trauma. Carrying the burdens of your childhood won't accomplish anything. Look ahead, Tuck. Look at me. Look at us…"

C asey said, "We know it's a hell of a problem."

Eileen Barrett removed her reading glasses and leaned toward him, her blue eyes fixed on his as she tapped her glasses on the table, and she spoke slowly, carefully enunciating, almost passionately, "No, Mr. McAfee, it's an epidemic. We have grandmothers selling pills in nursing homes and twelve-year-olds dying from overdose." She retreated a bit, perhaps realizing the unwarranted drama of her reaction. "It's really quite overwhelming. We have received some grant money to help with education and treatment, and programs are underway throughout the state. But unless we can identify and eliminate the sources, we are just putting out fires." She sat erect in her chair and brushed back the bit of red hair that had fallen across her forehead.

Mason had remained silent as he tried to discern the meaning of this carefully scheduled visit from the Virginia Department of Health and Human Resources. "Isn't that the responsibility of law enforcement?" he asked, immediately regretting the question.

"Like I said, Mr. Mason, it's an overwhelming situation. The DEA has task forces in action, but most of their attention is directed to Kentucky and West Virginia, and they have their hands full. The local police are essentially helpless."

"Well, as far as this site is concerned, we are in full compliance with the requirements of our contract and exceed almost every one of them when it comes to drug abuse."

She smiled briefly and replied, "I'm sure you are, but that is between you and the Commonwealth of Virginia, which, I assume, requires you by contract to have random testing. You are doing random testing, aren't you?"

Casey interjected, "Random testing, pretesting, inspections, background checks, targeted safety meetings, and distribution of educational materials. We do take it seriously."

"I'm glad to see that you do. Unfortunately, the state does not require private employers to do random testing. Some constitutional issues get in the way. Many do, but I have found a lot of employers around here that do nothing about drug abuse. So how is the testing going here with so many employees?"

"The subcontractors do their own testing according to our guidelines and report the results to us," Casey replied, clearly evading the question. "We have our own in-house department for our direct hires, including Tucker here and myself."

She rephrased her question, "What kind of results are you getting from the testing?"

Casey glanced at Mason before answering. "Well, based on what you're telling us and what we see on the news every night, pretty much of what can be expected."

Mason stepped in, noting Casey's awkwardness, "Actually, we are getting an alarming number of positive tests, not to mention the ones who disappear as soon as they are tapped for testing."

Eileen Barrett nodded slightly, saying slowly, "And what happens to the ones who have positive tests?"

"That depends on the employer and if a union is involved. Most of the employees at this site work for subcontractors and each company has its own policy. Our requirement from them is proof of clean testing for a twenty-one-day period. How they get there is up to individual policies, but most unions have some kind of rehab program available to get their members back on the job. Our own employees are sent to a local rehab facility for the first offense and get fired for the second."

"Which facility are you using?"

"Porter Clinic in Johnson City."

She rolled her eyes and made a clicking sound. "Lotsa luck with that."

Mason looked at his watch and then at Casey. "Ms. Barrett," he said as he leaned back in his chair, "what are you here for today?"

"Information," she answered immediately as if she were expecting the question. "As it stands right now, this construction site is the largest employer in this part of Wells County, and we want to know how deep your drug problem is and what you are doing about it. My hope was that we could take some ideas from you and pass them onto other employers in the area. You work for a large company. I would like to set up a dialogue among some of the other employers in the area. To share ideas and experiences. Maybe a monthly luncheon or something? Would you be acceptable to that?"

Mason slid his business card across the table. "I would be glad to," he said as he began to rise from his chair. "Just let me know when and where. Now if you would excuse us, we have a prison to build." Eileen stood up and straightened her navy blue suit. She was an attractive woman with fair skin, and Mason noticed a latent easiness about her now that her task was completed. He walked her to the door of the trailer after she closed her portfolio and grabbed her purse. She stopped on the landing and turned to Mason, speaking slowly, "I have relatives here and used to love coming here to visit. It's so beautiful. It just breaks my heart to see what's happening. It's a sad state of affairs, Mr. Mason, very sad."

Feeling obligated to respond in some fashion, Mason asked, "Where are you from?"

"Roanoke. Lived there all my life."

"Well, you have a fair drive ahead, but it's mostly highway. Thanks for coming."

She looked around her at the myriad of activity of the construction site. "Thank you, Mr. Mason. I'll be in touch. Is the e-mail address on your card okay?"

"Sure."

Casey stepped out of the trailer and shook his head. "Shit. Other jobs we would have a drug testing and some dumb kid who smoked a joint last night would get his tit in the ringer. Now we got 'em dropping like flies. Plumber is asking for some time relief while he tries to get help from another local. It's a real crock, Tuck. And what's worse is the shit they are getting into. Pills, heroin, meth, crack—really bad stuff. And I thought the worst we would have would be some hillbillies getting drunk on moonshine." He walked on into the swirling dust and noise of the site, still shaking his head as he slapped his hard hat.

Mason returned to the trailer and resumed his work, spending the rest of the morning on reports and e-mails. When he returned from lunch at Harley's, a patrol car was parked in front of the trailer, and an officer from the sheriff's department was waiting in the conference room. He stood up respectfully as Mason entered the room and introduced himself as Lieutenant Melker from the Wells County Sheriff's Department.

"What can I do for you, Lieutenant?" Mason asked, trying to conceal his annoyance with yet another distraction from his work.

"I'm looking for a man who works here. A James Carter. You know him?"

Mason shrugged his shoulders. "We have several hundred workers at this site and twenty-two employers. Do you know what trade he works in?"

"I just have a name," Lieutenant Melker said. "Don't you have some kind of roster here?" He was a lean, weathered man with an intensity about him that demanded attention.

Mason called Jamie into the room and asked her to find James Carter in the database. She returned and said that no one by that name is registered at the site. Casey entered the trailer as she was speaking, and she excused herself to ask for his help. Mason called for Casey to come into the conference room and introduced Lieutenant Melker.

"We're looking for a James Carter who we're told is working at this site," Lieutenant Melker said with some agitation beginning to show in his voice. "The lady said that he's not in your database. I don't know what trade he works, just that he works on this jobsite on the night shift."

Casey raised his eyebrows. "Night shift? We don't have a night shift here," he said.

"Well," Lieutenant Melker said, "that beats all." He began to stand up. "Sorry to have wasted you gentlemen's time. I'll—"

"Wait," Casey interrupted, "Jamie, call Miswell and ask if they have a guy by that name." He turned to Lieutenant Melker. "Miswell is our security company. They would be the only ones here at night. Our database is construction people only. Anyway, Miswell posts guards at each entrance at night."

Jamie could be heard on the phone in the next room as she politely ended her conversation and returned to the conference room. "Jenny at Miswell said James Carter is assigned here from four to midnight," she said.

"Then I know who he is," said Casey, "seems like a nice young guy. What did he do?"

Lieutenant Melker stood up. "We'll be here at four then." He looked intensely at Casey. "Please don't interfere, sir. This is sheriff department business."

Casey held his hands up defensively. "I have no intention to," he said.

At four o'clock, Mason looked out the window of the trailer to see two patrol cars pull up to the front gate. Lieutenant Melker approached the security guard while two deputies approached from either side. There was a brief discussion, and one of the deputies patted down the guard while Lieutenant Melker spoke to him. He was led away in handcuffs without any resistance. Casey appeared at the gate and spoke to one of the deputies while the other one placed James Carter into the back of his patrol car. He came back to the trailer after both cars had left.

"What was that all about?" Mason asked.

"Asshole's been selling heroin right in front of our site. Apparently, dope heads drive up at night and score like it's the pickup window at McDonald's. Jesus, what's going on around here?"

Mason looked out of the window across the room and observed one of the deputies as he drove up to the rear gate and questioned the guard there. After a brief discussion, the deputy drove through the gate and pulled up in front of the trailer, and Mason recognized him as Deputy Setty, who had been to his house to investigate the harassment. Deputy Setty explained the findings that they had about James Carter.

"Woman in Low Creek ratted him out when her son overdosed. He was scared to death when we arrested him. Not necessarily of us but of whoever he was working for. That's who we want to get, but I doubt he'll tell. Lot of rough heads working these drugs. Anyway, we need to impound his car. Can we get in the front gate with a tow truck yet tonight? I'm going to have to stay here with it until then."

Casey responded, "I called Miswell, and they are sending out a new guard. In the meantime, I'll have to tend the gate, so I can let your tow truck in."

Deputy Setty thanked Casey and headed toward the door but stopped and turned to Mason. "Haven't heard from you lately, Mr. Mason, so I guess the trouble at your place is finished."

"I think I'm okay for now, Deputy, but thanks for asking."

"Well, you know how to reach us if it starts up again," the deputy said as he reached for the door but stopped again. "It still bothers me that no one else saw or heard anything. I mean those two guys across the road are always either in the front room or on the porch, and they claimed to have seen nothing. Seems strange to me."

"Me too," Mason mumbled as he opened the door for the deputy. "Thanks for filling us in on James Carter."

Casey returned to the front gate, and Jamie left for home as Mason returned to his office and sat staring blankly at his computer. After a few minutes, he opened Google Earth, entered the address of his rented house. He had not gone beyond Two Stump Road on Mills Hollow for the simple reason that he had no reason to, the prison and the highway both being accessed from Two Stump, so he was not aware of the houses beyond on Mills Hollow. As Cavalone had pointed out, Mills Hollow rose up and down the mountainside and curled toward itself before dropping to another road that ran parallel to the highway. That put several of those houses in relatively close proximity to his and the Correl house, despite the distance that had to be traveling on the road. And there was that path between his house and the Correl house. Deputy Setty's comment was on Mason's mind as he considered the probability of his antagonists approaching the house from the woods behind it.

Deputy Setty returned the following morning with a list of names of workers at the prison site who the sheriff wanted to question. Mason passed the list to Casey, and asked the deputy if any information had been obtained from the security guard.

"Just those names on the list," Deputy Setty replied. "They aren't really suspected of anything yet. He just said that they were people that he knew here."

"Anything about his supplier?" Mason asked.

"Just a name. Carlotta or something like that. He claims he was buying painkillers from a friend but couldn't afford enough to feed his habit, so the friend hooked him up with this Carlotta to sell heroin like it was from a food truck. He gave us the friend's name, but we haven't caught up with him yet. Anyway, Carter seems terrified of this Carlotta guy for some reason."

Mason shook his head. "We're going to fire his employer. No excuse for an addicted drug pusher being here to protect our jobsite. And they made such a big deal about their drug testing and prevention program."

"Well, we see a lot of holes in drug programs and a lot of users slipping through," Deputy Setty said as Casey returned with contact information of the listed names. "This drug business is out of control, if you ask me," Deputy Setty said as he opened the door. "It's sucking up a lot of our resources, but it seems to me like we're only scratching the surface."

Mason returned to the reports that he had been working on, which took him some time to complete, long after the prison site had closed, and Jamie had left for home. A new security guard opened the gate as he left, waving to him in what seemed an apologetic motion. He stopped at the Kroger's on the highway for some groceries before heading for home, the new curiosity about the neighboring homes on Bright's Mountain that had emerged the night before still prevalent on his mind. It was near dusk when he approached Mills Hollow Road, and he stopped before turning right as always and instead turned left to where the road rose severely and then turned sharply back downward. An abandoned house with its roof caving in sat precariously close to the road on one side of the curve, close to what appeared to be a burned-out shell covered by overgrowth. Across the road was a mailbox near a trimmed driveway leading into a wooded lot. The only residents that he knew on Bright's Mountain were Cecil and Verna Lee, yet he was still surprised to see what appeared to be an inhabited residence at the end of the driveway. Not really wanting to engage in neighborly conversation just yet, he parked his car on the side of the road and got out, carefully approaching the driveway to see if indeed someone lived there. He walked slowly, and as he approached the house, he could make out the form of a small woman sitting on the porch steps. She didn't seem to notice him, and he was tempted to turn and walk away, although being seen escaping would certainly be worse than the intrusion itself.

Dusk was obscuring detail as he moved closer, but he noticed something peculiar about her posture, bent forward and slowly moving her head up and down in barely discernible dips as she lightly tapped her nose and chin, apparently unaware of his presence. The woman's hair was disheveled but pulled back, and as he got within a few feet from her, he recognized her as the woman who had held a shotgun on him a few weeks before at the Correl place. He stopped and looked around at the house and yard, all seemingly maintained at minimum levels but livable by many of the local standards that he had seen. Beside the house was a late model pickup truck with a hard shell and a severe gash in the right front fender beside a somewhat older Toyota Camry. Beyond was a wall of the same dense forest that encapsulated his rental house, the darkness of the forest giving the place an ominous appearance. There was a light in a back room of the otherwise dark house, and he detected some sort of movement, indicating that the woman was not alone. She then turned and looked in his direction briefly before leaning over on the step behind her, cradling her head in her right arm. He stepped back and walked toward his car, fighting the urge to run in the ensuing darkness.

The following morning, Mason again followed Mills Hollow Road past the house where he had seen the woman the night before and then past three other houses, all of which were obviously abandoned and in various stages of deterioration. The road followed a steep decline, leveling somewhat and running parallel to the highway where another house appeared. It was a larger and in better condition than most in the area, with a neatly trimmed front yard along an expanded driveway that contained a late model pickup truck and midsized RV. Mason drove slowly as a woman stepped onto the porch leading a teenaged boy who walked stiffly as he leaned into the woman's arm. The boy was no more than sixteen, and his right arm was in a sling below a large neck brace. The woman eyed Mason suspiciously as he passed because, he assumed, it was unusual for a strange vehicle to pass their house. He wondered if this could be the same "kid" who, according to Cecil, whacked off the mailbox at his rented house. And maybe he was Verna Lee's grandson as well, but maybe not, since Verna Lee had said that her daughter, presumably the boy's mother, had died. The road progressed into the town of Low Creek where Mason caught the highway and worked his way back to Two Stump Road and the prison site, the forested mountain creating a sense of intrigue as he crossed Mills Hollow Road.

XVI

"My mother told me how, when she was just a girl, she would walk past the place on her way to school and see Germaine and his brother, the one called Little Jim, and Little Jim's wife, Piney, all workin' on that house that they had been buildin' all summer," Verna Lee said as she nibbled an end off a piece of the boxed candy that Mason had brought. "Hmm, coconut." She placed the candy back into the box. "We'll let him set till later. Anyway, they had been livin' in a lean-to up until they got a roof on it, and my mother figured they was a right strange bunch, keepin' to themselves the way they did and all."

"Where did they come from?" Mason asked.

"I'm gettin' to that," Verna Lee replied as she surveyed the rest of the candy. "All I know is they came from Kentucky. Folks said they had some kind of trouble there, but that was just talk as far as I know. How they came upon this area is beyond me, but they had control of a pretty large piece of this mountain. But like I said, they started with that first house that they built themselves without no help. By the followin' spring, they had that whiskey still up and runnin' and then some more of them showed up to help Germaine build another house right on the very spot you're livin' on."

Mason interrupted, "I thought Ansel Newley built that house."

Verna Lee glared at him as she replied, "Who's tellin' the story, me or you? I'll get to that, so stop bein' so rude."

"Yes, ma'am."

"Well, they no sooner had that house finished when they started another just up around the bend and before long had themselves a nice little Correl neighborhood going. That's what I remember. Little Jim and Piney lived in the first house, Germaine and his wife, I don't know when he got married, lived in the second house, and their older brother Aaron lived in the last one with his wife and three daughters that came from Kentucky with him. Those girls was all older than me, but they had another about the time I was born, and she was called Marietta. Marietta and I was good friends along with her cousin Sarah Jane, who was Germaine's daughter about our age. Little Jim had one son with Piney, but Piney was sickly and passed away early. My mother felt real bad about Piney die'n since they had become good friends, but that was before I was born."

"Correls was good folks by my reasonin' back then. I spent a lot of time up there playin' with Marietta and Sarah Jane. There was a path that ran through the woods behind the houses, and we girls used to run about back and forth from one house to the other but not so much to Little Jim's 'cause them men, the three brothers, would be workin' that still and didn't want us kids in the way. Just the same, as far as I was concerned, Correls was just fine."

Mason shifted in his seat as Verna Lee sampled another chocolate. "What happened?"

Verna Lee munched the candy slowly, eyeing Mason as she chewed. "Well, I'll tell ya best I can from what I seen and was said by others and what my brother Henry told me. Henry worked for the Correls at the still now and then, mostly loadin' the truck and such. Knew 'em well, though. Correls did a lot of that, hirin' local boys, to make deliveries, that is." She looked up and chuckled softly. "Everyone knew that if you wanted a bottle, you could get one. Even ol' Abner Beckman, he was Cecil's father, carried a stash of whiskey in his trunk as he went about the honing business that he had. Anyway, it seems Little Jim was a bit of a bad egg after Piney died. Got into a lot of trouble, though I don't know what for, but folks in Low Creek had a low opinion of him, and word had got around that he was up to no good. He must have put on a good show elsewhere, though, because he got married again, and that wife was the only one I knew. Her name was Ruth, and to be honest, I was a bit afraid of her and Little Jim. They seemed like mean folks to me. Now Little Jim's boy Ez, he was a bit older than us, Ez didn't get along with Little Jim's second wife, and anyone could tell it. I remember seein' him and Little Jim and Ruth bickerin' more often than not.

"Ez and Joey, that was Germaine's boy about the same age, had the job of deliverin' whiskey when they came of drivin' age, and Ruth was in charge of routin' their deliveries. Well, as I heard it, she was always givin' Ez a hard time about it, and Ez got real resentful until one day he just had enough and smacked her right upside the head. That got Little Jim so upset that he told Ez to get out and don't come back. Ez did just that but took Little Jim's truck to do it. Well, that set both Little Jim and his wife off real bad, and she started on him so hard that he threatened to smack her himself if she didn't shut up. They was fightin' so bad that the other two brothers, who was workin' the still that day, had enough and just left those two there screamin' at each other, accordin' to Henry.

"Well, Ez got drunk and wrecked the truck, and Germaine and Joey had to go get him at the sheriff's the next day. They took him to Germaine's house and told him to stay there while they went to the still and settled Little Jim down. Sure enough, when they got there Little Jim was already workin' and there was no sign of Ruth, who Little Jim said got mad and took off, said she just walked away that morning, and he hadn't seen her since, and that was just fine. They didn't think much of it either, her disposition bein' as it was, and figured she would return in a better mood later. She did return, but in a sheriff's patrol car with a deputy, who was lookin' to arrest Ez for assaulting Ruth. Little Jim was mighty upset because that still wasn't all that well hidden, and he walked out to the patrol car and told the deputy that he didn't know where Ez was. Then Germaine came out and told the deputy that Ez was at his house because he didn't want the laws snoopin' around where the still was. The deputy then went up to Germaine's and arrested Ez."

Verna Lee looked at the candy on the table and sampled another as she peered at something in the yard beyond Mason. "Are you sure you don't want some lemonade?"

Mason acquiesced, considering the fact that he had absolutely nothing else to do on this Saturday afternoon and his fascination at the detail of Verna Lee's narrative, which could only be acquired by her brother's disclosure and waiting tables at the restaurant in Low Creek. He made some entries in his notebook while she moved about the kitchen with a pitcher and two glasses.

"Are you writing a book or somethin'?" she said, referring to his notebook.

"No, just interested."

"Well, I don't mind the company. You want me to keep going?"

"Please. What happened to Ez?" Mason remembered Sally saying that her mother had moved in with Ez Correl and assumed the connection.

"Little Jim had to bail Ez out of jail, and he stayed with Germaine until his trial. He did some jail time, but I don't think it was much. But Germaine and Aaron was mighty upset about Little Jim's missus bringin' the laws to his house with the still there and all and told him that they weren't going to be in business with him while that woman was there. Well, I'm told that Little Jim said that he had enough as well and was going to send her back to Kentucky. A week later, she was gone, and the still was back up and runnin', and things were going well for the brothers."

"So that's it?" Mason asked, fully expecting more.

"No, that ain't it. It all came apart when they found out what really happened. Ruth had a sister in Kentucky where Little Jim had said he sent her. But the sister come lookin' for her, and when she wasn't home, she, the sister, went to the sheriff's office and reported her missing because she never had showed up at her house like Little Jim had said. Well, that set off an investigation, and I'm told the Correl brothers had to dismantle the still and hide everything in the woods because deputies was coming to search the premises. It was big news around here, and Little Jim didn't handle it well, giving conflictin' answers and such and the investigators, they was from the state police now, got mighty suspicious."

"It was Dorl Lefly what brought things to a head. Dorl was an undertaker over in Norton, and he seldom come over into these parts, 'cept when he had business here, since there weren't no undertaker in Low Creek at the time. Anyway, Dorl liked to fish, and he had a likin' for a stream in the holler past where the four-lane is now. So Dorl come into Low Creek for business and was fishin' in that stream when he saw Little Jim draggin' somethin' heavy through the woods. It wasn't huntin' season yet, and Dorl thought it seemed peculiar, but everything about Little Jim was peculiar to Dorl, so he disregarded it. That was until he read about Little Jim's wife missin' and him being under suspicion. Well, Dorl told the investigators what he seen and then took 'em to the same place where he seen Little Jim in the woods. Sure enough, they found the poor woman buried there with her head busted. It was big news here for some time, but Little Jim got convicted, and they put him away for good."

"What happened to Ez?" Mason could see there was far more to come.

"Well, Ez stayed in the house and worked the still with his uncles and Joey. Did that for some years, along with some other business they had to go along with the whiskey. I never knew exactly what that other business was, but it got Ez and Joey put in jail a few times. That Ez was a rough character, but he had a way with women and eventually married one, a little gal from Bristol that he apparently met in a bar somewhere. Her name was Sandy, and she moved in and took her place workin' the still right alongside the men. I'd see her in town now and then, and she was right congenial. So Sandy and Ez had three kids. Two were girls who we seldom saw outside of school. The other was a boy named Billy Ray. There was a pistol, that boy. Smart in school, played football so good he got to go to college in South Carolina but got into some kinda trouble and had to come home. He was about to go into mine work when Ben Harley hired him to work in his restaurant. Did real well too. Ben made him an assistant manager and eventually made him the manager when Ben had his stroke and couldn't work no more. Ol' Billy Ray was on top of the world. Married a nice churchgoin' gal, had two young sons and good job. Then he blew it all."

"What happened to him?"

"Took to drinkin', takin' pills an' such. Got so bad that Ben had to fire him. His wife, I don't recall her name, tried to get him into some kind of rehab, but he just got worse. Ez finally came and got him one day and took him to a hospital, but he slipped out and disappeared for days until they found him dead outside a bar in Norton. I'm told he died from an overdose of some kind of drugs."

"And his family?"

"Ez took 'em in. Sandy had died of the flu the year before, so it worked out well for him anyway to have some help around the house. He and Joey was still runnin' the whiskey business, and the boys was helpful. They stayed a while, but Billy Ray's wife found another husband, and she and the boys moved to Low Creek. Don't know much beyond that."

Mason glanced down at his notes, opting not to ask about Sally's mother just yet. "What about Aaron?"

"He and his wife both had bad health and went somewhere, some said back to Kentucky. Marietta had died in a car accident, and two of the older girls married and moved elsewhere. Aaron left the house to their oldest daughter, her name was Rachel, and she sold it to Alf Moran. Then Alf sold it to someone else, and I don't know who has it now. Someone is livin' there, I believe, but I ain't met 'em or even seen 'em."

"So did Billy Ray's boys live happily ever after?" Mason asked without looking up.

"You forget where you are," Verna Lee replied. "They was some of the worst of the Correls. Germaine was gettin' too old to work the still, and Joey got arrested for something to do with their other business, so Ez had to run the still by himself. He tried to get them boys of Billy Ray's to help, but those two wouldn't have it. They found that sellin' pills and other drugs was far easier than workin' and caused a lot of trouble with it. Thane, the older one, sold some pills to one of Sally Wellman's boys once, and she made it a personal war against him. Followed him around and called the sheriff every time she thought he was up to somethin'. He eventually took off, and I never heard much more about him, 'cept that he might have been in Kentucky. Boone, the other one, was just as bad. I heard that a judge gave him a choice between going to jail or joinin' the army. I guess that's what he done because I never heard any more about him."

Verna Lee sat back in her chair and eyed Mason carefully. "I just gave you the skinny on a lot of Correl stuff and could stop right here," she said quietly. "But you ain't heard what you came for, have you?"

"No, ma'am."

"And you want me to tell you what I know and don't like to talk about, ain't that right?"

"What about Joey?"

"That's what I figured. Well, like I said, Joey had been in jail for a while and moved into a place in Low Creek when he got out. He got him a job and seemed to behave himself for some time. Even got married to Caleb Saler's daughter Mariel, and they had a daughter of their own, a pretty girl named Mary Louise or somethin' like that. Well, Joey sure enough returned to some of his old ways and lost the job, so Germaine got Joey and his family to move in with him and Germaine's wife, which made things kinda crowded, even though Sarah Jane had married and left some time before. So Germaine sold the house to Joey for one dollar, as I heard it, on the condition that he straighten out, and Germaine and his wife moved to a place in Low Creek. Died there a short time later. Don't know what eventually happened to his wife, but I know Joey didn't do much for his mother once Germaine passed on. Maybe Sarah Jane took her in, but I don't know."

"So Joey and Ez ran the still then. Joey was just as wild as ever and, among other things, got into some trouble for not payin' taxes. The mail man told me that he was gettin' a lot of important lookin' notices from the IRS. Now, accordin' to one of the folks that worked at the bank, Joey got scared that the government might take his house away, so he put it into Mariel's name instead of his. That was the only good thing that he done, at least that most could see, because that saved Mariel and the daughter when things got really bad."

Mason smiled at the obvious lead-in. "How bad?"

"Well, and this is how I heard it, Joey got to drinkin' and takin' drugs real worse than ever. Sometimes he would disappear for days at a time and not tell anyone where he had been or what he was doin'. That got Mariel upset for his not helpin' with the daughter and got Ez upset for not helpin' with the still. Just the same, Joey kept at his ways until one night Mariel got a call that Joey had been arrested in Johnson City. He had been accused of rapin' a woman he met in a bar there. Mariel couldn't afford to bail him out and had no inclination to, figurin' he was no longer worth savin' anyway. She let him set there and didn't even go to his trial when it come up. He got sent to prison for a long time, but Ez let her have what would have been Joey's share of the whiskey proceeds to keep up."

Verna Lee took a drink of lemonade and looked out at the lawn. "Now's when it gets bad." She looked at Mason across the table and sighed deeply.

"All the time Joey was in prison, Mariel would have nothing to do with him. Eventually, Ez helped her get a lawyer, and she divorced him. Well, it wasn't too long before she took up with Bradford Willis from Kingsport. Now Bradford's wife had passed away a year before when their third child was born, and it seemed a good fit for him, and Mariel to get together. So since Bradford had a job for the county in Low Creek, it just made sense for him and his three daughters to move in with Mariel. They made a nice family too, Bradford and Mariel and them four girls. I seen them in church on Sundays, and they was quite inspirin', Bradford's girls bein' such good choir singers and him such an uplifting deacon. We all thought that there was a redemption for the Correls after all. That is until Joey got out of prison and found out that Mariel was cohabitatin' with a stranger in what he still considered to be his house. He was mighty cantankerous, and Mariel called the sheriff several times and eventually got a restrainin' order to keep him away from her new family. Now Ez had no heart for Joey by now but let him stay with him just out of respect for what was left of the Correl family. But as I'm told, Joey had got hooked on some kind of drugs in prison and was more than Ez could handle, so Ez threw him out one night. Ez never got over the guilt that he felt for what happened later that night."

Verna Lee shook her head slightly and avoided Mason's glance. Mason asked softly, "What happened?" And she looked up at him, her eyes fixed on his.

"That Joey." She shook her head, still looking directly at Mason. "He got a can of gasoline and poured it on the house late that night whilst Mariel and her family was sleepin'. He burned that house down, and no one got out. When the fire department got there, the house was gone, and Mariel and Bradford and all four girls was dead, burned to death. He done that to his own house, killed his own daughter."

Verna Lee leaned across the table, and Mason could sense that she had had enough of the Correls for one day. "Folks, bein' as they are around here, said for a long time that if you was to go into that yard at night, you could hear those girls screamin'." She sat erect in her chair and smiled slightly. "Think maybe that's some of what you been hearin' up there, Mr. Tucker?"

Mason stood up and stretched his legs. "Well, I've heard some things, but nothing like that."

"I hope you don't," Verna Lee said as she stood up, rising slowly and wincing at some bit of pain. "I got the Saturday night shift this week, so I'll have to excuse myself. I hope I didn't bore you with my prattlin'."

"Not at all. I appreciate you taking the time, Verna Lee," Mason said. He started to head toward the door but stopped briefly. "One more thing before I go. What happened to Joey?"

"Overdosed on whatever he took to make him so crazy. Firemen found him dead on the lawn when they got there to put out what was left of the fire."

"Maybe he's what I heard."

"Maybe it is," Verna Lee replied as she opened the door. "But what I know is that whatever happens up there ends up in tragedy. Not a good place to live if you ask me. Of course, we have had that discussion before. Now you know why. Ansel and Thelma were just a continuation of the same, iffen you ask me."

Mason left Verna Lee's house and headed onto the highway toward Kingsport, preferring to have his dinner with Casey and not

189

the usual Saturday special at Harley's. Verna Lee's narrative of the Correl family's history on Bright's Mountain was still on his mind as he drove, but shocking as it was, it did not give any correlation to the occurrences at his rental house such as he had hoped for. Yet, the Correls seemed to have a thematic similarity to so much of what he had learned in the last few days. He felt a sense of emerging fatality as he thought about it: the degradation of Correls as they slid from the relative nobility of moonshining to drug abuse and distribution, the poor drug test results at the prison site, the nodding woman on his neighbor's porch, the drug-pushing security guard. For the first time, he realized the gravity of Eileen Barrett's passionate descriptions.

XVII

The heat on Sunday morning was already oppressive when Mason went for his run. After a short conversation with Cecil, he ate some breakfast and mowed the lawn, noticing with each pass the gap in the thicket that leads to the path he had followed. Verna Lee had said, "There was a path that ran through the woods behind the houses..." and he had followed it in one direction. Something beyond curiosity drew him there. Why didn't Cecil and Jeff ever see anyone approach the house? He had security lights installed in front of the house because that was the only access, but things were still happening. He stood before the opening, hesitating at first and then entering carefully where the shadowed pines revealed the paths beyond. He had taken the path to the right before, and someone pointed a gun at him, so maybe that was not the best approach. The other way seemed even more forbidding, but it appeared freshly worn, as if it had been used more recently. He moved cautiously, wondering to himself if this was a bad idea, given his previous experience in this place. The path rose steeply for a few hundred feet before dropping to another clearing, open and cavernous about a surface matted with leaves under a canopy of huge oaks. He moved forward to a worn path that continued narrowly through a briar patch and darkened beneath a series of pine trees, beyond which he could see light filtering through the diminishing brush. Peering through the foliage, he began to recognize the lawn and house that he had seen a few days ago with the drugged-out woman on the front porch. In the yard, sitting on an old stump in the shade of a maple tree, was the same woman.

Mason stood for what seemed to be a long time, wondering whether to approach her or turn around and forget anything he had seen. But her presence seemed to represent everything that he found perplexing about Bright's Mountain, and ignoring it could not lead to any conclusion. He stepped out of the brush onto the lawn, walking slowly, deliberately toward her, circling to avoid startling her from behind until he was within a few feet of the stump that she was sitting on. To his surprise, she was far from startled as she slowly turned to him with a strangely calm smile.

"You seem to like to wander around these woods and trespass on other people's property, don't you?" she spoke in a soft monotone while the smile continued.

"Well," Mason was struggling for something sensible to say, "I thought that since you weren't armed, I would try again to meet my neighbor."

"Maybe I should be armed with strangers creeping out of the woods uninvited." The woman closed her eyes and opened them slowly, looking at something beyond the driveway.

"I didn't mean to frighten you. It's just that I live around the bend, and I would like to know who I'm sharing the neighborhood with. A little girl showed up in my yard and told me to go away, and a lady at the house down the road pointed a gun at me for reasons I would like to know. That's kind of a bad way to get to know each other, don't you agree?"

"If you're looking to make friends in the neighborhood, take a walk down the other way. We're not looking for friends here."

"Okay, so we don't need to be friends. But you, or rather your little girl, approached me first. What was that all about?"

"Not about anything you can control now that you come sticking your nose around here. He wants you to go, so just go. We know what you do, so why don't you just do it from somewhere else and let things be as they are here."

Mason tried to catch her eye, but she still kept looking away. He thought carefully about what to say next, a sense of foreboding beginning to develop as he spoke. "Who is 'he?'" he asked, almost not wanting to hear the answer.

The woman looked upward and turned slowly, looking at Mason with what appeared to be subdued terror, her lips pursed as she squinted at the sun behind him. "I need to ask, no, *tell* you to leave now. You don't belong here. What gives you the right to come around acting like you're the goddamn Welcome Wagon when you're just some asshole hanging out long enough to make things difficult for yourself and everyone else. I tried to help you, and you just can't get it through your thick head that you can't be here. And don't ask me who 'he' is because you don't want to know. What I do know is that he will be back soon, and I promise you that you don't want to be around when he gets here." She turned back toward the driveway, her head dipping slightly but rising quickly as a side door of the house opened, and the little girl who had been in Mason's yard appeared. The little girl smiled and waved to Mason as if they were old friends. Mason waved back to her, and she giggled and disappeared back into the house.

"Is she your daughter?" he asked.

The woman began to stand up, slowly with an unsteadiness that would be more expected of someone much older. She was thin but shapely, and her hair and clothing was disheveled despite a latent attractiveness that, Mason surmised, was diminished by whatever drug she was using. She turned toward Mason again, blinking as if she were just now receiving his question.

"Yes."

"Is 'he' your husband."

She stopped briefly and again lowered her head.

"No. Now, what do I have to do to get you to leave?" She began to walk away toward the house.

Mason raised his voice enough to cause her to stop and turn to him again. "Maybe you can tell me why things have been happening at my house since I moved in. Maybe you can tell me why someone throws rocks on my roof at night and sets a fire in my yard and paints warnings on my shop building and throws animal body parts on my front porch. Maybe you have some idea who took a shot through my bedroom window, scratched my car, or blows an air horn in the middle of the night. It seems to me that you might be a little concerned to have things like that happening to a neighbor. Help me out with some of this and maybe I can leave you alone."

The woman stopped and stood still for a moment, staring at the ground as if stunned, perhaps, Mason thought, in the throes of her drug use. She spoke quietly, slowly raising her head to meet his gaze. "I can't tell you anything, mister, and I can't comment on shit that happens down the road from me. All I can tell you is that your living in that house is not necessary and not a good thing for you to be doing. You have had plenty of warning, so the rest is on you. I have nothing more to say to you, and I need to feed my daughter." She turned again and walked away slowly, her arms dangling and her head dipping forward as she shuffled into the house and slammed the door.

Having no desire to reenter the woods, Mason walked down the driveway to Mills Hollow Road, noting the address on the mailbox as he passed it and went home. After lunch, he drove to the Walmart in Norton, thinking as he drove of the strange woman who most certainly had knowledge of the activity he complained about. And why was she so concerned about "him" coming back. And who was he anyway? And how do you raise a daughter when you're spaced out on whatever? Maybe it was heroin if he recalled properly the videos that Eileen Barrett had shown on her tablet.

The questions had him distracted enough that he almost drove past the gas station and had to make a hard turn to enter it. He refueled the car and entered the adjoining convenience store for a bottle of water. The cashier, a tall slender woman in her mid fifties, was standing behind the counter with her head profoundly bent forward, apparently oblivious to his presence.

When he tapped the counter, she raised her head slowly with a subtle smile that reminded Mason of the woman he had visited earlier. The cashier blinked at him over constricted pupils and looked at the bottle of water. "What can I do for ya, honey?" she asked, raising her gaze slowly back to him.

"Just this," Mason said, her question seeming a bit ridiculous as he shoved the bottle of water farther across the counter.

She nodded slowly and said "okay" as she picked up the bottle and studied it before holding it to the price scanner. "A dollar twenty-seven," she said so softly that Mason could barely hear her. He handed her two dollars, and she carefully counted his change in her hand before passing it to him, stroking each coin and saying, "Ya want your receipt, honey?"

"No," and Mason exited the store, looking back at her as she continued to smile, her eyes fixed on something beyond him or maybe on nothing at all. As he pulled back from the parking space, he could see her in the window, still standing at the counter with her head dropped forward as it was when he first entered the store. Eileen Barrett's concerns were becoming even more alarming as he drove away.

The security camera that he had purchased at Walmart was more difficult than expected to install, but he had it operating above the back door along with motion-activated lights by the time he went to bed. He tested it the next morning, walking through the yard and watching himself on his iPhone, becoming somewhat obsessed with its potential for the revelation of something that he might not really want to see. The iPhone was placed on the table as he ate breakfast, on the sink as he showered, and on the car seat as he drove to the prison site. As he went about his work routine, the iPhone became such a distraction that he left it on his desk as he inspected the prison site with Casey and walked to the food trucks that were parked by the gate at lunch time. He was waiting in a food truck line when a laborer came running up to him saying, "Office lady says you gotta get up to your trailer right quick, boss."

Jamie was in his office with Casey when he got there, looking at his iPhone on the desk. "Looks like you caught a fish, Tuck," Casey said without looking away from the device.

Jamie was apologetic. "I would have sent for you earlier, but I didn't know where the sound was coming from."

"It's okay, Jamie," Mason said as Casey slid the iPhone to him.

"He's out of sight right now, but he'll be back," Casey said. "It looks like he's peeking in the windows."

After a few minutes, a man in a sleeveless shirt appeared, his back to the camera as he headed toward the gap in the foliage that led to the path behind the house. As he approached the gap, he turned, but the distance was too great for Mason to distinguish any features beyond a full beard as he turned back and disappeared into the woods. Mason retrieved the video portion and froze the image of the man's face. He was bearded, probably late-thirties, wearing a camouflage hat low on his forehead.

"Somebody you know?" Casey asked.

Mason continued to study the man's face. "I'm trying to see if I can recognize him as the guy who stuck his face through my windshield when I wrecked the car last spring. It could be him, I mean with the beard and all, but I really didn't get a good look at that guy and can't see enough of this one. The one thing that I do know is that he came out of those woods into my yard, and I'm quite sure I know where he came from."

"So what do you do now, take this to the police?"

"I could, but he really isn't doing anything but visiting a neighbor's yard. To tell you the truth, I did the same thing yesterday. I walked out of the woods into his yard."

"Was he there?"

"No. His girlfriend was there, though, and she told me under no uncertain terms that he wanted me out of there. No reason, just that I should leave. Pretty well let me know that he isn't a nice guy."

"Did she say why?"

"No. I actually think she might have been trying to help *me* more than him." Mason tapped the image on the iPhone screen. "But I also think she's a drug addict, though. Remember the video that lady from the state showed us last week, the one with the heroin addicts nodding off? She acted a lot like that."

Casey shook his head. "I still think you should get your ass out of there, Tuck. This is all looking too weird. Hell, you might be in more danger than you realize."

Jamie interrupted to announce the presence of a building inspector on the site, and Casey stood up and walked to the door, saying, "Get out of there, Tuck," as he left.

It was beginning to rain as Mason left the prison site at the end of the day, and he was sitting in his kitchen eating his dinner as the rainfall increased. He watched the news on television while keeping an eye on the gap in the brush beyond the backyard. There was no expectation of visitors in the rain, but the image remained of a man he suspected was causing the annoyances. That sighting was both gratifying and, he admitted to himself, terrifying. Maybe Casey was right. Just pack up and let "him" have it. It would be Cletus Wellman's problem then. Just move on once more, as always, and his mother's voice emerged beneath the memory: *This time it's just you and me, Tucker. This will be our home for good…* That was it, always moving on. Never a home but a place to stay. But not with Katherine. Then she died, and again, he moved on, again aimless and detached, and he had told himself "no more" when Leo gave him the prison and a purpose to remain. He had tasted the alternative to moving on and wanted desperately to find it again, however diminished from Katherine's presence, in whatever form it might take. Staying, not for this pathetic little house but for the stake-in-the-ground privilege of remaining on his own terms. He came here to build a prison. That should be all. The man in his yard represented no less than the burden of surrender he had known all his life, except with Katherine, and it was she who created the desire for home and for her that he would see it through. He looked through the window at the woods beyond. "Hell no," he said aloud, "hell no."

There were a number of owner lookup sites available as he sat at his computer. He picked the first one and entered 84 Mills Hollow Road and his ninety-five-cent payment to expose the bearded idiot who was trying to get him to leave. The report came quickly with the current owner, but it was not what he expected. Melanie McCall? Who the hell was that? Is the drugged lady in the yard actually the owner? Or is Melanie McCall some resident of Low Creek collecting rent from an aberrant couple with a child and a distain for neighbors. Verna Lee had said that Aaron's oldest daughter had sold it to someone else, and then it was sold again, apparently to Melanie McCall. He quickly began to scour social media for Melanie McCall and found a dozen or more women with that name, but none who matched the woman in the yard or lived anywhere near Wells County, Virginia. He sat back in his chair and stared again at the woods as frustration and anger began to eclipse reason, and he could feel the rage emerging from within, rage at the audacity of someone he had seen and didn't know running through his yard, and leaving ridiculous items on his front porch, and shooting out his bedroom window.

The rain was letting up, and dusk was setting in as he walked out the front door and toward 84 Mills Hollow Road, determined and apprehensive at the same time. This foolishness had to end. Some clown ran him off the road and was throwing rocks at his house and using it for target practice. Sally had said, "I don't have a clue as to who you saw in your yard." State police inspector had said, "I kinda wonder if maybe the paramedics was there when you came to, and you just didn't catch it all the way it was." Deputy Setty had said, "Seems strange to me." Casey had said, "Tuck, get out of there." Mason didn't know the drugged woman in the yard or the bearded man behind his house, and he had no particular agenda for discussion as he walked along the driveway to the front porch steps at 84 Mills Hollow Road. He felt adrenaline rising, and he sensed his fear of what was ahead, but was already preparing to tell her to go get "him" as he knocked on the front door and stood back in expectation of its opening. But there was no answer. A television was turned up in high volume somewhere within the house, and he caught the brief movement of a curtain in the window to the right of the door. He knocked again, imagining the woman moving slowly toward the door in a drugged stupor when he heard the click of a dead bolt, and the door opened quickly.

Mason felt the rush of his own breath as he instinctively gasped at the man who opened the door, a thin man with a full beard about what appeared to be facial sores and thinning hair combed straight back on his head, wearing the same sleeveless shirt that revealed his heavily tattooed arms and chest. The man glared at Mason severely with bloodshot eyes that seemed glazed in the dimly remaining daylight, saying nothing at first and then almost shouting, "What do you want?"

Mason struggled to compose himself as he stuck his right hand out weakly, saying, "I'm Tucker Mason, your neighbor from around the corner. I just thought—"

"You just thought what?" The man was still speaking loudly, his eyes fixed on Mason's. "That you'd come around beatin' on my door without an invitation. We ain't seein' visitors tonight, so go on back to where you come from."

Mason caught the door with his foot before the man could close it. "Well," he sensed the infirmity of his voice and tried to meet the man's intensity, "you didn't have an invitation when you came into my yard earlier today, so I just figured we were a bit informal in this neighborhood."

The man in the doorway started to breathe heavily, and Mason knew that he had struck his mark. "I don't know what the hell you're talking about," the man said in a somewhat quieter tone. "Now get the hell outa here."

"Well, I have a video here on my phone of you sneaking around my backyard," Mason pulled the iPhone from his pocket, unsure of his intention. He heard a door slam somewhere in the house, and the volume of the television increased.

The man pulled the door against Mason's foot. "Like I said, jerkoff, I don't know what the hell you're talking about. Now, get the hell outa here."

Mason pulled his foot from the door, and it slammed shut, the dead bolt clicking sharply behind it. He stood still for a moment, realizing that he was shaking and breathing heavily, and then turned to walk away with the same inclination to run that he had the first time he had approached the house. His antagonist now had a face, and he found that strangely troubling. But he had put the man on notice that he was watching, that he was not giving in to his childish encroachments, and that should be enough to end it. He walked slowly along the road, the bearded face, however, remaining in his thoughts, now menacing and threatening, then seeming comical and absurd.

Cecil's front room was lit, and he could see Cecil and Jeff moving about, probably sharpening someone's lawn mower blade, and he felt a subtle comfort in their presence. The rain began to pick up again as he walked down his driveway, and the motion-governed security lights were activated, blinding him until he reached the front porch. He sat in one of the wicker chairs and felt suddenly exhausted and overwhelmed, the events of the last two days seeming dreamlike and distant. Slowly, a feeling of insecurity began to take him, a sense of free falling as if into some bottomless chasm where darkness rose like a fog, and he felt numb and weak as the rain intensified. The wicker chair seemed to hold him, and he sat for a long time, missing Katherine, aching for her presence, for her quiet patience, her softness, her loving comfort, but the reality again intervened... *She's gone, Tuck*...and he was suddenly angry with the man who had so viciously dismissed him, with the drugged woman who lived with that man, with the ambivalence of local law enforcement, and the inexorable aloneness that plagued him as the rain drummed heavily on the porch roof.

XVIII

Rough weather in Trenton caused enough of a flight delay that Mason could not stop at the prison site before going to the meeting that Eileen Barrett had arranged at the Comfort Inn in Low Creek. He knew that the two days of mandatory home-office meetings of the Project Team would put him behind in his work, and he harbored a latent resentment for this affair. Eileen introduced the guest from the DEA, Special Agent Mike Willis from the Washington, DC, field office, two officers from the Low Creek Police Department, two officers from the Wells County Sheriff's Department, including Lieutenant Melker, whom Mason had met previously at the prison site, and the vice mayor of Low Creek, Ellis Wright. Thirty or more other attendees were crowded into the relatively small meeting room, including Cletus Wellman, who was the only familiar face besides Eileen and Lieutenant Melker that Mason recognized.

Eileen handled the meeting well, coaxing comments from the group after Mason presented the Doenitz Building Company's award-winning Twelve-Point Program, and the executive director of the Southwestern Virginia Alliance for Manufacturing spoke about member policies. Special Agent Willis then spoke about the depth of the opioid problem and specific activities of the DEA both in Wells County and the region in general. When he explained the typical supply chain of illegal drugs, a young man who identified himself as a reporter for the Kingsport Times asked, "Who is Carlotta?"

Special Agent Willis smiled. "News travels fast around here, doesn't it?" he said as he glanced at the police officers. "We briefed the local law enforcement agencies about her just this morning. Anyway, for the rest of the room, Carlotta is an operative for one of the Mexican drug cartels that my agency and the FBI have been tracking for some time now. She's responsible for establishing or taking over drug markets for the cartel, and she's very good at what she does. She enters an area, connects with or recruits a distribution system, and moves on, always just ahead of us or local law enforcement. She retains control for some time after leaving, though, which makes it hard to know exactly when she moves on. The difficulty with Carlotta is that despite our efforts to date, we still know very little about her, not even exactly what she looks like. Nevertheless, she's very ruthless and believed to have committed or ordered several murders to cover her tracks, including two possibly here. The popular theory is that she has some medical training and uses it to provide cover for her operations. She appears to have been acting as a visiting nurse in this area last year while setting up her systems, and we got fairly close to her. But she disappeared as usual and made sure no one was left who could identify her."

The reporter checked his notebook. "Was she the one who killed the Newley couple last fall?"

Lieutenant Melker interrupted, "That's an ongoing investigation. I'll be glad to brief you on it later, but it's not the topic of discussion here today." The reporter started to say something but stopped and entered something into his notebook. Mason was looking at Cletus Wellman, who was avoiding the contact as he stood up and cleared his voice to speak.

"This is all well and good," Wellman said as he stood up. "But I believe we all need to step up and give some real support to these fine public servants." He cleared his throat again and looked around the room, obviously getting bolder as he sensed the attention being focused on him. "I believe," he continued, "that all of us as employers have the ability to do a better job of getting information about the rats who are supplying drugs to our employees. I'm sure just about everyone in here has either had to fire or suspend someone for using pills, heroin, or whatever, and some of us even have lost people to overdose. I know that I have, on several occasions, had an employee who couldn't pass a drug test or showed up cross-eyed and sent him or her to rehab or just out the door without ever asking the simple question, who is selling these drugs to you? Maybe it's easier than we realize to ferret out some of the dealers and help stop the problem at the source." Wellman paused, acknowledging Eileen Barrett, who was nodding in apparent support of what he was saying. "Suppose," he said emphatically, "we establish a fund to reward those who are brave enough to tell us who the suppliers are. I know I have some on my payroll who would snitch on their own brother for a few hundred bucks. We would have to make sure that it's anonymous, of course. Anyway, I think we could make some real progress by letting the suppliers know that we're coming after them with money. And I will be glad to write the first check."

There was an uncomfortable silence in the room as most attendees sat looking at Cletus with neither approval or disregard, as family members might react to a beloved uncle's off-color remarks at dinner. Mason then could see the balance of respect and tolerance that this group had for the man who, based on what little he already knew about Cletus Wellman, probably had a distinctive reputation here despite his sometimes impulsive, and perhaps bizarre, actions.

There had been comments from Casey and others staying in Kingsport that Cletus perhaps had the same effect on the business community there, and even Sally had referred to him once as a bull in a china shop when it came to the standard protocols of behavior.

Special Agent Willis spoke, choosing his words carefully. "Well, on the surface, that might be a good idea. However, giving money to someone hooked on drugs often just gives them the ability to buy more drugs. There is no shortage of dealers on the street, and even if your employee identifies his or her supplier, there is another one immediately available to take his place. Also, in many cases, these dealers are users themselves who are just trying to make enough to support their own habit. The real sources of these drugs can be anything from pill-milling practitioners to sophisticated rings working for larger organizations, ruthless organizations, both American and foreign, who place little value on human life. I appreciate your desire to help, but pursuing drug dealers is best left to law enforcement. The agenda for this meeting, as I understand it, is to share ideas and best practices for controlling production and preventing losses due to drug use. I think this is a good group here, and we have had a lot of good input. Our law enforcement professionals will take care of the front line."

Cletus Wellman was still standing, now with his hands on his hips and almost appearing defiant as he spoke. "Understood, Special Agent Willis, but we are the ones who lose to these scumbags, as well as our families and loved ones. We need to be involved, and we have been. We ran one of those clowns out of this area some years ago, so I think we know what we're doing." He looked around the room. "A lot of you remember how my wife dogged Thane Correl until he packed up his pill business and left town. Maybe that's what we all should be doing. Let's jump on these monsters and show them the way out like we did Thane Correl. I'll tell you right now that the opportunity is right in front of us. I've had two people tell me that Thane's brother and partner in crime has returned and is most likely back in business. I say let's track this guy and make an example of him. Give him a taste of what his brother got. I'm willing to lead the charge for anyone who wants to join in."

Lieutenant Melker reached across the man beside him and touched Wellman lightly on the shoulder. "Cletus," he said softly but loud enough for the rest to hear, "why don't you stop by the Wells County sheriff's office and discuss your idea in detail with us? In the meantime, we can stick to the agenda at hand here."

Cletus looked at Lieutenant Melker for a moment and then sat back in his chair, apparently satisfied with his contribution, but Lester B. Karin, owner of L&S Feed and Supply, stood and interjected without regard to Lieutenant Melker, "Cletus, you and I go way back, don't we? So please don't take this as an insult. But most of us grew up here, you included, and either were involved in or at least knew about moonshiners. Criminals maybe, but they also were the same people who shopped in our stores and sat next to us in church. Aren't these drug dealers pretty much the same?"

One of the Low Creek officers interjected, clearly annoyed with Karin, a large awkward man with thinning hair and pale blotchy skin. "Lester B, you can go down to the ABC store and buy a bottle of whiskey today and, like as not, won't become an alcoholic, and you won't break the law. Moonshiners sell whiskey to folks who don't want to pay the commonwealth tax or just like moonshine. These days they are more of a novelty than anything else. Drug dealers know that almost everyone who buys from them is going to get seriously addicted. This ain't about folks having a good time. It's about the destruction of lives, of families, of businesses like yours. It's serious shit. Now, let's get back to the agenda, can we?"

Lester B obviously did not enjoy the privilege of exemption that Cletus Wellman had with the group and sat down amid the low grumbling, headshaking disapproval of the others.

The meeting continued with presentations from Lieutenant Melker and Officer Cook of the Low Creek Police Department, followed by a roundtable discussion and lunch. At lunch Mason had purposely seated himself next to Cletus, who again introduced him as the general manager of construction at the prison. Cletus then explained how he had been "taking care" of a lot of the prison builders at his rental units in Kingsport and placed the head man right by the construction site. The conversation drifted into inquiries about the prison, which Mason found a bit annoying but answered with civility.

As lunch was being served, Cletus leaned toward a tall man sitting at the opposite side of Mason, who had been introduced as Jake Morrow and owned Wells County Tool and Equipment Rental. "Jake," Cletus addressed him in a quiet, sympathetic tone, "How's the boy doing?"

Jake nodded slightly, "Much better, Cletus, although it appears that he might need another surgery on his arm. But his other injuries are healing up, and he's responding to therapy real good. It's keeping the wife pretty busy with all his doctoring and tutoring, but she doesn't complain at all, bless her heart. Treats him like he was her own son."

Cletus gave Mason the courtesy of inclusion in the conversation, saying, "Jake's boy had a bad car accident a few months ago, right up by where you're living." He turned to Jake. "Mr. Mason here rented the Newley place."

Jake looked surprised and then smiled at Mason. "Well, that makes us kinda like neighbors. I live in the flat ground on the other end of Mills Hollow Road."

Mason acknowledged, piecing in his mind some of the circular nature of things on Bright's Mountain as he recalled Cecil Beckman's voice, "Kid whacked it off night afore last when he missed the bend..." and Verna Lee's "Jake, that's his daddy, Jake an' me don't get along, much less talk, so I can't really say if the boy's doin' good or not." Mason mused to himself that perhaps he should go and tell Verna Lee that her grandson was all right. Verna Lee had said that her daughter had died of cancer, so he guessed at the revelation that probably evolved into local gossip, that of a mother bitter about the abject replacement of her dead daughter. The thought took him enough that he almost missed Jake's low response to Cletus. "Well, he's been laid up enough that he can't find drugs whether he wants them or not. I think he learned his lesson, but who knows with this addiction business. I don't understand that, Cletus, and it scares me."

Cletus again included Mason, "His boy, like so many kids around here, got into drugs, and we think Boone Correl supplied them."

"Well," Jake offered quickly, "That's how it appears. He said got it from friends at school. When we had the school investigate, none of the boys questioned would say much except that a guy what used to be a janitor there sold it to them and told them that, if they got caught with it, to keep shut because telling would upset Boone, and that would result in someone getting hurt bad." Jake raised his hand to Cletus, who was suddenly becoming animated, and continued to Mason, "That's all we know. No one ever said Correl, and the janitor disappeared before the police could question him."

"It was Boone Correl, sure enough," Cletus said.

"Who else saw Boone Correl?" Mason asked Cletus.

Cletus answered quickly, obviously satisfied to see that his premise was still alive. "Real estate agent, partner in our housing project on Bright's Mountain, said Boone approached him wanting to buy the house you're living in. Seemed to want it real bad, but there's no way we're going to have our first sale in the project go to a drug dealer. That wouldn't be a good way to entice other buyers now, would it?"

"What is the project?"

"Homes," Cletus replied. "Each of the houses we bought up there had a substantial amount of acreage attached to it. The one you're in has eleven acres. The old Correl place and the McCabe house across the road from you each had another twenty, give or take a few. The plan is for single family, duplexes, and an apartment building. A lot of folks are going to work at that prison you're building, and we intend to give them a quality place to live."

"What about the existing houses?"

"Might sell the one you're in or maybe tear it down. The other two gotta go."

"What about Cecil and Jeff?"

Cletus raised his eyebrows at Mason's concern. "We'll have a place for them. They'll be okay."

Mason smiled at the reassurance. "So you bought about fifty acres for the project."

"Yep, there's another twenty acres in Mills Hollow that we want to acquire at some point for Phase Two."

"You mean where Verna Lee lives?" Mason avoided eye contact with Jake, who reacted immediately to the name."

"Yep," Cletus said. "Ol' girl don't want to sell just yet, but her son said she probably would eventually."

Mason placed his napkin on the table and began to stand up. "Jake," he said, "nice meeting you, and it's good to see you again, Cletus. I would love to learn more about your project, Cletus, but I have one of my own that needs my attention." He found Eileen Barrett and thanked her for her efforts and started for the door, catching Cletus about to enter another conversation. "Cletus," he asked, "what does Boone Correl look like?"

Cletus seemed embarrassed. "Actually, I've never seen him myself. But I'm told he's about five-nine and has a full beard. Why do you ask?"

"Just curious."

Jake Morrow caught Mason as he was walking out the door. "Mind if I walk with you?" he asked as they stepped into the corridor.

"Not at all," Mason said as he checked for messages on his iPhone. "But I really need to get to work."

"No problem, I understand," Jake said as he kept pace with Mason, "You mentioned Verna Lee Capron. Do you know her?"

"Sure, I've been to her house a couple of times. Nice lady."

"She really is a nice lady," Jake said, "but she has no love for me."

"Why is that?"

"Well, I was married to her daughter until she passed away a few years ago. I just wanted to know how Verna Lee is doing."

Mason found the subject strangely uncomfortable, sensing a slight defensiveness in Jake's voice. "She seems all right to me," he answered, trying not to appear dismissive.

Mason stopped as he reached for the car door. "Cletus mentioned that Verna Lee has a son. Does she have any other family?"

Jake shrugged, "Well, I still consider myself family, but she apparently doesn't. She has a brother, Henry, here in Low Creek and another daughter who lives in Norton. The son's in Low Creek but is gone a lot. Over the road trucker. They all get together about once a month, grandchildren included. Of course, we're no longer invited."

"Mind if I ask why?" Mason asked, regretting his interest in the man's personal affairs.

"Did Verna Lee tell you how my wife died?"

"Said she had cancer."

"Yep, she had breast cancer. It was in remission when she died." Jake looked away and then back to Mason. "Mr. Mason, my wife died from an overdose of painkillers. She had been addicted for some time. Verna Lee just couldn't accept it, though, and when I told her she kinda went off the deep end. You know what I mean?"

Mason opened the car door. "I guess, I really didn't—"

Jake continued, "And when I remarried, well, that was the end of it. You know, a death in the family is hard on everyone. My son was close to Verna Lee. Stayed with her for a while. He took his mother's death pretty hard, and his grandmother was able to give him more comfort that I could, I guess. But he was getting into drugs while living with her, and she had no clue. Drug abuse killed my wife and almost killed my son, Mr. Mason. That's why things like this meeting are so important to me. That's why I can understand Cletus's desire to get involved." He shook his head. "That's a lot of the problem here. People just don't want to recognize that we have a serious drug addiction issue going on. I ignored it myself until it affected my personal life." He looked away and shook his head slightly. "I know you need to get to work, and so do I. I really didn't mean to belabor you with my personal issues." He reached out to shake Mason's hand. "It's a pleasure meeting you, Mr. Mason. I'm sure we'll see each other again."

As he drove away, Mason wondered why Jake Morrow was so eager to speak with him and why the man would want to unload so much of his personal burden on a stranger. Guilt, maybe. Mason knew the subject well. "Grief over the death of a loved one," Dr. Gutersen, the therapist who occasionally treated Mason, had said after the death of Mason's mother, "heals with time. But the guilt that so often accompanies it takes a lot of effort to overcome. That can be a heavy load to carry by oneself. It's best to get it out in the open, see it for what it is and deal with it." Much like the way, Mason thought, Katherine had pulled his demons from him and made him talk to her. But Katherine was gone now, and the demons had returned, and he had some sympathy for Jake Morrow.

Low Creek was around him as he drove by neatly arranged retail and other business establishments: the town hall, the Mountaineer's Museum, Harley's Restaurant, and others on open streets that crossed avenues where houses were assembled almost haphazardly, some well-kept and pleasant while others were dilapidated and pathetic. The town seemed to have a life of its own beyond the buildings and parks and surrounding mountains and residents who were going about their business or, having no business, seemed strangely disassociated from the world beyond Low Creek—an old woman sitting on a park bench, four young men standing on a corner without speaking, a man and woman emerging from a bank, sidewalk denizens moving in one direction or another in the late-summer sun. There was a peacefulness about the town, yet Mason could not help feeling a subdued tension that prevailed in the vacancy of expression that he noticed as he exited the main street on his way to the highway, past the poorer district where residents sat on porches and stoops or leaned on old automobiles in the shade of untrimmed trees, shirtless men and sleeveless women displaying tattoos on sunburned arms and shoulders while children played in bare yards and graveled driveways. Mason had the same sense of discord that he had experienced when he had first driven from the airport in April, and he found it somewhat troubling in light of what Eileen Barrett had called a sad state of affairs.

He took an unnamed road that ran parallel to the highway, knowing from a Sunday run that it led to Mills Hollow Road, past Jake Morrow's house and past Melanie McCall's house, where he drove slowly, contemplating the possibility that he had met Boone Correl there earlier in the week. "About five-nine and has a full beard," Cletus had said although that description suited a good percentage of the male population of Wells County. He mused at the possibility of Boone's return from wherever he had been. Verna Lee had said that she heard that Boone had joined the Army, but the individual at Melanie McCall's house didn't seem to fit the description of a career soldier although years had passed, and he could have been out of the Army for some time. But whether it was Boone or not, the question still remained that someone shot out his bedroom window and harassed him, and now that he had a face and perhaps a name, finding a reason became even more important. He considered his next move as he turned up Two Stump Road and took the access road to the prison site.

Jamie was setting water bottles on the conference table for his three o'clock meeting with an OSHA inspector as he entered the trailer. She leaned close to him and said in a low voice, "There's someone here to see you. I told her you had a meeting and were very busy, but she said that she would wait for you. She's in your office."

A tall woman, fiftyish with long dark hair and wearing blue jeans and polo-style shirt, stood when he entered his office and introduced herself as Leanna Dell, a name familiar to Mason as the author of a book about the history of Appalachia that he had purchased in Low Creek. "I'm writing a book about the evolution of industry and trade in the area, and I thought the construction of this prison would be a good example of modern construction methods being utilized. The architect's office gave me some general data, but I wanted to get some corresponding pictures and practical information. Is it possible for me to walk around the site for a bit?"

Mason smiled, "It is possible, but not alone. Jamie, get ahold of Casey and have him send someone up to escort Ms. Dell around the site. And get her a hard hat and safety glasses."

"Casey's on his way up here now for the meeting. I'll call him anyway," Jamie answered.

"We'll have an assistant superintendent escort you. Our insurance underwriter wouldn't be too happy to have you walking around by yourself. Besides, that way we can answer any questions that you might have as they come up. Now, if you will excuse me, I have a meeting to attend. Jamie will handle things from here."

After the meeting, Mason was in his office working when Leanna Dell entered the trailer. Jamie had already left for the day, and Leanna stuck her head into his office. "I just wanted to thank you for your kindness today. The young man who escorted me, Jimmy, was very informative and a real gentleman."

"Glad to be of service," Mason answered. "Let us know when the book gets published. It sounds interesting."

"Will do. Thanks, again, Mr. Mason," Leanna said as she turned to leave.

A thought occurred to Mason that made him impulsively call out to her as she opened the door. "Ms. Dell, you seem to be the most informed historian in the area. Is that a fair assessment?"

"It is. I was born and raised in Low Creek and have been studying Southwest Virginia nearly all my adult life."

"Well," Mason said already feeling embarrassment for the request, "I'm currently living just down the road here and am interested in the history of this mountain, particularly the people who have owned property here. I wonder if maybe I can steal a few minutes of your time at some point and ask a few questions."

"I would be glad to have the opportunity to return your consideration, but it will have to be at another time. I'm leaving for New York tonight and won't be back for a while. I live there now. However, if you go to the Mountaineer's Museum in Low Creek, you can find a number of resources that will help, including my first book, *The Barter Tree*." She turned to leave but stopped and said, "Better still, I have a lot of notes on my laptop. If you give me an e-mail address, I can put together a quick lowdown on the plane tonight if that's all you need. I actually would enjoy it. This mountain has some interesting history."

"That would be great. I don't want to put you to unnecessary effort, but if it's no problem, I would love to see it."

"My pleasure, Mr. Mason. I'll send it to you tomorrow." Leanna closed the door behind her.

Cecil was on his front porch while a shirtless Jeff worked at some weeds in the lawn when Mason turned into his driveway. He grabbed three beers from the refrigerator and walked across the road and sat in his usual chair, handing one beer to Cecil and placing another on the porch rail for Jeff. Cecil nodded and asked, "So how's that jailhouse comin' along?"

"On schedule so far," Mason replied. "As long as we're closed in before winter, I think we'll be okay."

Cecil looked at Jeff in the yard with one of his typical responses, "Yup." He flicked something from his arm. "Hot one today, weren't it?"

Mason couldn't resist the temptation to follow, "Yup."

They sat quietly for a few minutes in the warm breeze as Jeff put his shirt back on and took his beer and sat on the steps. Mason asked, "We talked before about Boone Correl. Did you know him?"

Cecil turned to him as if surprised by the question. "Nope. Knew of him. Lotta talk about him and his brother years back."

"So you never really met him."

Cecil scratched his neck, "Don't reckon I did until he come around here a couple of months ago asking questions."

"He was here?"

"Yup."

"What kind of questions?"

"Mostly about you and what you was doin'. I told him you was buildin' the prison and was a right nice feller. Wanted to know if you bought the house. I told him you was rentin' just until that prison was built."

"Then what did he say?"

"Nothin. Just turned and walked away. Headed that away on the road. I figger he's stayin' at ol' Aaron Correl's place since that's the only habitable place within walkin' distance. Seemed agitated, though."

"Have you seen him since?"

"I seen him drive by a few times in a pickup."

Mason looked at the road and then back to Cecil. "Why didn't you tell me this earlier?"

"You didn't ask."

The following morning, Mason took an early run, turning right from his driveway instead of his usual direction. A small school bus was stopped in front of Melanie McCall's house. Melanie hugged her daughter and helped her get on the bus. Seeing Mason approaching, she stood still and shook her head as the bus drove forward.

Mason spoke before she could, "Seems early in the year for school to start," he said, expecting a terse answer.

"Remedial classes. She didn't finish last year when…we moved." Melanie regained herself. "You keep showing up. All I can figure at this point is that you are really stupid," she said, looking away at the bus. "Your situation is so much worse now that you had to get him stirred up. I don't know what to tell you now. You need to leave us alone and go away." She appeared agitated as she looked briefly at Mason and turned to walk away on the driveway.

"His name is Boone Correl," Mason said, just loud enough for her to hear him. "Aside from being an awful neighbor, he's quite unpopular with a lot of folks in the area, people who aren't too happy about his return. I expect they would like to know where he's living. I guess that could be information that I could give them, couldn't it, Melanie? Maybe I should make some calls and let you and Boone deal with it. Do you think that's what I should do?"

She stopped and turned to him, "Okay," she looked up and shrugged her shoulders, "we need to talk. But not here. Not now." She turned back toward the house and started walking again.

"Okay, when and where?" Mason asked, raising his voice now.

Melanie kept walking, and Mason followed until she reached the front porch of her house. She stopped on the porch and turned toward him. "You really are annoying. Come in. I want to show you something."

She opened the door and walked in, leaving it open behind her as Mason continued to follow. The tiny front room was sparsely appointed with a couch on one side and two folding tables set in an L shape on the other side. On one table, small tools, gemstones, and other paraphernalia were neatly arranged in small containers and spread about felt pads. The other table was bare, except for a large wooden work surface. Mason pointed to the tables. "Who's hobby?"

Melanie turned with the subtle smile that he had noted before. "Mine, but it's not a hobby. It's what I do. I make custom jewelry."

"You sell it, like in stores?"

"Some. Mostly through my website. I do some shows when I can."

Mason looked back at the tables. "So how's business?"

"Okay. I'm building inventory now. The majority of sales comes during the holidays."

She walked through a small hallway and through the kitchen, where Mason noted her child's stickers and drawings on the refrigerator, to a closet door, which she opened after turning a key in the lock and then stood aside. The closet was empty, except for what appeared to be a hunting rifle with a massive scope, a pump-style shotgun and some kind of assault rifle. On a shelf above were a large set of binoculars, two handguns, and boxes of ammunition.

"This might give you an idea of whom you're dealing with," she said, eying Mason carefully.

"These are Boone's?" he asked, looking back into the closet.

"Yes."

Mason couldn't resist the next question, and he felt sure she would know what he was talking about. "Where's yours?"

Her subtle smile appeared, "Back in the shed where I found it."

"Why didn't you use one of these?"

She closed the closet door and locked it. "Like I said, we'll talk later. In the meantime, I suggest you stay out of Boone's way."

Mason shot back, "I just want Boone to stay out of my yard."

Melanie looked down and back at Mason. "I believe he's doing that. Staying out of your yard, I mean."

"Now that you mention it, I haven't had any events lately. That's a good thing."

Melanie walked past him into the kitchen. "Maybe. But probably not. Listen, I have work to do, and I need to pick up materials in Low Creek. Boone won't let me have anything delivered here." She picked up her purse from the kitchen counter and dropped her keys into it, moving out the front door, which she held open for Mason. "We'll talk later, mister…what was your name again?"

"Just call me Tuck,"

"We'll talk later, Tuck."

"When and where?"

Melanie opened the door of her car, "I'll find you."

A sense of defeat rose in Mason as he stood in the driveway and watched her drive away. He finished his run feeling frustrated and foolish.

XIX

Leanna Dell's e-mail arrived as promised, but Mason didn't get around to reading it until several days later. It was the simple narrative that he had hoped for:

> After the Revolutionary War, the Virginia Land Office began awarding bounty lands to military veterans who could show substantial proof of service. Once the last of the Shawnee villages was abandoned and the Iroquois turned their raids northward, William Bright, a retired colonel in the Continental Army and Virginia native of Scottish descent, requested a bounty warrant for a tract of land consisting of three hundred acres extending from the confluence of Maris Run and Bents Creek along defined parameters that comprise the entire western face of what we now know as Bright's mountain. Colonel Bright's intention was to establish a salt extraction business by exploiting the marshes at the lower end of the property. The land was granted in 1787, but according to the surviving fragments of Bright's journal, actual production was delayed until 1800.

In 1809, Bright's salt works was in full production, the colonel having by then resolved logistical issues of travel through the perilous and often flooding lowland marshes by constructing a road across the face of the mountain. In order to compensate for the steep terrain, the road was built rising and descending gradually in an inverted "V" pattern up and down the face of the mountain and connecting to the wagon trail and access to markets developing from the coastal origination points. Homes for employees of the salt business were located along the road, now known as Mills Hollow Road, with the production facility located on a level plot near the marshes now known as Mills Hollow (the name has no discoverable origin and probably was added by a cartologist or surveyor at some later point in time).

Records indicate that Bright sold his salt production business in 1822 to a larger producer in what is now West Virginia, probably due to his own poor health as he died a year later. Prior to his death, he had surveyors divide the land into three equal parcels. The parcel directly above and including the closed saltworks on the northwesternmost side of the mountain was sold immediately to a French immigrant named Charles Capron. The following year brought another Frenchman named Jean Ives Cordel, who purchased the parcel that comprised most of the area within the inverted "V" of Mills Hollow Road. The remaining piece was purchased by James Wilmont Wainwright, a second-generation Virginian of English heritage. Colonel Bright's family relocated to a family-owned property near Roanoke.

Charles Capron destroyed the abandoned salt facility and built a dairy farm after clearing adequate land for grazing. He apparently had two sons, one who died in an accident, and the other, Henry Louis Capron, worked the dairy farm with his father while also serving in the Virginia House of Delegates. Henry was married to Agathe Cordel, who was the daughter of his neighbor, Jean Ives Cordel, and had two daughters and a son. Little was recorded about the daughters, but the son, Durant Capron, was conscripted into the Confederate Army in 1862. Durant returned to the dairy farm after the Civil War was over and remained there with his widowed father, continuing beyond Henry's death in 1882. Durant had five children, four daughters, who married and left home, and one son, Oliver James Capron, who continued operating the farm well into the next century. Oliver had no children but married a widow from Low Creek named Mary Louise Mays in 1902 and adopted her two young sons, Phillip and Roger. When the United States entered WWI, both of Oliver's adopted sons were drafted into the Army. Roger was killed in battle, but Phillip returned to his wife, the former Melissa Cole Jamison, and their young son, Phillip Jr. Phillip had four more children and, in the following years, rebuilt the family homestead to accommodate his growing family. The dairy farm continued successfully for a while but barely survived the Great Depression, and Phillip Jr. had to manage the farm operations as his siblings left in desperation. The hard times continued to take their toll on the family, with all but one of Phillip Jr.'s children leaving home as they came of age except his youngest son, William, known as Willy Joe, who struggled to survive with his father for years afterward until they closed the farm in 1958 and found work elsewhere. Willy Joe married a woman from Low Creek named Verna Lee Barden and had three children, all of whom still live in Wells County. Willy Joe passed away some time ago, but I believe Verna Lee still lives in the homestead although she is pretty well up in years.

For reasons undisclosed, Phillip Capron had transferred a substantial part of his property that was not pasture to his widowed sister, Ella. Ella was then remarried to a blacksmith from Low Creek named Caleb McCabe. In 1902, they rebuilt a burned-out house on Mills Hollow Road and raised a family there. When Caleb McCabe passed away, the property was transferred to Abner Beckman. To my knowledge, Abner's son Cecil still lives there.

The rest of the original Bright grant was not quite as linear. James Wainwright built a house on Mills Hollow Road but never moved into it, and no further records of him have been found, except a letter thought to be sent by him to the Virginia House of Delegates decrying smuggling operations in Richmond. His property on Bright's Mountain remained unsettled with the exception of squatters who, in some cases, took possession by squatters' rights as allowed by law. Over the years, about a dozen families are thought to have lived there, in some cases for several generations, with the only legal activity being a broad easement acquired by the state of Virginia for the prison and a deed transfer in 2008 to Jacob Morrow for several acres at the lower portion near the highway.

Jean Ives Cordel cleared land for a corn crop and built a whiskey distillery on his property along with a house and several outbuildings. He had two sons, Burrel and Pierre, and a daughter, Agathe, mentioned above. The business flourished even through the Civil War, with Jean Ives's two sons and eventually their sons and daughters working the corn and distillery. Burrel had one son and two daughters (I couldn't find a record of their names), and Pierre had one son, also named Pierre but called Petey, and a daughter, Felicia. By all indications, everyone in the family worked at the distillery and in the corn field, except for Petey's two-year stint in the Confederate Army.

Things were going well for the Cordel family until the summer of 1873, when a fire broke out on a particularly dry day and destroyed virtually every structure and tree on Bright's Mountain, including all the Cordel's buildings, but excepting the Capron dairy farm in Mills Hollow. The family was able to escape, although Jean Ives passed away shortly afterward. Durant Capron wrote in a letter to a friend, "Everything reeks of ash and we cannot last but a few hours in the befouled air. Our cows and horses suffer with black ash about their snouts and the creeks run black. Only rain and time can save us."

Apparently, Jean Ives Cordel's deceased brother-in-law, Colonel Michael Townsend, had received a bounty award in Kentucky and his surviving family invited the Cordels to relocate there to start a new distillery. Having little choice to the contrary, Pierre and Burrel accepted, and the Cordels moved to Kentucky. That is out of my area of research, but there is a fair amount of evidence of a successful Cordel distillery near

Georgetown, Kentucky, operating right up to the time of Prohibition.

Bright's Mountain was quite deserted, except for the Capron dairy, for some time after the fire. As growth began to be restored, some squatters began to sparsely repopulate the area. Then in 1921, a document was presented by an Aaron Cordel to the Virginia Land Office claiming ownership by inheritance of the original Cordel property. Three separate documents were then produced dividing the tract into three separate parcels, with Aaron retaining one parcel and his two brothers, Germaine and James, receiving the other two. Interestingly, either by intent or a clerk's carelessness, the three new documents had the surname spelled "Correl." Regardless of intent, all future documents retained that spelling.

Now this part of the story is based strictly on unverified information and speculation because, as I stated earlier, Kentucky is out of my range of research. By several accounts, the Cordel Distillery disregarded the passage of Prohibition and continued in business until government agents destroyed its production equipment and arrested several members of the family. There also was some suspicion regarding a missing government agent. As I stated above, I have no evidence of anything in Kentucky, but I do know that the three brothers built homes on Bright's Mountain in 1921 and raised families there for some time..."

Leanna's further narrative of the Correl family was far less colorful than the stories Mason had heard from Verna Lee and Cecil. Mason skimmed it quickly and replied with his thanks.

"Turn your head and cough," Dr. Locke said as he held the stethoscope to Mason's chest. "Sounds interesting, the story, that is. Leanna has quite a name around here. She's a very successful writer and has done a lot to raise awareness of our part of the world." He held the stethoscope to Mason's back. "Breathe deeply. Okay, so you say she sent all that to you in an e-mail? Go ahead and put your shirt on."

"Yes," Mason replied, "it was quite impressive."

"Was there a particular reason for the e-mail?"

Mason stood and tucked his shirt in as he spoke. "She had come to the prison site for research, and I guess she just wanted to return the courtesy that we showed her. I had asked her for some history of Bright's Mountain. No reason in particular. I just found the place to be fascinating and she was a convenient source."

"Well," Dr. Locke said as he picked up the clipboard and a pen, "I've read some of her books, and Bright's Mountain has had some interesting goings on. Of course, you could just read the papers over time and tell that." He signed the form on the clipboard. "Do you want me to send this directly to the insurance company?"

"Yes," Mason pointed to the clipboard, "there's an envelope attached. I don't know why I have to do this every year, but the company pays the bill, so it is what it is. You said that you knew the people who lived in the house that I'm renting, the Newleys."

"Sure did," Dr. Locke said as he exited the exam room and handed the clipboard to his assistant. "Copy this and send it out, Berty, and good night." He turned to Mason. "You're my last today but walk with me." He closed the door as they exited through a small hallway. "We all grew up in Low Creek," he continued, "and Thelma and I went all through school together. Ansel was a few years older, but he was my patient from the time they were married until, well, until they died."

Dr. Locke stopped on the front stairs of his office building and looked down Davis Street into downtown Low Creek. "They were teachers. Met while teaching at the high school here. Because of dating rules, Ansel had to quit and moved on to the high school in Norton. Taught shop there until he retired. Thelma taught English literature here until she retired."

Mason leaned against the railing opposite Dr. Locke, realizing that the doctor was enjoying his discourse. "Is that when they built the house, the one that I'm staying in?"

"No, that happened long before they retired," Dr. Locke said as he turned to some distraction beyond the street below them. "They were living in a little house a couple blocks from here until the first child was born. That was a boy, Roy, I believe, is his name. I didn't know the kids all that well. Thelma preferred to have them treated by a pediatrician, which was fine with me. But Roy was a smart boy, works for a law firm in Kingsport now, I'm pretty sure. Anyway, Thelma inherited that property up there from a cousin she hardly knew. The cousin had died in a fire, and the property sat in probate for a long time before it settled to Thelma. They had that house built when the third child was born, Jane Louise was her name. She's a nurse at a hospital in Knoxville. Another boy, they call him Stewy, is a career army officer stationed in North Carolina. I saw all the kids at the funeral. They were a great family. Such a shame the parents were taken so suddenly."

Dr. Locke took a cellphone from his pocket and looked at it before returning it to his pocket. "Ansel was an accomplished wood-worker, and he had a little shop built next to the house. I believe it's still there, isn't it?"

"Yeah, it's still there," Mason answered.

"Well," Dr. Locke continued, "when Jane Louise got married and left home, Ansel took early retirement from teaching and started a little business building custom furniture. Had stores in Knoxville and Cincinnati that bought from him regularly, and he got custom orders from mailings that he sent out. He wasn't, of course, getting wealthy from it, but it was a nice supplement to his pension and Thelma's teaching salary."

"Then Thelma got sick," Mason said, almost as a question.

"Yes, she did. Had a stroke. Took her down a bit, but she was responding to rehab well. Ansel, being as he was, wanted the best and hired a rehab specialist to work with her. Her name was Connie, and both Ansel and Thelma thought the world of her. Then Connie just disappeared, and Carly showed up. They loved her just as well, but I guess that was a fatal mistake, considering what happened, or what is thought to have happened."

"You mean that Carly might have killed them."

"That's what I read in the paper. I don't know any more than that."

"Did you know Carly?" Mason asked, not sure of why he wanted to know.

"No. I never met either one. Just knew what the Newleys told me."

Mason looked toward downtown Low Creek. "Dr. Locke," he asked, "was there anything special about that house that the Newleys built that would make someone have a particular desire for it?"

Dr. Locke looked at Mason squarely as he responded, "I'm not sure of what you're getting at, but as far as I know, it's just a house that held a family that everyone around here admired. It's not that great as you well know. It's just what Ansel and Thelma could afford, and for them, it was everything. I think Cletus intends to sell it once he gets his housing project going. Is there a particular reason for asking?"

Mason mused at what he could answer but withheld his response. "Not really," he said, "just curious."

"Well," Dr. Locke said as he stood straight and stretched his legs, "I've told you what I know. If you don't mind, could you send me Leanna's e-mail. I'd love to see it." He handed Mason a card. "The e-mail address is right there."

"Sure," Mason responded as they walked down the steps to street level, "but one more thing. Did you know any of the Correl family?"

"No, I didn't. A lot of talk about them around here, but I didn't know them. A friend of mine is a psychiatrist in Kingsport, and he did a court-ordered assessment for one of them. Diagnosed a bipolar disorder. That's more than I should be saying, but well, that's what I know."

"Which Correl was it?" Mason asked, not necessarily expecting an answer.

Dr. Locke proceeded down the steps to street level. "Not sure… Bodie or Bowie. I'm pretty sure it was Bowie. Yeah, Bowie," he said. "Going to dinner. Care to join me?"

"Thanks, doctor, but I have some work to do yet," Mason said, regretting missing the possibility of not eating alone. "The company insists on these physicals but reports still have to be on time. But I would love to catch you later at some time."

"Please do," Dr. Locke said. "Guys like us need some company now and then, don't we?" He stopped on the sidewalk and looked back at Mason. "How did she die, Tuck?"

Mason responded impulsively, "How did who die?"

"Your wife."

Mason looked away briefly and then back to Dr. Locke. He never cared for answering that question, but Dr. Locke's bluntness seemed to make it easier. "She was shopping with her mother in downtown Denver, and a car jumped the curb. She was able to push her mother out of the way but couldn't save herself. She died from internal bleeding shortly after arrival at the hospital. They said that she had never regained consciousness."

Dr. Locke did not change his expression. "Drunk driver?"

"No. Old man had a heart attack. He died before she did."

"Well," Dr. Locke replied after musing briefly, "it was sudden and quick. Maybe that's better. My Ellie died a little more each day for seven months. Tough thing to see. Well, there's nothing good about losing a loved one. Have a good evening, Tuck, after you finish your work, of course."

Dr. Locke turned to walk away and stopped again, turning back to Mason. "You know what," he said, rubbing his chin, "now that I think of it, Ansel and the other Correl brother seemed to get along for a while. They were neighbors, as it were, since the brother was living in his grandfather's house just down the road from Ansel. Anyway, he, the brother, that is, used to drive Ansel's truck to Cincinnati to deliver furniture. The only reason that I know is because Ansel told me once that the Correl guy might have been using the truck to transport drugs. Even had the sheriff and some federal agents out to his place to inspect the truck. Of course, they found nothing, but Ansel was embarrassed and furious at the same time. You would have had to have known Ansel to get it." Dr. Locke laughed as he shook his head. "Ansel abetting drug runners. That's a good one. You sure about dinner? Harley's here has a great buffet."

"I would love to, doctor," Mason said, still regretting, "but I have to take a rain check."

Katherine intervened in Mason's thoughts as Dr. Locke disappeared into the parking lot across the street: *I'll be back in a few days unless the conference sucks. Go to Mom and Dad's for dinner. They would be thrilled to have you. I don't like it when you're alone...*

"Yeah, alone," Mason said aloud as he stood to leave, walking slowly toward his parking spot on Oak Street, stopping as some traffic passed, the last of which was a late model pickup with a hard shell and a severely gashed right fender, the same truck that he had seen at Melanie McCall's house. The windows were darkly tinted, obscuring the driver, and Mason watched as it proceeded on Oak Street and turned right into a narrow side lane. Mason followed in his car, parking on Oak Street and then continuing on foot as the pickup turned into a graveled driveway and parked by a small house. It was a short lane, holding a dozen or so small homes that were mostly well kept except for the couple of unoccupied disasters. Mason stepped behind a tree in a neighboring yard as Boone Correl got out of the truck and slid a large cardboard box from the bed. A somewhat disheveled woman opened the side door of the house and closed it behind Boone as he entered.

Mason sensed something at the house behind him and turned to see two young people who were oblivious to his presence in the yard. A boy, no more than seventeen, was seated on the porch steps, leaning back with his head lying awkwardly against the top step. The girl next to him was slumped sideways with her head in the boy's lap. Mason stepped out of the yard, again recalling his conversations with Eileen Barrett, perhaps a little more schooled now to her concerns. He walked carefully toward the house where Boone had entered and noted the address on the mailbox. The door opened again, and he turned to walk back to his car on Oak Street, writing the mailbox number on a slip of paper in the car.

It was nearly five thirty when Mason returned to the prison site. The James Carter incident had made him more conscious of the security services at the site, and he had made sure to get to know the guards posted at both entrances. The front entrance was handled by BJ Lawrence, a lifelong resident of Low Creek and a deacon at his church. BJ was talking with the driver of a white van with no markings as Mason pulled up. The van backed up and pulled away as Mason eased closer to BJ and opened the car window.

BJ leaned into the window and said, "Working the night shift, Tuck?"

"Yeah," Mason answered, "I need to finish some paperwork." He pointed at the van that was disappearing on the access road. "Who was that?"

BJ shrugged, "Delivery man. He shows up every week or so to deliver paint. Usually, when he comes, the painter foreman is here to meet him, but he's not here tonight. Anyway, this guy said he had orders to pick up paint that was delivered here by mistake. I told him he would have to come back when the painters was here, and he wasn't too happy about it. What else could I say?

"Well, you did the right thing. I'll get on the painters tomorrow about scheduling deliveries. Unmarked delivery trucks are unacceptable anyway, especially after hours," Mason said as he signed BJ's log and returned it.

"I didn't know that, Tuck."

"Didn't know what?"

"About unmarked delivery trucks."

"No problem, BJ, you do now," Mason said as he progressed into the site.

The curiosity about Boone Correl was distracting as Mason finished his work and submitted his reports. He pulled up a map of Low Creek and identified the street where he had seen Boone as Culver Lane. He then entered the address on Culver Lane that he had written on the slip of paper in his car into the same lookup site that he had used to find Melanie McCall's address. The name that appeared was surprising as he sat back and said it aloud, "Lilly Jane Correl."

XX

The inspector for the architect had Casey tied up for most of the morning. At around noon, Casey emerged from his office and entered Mason's, shaking his head. "That guy is a real piece of work," he said, referring to the inspector who had left the trailer. "Let's go to Harley's and get a decent lunch."

As they were leaving in Casey's truck, Mason said, "You need to get on that painter foreman. I was here last evening, and some character in an unmarked van was trying to make a delivery or pick up. He needs to get control of that stuff."

"Well," Casey returned, "first of all, the painters get their deliveries from a distributor in Knoxville. Arrives at the same time every Thursday morning, so I don't know what this after-hours delivery is all about. Secondly, Artie, the painter foreman, has disappeared. The company hasn't seen him for several days, and apparently there is a missing person report out for him in Pound, where he lives. I got on them yesterday to get someone in charge here, but I do feel kind of bad about Artie."

Not happy about the answer that he received, Mason turned to look out of the side window of Casey's truck and then forward, only to see the billboard at the exit to Low Creek. "Holy crap!" he shouted at the sight of a larger than life Cletus Wellman glaring at the highway with the caption, "Be aware, drug dealers, we're watching you." The sign was endorsed by the VaTn Coalition Against Drug Dealers.

Casey laughed and said, "He's got the same sign outside of Kingsport. I gotta give him credit for his guts. Seems like a good way to get your point across, though."

"I don't know," Mason responded, musing at the highway as he spoke, "seems like a good way to get hurt. He was warned not to fool with those people."

"Probably not a good idea, but I still love his guts. They also have flyers all around Kingsport offering rewards for information about drug dealers."

At Harley's, Verna Lee patted Casey on the shoulder as she poured Mason's iced tea. "Nice of you two to pull yourselves away from that food truck and visit us," she said as she winked at Mason. "We was missin' you."

"You know we wouldn't forget you, darling," Casey said as he patted her hand.

"Verna Lee," Mason addressed her as she took silverware from her apron pocket, "do you know who Lilly Jane Correl is?"

Verna Lee smiled. "I haven't heard her by that name in a long time. Goes by her maiden name of Mitchel now. She was married to Boone Correl once, but they've been divorced for some time now, and he's long gone as far as I know. Worked here for a while. Not a real friendly one, though. I never got to know Lilly Jane very well. How did you come across her?"

"The name just came up in conversation," Mason responded, not wanting to get into his issues with Boone.

He turned to Casey as Verna Lee walked away. "I'm a little concerned about this business with the painters," he said as he sipped his iced tea. "I'd like to know why the foreman is accepting after-hours deliveries from an unmarked van, apparently on a regular basis."

"Well," Casey replied, "we have to find him first. But I'll see what I can find out. By the way, Wellmans are having a cookout on Labor Day weekend, and you can expect an invitation. Millie's coming in, and she would love to see you, so don't squirm out when Sally invites you."

Millie was Casey's wife, an economics professor at Princeton University with a keen sense of humor and genuine warmth that was endearing to anyone who she met. She would often spend weekends at jobsite cities, and Mason had developed a particular fondness for her during those visits. He knew that refusing the two women in the world who could talk him into showing up, Sally and Millie, would be futile. "Thanks for the heads up," he responded to Casey, "I'll look forward to it."

When they returned to the prison site trailer, Jamie cornered Mason as he entered. "They insisted on speaking with you and Casey," she whispered. "I told them that they needed an appointment but…"

"It's okay, Jamie," Mason interjected, looking at Lieutenant Melker and Special Agent Willis who were sitting in the conference room. He motioned to Casey, and they joined the visitors.

After some brief discussion about the progress of prison construction, Special Agent Willis said, "Gentlemen, we're working with a man named James Carter. I guess you know who that is." Lieutenant Melker sat back in some sort of satisfaction as Mason and Casey nodded cautiously. "Well," Willis continued, "his statements plus others have led us to believe that the drugs that he was dealing might have come through this construction site. We think it's possible that someone inside here was receiving drugs and getting them out to the street in broad daylight. It's happened before, so we know it's possible."

Casey looked at Mason and then back at Special Agent Willis. "How the hell could that happen?" he asked, obviously taking some personal offense to the suggestion.

Willis responded, "You have a lot of material and equipment being delivered or picked up every day. What has happened in other cases is that drugs are transported to a construction site concealed with legitimate material and stored there. Someone on the site then takes small quantities and delivers them to a dealer. Money is handled the same way in reverse. We actually had a situation on a high-rise in Maryland—"

"Our subcontractors are all responsible for their own deliveries and logistics," Casey interrupted. "How the hell are we supposed to monitor that?"

"You can't, and we know that," Willis responded, "But you can help us track some things down. Carter said that the heroin he was selling was always in a toolbox just outside the front gate. He would pick it up when site closed down and return what he didn't sell along with the night's receipts to the same box. His commission was provided the same way. Right now, we are hoping to find out who owns that toolbox."

Casey was looking intently at Special Agent Willis. "I know about that box," he said, turning toward Mason. "It's one of those small gang boxes on wheels that can be moved closer to a workspace. Hell, they're all over the site. I saw a box like that just outside the gate several times when I left late, but it was always gone when I returned in the morning."

"What time do you usually arrive at the site?" Lieutenant Melker asked.

"Between seven and seven thirty."

"And when is the site accessible?"

"The security guard leaves at six. He unlocks the gate before he goes."

Lieutenant Melker looked at Special Agent Willis and back at Casey. "So it's possible that the toolbox that Carter was talking about could have been moved each morning before you got there."

"Yeah," Casey said slowly, "I guess that's true. But you caught Carter, so whatever was going on is over with now."

Special Agent Willis rejoined the conversation. "Not necessarily. Carter was moving a substantial amount of product from this location. When the sheriff's department shut him down, we should have expected a noticeable reduction of flow, at least until a new source could be established. However, that didn't happen. The volume continued, leading us to believe that someone replaced Carter rather quickly, and there was no change in the supply chain."

"Which means that you believe drugs are still somehow coming through this site," Mason said.

"That's right," Willis returned. "And we need to find out how and who is responsible."

There was an awkward silence in the room as Mason looked through a window at the activity of the building site. "I would start with the painters," he said quietly, still looking through the window.

"Why the painters?" Special Agent Willis asked after glancing at Casey.

Casey responded ahead of Mason. "Some strange goings-on. Tuck came here after hours, and someone was trying to make a delivery to the painters in an unmarked vehicle. The security guard sent him away."

"It wasn't the first time," Mason joined in. "The guard said that the painter foreman had received deliveries that way before, which is against our protocol. Actually, the driver told the guard last night that he was picking up an order that was delivered to the wrong place, which also seemed a little weird."

"It gets even stranger," Casey continued. "The painter foreman didn't show up for work this week. I'm told he disappeared, and his wife has filed a missing person report."

"Where was the report filed?" Lieutenant Melker asked.

"Pound," Casey responded. "That's where he lives."

"What is the foreman's name?"

Casey shrugged his shoulders. "I just know him as Artie," he said as he leaned back to call to Jamie in the reception area and request Artie's proper name. She entered with the name printed on a slip of paper. Casey smiled briefly as he read it. "Arturo Flores. Seems a far cry from Artie."

Lieutenant Melker stood up as he pulled a cell phone from his belt. "I'll call the Pound police and see what they know," he said to Special Agent Willis. Then he spoke to Mason as he walked toward the door of the conference room, "Any chance that security guard got a license number?"

"It will be on his report. Jamie can get it for you," Mason responded as Special Agent Willis pulled a laptop from his briefcase. "Can you give me a Wi-Fi password?" he asked Casey as he opened the computer. "I want to see if we have anything on an Arturo Flores." He worked intently on the computer while Mason checked messages on his iPhone. Willis eventually looked up. "Must be a popular name. We have seven Arturo Floreses in the database. However, none that would seem to correlate with this site or even this area, but that will take more research to confirm."

Mason returned the iPhone to his pocket. "You have to love the technology we have these days," he said. "It's amazing that you can search your database in a matter of minutes."

"Really," Willis returned. "When I started, it would take several hours after I made a phone call."

"So here's another name for you. I'm not sure if it has any correlation, but it's someone who has been harassing me directly, and I know is somehow involved with the illegal drugs."

Special Agent Willis sat up in his chair. "What's the name?" he asked as Lieutenant Melker returned holding a small notebook.

Mason responded, "Boone Correl," he said, spelling the name.

Lieutenant Melker turned quickly to Mason. "Do you think he is involved here?"

"I'm not sure," Mason said. "He lives in my neighborhood just a mile away from here. It turns out that he's the one who has been harassing me. Do you know him?"

"Know of him," Lieutenant Melker replied. "Cletus Wellman and his wife seem to be obsessed with him and insist he's dealing drugs, but so far he's done nothing wrong that we can see."

As Special Agent Willis typed the name into his computer, Lieutenant Melker said, "I spoke to the Pound police department. Arturo Flores is dead. They found him this morning in an abandoned building."

"Any idea as to the cause of death?" Willis asked as he looked up from his computer.

"Not yet. They just opened the investigation. They're a small department with their hands full, so it might take a while. The officer whom I spoke with said it looked like a drug deal gone bad."

Casey sat quietly, slowly shaking his head before saying, "Well, that's a shame about Artie. He seemed like an okay guy. You figure he was selling drugs?"

"Appears that way to the Pound police," said Lieutenant Melker.

"Then if Artie was selling the drugs and he's dead now, the problem is solved, right?"

Special Agent Willis looked up again. "Probably not. There's a good likelihood that Flores had an accomplice here. Whether he did or not, there's a strong possibility that there is a cache of heroin stored somewhere on this site and that someone will eventually want to claim it." He turned to Mason. "Okay. We'll start with the painters. We'll set up surveillance and get someone involved with them. Do they have a designated staging and storage area?"

Casey answered, "Yeah. They have space in one of the rec rooms."

"What is in that space?"

"Paint, tools, scaffold, ladders. Painter stuff."

Willis paused, staring at the computer at first then looking intently at Casey. "Cans of paint?"

"Yeah," Casey continued, "five-gallon cans mostly."

"Can I see delivery receipts, inventories, things like that?" Willis asked.

"Subcontractors are responsible for their own logistics and inventory. You would have to get that from the painters."

Willis looked at Mason and then back at Casey. "Who's in charge of the paint crew?"

Casey sat back in his chair and turned his hands upward, "Artie," he answered, clearly regretting the fact. "The contractor will replace Artie, but for the time being, we just have a couple of senior worker bees who won't be much help."

"Okay. Get us contact information for the painting contractor, and we'll start there," Special Agent Willis said as he turned to Mason. "We will have people here tomorrow and appreciate your cooperation."

"You will have it. How about Boone Correl?"

Willis studied the computer for a while and eventually spoke without looking up. "Boone Raymond Correl, US Army at Fort Bragg, expert marksman, medical discharge—"

"Medical discharge?" Mason interrupted. "For what?"

Willis looked up, "Personality disorder. That's all it says," he said, returning to his computer. "Tracked in Santa Barbara, California, arrested for possession in Los Angeles, tracked again in New Mexico, last seen by an informer in Cincinnati."

"Not much then," Mason said as Special Agent Willis continued to study the laptop.

"Well, maybe that's not so," Willis continued, still engrossed in the computer, then looking up. "FBI is watching Correl more than we are. Apparently, he's thought to have worked as an assassin for a Mexican cartel. I don't think you want to mess with this guy, Mr. Mason."

Lieutenant Melker sat, looking squarely at Willis, saying, "Well, we don't have anything on him here."

"I do," Mason said, obviously becoming agitated. "He spent the last three months harassing me."

Lieutenant Melker responded, "You've seen him?"

"I've met him."

"Have you reported this to Deputy Petty? That's an open investigation."

Mason struggled to avoid any facial expression. "Not yet, but I will," he said without looking at Lieutenant Melker.

Special Agent Willis interjected, "Apparently, Correl is from this area originally. Maybe he just wanted to come home. Why is Mr. Wellman so obsessed with the man anyway?"

Lieutenant Melker shrugged, "I don't really know. I do know that, according to Cletus Wellman, he had a bad reputation. I've only been with this department for three years, so I don't have any past experience with him."

Closing his computer, Special Agent Willis said to Mason, "Mr. Mason, it's critical that this matter stays among us meeting here today. We will have people here tomorrow to keep watch over that painter's staging area." He turned to Casey. "Any chance you could use another laborer here?"

"Sure, okay. But if you want someone here eyeballing the painters, I think we could—"

"We just need your cooperation, Mr. McAfee," Willis interjected.

Casey said, "Just have them see me when they get here. Jamie can find me if I'm not in the office."

Special Agent Willis packed up his briefcase and excused himself and quickly exited the trailer as Casey and Lieutenant Melker walked toward the painters' staging area. As Mason walked past the open office area, Cavalone called out to him, "What's with the police, boss?"

"Just some security issues," Mason responded as he returned to his office.

It was getting late in the day, and Mason could see various trades beginning to wrap up their work, returning tools to gang boxes and cleaning work spaces. The afternoon's events were distracting him as he glanced through requisitions that Jamie had put on his desk, and he began to feel a sense of subdued anger over the fact that the drug situation that seemed to grip Wells County had invaded his construction site like a parasite right in front of him. Drug abuse by employees and subcontractors was something that caused him and others like him to spend countless hours in boring training sessions, and the occasional occurrence was always something that was referred elsewhere and stayed remotely from his daily activities. But this was criminal activity occurring on his watch under his responsibility, and the violation was serious and personal.

He got Leo's voice mail when he called, and he left a message about the need to get the legal department involved to determine any liability for Doenitz Building Company resulting from drugs being distributed from the site. The requisitions on his desk took another hour to complete, and the prison site was almost deserted when he drove through the front gate, acknowledging BJ as he scanned the fence line for anything suspicious. Boone Correl returned to his thoughts as he drove down the access road. It seemed as if the more he learned about Boone, the more curious he was about the man. An assassin for a cartel? Mason suddenly realized that he had confronted a man who lived in a world that, to Mason, only existed in movies and on television. The thought was both disturbing and exhilarating as he turned off Mills Hollow into his driveway, immediately noticing two small figures on the front porch. His first inclination was that Boone was back to his old tricks, but as he pulled into the lot, he recognized Melanie McCall and her daughter sitting in the wicker chairs.

XXI

"W ell," Mason said as he sat down on the iron chair, "you found me."

Melanie smiled, "It wasn't hard to do," she said. "We knew where you live." The little girl giggled and drew her legs up on the chair.

Mason liked Melanie's subtle sense of humor although he felt strangely threatened by her presence on his porch, perhaps due to her connection with Boone Correl. "Can I get you something to drink?" he asked. "I don't get much company, so all I have is iced tea and beer."

"Thanks, but we just had supper. I'm good, and she brought her own drink," Melanie responded, indicating the juice box in the girl's hand.

"I've met you several times and still don't know your name," he said to the girl, who smiled and looked up at her mother.

Melanie said, "Tell him your name, honey."

"Jenna."

"Well, that's a pretty name, Jenna. Do you remember my name?"

"Tuck," Jenna answered and giggled again.

Mason turned back to Melanie. "You're not from here. Where are you from?"

"Ohio," Melanie answered quietly, clearly annoyed by the question.

"Ohio, really? So am I. What part?"

"Portsmouth."

"By the river?" Mason asked.

"On the river. And you?"

As was usual when asked about his origins, Mason felt a twinge of vulnerability. "Solon, originally," he answered.

"By the lake?"

Mason again noticed her sense of humor and Mona Lisa smile. "On the lake."

Melanie touched Jenna on the shoulder and said, "Take your iPad down on the steps so Tuck and I can talk." Jenna smiled at Mason as she climbed off the wicker chair, still clutching the juice box and holding the iPad under her arm as she descended the porch steps.

There was an uncomfortable moment of silence, but Mason began the conversation. "I asked a simple question, but you said we need to talk. I'll ask the question again. Why was Boone acting like a fool in my yard for most of the summer?"

"I'll tell you the truth, and you probably won't believe me," Melanie said, looking directly into Mason's eyes. "But you have to understand that I would not have risked coming here just to lead you on."

"Okay, go on."

"He thinks that there is something that belongs to him under the floor of that house that you're renting. He wants you to leave so he can buy or rent it himself and tear up the floor." Melanie said, again fixing her gaze squarely on Mason's.

He looked away and then back at Melanie. "And that something is?"

"Money," Melanie returned, still fixing her eyes on Mason's.

Mason slapped his leg and leaned forward toward Melanie, speaking so loudly that she drew slightly from him and Jenna turned quickly from her seat on the steps. "Are you telling me that all this crap is over buried treasure?"

"Yes."

Mason stood and turned away, leaning on the porch rail and staring into the yard. He noticed Jenna watching him from the corner of his eye, looking stunned and fearful. He smiled, waving slightly to her with his fingers. She smiled back and returned to her iPad.

"Well," Mason said as he returned to his chair, "I'm sure there's more to the story, or you wouldn't be here."

"I don't know you, Tuck," Melanie said as she regained her composure, "and I'm not in the habit of telling my life story to strangers. But since you don't seem to want to accept serious warnings, and since I could be implicated if Boone does something awful, which could well happen, I don't see much choice in the matter." She looked at Jenna and then back at Mason. "Jenna's father disappeared shortly after she was born. I was teaching at the time—"

"You were a teacher?" Mason interrupted, immediately regretting the inappropriateness of his reaction."

The smile returned as Melanie disregarded the insult. "Well, there is not much employment for a jewelry setter in Portsmouth, Ohio, so I got a teaching certificate and taught fourth grade."

Without trying to hide his embarrassment, Mason again interrupted, "A jewelry setter?"

"I actually went to school for it and worked as a setter for a company in Cincinnati for a while."

"And then you became a teacher?"

"No, I did that first and then got into jewelry."

Mason was mildly interested but also wanted to know what any of this had to do with Boone Correl. "Okay, sorry to interrupt so much."

Melanie continued, "Anyway, my mother was watching Jenna while I was at work and things were okay for a long time. But then my mother got sick and couldn't help anymore. I quickly found that the cost of day care on a teacher's salary was prohibitive, so I took a job as a work-from-home customer service representative. It was a substantial cut in pay but still better than the alternative. During that time, I also started my online jewelry business."

Jenna climbed up the steps and whispered into her mother's ear. Melanie said softly to her, "Well, why don't you ask him?"

Jenna stared at her foot, saying in barely audible tones "Can I use your bathroom?"

Mason showed her to the bathroom and returned to his chair. "When do we get to Boone and me?" he asked.

"I'm sorry," Melanie replied. "It's just that so much about Boone is so incredible that I need you to know that I am for real and not making it up and not abetting what he does. I know it looks pretty much like I am, doesn't it?"

Mason sat back and said, "Go on. You were working from home…"

"I was working from home, and one day I broke my foot playing with Jenna at a park last summer. It was a bad break. I had to wear a boot for a while, and it was very painful. My doctor prescribed Percocet, which helped with the pain, but was only in one prescription, which the doctor would not renew for me. My foot was still hurting, and since just about everyone in the apartment building where I lived was on something, I soon found a source for OxyContin. That source was Boone who lived in the building."

"So Boone was the dealer?"

"Well, that's not how I saw it at the time. He was just a nice guy who could get prescriptions and fill them. I knew it was illegal, but of course, like so many people, it was just until I get past the foot problem," Melanie said as she looked upward at the porch ceiling. She continued, "Anyway, we got to know each other and spent time together, just talking by the pool or in the lounge. Jenna was beginning school then, and I told Boone several times about my desire to get Jenna out of the school district we were in and maybe even get out of Portsmouth entirely, you know, to get a fresh start."

Mason was growing impatient and getting hungry, but he began to realize Melanie's desperation, her apparent necessity to enlist an ally. She was not just explaining her concern for Mason's safety, but pleading a case for some sort of redemption, as he saw it, to the only person in the world available to hear it. He nodded politely and let her continue.

"I also told him that I was getting concerned about my growing dependency on Oxy. He seemed sympathetic but continued to provide, and I was, well, too weak to resist. But he was always good company, a good listener with a sense of humor with a great Southern accent. I learned that he had been married once and was in the Army and that he had worked in a gun store in California. He also told me that his medication for some 'condition' kept him from doing certain types of work, but I never got him to elaborate on that. I really didn't press for more of his past, and he was the same way with me. Maybe that's why we could be so comfortable with each other."

"What brought him to Portsmouth?" Mason asked.

"He said that an old Army buddy of his was opening up a fire-arms training center and had invited him to be his partner. Somehow, that fell apart after he moved into town, though."

"So he started making his income selling drugs?"

"I guess so. I mean, I never wanted to ask that question, prob-ably because I didn't want the answer. Maybe it was my own loneli-ness that made me avoid the obvious truth about Boone. I was not romantically involved with him at that point although I could have been. He just didn't seem interested in that kind of relationship."

Jenna returned from the bathroom and leaned into her mother, whispering something into her ear. Melanie returned the whisper, and Jenna smiled and said okay before returning to the bottom step.

"They are so easy to please at that age. I made her a promise, so I won't be boring you much longer."

"I'm not bored." Mason said, noticing an evolving sense of dis-comfort as she spoke. "Please go on."

"There was a nice lounge area in our apartment building where we would congregate when the pool wasn't open. Those of us with children tended to stick together, but when Boone was around, I tended to migrate in his direction. So I was a little dismayed when he introduced JoAnn as his guest for the weekend."

"JoAnn?"

"I found out later that she was the ex-girlfriend of his brother, who apparently was in prison. Anyway, Boone told me that he and JoAnn had some business in Virginia, and I didn't see him for a cou-ple of weeks. That wasn't unusual, he would often take off for a week or two, I think now that he was coming here. Anyway, when he returned, he said that JoAnn had moved on, and he had a proposi-tion for me. That was when he revealed his scheme."

"His scheme?"

"He said that he wanted to return to the place where he grew up, that he had certain assets to recover there but needed a place to live in. There was a house he wanted to buy, but since he didn't have what he called a reportable form of income, he couldn't obtain a mortgage. I asked him why he didn't just rent an apartment, and he told me that there was nothing near where he wanted to be. Then he told me something peculiar. He said that the apartment that he rented in our complex was under the name of the friend that he was supposed to go into business with. He said that he didn't like his name on any kind of contract."

"Seems like an old habit," Mason said quietly, recalling Lilly Jane Correl.

"Beg your pardon?" Melanie said.

"Continue," he answered.

"His proposition was unusual, to say the least. He wanted me to buy this house, I mean, this house we're sitting in, for him and stay for a few months. I asked him why he thought I would want to move to Southwest Virginia in one of the poorest areas of the country, and he had his answer well prepared. He said that he knew that I wanted to take Jenna to a better place, and this was the stepping stone to get there. All I had to do was buy the house with money that he would give me and live in it so no one would get suspicious of what he was going to do, which was to tear up the floor and replace it. Apparently, he and his brother had come into a sizable amount of cash some years ago, and he, the brother, took it to the house he was living in, the same house where you and I first met. Then the brother and his girlfriend took off to Kentucky. Boone assumed that the brother had the money with him, but the brother told him that he had hidden the money and wouldn't tell Boone where until he got out of prison. I guess there's not a lot of trust in that family."

Jenna began to walk around the yard as Melanie watched her briefly. "Apparently," she continued, "the brother dumped JoAnn while he was still in prison, and she felt that she was going to be cheated from sharing the money, so she contacted Boone and said that she would show him where it was if he agreed to share it with her."

"So," Mason interrupted, "JoAnn brought Boone here to show him where the money was."

"I guess, although I don't know what she needed Boone for if she knew where it was. I think he made the same offer to her before making it to me," Melanie said as she looked away again at Jenna in the yard. "The deal was that I could sell the house and share in the hidden money. I turned that down because I didn't know where that money came from. Instead, he agreed to provide the down payment for the house and make the mortgage payments, which he would give me in cash. I figured I could handle a few months here rent free and take the proceeds from selling the house and move back to Ohio, probably Columbus. I have family there."

"Your parents?" Mason asked.

Melanie shook her head slightly, "No. My mother passed away last year, and my father died a long time ago. I have a brother there. He's an administrator at Ohio State."

Mason shook his head slightly. "I'm still having a hard time with this. You are obviously a smart lady. How does someone like you end up with a guy like Boone?"

She lowered her head a bit and looked out at Jenna who was wandering around the lot and yard. "Sometimes, things just take their course. Boone was good to be around. Oh, I knew he was into some bad things and that I had to get distance between me and him eventually. But he was offering something that could be good for me and Jenna and, to be honest, a bit of an adventure." She looked out at the yard again and said quietly, "But then it all changed. He became a different person."

"What caused the change?" Mason asked.

Melanie was looking down at the floor now and appeared to become even more agitated. Her body seemed to be twitching slightly as she spoke. "Meth," she said, almost in a whisper.

"Methamphetamine?" Mason said, recalling the literature that Eileen Barrett had left.

"Yes," Melanie replied, still looking down. "I think he makes it somewhere around Low Creek with others who I have never met. Anyway, he told me that he had quit his medication and switched to the meth because it worked better. I don't know whether that was it or not, but he turned into someone else. I'm actually afraid of him now, and," she raised her head, "you should also be afraid of him."

"Where is he now?"

"I don't know. He shows up every so often and stays for a couple of days and leaves again. He does strange things, like sitting up all night watching television or sleeping for twenty-four hours. He never eats with us and mostly ignores us. But I never know when he's going to show up. You caught him there last week, and I wish you hadn't. It really set him off."

Mason noticed that she was quivering more now and appeared to be ill. "Are you okay?" he asked.

"Actually, I need to get Jenna home. I promised ice cream, and she needs a bath. It's a school night. Can we continue this conversation tomorrow?" she said, folding her arms tightly around her body and standing up without waiting for an answer. "Thank you for listening, Tuck. I'll come back tomorrow. There's much more to tell. And please turn on your alarm and lock your doors." She walked unsteadily down the porch steps, picking up Jenna's iPad and juice box on the way. Mason noticed the same belabored walk that she showed when he had visited her in her backyard. Jenna called, "Bye, Tuck," as her mother took her hand and walked her to the driveway without looking back at Mason. Clearly, Mason thought, she was going through some kind of withdrawal from her drug use.

His dinner was eaten slowly as Mason considered the day's events. Drugs flowing through his construction site, a woman he barely knew enlisting him into her personal life, Boone Correl out there somewhere with some sort of malicious intent, and other minor issues occupying his thoughts made him both apprehensive and intrigued.

But Melanie kept the rule of his consideration. Her latent prettiness, her enticing smile, her vulnerability, the abject baring of her personal life, all seemed to draw him to her. Perhaps it was a sense of shared loneliness that had him looking forward to hearing the rest of her story or maybe just his usual interest in the histories of people and places in general. But her story was hard to swallow despite her genuine approach in telling it. Portsmouth, Ohio, may not be the land of opportunity, but Wells County was clearly not a place where people come to improve their futures. And why would anyone follow a man like Boone Correl to any place at all? Was she that much in love with him? It certainly didn't seem that way. Like she said, sometimes, things just take their course. Regardless of her initial intent, she saw herself as extremely vulnerable and helpless in a strange place where she knew no one except the changed man who brought her here. Mason then realized that her concern for his own safety, which was borne of the jeopardy to herself by her association with Boone, was evolving to a cry for help to the only passerby she could see.

Yet there was Jenna, the ultimate victim of a loving mother facing something that Mason could only see as disaster with an association that was obviously becoming critical. It should not be that way. The child should not have to bear the risk of her mother's gamble, which seemed unnecessary and irresponsible. Melanie could choose to walk the tightrope that she was on, but Jenna had no say in the matter. It was simply stated that we are going to a new home, perhaps just for a while, and not said that the new home is on a mountain where there are no other children to play with and a mother with an increasingly dangerous drug addiction. He knew the routine only too well... *We need to pack, Tucker, we're moving to a new home tomorrow.* Even under the best of circumstances, Jenna's situation could only get worse as her mother's spiraling loss of control continued.

And the money supposedly hidden beneath his feet. Such a preposterous idea might work as a fraternity prank, but the belief that Thane could break into Ansel's house, pry up the floor, insert his treasure chest, replace the floor, and escape unnoticed was more than ridiculous. However, JoAnn believed it so much that she sought out Boone to come here and retrieve it.

His sense of curiosity and training prevailed, and despite his skepticism, Mason began to scope the floors. The front room was recently carpeted, and the kitchen floor was covered in what builders call sheet goods. Both bathroom floors were tiled, and the three bedrooms had the original hardwood, which Mason believed probably existed under the front room carpet as well. The wood floors were solid top-nailed oak boards that Ansel probably made himself. Fitted tightly originally, temperature and humidity swings over the years had caused many of the boards to separate, slightly exposing the tongues that joined them. Ansel, the shop teacher and consummate builder, would not cheat on something so important as a floor. Mason knew from his own training that beneath the hardwood would be a subfloor, probably plywood given the time of construction, resting on two by four sleepers on a concrete slab. That would indeed create a nice space to hide money. However, cutting through the joints and subfloor in such a fashion that the removed pieces could be replaced unnoticed would require tools and expertise that Thane Correl would not likely have. But Ansel would have that ability. So if despite Mason's skepticism of the possibility, something was hidden, could Ansel have collaborated? That certainly would explain Ansel not noticing that his floor had been cut open.

The next day's events bore heavily as he got ready for bed. He set the alarm system as Melanie had advised, turned on the outside floodlights, and checked the windows and doors before retiring. Melanie had instilled something that had not been present before. It was no longer an annoyance of someone trying to disturb his peace but the possibility that someone might be wanting to harm him that invaded his thoughts now. He lay in bed, keeping an eye on the window of his bedroom and wondering where Boone Correl might be now. He slept fitfully, dreaming intensely and waking often as he longed for Katherine's presence in the bed beside him.

Mason arrived at the prison site early in the morning to face a full agenda. It was Cavalone's last day, the heavy site preparation work having been completed, and Mason needed a final download. There were also inspections and month-end reporting to be dealt with. But the presence of illegal drugs on the site still prevailed in his mind.

Ed Ronan, the assistant corporate attorney, had texted him the night before: "Hey Buddy, Leo says you have some things going on that might need my attention. I'm looking at coming in tomorrow. Can you arrange for someone to pick me up at the Tri Cities Airport and Bait Shop? And let me know where to leave my shoes and how to say sumbitch properly."

To his own surprise, Mason was offended. He responded to Ronan, "Send me your flight information and I'll pick you up." He thought of several other responses but stayed reserved. He disregarded Ronan's immediate response and asked Jamie to work out the details with Ronan's assistant, wishing privately not to have to deal with the man at this time. For reasons he couldn't identify, Ronan had made him feel defensive for the environment about him, for Wells County and Bright's Mountain and the warped kinship that seemed to be developing, for good or bad, with its inhabitants, now and before.

By noon, Albert, the new laborer who had reported to Casey at 7:30 a.m., had proven to be a worthy addition. Aside from the tasks that Casey had assigned him, he had managed to install three wireless cameras that were invisible even to Casey. A fourth camera had been installed earlier outside the main gate, focused on license plates of vehicles entering and leaving the site. A fifth camera was in similar position at the rear gate. Albert was a good-natured individual who seemed to get along well with others at the site and was clearly in fellowship with the locals. "I gotta tell you, Tuck," Casey said as he unwrapped his sandwich from the food truck, "there's no way that I would have guessed him to be a government agent if I didn't know better."

The words "government agent" was slightly disturbing to Mason as he explained the drug distribution possibility at the prison site to Ed Ronan on the way back from the airport. It was three thirty before they sat in the conference room with Casey. Ronan's demeanor had changed considerably, and he listened intently, taking notes on a yellow pad as Casey explained the situation from his own point of view.

"First of all," Ronan said to Mason as he leaned back in his chair, "I wish we knew more about this earlier. Leo had told us that a security guard had been arrested for selling drugs outside of our gate. That, in itself, might create a liability for the company he worked for but not necessarily for Doenitz. However, drugs possibly being delivered to our site and distributed under our supervision could present a liability for Doenitz. Someone who overdoses from drugs obtained from this site could have a lawyer salivating over a big company with big pockets allowing the distribution of heroin from its domain to contribute to the detriment, or even death, of their client."

Ronan continued with his inquiry, gathering information about the visits from the sheriff's department and the DEA, as well as the suspicion of the painting crew and Arturo Flores, emphasizing the need to be cooperative in every way with the efforts of law enforcement. He walked the site with Mason and Casey, taking pictures and notes at the painters' staging area. After returning to the trailer, Ronan said, "I'm going to need a place to stay tonight, near the airport, if possible."

Casey replied, "That would be Kingsport. Twenty minutes to the airport. There's a couple of hotels there, but I have room at my place, and you're welcome to stay there." They drove into Low Creek for dinner at Harley's, Mason driving separately so Casey and Ronan could continue to Kingsport.

Ronan continued to query and instruct through dinner, repeating himself enough that Casey finally interrupted, "Tuck, any more raids from the wild man behind your house?"

Mason answered quickly, sensing Casey's ulterior intention, "No, as a matter of fact. But I know who he is, and I've confronted him about it."

"That's the guy you were asking the DEA about?" Casey continued. "Sounds like someone you don't want to mess with."

"Well, I found that out after the fact," Mason said as he turned to Ronan, who was obviously confused. "I rented a house about a half mile from the site on Bright's Mountain. This character, who apparently grew up in this area, moved into a house close to mine. He spent the summer doing everything possible to get me to leave. His girlfriend gave me some story that it was because there is money hidden in my house, but I'm not really buying that story just yet."

Ronan turned to Casey and said, "Why is he someone not to mess with?"

Casey ordered coffee from the waitress, and Mason answered ahead of him, "He's thought to be a drug dealer and maybe worse."

Ronan ordered coffee and turned back to Mason. "Have you talked to the DEA about this guy?"

"Actually, they gave me some information about him. I did report the harassment several times to the local sheriff's department, but they were fairly useless," Mason replied.

"The DEA gave you some information, but what did you give them?" Ronan asked as he eyed Mason intently.

"What do you mean?"

"Well," Ronan continued as he stirred his coffee, "we're trying to prevent our site from becoming a drug distribution center, and you have a suspected drug dealer living less than a half mile away and interacting with you. That might not look so good if some lawyer picked up on it. Has this guy ever been to the site?"

Mason shrugged his shoulders. "I don't think so. At least I have never seen him there."

"But he could have been there," Ronan said flatly. He turned to Casey. "If this guy ever came to the site and just mingled with say, the painters, he could do it easily, couldn't he?"

"What are you getting at, Ed?" Mason interjected.

"I'm just covering the bases. You have camera surveillance going on now. If we were to give the DEA a heads up about this guy, like maybe a description of the vehicle that he drives and what he looks like, at least we would have some positive reaction on record to his potential involvement," Ronan said as he looked at his watch.

Mason said, "Well, he looks like half the people on the site. I know what he drives, but the gate surveillance only captures license plates."

"Can you get his plate number?"

"I guess I could."

"Then I suggest that you get it and report it as a potential suspect to the DEA, so they can flag the surveillance," Ronan said as he turned to Casey. "We ought to get going. I want to consolidate my notes yet tonight."

After dinner, Mason drove down Oak Street and parked his car at the same space where he had parked when he followed Boone Correl to Lilly Jane's house. Dusk was beginning to set in as he walked slowly, seeing Boone's truck in the driveway. Unsure of how to accomplish his intention, he stopped, noticing the boy who he had seen with a girl the last time he had been there. The boy was sitting on the porch, this time alone in a chair, smoking and staring at Mason. Mason approached him carefully, not wanting to appear intrusive. He stopped again at the porch steps, carefully addressing the boy. "Hi, my name is Tucker. Do you mind if I ask you a question about your neighbor two doors down?"

The boy took a drag of his cigarette and flicked it into the side yard. "Don't mind," he answered blankly, looking into the yard beyond Mason.

"Do you know them?" Mason asked.

"Known Lilly Jane most all my life. Nice lady. Don't say much."

"What about the man with the beard. The one who owns that truck?"

The boy looked at Boone's truck and back at Mason. "Don't know him. Seen that truck there a lot lately."

"Well," Mason said, "I'm interested in that truck. I would like to get a picture of it, but I don't want the owner to see me take it. Do you think you might help me out with that?"

The boy took another cigarette out of the pack on the table next to him and lit it. "Why should I help you?" he said, expelling the smoke as he spoke. "I don't even know you."

Mason pulled his wallet from his back pocket and extracted a twenty-dollar bill, which he handed to the boy. "Maybe we can get to know each other better," he said as the boy grabbed the bill."

"Maybe we can," the boy answered, his grin showing serious issues with his teeth and his pupils so constricted that Mason wondered about his vision. "Gimme your camera, and I can gitcha a picture," he said as he stood up.

Mason set the iPhone camera and gave the boy some instructions. The boy took the device and started to walk away, studying the iPhone with the cigarette still hanging from his lips.

"And make sure you get the license plate clearly," Mason said, impulsively, he thought to himself.

The boy stopped and turned to him. "Aww, mister, you know we charge for add-ons. Let's not fuck around here."

Mason realized that his counterpart was more sophisticated than he had anticipated and pulled another twenty from his wallet, which he held out to the boy. "Just negotiating," he said as the boy grabbed the bill.

"Just business," the boy said as he flicked the cigarette into the street and moved on toward Boone's truck.

An immediate sense of regret began to overtake Mason as the boy walked openly down the street and took pictures from the front yard, the driveway and the little stoop at the side door, then holding the iPhone up to Mason and grinning with his broken teeth as he returned.

"Here ya go," the boy said as he handed the iPhone to Mason. "Gotcha some goodies."

"You could've been a little more discrete," Mason said as he retrieved the iPhone.

"What for?" the boy said, whipping the bills in his hand. "They ain't there anyway."

"What do you mean?" Mason responded.

"They took off this morning in that RV."

"What RV?"

"The one they keep in the alley behind Lilly Jane's house."

"An RV?" Mason looked around and considered the possibility that someone in this neighborhood could own anything beyond what might feed and hope to educate their children.

"I need more information," Mason said, expecting the inevitable.

"Yeah, mister, and I got more. But like you, I need more."

Mason opened his wallet, finding fifteen dollars, which he offered to the boy.

"That'll get me through school tomorrow," the boy said as he took the bills. "You're not as generous as the other dudes."

"What other dudes?" Mason asked.

The boy folded the bills into his pocket and grinned. "The guy on the billboard and the tall one. You're with them, ain't ya?"

"You mean Cletus? And what other guy?"

The boy seemed distracted with his own body, scratching and wriggling as he spoke. "That tall guy with the little mustache. Goofy fucker, don't know what he's up to."

Mason realized that Cletus Wellman had been shadowing Boone Correl to no surprise. But the boy's description of the accomplice was obviously of Jake Morrow. Cletus was apparently obsessed with Boone Correl, but for no specific reason other than what he probably considered his civic duty. Jake, on the other hand, had a personal reason to distain Boone Correl. However, as Special Agent Willis had explained, Boone Correl was no one to take lightly. Melanie McCall had given Mason enough to be concerned about his own safety regarding Boone, but Cletus and Jake had no idea of the danger that they might be creating for themselves, perhaps even more so than Mason had considered for himself.

The boy scratched his neck vigorously. "Well, mister, I got things to do, and it looks like you're out of cash." As he spoke, a car passed them slowly, and an attractive woman in her early thirties waved to the boy who returned the gesture.

"Who's that?" Mason asked as the woman parked the car in front of Lilly Jane's house.

"Lilly Jane's sister. Lived with her for a while." The boy smiled as the woman got out of the car and walked toward Lilly Jane's house. "Got her a sweet ass, don't she?" He walked toward Oak Street, calling back as he spoke, "Nice meetin' ya, mister. Come by anytime."

After his usual Saturday breakfast at Harley's, Mason walked to the municipal park behind the Mountaineer Museum as requested by the handwritten note that he had found stuck in his front door handle the night before. He found Jenna first, playing on a Jungle Gym with two other girls about her age. Melanie was sitting alone on a park bench close by. Jenna called, "Hi, Tuck," as he sat beside Melanie.

"Thanks for coming," Melanie said while still staring ahead. Mason noted that her voice seemed different, perhaps softer than the other times he had spoken with her. "Boone was at the house yesterday," she continued. "He left, but I didn't want to chance getting caught speaking with you."

She turned to Mason who noticed that her pupils were constricted, not as badly as Lilly Jane Correl's young neighbor's but seemingly more than before. "Some of us mothers got together to let these girls play with each other here since we all live so far away from each other. We take turns watching them. Sometimes girls from the neighborhood join in as well. Jenna loves it."

"That's a great idea," Mason said as he watched the girls running through the park. "So," he continued after a pause, "if I got it right, Boone found out from JoAnn, who apparently was a former girlfriend of his brother, that money was hidden under the floor in the house that I am renting. His plan was for you to buy the house to keep him under the radar of, I guess, the IRS and maybe law enforcement. That couldn't happen because the owner didn't want to sell and rented the house to me instead. At the same time, Boone has flipped out on methamphetamine that he was using as a substitute for some medication that he was taking. So in his lunacy, Boone performs his clown act in my yard to get me to leave so he can get to the hidden money. Is that pretty close?"

"There's more," she said slowly.

"I'm sure there is," Mason returned. "How did you end up in the house that you're living in?"

"I guess because it was available and close by. I guess he figured he could keep an eye on your house while it was being renovated." She smiled and shook her head, "He was over there every day, mostly watching from the woods and peeking in the windows after everyone left in the evening to make sure the floors were intact. He actually broke in once, but that set off the alarm. After you moved in, he was able to see the armed alarm panel through the kitchen window. You really pissed him off when you set that alarm whenever you left."

"When Jenna came into my yard," Mason asked as he looked at Jenna and the other girls, "why did she lead me to that other house?"

"She didn't," Melanie said with a slight smile. "You went the wrong way. I took Jenna home and still got ahead of you on the path while you were thrashing around in there."

"Why the shotgun?"

The smile returned briefly. "I just wanted to scare you. I was really worried that Boone was getting out of control."

"Well, you did scare me," Mason said as he turned toward her again. "He ran me off the road, didn't he?"

"Well, I guess so," she said. "He had me pick him up near the highway and drive him to the construction site to get his truck. When I asked how he got so far away, he said it was none of my business."

"You're right. This is getting bizarre."

"He was creeping around in the woods when he saw the owner showing you the house. I think he believed you were buying the house. Now," she continued catching Mason's eye, "I told you that this gets worse. Boone saw you there and freaked out. He ran home, grabbed his rifle, and hopped into his truck. He waited on the side of the road and followed you to your construction site. I had asked him what he intended to do, and he said he intended to scare you off."

"With his rifle?"

"Well, I don't think he had anything specific in mind, but he told me that he climbed a rise near the site while explosions were going off on a regular basis. He timed a shot to go off during one of the explosions. No one heard the shot, but according to Boone, you lost a tire. Anyway, I think it was practice. I really think he figured that he could eliminate you that way if it became necessary. My concern is that eliminating you might be becoming necessary."

"Why is eliminating me becoming necessary? Why doesn't he just wait until I leave? Why the urgency?" Mason felt a chilling sensation as he spoke.

Melanie called to the girls to stay out of the creek that ran through the park and where she could see them. "Because his brother has been paroled and would likely go for the money as soon as he was released from parole, in Kentucky, I believe. Apparently, they had a falling-out while the brother was in prison."

"So then I might have two Correls dancing in my yard."

"Well, that could happen, I guess."

"And JoAnn just disappeared?"

"I never said that. I just never saw her again."

"And there's still more?" Mason asked without concealing his sarcasm.

She smiled as if to acknowledge his disbelief. "You asked me before why I would link up with a guy like Boone. I guess there are reasons that I really can't explain even to myself, but there was a business aspect beyond the house deal."

"I almost hate to hear it," Mason said quietly as he stared at the ground in front of him.

"No, it had nothing to do with drugs."

"Okay, go on."

"It was about diamonds."

Mason turned sharply toward her. "Diamonds? You mean like jewelry?"

"Not jewelry, just diamonds. He said that he had a collection of small investment-grade diamonds, like half carat or less, that he wanted to cash in on. I asked him why he didn't just take them to a broker, and his answer was, to me, quite legitimate. He said that a broker would have to report the payments, and he would lose too much to taxes. Instead, if I were to make jewelry with them, the IRS and state would not know that he ever had the asset. I knew that there was something illegal in it for both of us, but the possibility of expanding my business into a diamond collection was very attractive. I never could afford expensive stones for my inventory, so I always had to remain in the low-end of the costume jewelry business. If he actually had the quantity that he spoke of, I could kick-start a much more profitable enterprise. His offer was to split the sale of diamond jewelry fifty-fifty."

"And once again, Boone operates without anyone knowing he's there. I have to admit that the guy is good at being nowhere. So have you seen the diamonds yet?"

"No, and I don't think I want any part of them now. Who knows where they came from at this point?"

Mason was watching a couple on a bench nearby profoundly nodding forward and raising their heads slowly. "Seems like a lot of that going on around here."

Melanie shook her head slowly, "Like I told you, I came here hooked on OxyContin. Boone told me that his pill mill contacts had to be reestablished. The heroin was supposed to just be a short-term substitute."

"Heroin?" Mason knew that his feigned surprise was not well demonstrated. "Does Boone supply it?"

"He did at first," Melanie replied while staring straight ahead.

"So how do you get it now?"

She turned back to Mason. "Tuck, finding drugs in Low Creek is about as easy as buying a hamburger, and you likely won't pay much more." She stretched her arms in response to Mason's obvious checking. "I don't inject. I…well, there are other ways."

"You know, there are—"

"I know," she interrupted. "I just don't know where to start. I don't know what to do about Jenna. And Boone is still out there somewhere."

"Why can't you tell the police about Boone?"

"A drug addict walks into the sheriff's office with her daughter to complain about someone who really has not done anything to harm her. I'm afraid to take that risk."

"What about your family? Didn't you say that you have a brother in Ohio?"

Melanie sighed deeply as she watched the girls who were sitting in the grass and talking. "He's very judgmental," she said slowly, "but he's a good man. I could let Jenna stay there, but there is a problem with school. She's a bright girl but still behind because of the move here."

"I don't know anything about children, but I would guess that, at her age, she could catch up fairly easily," Mason said, weakly, he thought.

She said nothing and stared at the ground as her lower lip quivered. They both sat quietly for what seemed to Mason to be a long time. He spoke eventually, "I know someone who can probably send you in the right direction. Just a phone call."

Melanie turned to him, and he noticed a tear running down her cheek. "Tuck," she said softly, "I don't—"

"Jenna does," Mason interrupted. "Having a mother is far more important than keeping up in school." The words seemed to tumble forth as something echoed from his past, rising in him and dissipating like Melanie's whimpering sigh… *Stay with Grandma and Grandpa, Tucker, until I get better.…* You need to think of her first. I can help with rehab, but you are going to need to reach out to your brother." He touched her on the shoulder and said softly, "Melanie, you need to clean this up and get clear of Boone before things get worse. And as I see it, things can only get worse."

A woman had been approaching as he spoke, and he noticed her gesturing to one of the girls. She was a short woman, somewhat overweight with bright red dyed hair and indistinguishable writing tattooed on one arm. Mason noticed that her canvas shoes were worn through at the toes. Melanie introduced her as Connie Jo's mother, Mavis, who smiled amicably despite her missing tooth and stretched out her chubby hand to Mason. Melanie had introduced him as "my good friend, Tuck." Mavis and Melanie exchanged some conversation about the girls and some issue at school before Mavis and Connie Jo walked away. Mason and Melanie exchanged cell phone numbers, and he stood to leave.

"I'll make some calls after the holiday. You have a call to make, Melanie. Your brother is an important first step."

She said nothing as he turned to leave. Then she called, "Tuck!" and he turned to see the tears streaming down her cheeks. "I will," she said as she pulled a tissue from her purse. "I will."

Mason spent the rest of the afternoon with yard work, but Melanie and her daughter were heavy on his mind as he worked. Melanie was pathetic and yet so captivating with attractiveness that he could not identify. She was in a hopeless situation without some external help, and he was compelled to provide it, not only for her but for Jenna, whose unknowing involvement in her mother's poor decisions was the ultimate tragedy in the spiraling vortex of circumstances that Melanie had created. It should not be this way. It had to be fixed quickly and permanently. Something was rising in him, creating the urgency of the matter, something heavy that pulled at him as he thought of Jenna... *It's just you and me now, Tucker... You have to move in with your dad, Tuck. Grandma and I have no say in the matter. Your mother is...well, he's going to take good care of you. I promise...*

XXII

It was apparently a tradition for Sally and Cletus Wellman to celebrate Labor Day on Saturday to allow their sons to their own pursuits on the actual holiday. This event was a considerably smaller gathering than the Fourth of July party with about twenty-five invitees, including Casey and his wife Millie, some other construction personnel who did not go home for the holiday, the two sons and some other friends who were introduced comfortably in Sally's inimitable fashion.

Dinner was served to three larger round tables by the catering company that had cooked ribs and chicken on grills near the patio that overlooked Kingsport. Mason was seated next to Millie who, by request, explained the theme of her new book. When asked if he had read it, Casey stated to laughter that he doesn't read any book that has a title he can't pronounce. Others at the table were Sally's son Zach Hendy and his wife, Jimmy Cahn, and a couple, Bobby and Melissa Surtemp, who had a local law firm practicing in Tennessee and Virginia.

Jimmy Cahn asked Millie how a college professor links up with a "construction guy," and she explained how Casey was a carpenter foreman on a project near her classroom when she was a graduate student at Temple University, and the two just somehow found "their chemistry." After twenty-eight years, two children and a grandchild on the way, she deferred to Casey who said, "It's been a damn good life."

Jimmy continued his query, asking how they deal with Casey building buildings away from their home in Princeton, and Casey explained how Doenitz gives a generous allowance for him to go home some weekends and Millie to visit the site locations, which she considered vacation time. He continued to explain how housing is always a challenge and how Cletus's accommodations were much better than normal. "Of course," he said, gesturing to Mason, "our boss here got special treatment with a mansion near the jobsite."

Bobby Surtemp turned to Mason. "Near the jobsite? Where are you staying?"

"Cletus rented me a house on Bright's Mountain about a mile from the site," Mason responded.

"So," Bobby said, "you're the one who rented the Newley place. Sally said you had some trouble there."

"Yeah. Some nutcase was harassing me to leave so he could buy or rent the house. But he seems to have given up."

Casey interrupted, "Tuck put a camera on his backyard, and we all got a chance to see this guy. He was like a wild man. We felt bad for what it was doing to Tuck, but it still was almost comical, the way he was acting, that is."

Mason gave a look to Casey and continued, "Well, as I said, he seems to have given up for the time being."

Bobby looked intently at Mason without dampening the lightness of the conversation. "Any idea as to why he wanted you out?" he asked.

"Well," Mason said as he rolled his eyes as he smiled over to Casey, "his brother's girlfriend or I guess she's his former girlfriend, says she believes that money that belongs to him is hidden under the floor."

Others at the table laughed, but Bobby turned to his wife, who seemed to share something privately with him.

"Ever hear one like that?" Casey said as he held his wine glass to the waiter who had approached the table.

Bobby looked again at his wife who was smiling broadly without looking at anyone else at the table. He turned back to Mason and said, with a side glance to Melissa, "Actually, there *was* money hidden under the floor there."

Everyone at the table became quiet, and Mason turned to Casey and back to Bobby.

"What?"

Sally and Cletus interrupted with the niceties of hosting, with Sally pulling a chair between Mason and Millie as the waiter cleared the table, and she made some conversation with Millie with the inclusion of the rest of the table. Cletus leaned in between Bobby and Melissa with some issue of business. As coffee was being served, the Wellmans moved to another table, and Casey said to Bobby, "What the hell, you mean that there was buried treasure in Tuck's house?"

"Yes, there was, but it's not there now," Bobby said. He looked at Mason who seemed paralyzed by Bobby's previous statement. "It's a long story—"

"We have time," Casey interrupted.

Bobby laughed, noticing that everyone at the table was intently interested. "Well, here's the short version. We have a small office in Low Creek. I'm there twice a week for clients in the area. Some years ago, I represented a young man there on some minor drug charges. He was convicted and spent some time on probation. That was the only interaction that I had with him until last summer when I received a call from a chaplain at a prison in Kentucky requesting that I accept a visit from him regarding the young man who I had represented in the case that I just described—"

"Thane Correl," Mason blurted to his own embarrassment. "Your client was Thane Correl."

Bobby looked at his wife and back to Mason. "Yes, it was Thane Correl. Anyway, this chaplain said that he was prepared to pay for my time on Thane's behalf. I told him that I don't practice in Kentucky, and he explained that he was not looking for legal counsel for Thane but personal representation in another matter. Maybe out of curiosity more than business interest, I agreed and met with the chaplain, a Reverend Yost, a week later. Here's what he told me. There was a doctor, his name was Raphael North, and some of you might remember reading about him who ran a pill mill in Pleasantville.

Apparently, Dr. North's business was so robust that he hired Thane and his brother to run some of his distribution. Now, one problem any drug dealer has is managing the substantial amount of cash that they tend to accumulate without drawing attention. The doctor had a unique approach to that problem. He would make regular trips to New York to buy diamonds on the street in small quantities. I guess he intended to convert them gradually, but I don't know. The doctor apparently kept his diamonds and cash in a safe in his office."

A waiter came to the table with a dessert cart, and the conversation changed to the selections of tarts and cakes. Casey took a bite of his dessert and said, "Okay, sir, please go on."

"Well, as I was saying, the doctor had his stash in a safe in his office. So he got a tip one day that the DEA and local police were about to raid him. Thane was there at the time, and the doctor opened the safe and asked him to take his stash and hold it for him until the heat was off. Thane left there with a knapsack full of pills, cash, and diamonds."

Bobby ate some of his dessert and took a drink of coffee. "You have to realize that I got all of this from notes handwritten on a yellow pad that Reverend Yost gave me. It was effectively a de facto affidavit from Thane for reasons I, to this day, don't understand."

Melissa interrupted, "He still has the notepad."

"Anyway," Bobby continued, "Thane took the knapsack to his house that his great-granddaddy had built just down the road from where you're staying, Tuck."

Cletus had pulled a chair to the table. "Ah, the drug money story," he said as he placed his hand on Mason's shoulder and laughed. "We bought that house too late. The goodies were gone by the time we got there. I need to have a word with this gentleman," he said as he stood up, tapping Jimmy Cahn on the shoulder.

Casey said, "Go on."

Bobby continued, "So Thane took the knapsack to his house and separated the pills into another container for reasons he didn't disclose." He raised his eyebrows and shot a glance at Melissa. "Now it gets good. The next day, Thane's brother called him and said that he was tipped off about upcoming raids at both brothers' homes.

Thane threw the pills into his girlfriend's car and sent her off. But he apparently didn't trust her with the cash and gems. Well, the girlfriend made it out, but Thane saw the DEA vehicles approaching before he could leave. So he took the knapsack and ran out the back door to a path in the woods that he had used as a boy. That path led to Newley's house. Now Thane had done some work for Ansel Newley, I don't know exactly what kind of work, and he knew that Ansel never locked his shop door. That gave Thane the idea to hide the knapsack in Ansel's shop. He snuck into the shop, moved Ansel's table saw, and pulled up some floorboards with Ansel's tools. That's where he hid the knapsack under the table saw."

"The shop!" Mason exclaimed. "It was in the shop."

The others at the table turned to Mason and Casey said, "Why is that so important?"

"Because," Mason said, "Boone..." he turned to Bobby. "The guy who was harassing me was Thane's brother Boone, and..."

Bobby and Melissa looked at each other. "Are you sure?" Bobby asked, apparently surprised.

"Positive. I actually met him."

Bobby sat back in his chair. "Well, maybe you have a better story than we do."

Casey put his hand on Mason's arm. "Let him finish, Tuck."

"Please go on," Mason said without concealing his embarrassment.

"Okay," Bobby continued, "so as Thane was nearing parole, he got a sudden attack of conscience or, at least as we believe, made it look that way. Anyway, he asked Reverend Yost to approach me, I guess since I'm the only one in the Low Creek area whom he could trust, and have me go to Ansel and show him where the knapsack was hidden. Well, I asked the reverend why he didn't just go to Ansel himself, and he said that it was Thane's wish to have me do it."

Jimmy Cahn returned to the table, and Zach Hendy excused himself to use the restroom. The waiter offered more coffee and took some drink orders as the conversation drifted into lighter topics. Zach returned with a tray of drinks supplied by the waiter and asked, "What did I miss?"

"Nothing," Casey responded, turning to Bobby. "Don't leave us hanging here. Did you go see what's-his-name?"

Melissa laughed and poked Bobby in the ribs. "Go on. Finish what you started."

"I did go to see him," Bobby continued. "Fortunately, I knew Ansel fairly well from some legal work that I had done for his furniture business. Boy, I gotta tell you, he was not happy when I brought Thane's statement. You would have to know Ansel to guess his reaction. When he read the statement, he threw the pad down, grabbed me by the arm and dragged me into his shop. But when we were in the shop, he just stood there staring at his table saw. I guess he was just trying to collect his thoughts, but I didn't want to wait any longer and moved the saw myself, which wasn't easy. Thane actually had done a poor job of replacing the floorboards, and they came up fairly easily with a pry bar that Ansel had handed me."

"And the money was there?" Casey asked.

"Yes. A big knapsack that Thane probably had to work hard to get in between the joists. Anyway, I pulled it out, but Ansel wouldn't have any part of it. He wouldn't even touch it but stood back, and while I opened it, it was full of cash and several velvet bags full of diamonds."

"So," Casey asked, almost animated by the story, "what did you do with it?"

"Well," Bobby continued, "You would have to know Ansel to understand how things were at that moment."

Zach Hendy laughed. "We knew Ansel. That had to be the worst thing for him to see, drug money in his shop."

Bobby nodded to Zach, "Really. He was paralyzed. Anyway, once I got Ansel settled down, I took the knapsack to the sheriff's office because, as I saw it, it was evidence in a drug deal. Well, Sheriff Rafe Miller didn't see it that way. He was up to his ears with other drug issues, and this is the corker, Dr. North, was dead."

"Dead?" Mason said, drawing the attention of the table.

"Dead. Rafe said that any investigation into Dr. North was closed, and if Ansel found something in his shop, it was his. As an attorney, I can tell you that this was a blatant breach of policy, but given the handful that Rafe's office had and still has, I guess I can see his point. Anyway, I brought the knapsack back to Ansel, and he wouldn't even let me take it out of my car."

Zack Hendy laughed again, "Oh man, I could just see Ansel's face..."

"I did," Bobby continued, "and the man was beside himself. Now Thane's statement included a request for Ansel to take whatever he needed and give the rest to charities of Ansel's choice, which Ansel left up to me, not wanting any part of it. My fees were also to come out of the take. Well, Ansel would have none of that either, and he eventually wrote me a check for the fees, which I billed fairly but had to include the brokers that I hired for the diamonds and the charity distribution. So that was it, Tuck. There really was buried treasure under the floor of your house."

Mason nodded, saying nothing at first and then, "How did Dr. North die?"

"Well, that's another story that I looked up after the fact. He was arrested on several charges but got out on bail. It was only several hours after placing his bond that he was murdered, shot in his car in front of the courthouse in Pleasantville."

Casey stood up and said, "Well, if I was you, I would take that notepad to a movie producer and cash in on it. Anyone need a drink? I'm going to the bar."

The people at the table broke up into conversations with others on the patio, and Mason got engaged with a discussion about college football with Zach Hendy. As the evening progressed, he tried to make his obligatory regards to Sally and Cletus, but Cletus pulled him aside and said, "Bobby tells me that you might know something about Boone Correl's whereabouts."

"I did know where he was staying sometimes and actually met him. I'm not sure where he is hanging out now," Mason spoke carefully, still concerned for Cletus's safety.

"Where was he?"

"The house around the bend from mine. The first one on the right."

Cletus rubbed his chin. "Yeah, we weren't interested in that one," he said.

"Why not?"

"Sewers," Cletus said. "The properties that we bought can tie into the treatment plant for the prison. Sewers is a big selling point for housing these days. Is he still hanging around there?"

Mason didn't want to make things worse for Melanie despite his aversion to lying to Cletus. "No, I don't think so. I believe he spends a lot of time in Low Creek with his ex-wife."

"Yeah," Cletus said, apparently frustrated. "We knew about that. It seems that he shows up and disappears quickly. We even talked the police into questioning him when we knew firsthand that he was in there, but he was always gone before they arrived. The man is like a ghost."

"Cletus," Mason said, trying to choose his words carefully, "why so much focus on Boone Correl? I'm sure there are plenty of drug dealers to spotlight."

"There are, and we have had some success in identifying them. So far, we can claim two arrests and a disappearance in Kingsport, and we're getting a lot of activity in Low Creek and other places in Wells County. Boone, on the other hand, doesn't stir much interest with any authorities because they have nothing on him. His name comes up now and then, but someone else is always in front of him."

"So why the strong interest in him?"

"Kids. Whenever someone mentions his name, it's someone under the age of eighteen. It also has a lot to do with my friend Jake Morrow. His son was approached for drugs on the first day he returned to school, and Boone was mentioned. That's how it seems to be with him. His name comes up, always the first name only, but nobody can or will actually say that he supplied the drugs that the kids are buying."

Mason attempted to conceal his concern. "Seems like your program is having some impact. That must take a lot of your time."

"Not really," Cletus said as he shook the hand of a leaving guest. "We actually are little more than a tip line for the authorities. I have a girl in our real estate office who takes calls and passes the information to the various police and sheriff departments."

"You mean you don't actually follow suspects around?"

Cletus gave a surprised look. "Shoot no. Now Jake was trying to shadow Boone, and I even went with him once, but it was always a dead end, and I talked him into backing off. Our mission was originally to get information from affected employees and pass it on to authorities. It just blossomed on its own into what it is now. We get about twenty calls a day from employers, teachers, mothers, and just about anyone else who is sick of seeing these drugs ruin lives."

"Well, I commend you for what you're doing," Mason said, still concerned about the billboards near Low Creek and Kingsport. "For what it's worth, I had some research done on Boone Correl. He's no lightweight and not exactly a stable thinker. Not a guy that I would want to piss off. Thanks for dinner, Cletus. I had a great time."

He paid his regards to Sally and caught Bobby Surtemp on his way out. "Thanks for the update on my house, Bobby," he said. "By the way, how much money was there in that knapsack?"

"Four hundred eighty grand and change in cash," Bobby replied, "and another three-fifty for the diamonds."

"That's a lot of money. No wonder Boone was so anxious to get at it."

"Well," Bobby said, laughing, "if he wants any part of it, he can apply for the scholarship in Ansel's name at the Virginia Institute of Technology. Or he can check into the drug rehab facility that Ansel's son is running in Florida. Good night, Tuck. It was nice meeting you."

Mason drove home with Bobby Surtemp's revelations weighing on his mind as he passed Cecil's darkened porch and turned into his own lighted front lot. He felt some victory in learning about Boone's objectives but was more concerned than ever about Boone's current motives. Perhaps, he thought, Melanie could tell Boone that the money was gone. But given the state of mind that she had described, that could set him off and put her into imminent danger. He watched the local news on television and went to bed, still uncertain about what to do with Bobby's story, about how to help Melanie and Jenna, about the heroin sitting somewhere on his jobsite, about Boone Correl lurking somewhere in the periphery.

He spent Sunday with Casey and Millie, visiting the Mountaineer's Museum and others in Johnson City, Wytheville, and Bristol, ending up for dinner at a restaurant in Kingsport. On Monday, he had breakfast at Harley's and walked to the park where he knew from her text that Melanie would be with Jenna. There was a half-dozen girls in the park and three mothers, including Mavis, besides Melanie near the picnic area. Melanie made the appropriate introductions and walked away from the others with him on the path that circled the park, saying nothing at first as she glanced at the playing girls.

After a while, she said, "Nice weather for the holiday. Thanks for coming."

"No problem," Mason said as he looked around the park. "Were you able to make a phone call?"

"Yes," she answered distantly.

"Your brother is okay?"

"He said that he would be glad to take care of Jenna while I got straightened out."

Mason suspected that she was holding something back. "What did you tell him?"

"Only that I had an addiction problem stemming from that foot accident and wanted to go through rehab. He offered to help, and I told him that I had things in order. Our father was an alcoholic and spent a lot of time in rehab, so it wasn't hard for him to process."

"I get that," Mason said as something from the past flashed in his mind. "I guess there was no need to tell him that you were living on a mountain in Virginia."

"Tuck, please," she said as she looked directly at him.

"I'm sorry," Mason returned. "I told you I would help, and I will."

"It's just that Phillip, that's my brother, is a bit…"

"It's okay, Melanie. Enough said. We'll get Jenna to Phillip's house, put you in rehab, sell that damn house, and you and Jenna can restart."

They continued walking, and Mason knew that her effort to look away had more to do with the tear running down her cheek than watching the girls. He had noticed when he first approached her how different she appeared with her brown hair brushed and lightly touching her shoulders and that the T-shirt had been replaced by a crisp blouse and the baggy blue jeans had given way to a plain blue skirt. She wore fashionable sandals instead of worn-out Keds, and he could catch a faint scent of perfume when the wind allowed. He pulled a handkerchief from his pocket and stopped her to wipe the tear from her cheek. "You look real nice today," he said, feeling awkward. "I like your hair that way."

"Thanks," she responded with the little smile that he had always found so attractive.

"I guess I owe you an apology," he said after a brief silence.

"For what?" She was watching the girls running through a flock of pigeons.

"For doubting you, or at least for doubting what Boone told you." He stopped and grasped her shoulder lightly. "There *was* money hidden in my house. It was under the floor in the workshop."

"You said 'was.'"

"It's gone now. Boone's brother had someone get it for him, and it was given to charity."

Melanie looked back at the girls. "Now I'm the one who should be doubting."

"His name is Thane," Mason said. "He contacted a local attorney through a prison chaplain and had the attorney go to the house and show the owner where it was. The owner had it all given to charity."

"Why would he, Thane, do that?"

"I don't know. My guess is that he was coming up for parole and wanted to impress someone with his moral resurrection. But it was a lot of money to give up, so it's hard to speculate."

Her smile returned. "I have this suspicion that Boone's diamonds were there as well."

Mason nodded. "Enough to start a nice little enterprise. I'm sorry."

"Well," she said as they started walking again, "as much as you and I would both like to dump this on Boone, I'm afraid that would be like lighting a fuse."

"From what I know about the man, I have to agree," Mason said.

They continued walking quietly around the full circle of the park until they approached the other mothers where Mason made his regards and lightly gripped Melanie's arm as he said, "We'll talk tomorrow." She said nothing but gave the smile again as Jenna called, "Bye, Tuck," from a seesaw.

Eileen Barrett returned his call early the next morning and recommended several rehab facilities, which she e-mailed to Mason with website links and her personal commentary. He had just finished thanking her as Special Agent Willis entered the trailer.

"Well, Special Agent," Mason said as he indicated the guest chair in his office. "It's been two weeks. Anything to report?"

"Just that it's ongoing. We have tracked a couple hundred license plates and conducted dozens of interviews, some of which have contributed to other cases."

"Aren't we supposed to be advised of these things?" Mason asked.

"You really aren't involved at this level," Special Agent Willis responded to Mason's surprise and frustration as he withdrew a tablet from his briefcase.

"Give up on the laptop?" Mason said, referring to the tablet.

Willis looked over the rim of his glasses, "It's in the car. Actually, despite my doubts, this thing has been working pretty well."

Mason looked at the tablet. "Those things are getting more useful quickly. I'm about to upgrade mine, and it's only two years old. You're still convinced that there are drugs stored on this site?"

"Oh yeah, I'm quite positive of it. That's all I can say at this point."

"So what is today's visit for?"

"Just touching base. We don't want to be interfering with your business, and I'm required to check in with you occasionally. Also, I wanted to talk with you about the license number that you gave us for this Boone Correl character."

"Okay, so what did you find?" Mason said as he leaned forward over his desk.

"Well, we haven't seen him visiting the site, but we did run the number."

"And?"

Willis looked down at the tablet. "It's not his truck. It belongs to a person named Calvin Ebert."

"Who?"

"Calvin Ebert. I doubt he's anyone familiar to you," Special Agent Willis said as he looked up from his tablet, "because Mr. Ebert is a patient in a nursing home in West Virginia and is quite incapable of driving."

"So what the hell is Boone doing with his truck?"

"Probably driving it with permission. Mr. Ebert has a history of opioid addiction as well as some minor drug-related convictions. It happens more than you would expect, a person incapacitated or incarcerated lends out his vehicle and identity in exchange for Fentanyl or whatever."

"His identity?"

"I would expect Correl has a driver's license that has his picture and Ebert's name."

"Damn," Mason said quietly, "always the ghost."

"Yeah," Special Agent Willis said, "I guess that's a good way of putting it."

"Like Carlotta."

Willis put the tablet back into his briefcase. "Not quite in her league, but yes, she's a good example. Never underestimate the cleverness of the criminal mind. On the other hand, we also get our share of losers, but those are generally small players. Anyway, now you can see what we deal with every day." He stood and slid his chair out of his way. "By the way, Mr. Mason, Lieutenant Melker says that you are apparently the only person who can actually verify that Boone Correl was in the area."

Mason looked past Willis to the window. "Not necessarily the only one," he said, regretting his disclosure.

"Well, I wouldn't be surprised if the sheriff or one of the local police departments would want to have a discussion with you at some point. He's been coming under a lot of suspicion lately," Willis said as he started for the door.

"So," Mason said quickly, "we are going to continue twenty-four-hour surveillance?"

Willis shook his head. "Not twenty-four hours. The cameras set alarms by motion, and you have an after-hours security guard here when the site is shut down. Casey made sure the shift schedule was tightened up, so the guard doesn't leave until we're in place. The back gate appears to be sealed, so we're only focused on the front gate. Anyone, by your order, will be turned away after hours. We still think that whoever owns the drugs here knows that there is no way in except the front gate. It is, after all, a prison."

Mason stood up and leaned across the desk. "The back gate wasn't necessary once excavation work was finished. Special Agent Willis, if there are drugs hidden on this site, then please find them and get them off the site. If your hunch is wrong, then, well, I have a prison to build, and we are already facing some scheduling issues. I believe you know what I am getting at."

"I understand your frustration, Mr. Mason, but we have good reason, not just a hunch, to believe that there is a cache of heroin either here or destined to be here that has a street value probably greater than any single delivery this region has ever seen. It won't be ignored by whoever owns it, and we intend to identify that source."

"And it's not in the painters' inventory?"

"I didn't say that. Now, if you will excuse me I have to run up to Roanoke yet today," Willis said as he turned again to leave.

Mason finished the morning returning phone calls and had lunch with Casey and some of the subcontractor representatives at Harley's. He left the site shortly after lunch with the printouts from rehab facilities that Eileen Barrett has recommended. He had wanted to take them to Melanie and discuss applications before Jenna got off school, but Melanie asked to meet him at his house because of the unknown intentions and whereabouts of Boone Correl. After an hour discussing the options, she settled on a facility in Bristol.

She stood to leave, her eyes intense despite the constricted pupils. "Tuck...I don't know what to say," she said, quivering slightly in the breeze. She was standing close to him and he again noticed a faint trace of perfume.

"You don't need to say anything, Melanie," he said softly as he touched her shoulder. "Just get well."

She leaned forward and he pulled her closer as she pressed her head to his shoulder. "I'm scared," she said as he held her.

"It'll be okay," he said as he gently held her away. "You need to get home before Jenna gets there." She turned and walked quickly across the lot to the driveway, smiling briefly as she disappeared beyond the trees.

The local news was on the television in the living room as Mason cleaned the kitchen and dressed for a run on the following morning. He seldom paid much attention to local affairs but left the news on more for the company that the television provided than the banalities of the Tri-Cities area. The report about a body found in Low Creek was old news, and he was about to turn the television off when the update registered with his memory, and he almost dropped the bottle of juice that he was holding as he ran out the front door, stopped, and returned to set the alarm and ran out again, locking the door behind him. He ran at full speed eastward on Mills Hollow toward the school bus as Melanie kissed Jenna and pointed to Mason. Jenna called, "Hi, Tuck," as she boarded the bus, and the bus was just pulling away as Mason grabbed Melanie by the shoulders, her smile disappearing as he caught his breath and spoke, almost shouting, "Boone killed JoAnn!"

XXIII

The Low Creek police department was located on Miner Street across from Gender's Market, where Mason and Jenna sat on a bench in front of the store eating ice cream. It had been two hours since they had lunch at McDonald's and Melanie proceeded into the police building. After they finished the ice cream, Jenna announced a need for a bathroom, and they walked back to McDonald's and returned to the bench in front of Gender's. Another hour passed as Mason recalled the frenzied morning and the confusion in Melanie's face as he explained what he had heard and the fact that she had no choice now but to talk to the police. She was too frightened to go alone, so they took Mason's car and pulled Jenna from class because of the uncertainty of the time required, and the three of them entered the police department where Melanie declared her knowledge of the case, and Mason took Jenna to wait for her.

The television report remained on his mind as the reporter's words seemed to echo in the background: "Police in Low Creek reported that the partially decomposed body found in an abandoned cistern last month is that of JoAnn Healy, formerly of Low Creek and more recently Lexington, Kentucky. Ms. Healy was originally reported missing last March when she failed to return to work after a vacation. The Wells County coroner has not determined the cause of death, although Low Creek police Chief Edgar Moore reported that her death was suspicious. The FBI has been called into the case…"

Melanie finally emerged from the police building at around 3:00 p.m., appearing uncomfortable and distracted. "They said he is a person of interest in this and other cases," she said as she rooted through her purse for a tissue, "but so far, they haven't been able to find him. I live out of their jurisdiction, so I'm to call the county sheriff's office if Boone returns."

"Do they consider him as dangerous?" Mason asked.

"They said they have no reason to because he hasn't done anything that they can prove. They want to talk to him only because he might have been the last person to see JoAnn. They emphasized 'might have been.'" Melanie was clearly distracted as she helped Jenna into Mason's car and climbed into the front seat. Mason began to realize that she was going through some kind of withdrawal. "We talked a lot about Boone's drug use and possible dealing," she continued, "but they said that they still had no evidence of wrongdoing and couldn't arrest him even if they could find him. They actually seemed annoyed by Boone's name being mentioned. One officer even complained of getting sent on wild goose chases for Boone Correl."

Mason started the engine and pulled on to Miner Street. "There are people in the area," he said, carefully choosing his words, "who know Boone and think he is dealing drugs to high school kids, among other things."

Melanie said nothing as she gently rubbed the base of her neck and looked ahead as Mason turned down Oak Street toward the highway. As they drove through the poorer section, Melanie seemed disturbed by something she saw. Mason didn't notice the woman on the opposite side of the road until she appeared in the rearview mirror, sitting on the ground by the road with her head dipping profoundly toward her knees.

"It's bad," Melanie said, as she looked back at the woman and smiled at Jenna, then back to Mason, "what Boone's doing. It's really bad, isn't it."

"I don't know, Melanie. I have heard a lot, but I only know that he spent a lot of time in my yard. Other than that, it's just what people seem to suspect. I suspect that he killed a woman who I only know by name. Maybe that's wrong, but I don't think we should take any more chances with him."

Mason dropped Melanie and Jenna off at their house and left, knowing that Melanie would probably secure Jenna in front of the television while she resolved her withdrawal problem. A tremendous sense of urgency was evolving within him as he drove to the prison site for a scheduled late meeting with the plumbing contractor. The meeting lasted longer than expected as Casey and the plumber argued over a number of change order requests as Mason reviewed each one and made decisions accordingly. It was already getting dark when he arrived at the Lowes store in Norton, where he picked up two door-bell cameras, replacement door locks, a trail camera and other alarm equipment.

Jenna was sitting on the front porch steps when he finally returned to Melanie's house. The porch light was on, but the rest of the house was dark. She was staring straight ahead as if something had terrified her and made no effort to look at Mason, who tried to get her attention. "Where is your mom, Jenna?" he asked gently, a sudden feeling of anxiety rising within him as he spoke.

"In there," Jenna answered, still staring ahead.

Mason walked to the front door but stopped before opening it. He could feel a tightening in his chest as he turned back to Jenna and asked, "Was Boone here?"

"Yes."

"What did he say to you?"

She continued to stare straight ahead. "He said to wait here and don't move until he comes back."

Mason opened the front door and rushed inside the house, fumbling in the darkness for a light switch, which he found on the wall by the door. The bedroom doors were all closed, and he quickly opened the closest one, which was obviously Jenna's. In the next room, he found Melanie sprawled on her back on the bed, her eyes open but barely breathing. He tried to sit her up, but she was completely unresponsive, and her breathing stopped entirely. Gently laying her back on the bed, he dialed 911 on his phone and gave the appropriate instructions before attempting chest compressions and then mouth breathing, as he had been trained to do in a required first aid class in Trenton years before. Melanie responded briefly and intermittently, but her breathing abated or stopped entirely whenever he stopped the procedure to call out to Jenna, who was still on the porch step waiting for something that Mason could only consider a terrible fate. He finally laid Melanie back down and ran to the porch, calling Jenna firmly but softly to avoid frightening her any more than necessary.

"Jenna, I need you to come inside with me," he said, realizing that he was beginning to tremble. Jenna looked at him, clearly terrified as she looked back at the driveway and then back to him. "Please, honey," he continued, "Boone won't be back. He can't hurt you now. Please come into the house."

Jenna stood up and walked toward him, slowly at first but then running to him with her arms outstretched. She sobbed loudly as she wrapped her arms around his neck, and he could feel the wetness of her tears as he carried her to her room and sat her on the bed. "Your mom is sick, and I have some people coming to make her better," he said as he wiped her cheek with his handkerchief. "I need you to wait here and don't open the door for anyone until you hear my voice." Jenna said nothing as he ran to the next room where Melanie lay as he had left her, her eyes staring straight ahead with severely constricted pupils.

It took another twenty minutes for the ambulance to arrive, and he ran to the front door and led two EMTs to Melanie's room, explaining the procedures that he had been applying and answering their questions as one of them opened a kit marked NALOXONE. He stood back as they treated Melanie and eventually opened Jenna's door and took her hand. "Come with me, Jenna," he said gently as she slid from the bed and walked with him to the front porch. She stopped and asked to go to the bathroom, and Mason held the door for her as she went back into the house. As he sat on the top step, he looked past the lights of the ambulance into the darkness beyond it where the ghostly image of a car with no lights on was parked perpendicular to the driveway. The car began to move, slowly at first, then quickly, and he could see its headlights come on through the trees.

"You bastard!" he said under his breath as the headlights disappeared.

Jenna returned, and they sat on the porch steps for what seemed a long time before one of the EMTs came out of the house and descended the steps in order to face Mason. She was a short woman with a caring expression as she smiled at Jenna and then turned to Mason. "Sir," she said, "can I have a word with you?"

Mason stood up, patting Jenna on the arm and assuring her that he would be right back. He took a few steps into the yard with the EMT, who asked, "Do you live here?"

"No," Mason responded.

"And the little girl?"

"Her daughter."

"Are you a family member?"

"No, just a neighbor."

"Are you the one who called this in?"

"Yes. What is this getting at?"

"We're going to have to take the lady to a hospital. She has suffered an overdose of what we assume is heroin, considering the needle mark on her arm."

"Needle mark? She doesn't use needles," Mason responded quickly, stopping the urge to raise his voice.

"Well," the EMT said, "apparently she decided to try it this time. However, we can't find the needle or any other paraphernalia. Did you remove anything?"

"No, of course not."

The woman said something into the device clipped to her collar and someone answered. "Sir," she continued, "you did a great thing keeping her breathing. Definitely saved her life. But she apparently has had more involved because she is not responding as well as she should. And the fact that there is no sign of the equipment used to administer, the contusions on her arm and—"

"Contusions?" Mason interrupted, this time raising his voice.

"Please calm down, sir. We're just trying to help the lady here."

The front door opened suddenly, and the other two EMT's emerged with Melanie on a gurney. They quickly opened the rear door of the ambulance and loaded her into the ambulance, which started immediately and proceeded down the driveway. Mason held Jenna's hand and turned to the woman in front of him. "Aren't you going with them?" he asked as the ambulance turned onto Mills Hollow road."

"No," she responded. "I'm going to stay here until the others arrive."

"Others?"

The woman looked at Jenna on the steps and back at Mason. "The sheriff's department and Child Protective Services. There may have been a crime here, so the sheriff will want to ask you some questions. Also, since you are not a family member and the patient could not identify you as a responsible guardian for her daughter, Child Protective Services will have to take temporary custody of the little girl."

Jenna gripped Mason's arm as he sat down on the step next to her. The EMT reentered the house and returned to the porch, sitting on the opposite side of Mason on the porch step. She sighed deeply and shook her head. "This is number five for us today," she said, looking into the darkened yard. "We lost one. She was only seventeen. OD'd in the restroom at school."

"What about this one?' Mason asked, regretting the insensitivity of his approach.

The EMT looked briefly at him and then back to the yard. "I don't know. I wish I could give you a better answer. We see a lot. She has something else going on besides heroin. I just don't know. It's up to the doctors now. Something happened here beyond just a heroin fix."

"Yes, I believe something did happen," Mason said slowly. "I'm quite sure of that."

She looked back at Mason again. "My name is Mary," she said blankly.

"Tuck."

Mason patted Jenna's hand, and Mary leaned over to speak to her. "You're a pretty one," she said softly. "My little girl is all grown up. I'll bet you will grow up all pretty like she is." She sat back, and Mason could tell from the weariness in her voice that she was exhausted.

A sheriff's patrol car turned slowly into the driveway and parked in front of the porch. Deputy Gabe Setty got out of the car and acknowledged Mason before offering a hand to Mary, who was standing up stiffly and regarding the deputy with a sense of close familiarity. Setty and Mary entered the house, leaving Mason and Jenna on the porch steps. After a short time, Deputy Setty asked Mason to come into the house while Mary took his place next to Jenna.

The deputy questioned Mason extensively, taking pictures of Melanie's bedroom with a smart phone and looking around as he spoke. Mason explained the day's activities, including his belief that Boone had committed a murder, how Melanie had spent several hours at the Low Creek Police department, how he had left them to purchase alarm equipment, and how Jenna had told him that Boone had been there in the meantime. Deputy Setty took extensive notes on a small pad, which he eventually inserted into his belt and asked Mason if any family was around to help identify Melanie in the event that she couldn't do it herself. Mason indicated her purse on the kitchen counter.

"I can't take that without a warrant," Setty said as he opened the front door. "It would be helpful if you would stop by the hospital later or in the morning. Also, I'm sure the sheriff would like to question you further, depending on the outcome of this." He looked around the yard and back to the house. "I can't declare this a crime scene. Can you be a good neighbor and lock up after we leave?"

"Sure," Mason replied, once again resenting Deputy Setty's attitude.

Mary and Jenna seemed to be having a conversation on the steps as Mason approached, and he realized that Mary, as a mother herself, was putting Jenna to ease about Melanie's condition.

Deputy Setty made several telephone calls from his patrol car but remained there as another car slowly proceeded down the driveway and parked next to him. Two women got out of the arriving car. Mary stood, patted Jenna on the shoulder and approached them and

Deputy Setty joined them as well. After conferring together, one of the women approached Jenna without acknowledging Mason. She was a portly woman but well dressed and clearly professional. She introduced herself simply as Julia and explained that she was going to give her a place to stay until her mother got better. She extended her hand and asked Jenna to come into the house with her to get some things to take with her. Jenna grabbed Mason's arm tightly and looked at him. "It's okay," he said, gently taking her hand from his arm. "I'll be right here."

Julia and Jenna returned with a shopping bag full of clothes and other items. Jenna ran to Mason and threw her arms around his neck, sobbing but saying nothing. Mason looked up at Julia and said, weakly, he thought, "She can stay with me. I just live—"

"You know I can't do that, sir," Julia interrupted. Then to Jenna, she said, "Come with me, sweetie. It's okay."

"It's okay," Mason repeated as he touched Jenna on the cheek. "We'll take care of your mom and come to get you real soon. I promise."

Julia placed Jenna in the back seat of the car next to the other woman and took her place in the driver's seat, speaking into a cell phone as she drove away. Deputy Setty followed with Mary in his patrol car.

Mason retrieved Melanie's purse from the kitchen and sat again on the step, the evening's events now weighing heavily on his mind. It should not be this way. The child needs her mother, but the mother was not there…not there because of the spectral influence of another, the beast who had emerged into their lives and created the crisis that now separated them. He thought of Melanie, lying like a rag doll on the bed, her eyes staring, lifeless as the past arose… *Where, honey…in our yard? Show me… George, he's turning blue, call 911…and he could hear them beyond the yellow light that encircled the door… He's a little boy, Cam. He didn't know what to do… Damn you, Cam. He's a little boy. He was just trying to…*

Mason jerked his head upward, realizing that he was sobbing. Melanie's eyes were in front of him now, and he looked up into the darkened sky. The chill of the Appalachian night seemed to envelope him as he tried to sort through it. He had some business to do, and he just wanted to make them safe. Maybe he should have... *For god's sake, Tucker, why did you leave him? He's a little boy, Cam. Damn you, Cam...*

"Maybe she's okay," he thought, as the darkness seemed to close in around him. "Maybe she will respond. I should not have left them."

XXIV

letus Wellman's death was first reported on the WEMT early news as an unidentified man found dead by an apparent homicide on a highway ramp in Kingsport. Mason thought little of it as he blankly watched the television in the emergency waiting room at the Mountain View Medical Center. It was an hour later, when the news resumed, that the deceased was identified as Cletus Wellman, a well-known businessman from Kingsport. Anyone with information about the incident was asked to contact the Kingsport police department or the Tennessee highway patrol. Mason felt numb as the anchor went on to another report. He called Casey who had heard the same news but knew nothing else.

"I'm helping a neighbor out this morning," Mason said as he looked at the television, not expecting Casey's usual commentary about his living environment. "I'll be in later. Let me know if you hear anything."

A text message appeared on Mason's phone from Philip McCall, who Mason had reached the night before. The cell phone in Melanie's purse was locked, so Mason had to do several searches for Philip McCall in Columbus, Ohio, finding two with that name but not Melanie's brother. He finally found the right Philip in Dublin, who was very resistive at first and threatened to call the police. Mason gave him the phone numbers of the Wells County sheriff and the hospital, and Philip abruptly disconnected the call. It was only ten minutes later that he called back and asked what he should do. Philip was due to land at Tri-Cities Airport at 10:12 a.m.

A young doctor stepped into the waiting room and called, "Melanie McCall." Mason stood to approach her with a sense of trepidation. "She's out of the woods," the doctor said as she walked with Mason to an unoccupied corner of the room. "She apparently overdosed on heroin laced with what we suspect is fentanyl. But there is something else that we're not sure of, considering her fever and the infection on her injection site. It could be the result of a dirty needle or something toxic in her dose, but we need to keep her here for a while until we clear up whatever is causing the fever."

"How long is 'a while,' doctor?" Mason asked.

"Hopefully just a day or so. She needs to be hooked up to an IV in order to get the antibiotic that she needs. The nurse said that you were trying to find her relatives. Have you had any luck with that?"

"Yes, her brother is on his way from Ohio. By the time he rents a car and drives in, I guess he will be here around noon at the latest," Mason answered. "Can I see her?"

"She's sleeping now, and we have to do some tests to make sure there is no damage to her brain or vital organs. EMTs reported that she might have stopped breathing for a long time, and we have to make sure that there is nothing permanent going wrong." The doctor quickly checked her cell phone. "By the way," she said as she looked up from the phone, "a sheriff's deputy who apparently accompanied her last night has requested to be notified when she can talk. I expect we will call him this morning."

Philip arrived at 11:50 a.m. and walked directly to the emergency desk to request information about Melanie. Mason interrupted and, after introducing himself, led Philip to where he had been sitting. Philip listened intently as Mason explained, as briefly as possible, how Melanie had come to the situation that she was in. When Mason answered the question about Jenna's whereabouts, Philip became agitated until Mason gave him Julia's card.

Philip sat back in his chair, slowly shaking his head as he tried to process all the information that Mason had given him. He was a slight man with thinning brown hair and features so similar to

Melanie's that Mason had recognized him immediately as he walked in. "So," he asked Mason, looking out of the window at the mountains in the distance, "how do you fit into all of this?"

Mason thought of all the information that Philip still didn't have and considered the overwhelming amount already dumped on the man. He answered as matter-of-factly as possible. "I'm just a neighbor. We became friends, and I was helping her to get into a rehab facility in Bristol."

"Well," Philip said as he turned back to Mason, "we can forget about that. I'll get her into a rehab facility in Columbus. I want to get her out of this godforsaken place as soon as I can." He checked his phone and said, "I really appreciate what you've done here, Mr. Mason. I can take care of things here now. I'm sure you need to go to work."

"I have some things to take care of if you don't need anything from me now. Melanie won't be available for a while, so you might want to go to the cafeteria or something," Mason said as he stood to leave, realizing that Philip needed to get in control. He handed Melanie's purse to Philip. "There is more to talk about. I'm sure she will tell you, but I'm available to help as much as I can."

"You've done plenty," Philip said as he looked at his phone, which was buzzing. "My wife," he said as he held the phone up to Mason. "Please excuse me."

Mason arrived at the prison site as the trades were returning to their work after lunch. Casey was in the office trailer discussing business with Ralph Watson, the scheduler. Ralph was also a tenant of Cletus Wellman, and the three of them compared information gained about Cletus's death with Mason offering what he had heard on the radio on his way from the hospital.

"I don't know anything, Tuck," Casey said as he stood to leave, "but I gotta believe that those billboards didn't do him any good. Do you think those drug nuts killed Cletus?"

Mason looked out at the fence crew working near the front entrance to the site. "I don't know anything either, Casey, but I have to agree that if anyone had a grudge against Cletus, it would be drug dealers." He pointed to the fence crew outside. "They're pretty far along. Is the site secure yet?"

"All but the front gate. That probably won't happen until spring, but the temporary gate is locked at night, and we have a security service at night," Casey answered.

"And the DEA is still surveilling the delivery traffic."

"Yeah, we've been inventorying everything that comes and goes, and I've had Albert rooting through every trade's staging area, but nothing has turned up so far."

Mason continued looking out the window. "Yet they still insist that there is a cache of drugs here that someone will come after."

"I guess so," Casey continued. I guess that security guard they arrested told them something. They figure Artie was responsible for it and that special agent is absolutely convinced that there's a load of dope here."

"Well, they aren't affecting production that I can see, but I'm still not convinced that there are drugs hidden here," Mason said as he looked at his watch. "Of course, I've been wrong before about buried treasure."

"I wasn't going to mention that," Casey said as he walked out.

The hospital information desk reported that Melanie had been admitted, and Mason found Philip in the hallway near her room. "Some kind of counselors are talking to her," Philip said in response to Mason's inquiry. "A sheriff's deputy was here earlier. She seems all right, but she still is hooked up to an IV." He looked at Mason and shook his head. "I know you're her neighbor, and I don't want to be insulting, but I can't believe that she actually owns a house here. I mean, Portsmouth was no paradise, but what in the world is she doing here?"

"That's an interesting story that she will have to tell you herself," Mason said as two women exited the room comparing notes in low tones.

"Well," Philip continued, "as far as I'm concerned, she needs to get rid of the house and get the hell out of here."

"I agree with getting her out of here but selling her house will be difficult until the prison is finished."

Philip held his hands outward. "Prison? What prison?"

"The one being built a mile from Melanie's house. I work for the company that is building it. I rented a house near Melanie's to be close to the job."

"So you're not a local? Where are you from?"

"New Jersey before I came here," Mason said, regretting the question as always.

Both men entered the room, and Melanie smiled at Mason but turned quickly to Philip. "What about Jenna?" she asked. She appeared exhausted and perhaps sedated.

"She's fine." Philip said, "I spoke with the Child Protective Service. You and I have to meet with them to verify Jenna's safety as soon as you can get out of here."

Melanie frowned and looked at the IV bottle beside her. "That looks like tomorrow." She turned to Mason. "A sheriff's deputy was here before. I filed a complaint against Boone. He would like for you to call him when you get a chance. He said you have his number."

"Deputy Setty, yes, I have his number."

Melanie asked for a pen and paper and made a list of clothing items that she wanted from her house, and Mason agreed to accompany Philip to get the listed items.

"You have got to be kidding me," Philip said as they turned into Melanie's driveway. "What the hell is she doing with this shack in the middle of nowhere?"

Mason said nothing as he exited the car and unlocked the front door. He handed the key to Philip, saying, "She can put the house up for sale, but I doubt anyone will be interested until spring when the prison is closer to opening. The prison will need about five hundred employees, so this house will be in a desirable location for someone on the payroll there. If she can handle the mortgage payments, I can keep an eye on the house and help with showing it. She should make a nice profit on it." Mason refrained from explaining that Boone had provided the down payment.

Philip looked around the house. "I can't imagine the payments as being much here. I guess I can help with that. Well, I need a place to stay tonight. I guess this is as good as it will get."

"I wouldn't recommend it," Mason said, shaking his head. "The guy who caused all this is still out there. He's ruthless and irrational and likely to be back. There's a couple of motels near the hospital. I suggest that you check into one for tonight."

"That's hers," Mason said, indicating Melanie's room. He remained in the front room and checked some messages on his phone as Philip packed the items on her list into a grocery bag.

"I think," Philip said as they drove back to the hospital, "considering the difference in our ages and the fact that our father died so early, that Melanie looks to me more as a father figure than a brother. I'm nine years older. Maybe that's why she kept all this so secret. I mean, we texted each other occasionally, and she even called me on my birthday. I invited her and Jenna to Columbus for the Fourth of July holiday, and she just said she had other plans. I thought she was still in Portsmouth until you called last night. Maybe she was afraid of disappointing me."

"She saw this as a stepping stone to something better," Mason said. "I'm sure she'll explain it all to you eventually."

They returned to the hospital to find a resident doctor leaving Melanie's room who explained that she had no permanent damage and was getting something to ease her withdrawal symptoms. "She said that she's going to rehab as soon as she leaves here. That's imperative. She's motivated, and we want her to keep that attitude. Her fever is reducing, and assuming that continues, I see no reason to keep her here past tomorrow morning."

Mason went to the jobsite early the next morning to catch up on paperwork. The copy of the Kingsport Times that Casey had left on the conference table had Cletus Wilbur Wellman's obituary featured: Fifty-eight years old, leaving his wife, two sisters, his mother, and two stepsons. The article continued:

> Cletus grew up in Low Creek and attended Samuel Ellison High School. Upon graduation, he took a job as a mechanic's helper at the Wallace GM dealership in Pleasantville at the urging of his father, a mechanic at the same dealership. After convincing the management that he was not cut out for the repair shop, he became a sales assistant and eventually got the distinction of being the youngest used car salesman in

the region. His success in that role eventually led to his own dealership near Low Creek, which is still operating. Despite his financial success in car sales, Cletus's ambition and energy led him to an interest in real estate. He began to purchase distressed properties in Kingsport and Johnson City, successfully building a portfolio of apartments and retail facilities, as well as the Holiday Inn Express in Kingsport, a reclaimed furniture business, and other retail ventures. He was also a principle in a partnership planning a housing development near the Low Creek Maximum Security Prison scheduled to open next summer. Cletus is perhaps best known, however, for his charitable work. Aside from generous donations to various charities, he founded the Willy Joe Wellman Foundation, a fund named for his father to help retrain displaced coal miners; Caring Cars, a volunteer ride service for seniors and disabled individuals; Rent Righters, a rent assistance program for low-income families as well as other charitable endeavors. Recently, he had started a call-in program for the anonymous identification of drug dealers...

Philip's text interrupted Mason's reading. Melanie was to be released today, and he already had booked a flight to Columbus that was leaving later in the day, and they were gathering her things in the meantime. Melanie had requested to see Mason before they left. It was almost two hours before he could clear business enough to go to her house. Philip was loading a suitcase into the trunk of his rental car as Mason approached.

"She said that you saved her life," Philip said as he checked his watch. "I didn't know that. But anyway, I want to thank you for helping her." He looked at Mason and then back at the house. "My wife and I are coming back in two weeks to meet the packers and movers.

We can put her furniture in storage until she gets back on her feet. I spoke with a realtor this morning. You were right about the timing, but he thought that there might be a first-in opportunity, so we're going to list it right away."

"What are you doing with Boone's furniture?" Mason asked as Philip slammed the trunk.

"A filthy bed and a couple of chairs. We'll pitch them when the movers are here."

"What about her car?"

"We'll sell it here when we come back," Philip returned. "I just want to get her out of this hellhole and back on her feet. This is such a mess. Jenna will be in her third school in two years."

Jenna stepped onto the porch, calling, "Hi, Tuck," as she ran to him and took his hand. "We're going to Uncle Philip's house. I like it there."

Melanie emerged from the porch with a laptop computer and locked the front door. She smiled at Mason as she approached and placed her hand on Jenna's shoulder. "I'm going to miss a lot of business," she said as she tapped the computer. "Tuck, I…" She was obviously struggling with her words.

Mason interrupted her, lightly touching her lips. "You get well, Melanie," he said gently as he patted Jenna's head. "She needs you."

Melanie leaned up and kissed Mason on the cheek, the tears in her eyes glistening in the late-morning sun as she helped Jenna into the car and climbed into the passenger seat. Jenna opened her window and called, "Bye, Tuck," as the car pulled away.

"Goodbye, Jenna," Mason said quietly as he stood alone in the driveway.

XXV

According to news reports, Cletus Wellman was shot as he entered the ramp to the highway near his house. Police theorized that his death was an assassination, the shooter having been positioned at a location that would take substantial planning to consider, including Cletus's daily habits. The investigation was ongoing with the expectation that the killing was a professional job and had the markings of an organizational hit.

Cletus's funeral was on Friday evening. The funeral director in Kingsport had anticipated a larger crowd than his facility could accommodate, so Cletus's visitation was held at the church of the Holy Communion. Cecil and Jeff rode with Mason to the event, which was also attended by hundreds of people from all walks of life in the area. Cecil fidgeted on his crutches and talked to anyone who would listen as they waited their turn in line to pay their respects to Cletus and condolences to Sally. Sally was gracious as ever, greeting and accepting hugs as each person approached her, thanking Mason for bringing Cecil and Jeff in the genuine but numb manner of a grieving wife.

They remained briefly as Cecil circulated in the crowd, and Mason distanced himself as much as possible, his discomfort with crowds as prevalent as ever, pondering the irony of two funerals. Two deaths, two car dealers. One admired for his rise to prominence that he instituted from the middle step, his past removed like pages torn from a book and his legacy carefully crafted and forever revered by those who only knew him from his rebirth. The other admired for the honest and forthright existence that had no secrets. One died from the enigmatic end that all face eventually. The other cheated from life for reasons that had yet to be identified. Mason's resentment of his father seemed to swell within him, and he notified Cecil and Jeff that it was time to leave.

Mason waited outside as Cecil was having one last conversation with a couple of Low Creek shopkeepers. A tall man separated himself from the crowd and started walking toward Mason, who recognized the man as Jake Morrow. Jake made some small talk about Cletus and then looked intently at Mason. "I think you and I both know who did this," he said.

"If you're talking about Cletus's murder," Mason said, "I don't know who did it. That's up to the police to find out."

Jake smiled briefly and continued, "Cletus told me about your problems with Boone Correl at your house. I also know that you have met Jimbo."

"Who?"

"Jimbo. At least that's what he calls himself. The kid who lives near Lilly Jane Mitchel. He told me that you were checking up on Boone."

"I was only getting his license plate number," Mason said. "We have some concerns with the possibility of drugs passing through our jobsite. Since Boone lived so close by and was so highly suspect, our legal counsel wanted us to register his truck with the people surveilling the site."

Jake seemed to disregard the statement. "Did Jimbo tell you about the RV?"

"He told me that there was an RV parked near the house. That doesn't mean anything to me. If Boone's ex-wife owns an RV, that's none of my business."

"Well," Jake continued, "it seems a little strange for someone in that neighborhood to own an RV. Most of those people can't afford groceries."

"Like I said," Mason said as he motioned for Cecil to come, "I was just there to get his license number."

"Do you know what a rolling meth lab is?" Jake asked as Mason started walking toward his car.

The word "meth" associated with Boone Correl brought Melanie's admonitions into Mason's thoughts. Eileen Barrett had briefly mentioned rolling meth labs. "Not really," he answered. "I know that it's an RV where people make drugs. That's about it."

"I think Boone Correl has a rolling meth lab. I think that's what the RV in the alley behind Lilly Jane's house is," Jake said, now becoming somewhat animated.

"Isn't that something for the police?" Mason was watching as Jeff helped Cecil into the passenger seat of his car.

"You would think so," Jake returned. "I've been to them several times and even got them to visit Lilly Jane's house when I knew Boone was there. They tell me that there was no Boone and no RV whenever they got there. Chief Moore got irritated with me. Told me not to come back unless I had hard evidence of illegal activity and to stop snooping on Low Creek citizens."

"Maybe he has a point."

"Maybe he does, but I might just be able to get that evidence," Jake said as he looked briefly over his shoulder.

"How is that?" Mason asked.

"I use GPS tracking devices on large equipment and trucks that I send out in my rental business. They're great for loss prevention. Anyway, I had Jimbo attach one to Lilly Jane's RV. I know when it leaves and where it goes. I know where it is right now, and it's not behind Lilly Jane's house. Hasn't been there for a couple of weeks."

Mason held the car door open but did not get in. "Where is it?"

"It moves around but always ends up on an old road on the edge of town."

"Have you been there?"

"Yes, but I didn't have the balls to get further than a drive-by. I need a lookout so I can check it out."

Getting into the car, Mason returned, irritated with Jake's veiled request. "I'm here to build a prison, Jake. When that's done, I will move on. Your issues with the local miscreants are, well, your issues. I can't help you."

Jake stopped the car door from closing. "And I can't help you. He killed the man who owned the house that he's been trying to get you to leave. What's next?" He handed a business card to Mason. "Give it some thought. For me, it's a matter of kids getting drugs, and I have a son who is vulnerable. I know that Boone is directly responsible for the jeopardy created, and that makes it personal. For you, it might be something just as personal. I just want to get him arrested."

Jake walked away as Mason started the car and drove from the church, asking Cecil, "Did you find out anything?"

"He's been about," Cecil said as he gazed out the window. "Fergis said he come into his store now and then but ain't seen him lately. But Joe Otten Beasley, he drives the trash truck in Low Creek, Joe Otten says Boone done shaved his beard and his whole head too. Said he lookin' like a goddamn light bulb. That's all I got fer ya. The rest was all about Cletus."

"That's fine, Cecil. Thanks," Mason said, satisfied that he had engaged the services of an accomplished gossiper to get an idea of Boone Correl's current whereabouts.

Mason had a beer with Cecil and Jeff before returning to his house to do some laundry and go to bed. He picked up the small package that Melanie had pressed into his hand as she was leaving a few days before. It was a note wrapped around three keys with the words, "Please be careful" written on it. His thoughts began to turn to Boone Correl, the man who had harassed him for months, who had tried to cheat his own brother, who had likely killed his brother's girlfriend, who might have killed Cletus Wellman, who tried to kill Melanie, who threatened a little girl, who eluded law enforcement in broad daylight, and he realized that no one understood just how dangerous Boone was except Melanie and himself. Jake Morrow's crusade against Boone Correl was borne of his concern for his own son and other young people exposed to a burgeoning presence of drugs. But, as Jake had so poignantly pointed out, Mason's issue with Boone was personal, and Jake's preposterous idea of checking out an RV like a couple of schoolboys suddenly made some relative sense. He sat for a while, staring at the television as anger once again seemed to rise slowly within him as he considered the possibility of being added to Boone's list of accomplishments while law enforcement shrugged and looked away.

"So when do you want to go?" he asked when Jake answered the phone.

"Sunday. I'll pick you up. Around noon, okay?"

He woke early on Sunday but skipped his usual run, instead driving to Melanie's house with the three keys that she had given him. One key was for her car. Another opened the front door, and he entered the house. The third key, as he suspected, opened the closet that contained Boone's guns where the hunting rifle and one handgun were missing. He replaced the front and back door locks and installed the doorbell cameras that he had purchased at Lowes. The trail camera was mounted on a tree facing the driveway. He registered the cameras to his iPhone and returned to the closet, pondering the remaining handgun. Having only fired a gun once on a trip to a shooting range with Jack Murray, he had some trepidation as he retrieved the gun and two magazine clips from the closet shelf and returned home. He put the gun and clips in a kitchen cabinet.

Jake arrived at noon, and they had lunch at Harley's before driving to a place beyond the Low Creek business district where a severely potholed road crossed an abandoned railroad track and faded into a wooded area and then a clearing. A half dozen houses were located on a narrow lane at the foot of a rise that rose sharply to the mountains beyond. Four of the houses were clearly abandoned and deteriorated, but the two nearest the road appeared to be inhabited and in relatively livable condition. Boone's truck and a late model SUV were parked in front of the houses. An older model RV was parked behind the houses and partially obscured by trees. Jake drove past the lane and turned into an area close to the road but out of sight of the houses where he stopped the car and produced a wireless ear bud. He had Mason call him and leave the call open.

"I'm going to move in and take some pictures," Jake said as he exited the car. "You follow about twenty yards behind me and let me know if anyone is around who could spot me."

Mason followed Jake's instruction, feeling a bit foolish as he watched Jake enter the overgrowth near the houses. He found a position behind two trees where he could see the two inhabited houses and Jake, who was taking pictures of the houses and RV. After a few minutes, the front door opened on the nearest house, and two men emerged as Jake disappeared behind the houses. Both men were wearing hats, and Mason was unsure of which one was Boone. After quietly warning Jake on the phone, he moved in closer but still obscured and saw the tattoos that he recognized on Boone's arm. He photographed the two with his phone as they were unloading boxes from Boone's truck and moved to another location to get a better view of Jake's position. Jake was crawling behind the RV as Mason noticed a large poorly dressed woman sitting on the back porch of the second house, who, despite her thick glasses, seemed to be watching something in the woods beyond the RV. Mason whispered a warning to Jake to stay low behind the RV. The woman continued to stare for a couple of minutes and then slowly nodded forward, giving Jake the opportunity to back away from the RV and move in the direction of the car.

When they got to the car, Mason was amazed at the photographs that Jake had taken. Apparently, the house was the meth lab, and the RV was a traveling dispensary. The kitchen counter was filled with labeled containers including acetone, anhydrous ammonia, hydrochloric acid, and lithium, as well as other paraphernalia, which, Mason thought, explained the acidic odor that prevailed about the place. The RV was neatly arranged, with cabinets and a countertop stocked with small packages. About twenty feet from where the RV was parked was a ditch partially filled with spent containers, rubber gloves, stained cloths and other items that were partially buried.

"What now?" Mason asked. "Do you take these to the county sheriff?"

"I wish," Jake said as he started the car, "this is still Low Creek. I'll take them to the police, but that chief will probably throw me out if I mention Boone Correl again."

"Then don't mention him. It's a meth lab in his jurisdiction. He can't ignore these. I'll go with you and maybe we can get some credibility."

The duty sergeant asked them to have a seat in the interrogation room where they waited for a fairly long time before he returned with a yellow pad of paper. "Sorry for the wait," he said. "Our weekend dispatcher went home sick, so we had to call in our regular lady, and there is a lot going on today. We're a small department, but we still need someone calling the shots."

An officer came into the room and showed something to the sergeant who excused himself and left the room, promising to be right back. Mason stood up and looked through an observation window to the dispatch office. "Aren't these usually one-way mirrors?" he asked Jake.

"On television, I guess. I don't spend much time getting interrogated in Low Creek," Jake answered as he paged through the images on his phone.

Mason continued watching the individual in the dispatch office, noting some vague familiarity that couldn't quite identify. He sat down and Jimbo strangely came into his thoughts. There was something that Jimbo had said, something that the woman in the dispatch office seemed to bring into his recollection. And it suddenly emerged: "Got her a sweet ass, don't she?"

Mason stood up suddenly and tapped Jake on the shoulder. "Let's get out of here," he said looking back at the window.

"What?" Jake responded without getting up.

"The dispatcher is Lilly Jane's sister," Mason said in a whisper as he leaned to Jake's ear. "That's why Boone is always gone when you blow the whistle."

"How the hell do you know that?"

"Jimbo. Let's go."

They walked out quickly, Mason telling the sergeant that they would return later. Neither Mason or Jake spoke until they got into the car. "What the hell was that all about?" Jake asked as he pulled the car onto Miner Street.

Mason explained how Jimbo had pointed out the sister as she entered Lilly Jane's house. "You said that when you got the police to visit Lilly Jane's house, Boone or the RV were missing. Doesn't it make sense that someone inside might be making a phone call to warn Boone that the police were coming?" Mason did not mention his suspicion that the same thing probably happened when Melanie made her disclosures to the Low Creek Police Department that Boone tried to kill her to prevent any further exposure.

"So now what?" Jake asked as they pulled onto the highway.

"I don't know. Neither one of us actually knows the processes here. A woman whom I know filed a complaint for assault against Boone in Wells County, so there is probably a warrant for him there. Like I said, I don't exactly know how things work, but maybe you can go to the sheriff's office. I have to admit, though, they've been fairly indifferent to my own complaints about Boone Correl."

Jake shrugged his shoulders. "Okay. Maybe that's still a good idea. I have him marked in a half dozen places in the county—"

"Wait," Mason interjected, "I have a better idea." He pulled the iPhone from his pocket and began to enter something. "I'm sending you the contact information for the DEA special agent who handles this area. I'm pretty sure he would be interested, and he already has some knowledge of Boone." Mason realized that his hands were shaking as he worked the iPhone. "I can tell you, though, I've had enough of this detective work. Show your pictures to someone who knows what they're doing and let them handle Boone."

It was late afternoon when Jake dropped Mason off at his house. Cecil was sitting alone on his porch. Jeff and the truck were gone, apparently on an errand. Mason took part of a six-pack and sat next to Cecil, saying nothing at first.

"You look to be flustered," Cecil said as he wiped his mouth. "Whatcha been up to?"

Mason looked across the road to his driveway and then toward the bend in the road that led to Melanie's house. "I've been snooping on Boone Correl," he said, still looking at the road. "Cecil, how many cars have passed by here today?"

"Just the one what picked you up this afternoon and Verna Lee on her way to work. I ain't been here all day, but there ain't much reason for folks to drive here what don't live here or visitin' folks what live here."

"Where's your cell phone?" Mason asked, now turning toward him. He was referring to the phone that Sally had given him that he never received a bill for.

"In the house. I don't make many calls."

"Do you mind if I go and get it?" Mason said as he stood up.

"Don't mind. It's on the bench in there. Ya need to make a call?"

Mason returned with the phone and showed Cecil the speed dial number that he had entered into it. "If you see a car go by here, you just enter zero one, and the phone will automatically call me. Will you do that for me?"

Cecil looked carefully at Mason as he nodded. "Sure. Ya got your tail in the wind. Ya got some kinda worries over there?"

"Just interested in who comes by here."

"Ya mean like that Boone Correl feller?"

"Yeah. I'd like to know if he comes back," Mason said as he stood up to leave.

* * *

The television news included an update on Cletus Wellman's death, with a statement that the Kingsport police were receiving dozens of tips for the ongoing investigation, but no suspect had been identified at the time. The murder was still considered to be a professional hit.

Mason changed the station to a college football game and made a light supper as the day's events began to play out in his mind. The obsession that Cletus and Jake Morrow had over Boone Correl seemed to be affecting him as well, and he felt frustrated with the man's elusiveness. He finished his supper and sat back to watch the game, feeling spent and exhausted as his iPhone announced a call. Cecil was brief and to the point: "Car pullin' into your driveway now."

It was dusk, and the motion-controlled light above the front porch came on despite the adequacy of remaining daylight. Mason felt a rush of adrenaline as he stood up and set the iPhone on a table next to the door. He thought of the handgun that was in the kitchen cabinet as he peered through the front window behind a curtain, fully expecting to see Boone's truck. But the car entering was a white Ford Explorer. He felt some relief as two men got out of the car and walked up to the porch, probably having something to do with the prison construction. A union representative had recently asked to speak with him off-site. Perhaps that was it. But as he opened the door, it suddenly flew past him, causing his hand to fly backward, and he lost his balance briefly as something hard pressed against his forehead. He stood, frozen with the realization that the object against his head was a gun as he tried to focus on the man holding it. The man spoke, almost shouting in what Mason recognized was Spanish, "Llevanos a la prision!"

XXVI

"Please excuse my friend here," the other man on the porch said as he raised the arm of the man holding the gun. The gun holder stepped back but continued to point the gun at Mason. "They're all pretty much like that. A really rude bunch, most of 'em. I guess it's from lousy bringinupin'. Ain't like folks from around here." He was a thin man in his early thirties, wearing a John Deere hat and sleeveless shirt with a tattoo that said, "Only You" on one arm and a picture of an angel on the other. His eyes narrowed as he looked sharply at Mason. "Where's your car key?"

Mason was frozen, feeling unable to move or talk at first as he eyed the gun being held on him, then answering, "On the table next to me." He stepped back as the gun holder raised the weapon higher and the other stuck his head in the doorway to see the table.

"Git it," the man said, and Mason reached for the keys and his iPhone. "Leave the phone. You ain't needin' to make no calls up there." He motioned for Mason to come out. "Go get in the car. You and Chico are going up to your prison."

Chico said nothing as he got into Mason's Jeep on the passenger side. Mason got in and started the car as Chico stuck the gun into his ribs on the right side. As he pulled out of the driveway, Mason noticed that there was a passenger in the back seat of the Explorer, which the other man was entering on the driver side.

300

The drive to the prison site seemed to take an eternity. Mason's hands were shaking visibly as he pulled up to BJ's position and opened the window. BJ entered a code into the gate operator and stuck his head into the car window as the gate opened. "Workin' late again, Tuck? You sure put in some odd hours. Ain't you got better things to do on a Sunday night?" He handed a sign-in sheet on a clipboard to Mason, only then noticing Chico. "How're y'all doin', buddy. Tuck crackin' the whip on you as well?"

The gun rose as Chico pushed Mason's face back with his left hand and fired quickly before BJ could react. BJ stood erect for a second, with a round hole appearing on his forehead, and stumbled backward before falling fully on his back. The Explorer suddenly appeared and drove past them into the prison site. Chico said, "Seguir," as he stuck the gun back into Mason's ribs. They followed the Explorer, which drove directly to the electrician's staging area.

Both men exited the Explorer, and Chico indicated for Mason to hand him the car key and then get out of his car. They followed the other two into a designated warehouse section where some large light fixtures were stacked. The back seat passenger of the Explorer carried a tool belt and approached the fixtures, saying something to the Explorer driver who began to remove the cardboard packaging from the fixtures. The tool carrier immediately removed the ballast housing from one of the fixtures, revealing a number of small plastic containers full of a white substance. As he continued to open more fixtures, the other man apparently finished opening the relevant boxes and started to load the containers into one of them. He dragged the containers to Mason's Jeep and stacked them neatly into the rear compartment. They continued loading until all the revealed containers were in the car.

As Mason watched, he suspected that he was going to be instructed to transport the drugs somewhere. Why else would they be loaded into his car? Chico, who had been sitting on a box while holding the gun on Mason, stood and said something in Spanish as he approached the man with the tools, who looked at the other man and said, "What the hell is he saying?"

The other man laughed and replied, "He said 'Carlotta says thanks.'"

Chico fired three shots into the man's chest and stood over him as the man fell to his knees first and then forward. Mason saw an opportunity and took it, turning and running out of the warehouse into the now-darkened site. Another shot was fired, and he kept running, avoiding the dim security lights and staying in the shadows of the nearest cell pod. He heard Chico running behind him and shouting in Spanish. The man behind Chico was then shouting to Chico, "Let him go, you stupid spick. He ain't shit to us, and we're out of time." Mason looked back from behind a scaffold and saw Chico standing in the open, holding the gun. Chico then ran to Mason's car that was now running with the other man behind the wheel. They drove out quickly through the front gate and then down the access road at a high rate of speed.

Mason walked slowly back to the warehouse, still unsure that the two in his car would not return. The man who Chico shot was lying face down in a deep pool of blood, obviously having bled to death. He walked slowly to the front gate, where BJ was lying motionless on his back, the gravel surface around his head glistening with blood in the glare from the security light above him. Mason sat on BJ's chair and tried to control his trembling and figure out what he should do. BJ would probably have a cell phone in his pocket. He caught his breath and walked to BJ. There was no phone in his front pockets, so he tried to turn the body over, which proved to be more difficult than he expected.

A siren suddenly sounded in the distance, coming closer as he knelt to get a better grip on BJ's body. As he turned the body over, a patrol car appeared with blue lights glaring and stopped at the gate. An officer got out of the car, but Mason could not see him well through the blinding blue light. Mason knelt motionless as the officer approached with his gun drawn, shouting, "Lock your hands behind your head. Now!"

Mason complied with the order, saying, "It's Tucker Mason, Deputy Setty. I believe you know me by now."

It was 4:00 a.m. when a deputy drove Mason to his house after hours of questioning by sheriff's deputies and DEA agents. His car

302

had been found but was impounded for investigation. He lay on the bed still fully clothed, the previous day's events swirling in his mind as he fell into a deep sleep, awakening with a start two hours later. After some coffee and a shower, he called Casey for a ride to the prison site, which was already in disruption with the police investigation. The electricians' and painters' staging areas were isolated by yellow police tape, and the spot where Chico had shot the man with the tools the night before was enclosed by canvas screens. A black bag carrying BJ's body was being loaded into a coroner's vehicle. A tow truck operator was loading the Ford Explorer onto his flatbed. Two sheriff's deputies and several DEA agents were milling about the site. Small groups of electricians and painters were assembled near the staging areas.

The electrician foreman was waiting in the trailer. "How long is this going to go on?" he asked Casey but included Mason in his glare. "I'm going to have to send thirty men home with show-up time recorded. Who's going to pay for that?"

"We can't tell you anything yet, Ray, because we don't know anything yet," Mason said as Casey opened the door and motioned for the man to leave. "Let us get caught up here, and we'll get you some answers." The foreman left, muttering to himself as he descended the stairs.

"I'll see if I can find out anything," Casey said as he walked out of the trailer.

Mason entered his office where he left a voice mail for Leo and began typing a report for the home office, regretting the inevitable visit from Ed Ronan. Jamie came in and announced Special Agent Willis, who followed and sat across from Mason's desk.

"Mr. Mason," Willis said slowly, "I want to thank you for all your cooperation. I'm sorry you had to go through all this."

"How long will all of this go on?" Mason asked as he indicated at the activity outside the window.

Willis pointed to two FBI agents who were talking to Sheriff Miller. "It's up to them now," he said. "We're finished here. It's a murder scene now."

"Did you catch them?" Mason asked.

"No."

Mason leaned across the desk. "You mean that with all this crap going on for the last two weeks, you let them get away? What about the drugs?"

"Probably on the street in West Virginia by now. We don't always win, Mr. Mason."

"So they just got away with it? Isn't there any effort to catch them?"

"There is. But the Mexican is likely already out of the country. The other guy probably is as well, since he didn't seem to care about being identified."

"How the hell could they get away with it? I thought you had this all wired."

Willis shook his head. "It was extremely well planned. The stuff apparently came packed in light fixtures. We think it was leaving a little at a time in a private vehicle. The man who was shot over there was on the electrician's crew. He probably took a little at a time in his lunch pail or, for that matter, in any container that worked. You said last night that they seemed to be in a hurry. Well, the sheriff's department tracks response times. It took twenty-four minutes for the first deputy to get here from the time his dispatcher got the call. Our theory is that they rehearsed that response time. They knew that our cameras would trigger a call to the sheriff and us. So add five minutes for that to take place and deduct six for the time it would take to clear the access road, and they had about twenty-three minutes to get in and get out without running into the deputy. Even the day of the week was considered. Sunday night would be an unlikely time for anyone to be at the site."

"Why did they take my car?" Mason asked.

"That's a common approach. They probably parked a car by the highway and stole the Explorer. Then they left the Explorer, which might have been reported stolen and on a watch sheet, and took your car, which wasn't reported since you were here either dead or, as it turned out, alive but with no communication. The deputies found your car on the ramp to the highway."

"So all along we thought it was the painters."

"It was," Willis continued, "until Arturo Fuentes died. Our guess is that this electrician took over once Fuentes was out of the picture. We're still pretty sure heroin was coming through here in paint cans when Fuentes was alive."

"So for all we know, someone else could take over."

Willis shrugged and stood up. "I wouldn't rule it out, but I doubt it with all this attention. Thanks again, Mr. Mason, for your cooperation."

Jamie entered as Willis was leaving. "Tuck, there are two reporters here wanting a statement."

"Tell them I will have a statement later this morning," Mason said, knowing that a conversation with Ed Ronan had to come first. He looked out the window and saw a WEMT sound truck coming onto the site.

Mason finished his report and sent it to Leo. Ronan called at ten o'clock, and Mason prepared a statement for the press and had Jamie summon the reporters, which numbered about ten at this point. He addressed them from the trailer porch.

The afternoon was spent meeting with trade foremen and union officials while Casey worked with the investigators to permit some production in the affected areas. By four o'clock the site was relatively back to normal, and Casey reported that full production was possible the next day. Mason had Casey drive him to the airport to rent a car, which he drove to the sheriff's office for more questioning, this time including FBI agents. When they were finished, Lieutenant Melker came into the interrogation room.

"Any sign of Boone Correl lately, Mr. Mason?" Melker said as he sat at the table.

"I saw him yesterday in Low Creek."

"Where in Low Creek?"

"A meth lab at the edge of town."

Lieutenant Melker looked surprised. "Did you tell anyone?"

"Low Creek police don't seem to be very interested in him," Mason said. "I believe Jake Morrow has some information for you, though."

"I'll contact Jake," Melker said. "We would like to get Correl in here for questioning."

"Is this regarding Melanie McCall?"

"Well, that and a few other things. As far as Ms. McCall is concerned, I'm not sure how the judge is looking at it. From Deputy Setty's report, it looks like a drug addict on a bed with, perhaps, Boone Correl. Maybe something went wrong, and he took his toys and left. Maybe she just got pissed at him and accused him of something more."

Mason stood up, obviously disgusted with the law enforcement system in Wells County and Low Creek. "Call Jake, Lieutenant. I don't expect to see any more of Boone Correl, but I will certainly let you know if I do."

The sandwich that Mason had made was only half eaten when he lay across the bed and fell asleep, sleeping deeply for several hours and then fitfully dreaming intensely and waking with the troubling events of the past two days heavy on his mind. The images of BJ's broken face and the gun pointed at himself emerged and seemed to float about his consciousness as he tried to sort through the events and make sense of what he had experienced. As the sun was rising, he sat up in his bed, and the realization hit him with brutal clarity that it was not over. An armed Boone Correl was still out there. Jake Morrow's information might ignite some interest from law enforcement, but Boone was fully aware of Mason's relationship with Melanie and the fact that he could be a liability, and Mason knew well how Boone handled liabilities. He looked out of the bedroom window at the gap in foliage that indicated the path connecting the former Correl homes and realized that he was terribly afraid. He got up and went into the kitchen where he opened a cabinet and retrieved Boone's handgun, placing it on the counter. He dressed for a run and stepped out the front door but stopped and returned to the kitchen to set the alarm, which ticked a countdown as he walked out. When he returned, he picked up the gun and returned it to the cabinet, realizing that he didn't know how to use it.

XXVII

The light fixtures that had been impounded were returned on Thursday, but Mason's car was still being investigated. There was apparently no progress in identifying Chico and the other man, and the FBI agent in charge did not seem too hopeful. Leo had offered to take over for a few days to let Mason recover from the traumatic experience, but Mason refused, stating that he would rather keep busy. Ed Ronan had arrived on Tuesday and spent the day Wednesday meeting with the sheriff's deputies and the FBI agents, as well as members of the press who gave reports at a place near the front gate that Ronan designated along with a warning about photographs. The security company that managed the front gate canceled their contract in light of BJ's murder, but Jamie was able to find another without missing a night. Ronan left on Thursday, and the site, in Mason's opinion, was in good order by Friday, all things considered.

Jake Morrow called midmorning on Friday. The DEA and Wells County sheriff could not acknowledge his photographs due to privacy laws. But they acted on his tips and raided the house in Low Creek. Two people were arrested although neither was Boone Correl. The sheriff's office noted the locations where the RV had been located and said that a warrant had been issued for Boone on another matter. "Anyway," Jake said, "it appears that we are closing in on Boone."

Two FBI agents arrived as Mason was finishing the lunch that Jamie had picked up for him. He had tried to stay in the trailer as much as possible to avoid the group of reporters who were invading the site since Ed Ronan was no longer there to rein them in. The agents reviewed Mason's statements and explained some of the progress in the case. The Explorer had been hijacked in West Virginia, and the owner had been shot to death. The man who accompanied Chico was identified as Jack Dauper, a former convict currently wanted for drug trafficking in five states and a known operative for Carlotta. Prior to this incident, he had last been spotted in Cincinnati, but his current whereabouts were unknown. The electrician who was killed was from Knoxville and had no prior convictions but went through two sponsored drug rehab programs to keep his job. Those who worked with him apparently were not aware of his drug activities and considered him to be a good journeymen electrician.

It was three o'clock when Mason's iPhone signaled movement on Melanie's driveway from the trail cam that Mason had installed earlier. It had happened before, so he did not experience the adrenaline rush that occurred when a deer and raccoon had passed earlier. But this time it was Boone Correl in the SUV that Mason had seen at the meth lab in Low Creek. He must have abandoned the truck once he was made aware of the warrant for him. A very bald Boone exited the car, and Mason lost sight of him until the doorbell camera picked him up. As Boone was attempting to enter his key in the door lock, Mason called the Wells County sheriff's office and asked for Lieutenant Melker, who was not in, but returned his call from the field within minutes. He gave Melker Melanie's address and told him that Boone was there and also described the SUV that he was driving, along with the partial license number that the trail cam had captured. Melker thanked him and stated that a deputy would be dispatched immediately.

In the meantime, Boone had been attempting to open the back door and was checking around Melanie's car. Twenty-three minutes, Mason thought, as he considered the amount of time it would take for the deputy to arrive if he was coming from the sheriff's office.

He needed to keep Boone there long enough for the deputy to catch him. He spoke through the speaker on the doorbell camera. "They're gone, Boone, and she's selling the house."

Boone stood back and looked around the porch. Mason continued, "Pretty sloppy work on your part, Boone. They've moved away and won't be back. We know that you tried to kill them. We also know that you killed JoAnn and probably killed Cletus Wellman." Boone continued to look around, obviously confused by the voice coming from apparently nowhere. "Oh," Mason continued, "and I found the money and diamonds. I guess I could retire on it, but I think I'll give it to the folks who own the house. It's the right thing to do, don't you think? I want to do that before Thane shows up. I don't think he's as stupid as you are."

Boone backed up on the porch and missed the first step, falling back to the driveway. He stood up, looked around, and ran to the SUV, which he started and turned around, leaving the driveway at a high rate of speed. Deputy Setty arrived about five minutes later and approached the house. Mason spoke to him through the doorbell, "He turned right onto the road, probably headed to the highway." Setty returned to his car, speaking into his communication device as he sped out of the driveway.

Mason finished the day and left the site, stopping to meet with the new guard, a retired police officer named Joe-Bob Benson. After picking up some groceries at Kroger's, he drove home, feeling somewhat safer, now that the police were actually going after Boone Correl. Cecil called as he turned onto Two Stump Road. "Car goin' into your driveway. Look like Sally's." Mason turned into his driveway slowly, felling considerably relieved as he recognized Sally's Cadillac. Sally was sitting in one of the wicker chairs on the front porch, wearing a light sweater.

"Startin' to get a chill in the air," she said as Mason approached the porch.

"Would you rather go inside?" Mason asked.

"No. I like it out here," she answered and then said in a lower voice, "I knew you, of all people, wouldn't say it."

"No, Sally, I won't say it. By now you've heard it enough."

Sally sighed and looked at the darkening forest. "Partnership didn't want to continue with this project without Cletus, so they are selling to an outfit in Knoxville. The new group wants to speed up the construction and use this house for a headquarters. You have a month-to-month rental agreement, so you'll be getting a thirty-day notice fairly soon. Marty Cavalone's place is available if you want it. It's right next to Casey's. I just wanted to tell you in person, so you didn't feel mistreated."

"I appreciate that, Sally," Mason said. "What about Cecil and Jeff?"

"I don't know," Sally said, shrugging. "I imagine Cecil will get the same letter 'cause they intend to clear and survey that side so they can start excavation in the spring. Cecil has money in the bank from the purchase of his property that he can use to buy a place. I know he wants to stay on Bright's Mountain, but we'll probably have to move them to Low Creek."

"The house around the bend from mine is going up for sale," Mason said quickly.

"Really?"

"Really. I know the lady who owns it. I'll have someone get in touch with you."

"Please do."

Sally continued to look at the trees briefly, and then to Mason. "Remember how I told you once that I knew exactly how you felt when your wife died?"

"Yes."

She paused and looked back at the trees. "I was just out of high school, workin' the vegetable stand with Mama. There was some road construction going on. He was a little older than I was but big and strong and good lookin'. I could see him out there, all sunburnt and glorious while he was handlin' tools and machinery. He came to the stand on his lunch breaks and bought peaches and such but mostly just talked with me. When the project was finished, he would come down from Knoxville, that's where he lived, just to see me. I married him a week before my nineteenth birthday and moved to Knoxville with him. We was so happy, him workin' outside like he loved to, and

I had a part-time job in a grocery store. His mother helped with the babies, and I loved her too. It was good times."

Mason looked at the yard and back to Sally. "What happened?" he asked softly.

Again, a pause. "He fell off the back of a truck and hit his head. He lived for a few days but died, and the doctors said that was a blessing. He had enough insurance to bury him, but I wasn't makin' enough to keep the rent up and feed my boys, and his mother was so put out about her son she couldn't help no more. So I moved back to Virginia and stayed with my sister Emma for a bit until I found a job. I was as a file clerk at Cletus's dealership."

"And you met Cletus."

"Not at first. The person who hired me brought me in to meet him, and he, in his usual Cletus fashion, shook my hand without really looking at me and welcomed me aboard. I hardly ever saw him much after that, with him rushing around and in and out so much and me just trying to do a good job."

"What changed?"

"Sadie, she was my boss, liked me and gave me a lot of help. When I told her I was havin' a hard time findin' a place to live with no credit and a new job, she told me to just leave it to her. Well, a week later she told me to go see Cletus in his office. He offered me a job managing one of his apartment buildings in Kingsport, just on Sadie's recommendation. A rent-free apartment and day care for my boys was included in my salary. I told him that I really didn't know anything about managing property, and he just said few people in his organization knew what they was doing when they got there, and I would figure it out. Well, makin' a long story short, he was happy with my efforts and kept givin' me more responsibility and before ya know it, I was handlin' most of his apartment properties and helpin' out at the Holiday Inn Express. Cletus and I was workin' real close every day and got real familiar with each other. When he asked me to marry him, I thought I was the luckiest girl in the world."

"That's a great story." Mason said.

"He was a good man and a good husband, Tucker," she said quietly.

"As was your first husband."

Sally looked out at the darkening tree line. "Yes, he was a good man and a good husband and a good father," she said as she continued to look away, pausing and then with a sigh. "I was so in love with that man."

"You still are."

The breeze increased and was noticeably cooler as Sally continued to look away. "Yes," she said, almost whispering.

They sat quietly for a while before Mason asked, "What now, Sally?"

"Well, I guess just keep goin'. Cletus had me cashed out of everything except the inn. That's pretty much my home base now, so I guess I'll just keep doin' what I do. I'm goin' to be a grandma in the spring, so I guess I'll be spendin' some time in Lexington."

"A grandma!" Mason said quickly, his voice somewhat louder now. "Congratulations."

Sally smiled and looked up at him as she spoke. "Thank you. What about you, Tucker, what with all the misery you've been through? Casey has kept me up to date."

"I still have a prison to build."

"Dumb question."

"You're welcome to stay for dinner," Mason said, ignoring the comment, "if you can handle my cooking."

Sally began to stand. "I would love to," she replied as she reached for her purse on the floor, "but I got a houseful of well-wishers what are probably startin' to worry about me."

Mason walked her to her car and opened the driver side door for her, "Thanks, Sally," he said as she stepped past him.

"You take care, Tucker Mason," she responded as she touched his cheek and slid into the car. She backed up and drove out on the driveway as Mason watched her taillights disappear in the trees and brush. He stood there for some time, a certain sense of peacefulness coming about him until he heard the crash of glass behind him.

Bolting through the open front door, he could see a hand reaching through the broken pane of the rear entry door to the kitchen for the latch that held it. He quickly pushed the table into the door, which heaved against his force and then closed. Mason continued to hold the table in place with one hand while reaching back for the panic button on the alarm panel. Still a few inches short of the panel, he released his grip on the table to reach it, but the door then flew open, crashing the table into him and pushing him into the front room. Regaining his balance, Mason shoved the table again, this time catching Boone's arm and leg part way in the door as it opened briefly as before and then heaved again, this time the table knocking Mason to the floor of the front room. Getting back onto his feet, he could see Boone in the kitchen, looking wild and emaciated, the gun in his hand appearing unusually large and awkwardly held as he worked his way around the table in the small kitchen. Mason now ran through the open front door, slamming it behind him, and ran into the front lot. But the motion-controlled lights came on, causing him to return to the porch to avoid exposure in the yard. He grabbed the iron chair and propped a leg into the door handset just as Boone attempted to open the door.

"Open the fuckin' door," Boone called from inside. "You can't get away."

Mason pressed against the wall by the door to assess his next move but then realized the uncanny strength that Boone had demonstrated with the kitchen door, and he began to run toward the shop. He opened the shop door but changed his mind as the iron chair exploded, and the front door began to swing open. Mason ran around the shop and stopped, terrified and unsure of what his next move would be as he heard footsteps inside the shop, stumbling perhaps. A light came on in the shop, and he ran back around to its door, closing it and turning the latch with trembling fingers.

He ran back to the front door of the house with the intent of hitting the alarm panic button as Boone thumped loudly against the shop door. His iPhone and car key appeared suddenly on the small table near the front door, and he grabbed them instinctively as he moved toward the kitchen. The table had been shoved against the wall where the alarm console was located. He pulled the table away from the wall and shoved it toward the back door just as Boone kicked the door open, and he, once again, caught Boone's arm with the door. Boone shouted something as he crashed the door open, and the table came sliding into Mason's leg. Mason then upended the table and shoved it into Boone who fell backward through the doorway.

Running through the front room, Mason reached the car that he had rented since his was impounded as the outdoor lights again reacted to his motion. The sharp report from Boone's gun seemed to coincide with the exploding side view mirror, and Mason dove to the bruising gravel of the lot, crawling around the rear of the car before running headlong into the thick brush that lined the lot and driveway. Thrashing about in the darkness of the forest, he could faintly see that the front outdoor lights were still on, indicating Boone's presence in the lot. But then the rear yard lights came on, and Mason realized that Boone was shadowing him as he stumbled noisily through the thicket in the impermeable darkness. He stopped, hearing nothing but his own breathing, waiting for Boone's next move and feeling hopelessly trapped. The front lights extinguished suddenly as he tried to regain his composure. Then after what seemed like an interminable amount of time, the rear lights turned off as well.

Mason slowly dropped to his knees, wondering whether Boone had simply given up or was carefully threading his way through old familiar territory toward Mason's undetermined location. Slowly and deliberately, Mason began to retrieve the iPhone from his back pocket, but the device fell from his trembling hand into the thick undergrowth below. Being already entangled in the rotting vines and briars, he turned on his knees and fell head first into the undergrowth, inflicting deep scratches on his hands and face. He lifted himself carefully, still listening for Boone in the darkness, and began to feel around the musty ground cover for the iPhone for some time until it lit up at his touch. Concerned that the lighted phone could serve as a beacon for Boone, who might be seeking him out from some familiar pathway, he placed his hand over the screen until it again went dark. Then, his left hand still offering cover, he pressed the lock button five times quickly with the fingers of his right hand to get to the swipe screen, not wanting to risk any noise from entering numbers. But the expected SOS slider did not appear, and he then noticed the absence of bars in the upper right corner, indicating the unavailability of service. Clearly, there was no chance of making a call without getting back to the house and the satellite Wi-Fi. He picked up the phone and returned it to his pocket.

The rear yard lights came on again suddenly. A smaller, brighter light was bobbing through the trees, and Mason realized that Boone had a flashlight, probably one he retrieved from the kitchen drawer, and was entering the forest, undoubtedly through the entrance from Mason's yard into the paths beyond that Boone knew so well. Mason watched the light as it appeared and disappeared among the trees as Boone was obviously searching for him. The light continued to move, diminishing in its intensity as Mason realized that Boone was actually moving away from him on a path. He stood up slowly and began to feel his way through the entangled brush toward the location where he first saw Boone's flashlight. He continued slowly, the briars scratching his arms and small branches whipping his face until he found himself in a clearing that, after feeling around, he knew was apparently a path. Walking blindly and feeling his way with his hands until he could see moonlight amid the trees, and he realized that he was approaching his backyard, which was dark now except for the moonlight that reflected softly about the house.

Boone's light was no longer visible as Mason stepped out of the thicket but remained close to the forest wall in order to avoid activating the motion sensor that would bring the lights on. Moving slowly, he worked his way along the perimeter until he got to the point where the shop was directly between him and the house and neither motion detector could reach him. He walked directly to the side of the shop and around it as he held close to the shop wall and then the end wall of the house until he got to the back door, which was still open. Turning off the kitchen lights, he tried again the 911 call, which went through, and he stated his predicament to the dispatcher. The closest chair scooted a bit as his full weight fell into it, attempting in vain to stop the convulsive trembling of his body. "Twenty-three minutes," he said softly as he looked across the backyard. "Just stay in there for twenty-three minutes, you son of a bitch."

He sat quietly in the darkened kitchen, the trembling slowly receding as he began to catch his breath and collect his thoughts. The house and yard seemed surreal in the extreme quiet that prevailed, and even the subtle, usually inaudible hum from the refrigerator was pervasive and foreign to him. Carefully scanning the periphery of the backyard, he realized an overwhelming sense of anxiety over the possibility that Boone would show up first, that the deputies were busy chasing drug deals. "Are you in a safe place now, sir?" the 911 dispatcher had asked. The concept of a safe place now seemed almost comical as he considered the maniac searching for him in the woods. Boone must have approached the house from the side as Mason had to avoid the motion sensor above the back door. Undoubtedly there while Sally was on the front porch, Boone must have waited for Sally to leave, standing there noting that the alarm console had a green light indicating that it was disarmed, taking that perfect opportunity while Mason was alone in the front lot to break through the locked door. *A safe place*, Mason thought. *Probably not.*

He sat for what seemed a long time but was actually eight minutes by his watch when the backyard was suddenly illuminated, and he could see Boone, hunched forward but moving quickly toward the house. Mason's first inclination was to run through the front room, but that would only reenact the previous scene, and the sheriff's deputy might show up with him and Boone deep in the woods again. Trying in vain to avoid panicking, he stood up quickly and opened the cabinet that held Boone's other handgun. He withdrew the gun with a shaking hand, attempting desperately to recall the basics that Jack Murray had given him on his single one-hour excursion to a shooting range. Boone appeared in the doorway, his gun preceding him ominously as he entered the dark kitchen. Mason held his gun in one hand and then clapped his other hand to it as Jack had shown him. He could hear something from Boone's direction, like scratching at the wall, and he realized that Boone was searching for a light switch as the overhead fixture came on, the sudden brightness temporarily blinding him as he pointed the gun toward Boone, who was searching the room with his gun leading. As Boone turned in his direction, Mason raised his gun and squeezed the trigger, which would not move. The safety was on! He pressed a small button on the side of the gun and quickly raised it again as the magazine slid out and clanged noisily on the floor. Boone lowered his gun briefly but raised it again with a hoarse laugh.

It was some time before Mason could actually recall exactly what happened next, realizing that it was nothing more than Boone's head snapping sharply forward as the gun discharged, and the crash of dishes as the shot struck the cabinet directly behind Mason. Boone then disappeared from the door amid some commotion and what sounded like a loud grunt, followed by a shuffling sound and then silence. Mason dropped the useless gun from his hand and stood still briefly, frozen by fear and uncertainty. He stepped forward gradually getting the courage to move to the door. He hesitated briefly and then stuck his head cautiously through the opening, seeing Boone first, sprawled facedown on the ground near the shop, bleeding from his head and his arm twisted unnaturally behind him.

Jeff stood motionless over Boone, looking up briefly but not directly at Mason. "Cecil tol' me to keep a eye on ya," he said as he returned his gaze to Boone.

Mason retrieved the buzzing iPhone from his pocket and answered Cecil's call. "Deputy car turnin' into your driveway," Cecil said as the front lights came on.

Mason sat on the porch stoop, again trying to regain his composure. He could hear the car door slam in front of the house as he watched Boone writhing on the ground in front of him. He looked up at Jeff and asked, "What did you do to his arm?" Deputy Setty appeared around the corner of the house and stopped, looking confused.

Jeff answered, still looking at Boone, "Yanked it."

Mason looked at Setty and then back to Jeff. "You figure it's broke?" he asked while ignoring Setty.

Jeff continued staring at Boone as he shuffled a bit and said, "Yup."

XXVIII

June 2018

Barbara Jean Canter graduated at the top of her class at Lower Merion High school near Philadelphia with a full scholarship to Drexel University where she majored in clinical psychology. Post-graduate studies included a master's degree in forensic psychology from New York University followed by a PhD at Drexel. Currently tenured at Drexel, her résumé included numerous awards for research papers, two textbooks, speaking engagements, several lecture series, and a controversial testimony before Congress. At least, that is what Mason learned from the bio that he skimmed when she requested an interview to support her research of the effects of certain drugs on mentally ill specimens, which was funded by the National Institute of Mental Health. Her request was regarding the behavior of Boone Correl as witnessed by Mason. Boone, she stated in her request, was an important study, having been previously diagnosed with bipolar disorder and addicted to methamphetamine. "A colleague of mine is working directly with Mr. Correl to determine a more accurate diagnosis," she said as she finished the interview. "His intense drug use makes it more challenging, but we have a preliminary diagnosis of schizoaffective disorder, which is a kind of intermediate state between schizophrenia, which is mental illness, and bipolar mood disorder. He's a fascinating subject."

"For you maybe. For me, he's a crazy bastard who pestered me and tried to kill me," Mason said, regretting his tone.

"Understood. I want to thank you for your time, Mr. Mason," Dr. Canter said as she closed her laptop and stood to leave. "I realize that you are preparing to travel, so I won't take up any more of it. Where are you headed to your next project?"

"Actually, I'm taking some time off first," Mason said as he walked her to the door of the tiny office that he had commandeered near the prison commissary. "Then I have a facility to build at West Virginia University."

"One of my favorite places to visit," she said as she cleaned her glasses, "It's beautiful there. Did you find a place to live yet?"

"I've rented an apartment in Morgantown. My things are already there, so I'm ready to move in."

"Do you specialize in building in the mountains?" Dr. Canter asked with a subtle smile.

Mason was amused by her sense of humor. "Well, somebody apparently thinks I do." He continued to walk with her down the narrow hallway where a guard waited to escort her. "How about you? Headed back to Philly?"

"Not yet. I still have a prostitute in Low Creek to speak with."

"Prostitute?"

She smiled and shrugged her shoulders. "Yes, she's number four. It's not unusual. Meth addicts are often sexually hyperactive."

"Is it hereditary?" Mason asked.

"Is what hereditary?" Dr. Canter returned, apparently surprised by the question.

"Mental illness like Boone Correl's problems."

"There are specific genetic ties identified to certain conditions like schizophrenia. Bipolar mood disorder is a bit more complex, although several studies indicate the possibility. Why do you ask?"

"Just curious," Mason replied as he looked at his watch.

"Any travel planned in your time off?" she asked as he signed the guard's clipboard.

"Just a stop in Columbus, Ohio."

"Not exactly a vacation spot," she said as she removed the visitor tag from her lapel. "Nice town though. I've lectured at Ohio State several times and, of course, spent a day interviewing Melanie McCall about Boone Correl. Something special there?"

"Yeah," Mason said as he held the door for her and the guard. "Something special."

As Mason returned to the commissary office, he noticed a young woman escorted by a guard, and he realized that, after consistently rejecting her requests, he had finally given in to her persistence and offered her a quick interview depending on his schedule and the drop-dead necessity to begin the six-hour drive to Columbus. Letta Claire Doset's résumé was somewhat different from Dr. Canter's: graduated from Robert C. Byrd High School somewhere in West Virginia and earned an associate degree in journalism. She was currently on assignment for the Bristol Herald Courier. Unlikely as she was, her honest and unassuming approach was refreshing compared to the arrogant cable and network news producers and newspaper writers that he had turned down so consistently over the past several months. She appeared as he expected, a small freckled woman with red hair pulled to a soft knot and loose-fitting suit that clearly did not come from the Nordstrom's where Katherine shopped in Denver. Nevertheless, she had an air of self-confidence that Mason found convincing as he led her into the commissary office.

"I really appreciate you giving me some time, Mr. Mason," Letta said as she took a spiral notebook from a canvas bag. "You're kind of a local hero, abducted by the cartel and escaping and catching Boone Correl like you did."

"I really didn't catch him. Jeff Trapp caught him. I was hiding in the kitchen."

"More fun for my peers to say it was you. I tried to interview Mr. Trapp. Believe me, you're the better choice."

Mason admired her dry humor and began to become less annoyed by her presence. "What specifically can I help you with, Ms. Doset?"

The interview went on for over two hours, well beyond the time he had expected to allot as Letta prefaced with the evolution of drug abuse in Appalachia, emphasizing in a charming regional accent the disastrous prevalence of methamphetamine that gave way to opioid painkillers, which she said was proliferated by greedy drug companies, and eventually heroin, which was aggressively marketed through operatives of a Mexican cartel, graciously acknowledging Mason's personal experience. She then established her premise for the questions that she would ask about the drug transfer through the prison site. Her questions were well prepared and pointed, though respectful, and Mason answered as completely as possible despite his latent embarrassment about the matter.

"So," Mason said as she finished writing in her notebook. "If opioid pills and heroin are the drugs of choice, why didn't Boone Correl deal in them?"

Letta smiled. "That's a good question. There still is a strong market for meth, especially with young people. Boone Correl had a traveling dispensary that he would park near schools and businesses, kind of like a meth food truck. The police in Low Creek raided it last year and arrested his ex-wife and her sister. It was all over the news."

"I purposely don't follow the news around here anymore. I'd just as soon put all the bad stuff behind me. But I heard the van was impounded, and Lilly Jane and her sister were arrested," Mason said, recalling his conversations with Jake Morrow. "Once again, Boone slithered away. The man was amazing in his ability to be invisible."

"Well," Letta said as she returned the notebook to the canvas bag. "His luck appears to have finally run out. I've been assigned to follow his case, or cases, as it were. Wells County has already convicted him of multiple drug charges and rape, not to mention his assault on you. There are also drugs and a murder charge in Low Creek and drugs in Mt. Pleasant, Pound, and Norton. And then there's an extradition request from Ohio. Apparently, they think he killed a business partner and dumped his body in the Ohio River near Huntington."

"What about Cletus Wellman?"

Letta shook her head and said, almost reluctantly, "Two prostitutes brought Correl into the emergency room in Huntington the night before Mr. Wellman was killed. He apparently overdosed while having happy with them. Anyway, the speculation was that the cartel had Wellman killed as an example. Tell me that don't give you the chills."

As she stood to leave, Letta thanked Mason for his time and said, "It's important to get this out, what's happened here. I keep thinking things will get better, but it just seems to be getting worse. Goodness, I actually saw a woman smoking heroin in front of a gas station on my way here."

"I can see that this is very personal for you, Ms. Doset," Mason said as he stood to escort her out.

Letta looked at him intensely with deep blue eyes that carried a sadness beyond her confident demeanor. "My older brother was high on meth when he wrecked his truck and died. My younger brother died of an overdose of fentanyl last year. My best friend in high school died of an overdose of heroin in January. Yes, Mr. Mason, it's very personal."

Mason put some things from the desk into a small backpack that he grabbed along with his computer case and walked with her to the guard station. Letta asked, "Are you leaving for good now?"

"Yes. I'm going to put these in my car and pay my respects to the warden. Then I have a six-hour drive that I'm not looking forward to."

She looked around the hallway. "When do the prisoners show up?"

"They'll start arriving in about three weeks, a group at a time. A lot of training and preparation has yet to occur. Good luck on your feature, Ms. Doset."

Christina, the warden's assistant, said, "He's on a call. Please have a seat, Mr. Mason. I'm sure he will want to see you before you leave." Mason sat in the anteroom and was checking his e-mails on his iPhone when a man dressed in clerical clothing came in and asked if a Mr. Mason had been there. Christina politely said, "He's right there, Reverend," indicating Mason to him across the room.

"I'm so glad that I found you, sir," the reverend said. "I'm an assistant chaplain here. Mind if I sit?"

The reverend sat, saying, "I've been tryin' to catch up with you. They told me you was leavin', and I was afraid that I wouldn't be able to see you before you left."

"What can I do for you, Reverend?" Mason asked, trying to conceal his annoyance.

"Just this, sir." He pulled a hardbound book from a small shopping bag. "I'm stayin' at the Comfort Inn in Low Creek until my permanent place is ready. Anyway, I met a lady there who is well known around these parts, and we had a nice conversation, me bein' from around here as well. So when I told her that I was assigned to this prison, she asked if I would deliver this book to you since she wouldn't have time to see you herself."

Mason took the book and studied its cover. It was titled *The Mountain Movers: The Inevitable Transformation of the Appalachian Region*. The author was Leanna Dell. Inside the cover was a short inscription above her signature, "Keep building our world, my friend."

Christina interrupted, saying, "The warden can see you now, Mr. Mason." Mason stood and thanked the reverend as he entered the warden's office.

It was almost noon when Mason emerged to the pedestrian gate system. He was about to request access to the second swing gate when he noticed the group of about thirty reporters assembled in the parking lot for the scheduled press tour. Having no desire to encounter the group, many of which had been trying aggressively to interview him for months, he returned through the primary gate and entered the administration building where he stood in a hallway to wait for the tour to begin and hopefully move in a different direction. As he peered through the small window on the door, he felt a hand clasp firmly on his shoulder. Mason turned to see the reverend whom he had met in the warden's office earlier.

"I think you might be doin' the same thing I'm doin'," the reverend said as he adjusted a strap on his backpack. "The warden suggested that we should leave before the tour started, but I didn't get out in time." He opened the door and walked out slowly, looking carefully around the corner toward the pedestrian gates. "Not yet," he said as he removed his back pack. He indicated the chapel door. "Let's sit in here for a bit."

Once they were seated, Mason struggled for common ground for conversation, finally saying, "Chaplain in a prison. Seems like a tough job. Were you assigned or did you volunteer?"

The reverend smiled and replied, "Assistant chaplain. It's my first assignment. I was only ordained last month. And yes, I volunteered."

"Well," Mason continued, "I admire your dedication. I'm not sure I could do that."

The reverend smiled again and looked directly at Mason. "I found Jesus in a prison cell, Mr. Mason," he said with an air of humility. "It just seems appropriate that I help others find Him in the same place."

There was a shuffling sound outside and the reverend stepped out into the hall. He returned, grabbing his back pack. "I think we're good now. They're headin' toward the pods first."

They walked through the pedestrian gates into the visitor parking lot. The reverend stopped and turned toward the buildings. "It must be a real feelin' of accomplishment to see such a massive project completed."

Mason stopped with him. "Yeah," he said as he also looked back at the buildings, briefly realizing that he was standing on the spot where his office trailer had been, and he remembered the first day that he walked onto the site amid the dust and noise. There was a slight twinge of regret as he recalled the progress of the job that led to some anxiety to get started on the next project. "It's a good feeling to finish, but I'm a builder, so I'm ready for the next project."

"Another prison?" the reverend asked.

"No. College dormitory."

The reverend continued to look at the buildings. "Such a magnificent facility. Sad to think of what it is intended for. In a few weeks, the state of Virginia will send its worst offenders here, and it won't seem so magnificent anymore." He looked away and scanned the adjacent mountains and valleys that the prison overlooked. "I was born here, but I still think it's the most beautiful place on earth. It's a shame so many of us did so much to spoil it." He stood quietly for a moment, shaking his head. "Twenty-five percent of the people comin' to this facility are here because of drugs. Of those comin' from this part of the state, it's more like forty percent. That shame, that curse will remain forever."

"Well," Mason said as he turned to the reverend, hoping to break out of the awkwardness of the reverend's rather esoteric emotional moment, "I need to get on the road. It's been a pleasure meeting you, Reverend. Thanks again for your help."

The reverend seemed to recover quickly and smiled again. "The pleasure was mine, sir. If you're ever in the area again, please look me up."

"I will," Mason said, realizing the remoteness of any possibility that he would ever return to Wells County, Virginia. "By the way, Reverend," Mason said as he shook the reverend's hand, "I didn't get your name."

"My apologies," the reverend said, still gripping Mason's hand, "Thane Correl."

Mason stood still for a brief time, hoping that the shock of hearing that name was not evident on his face as Thane Correl turned and walked across the parking lot. Getting into his own car, Mason looked once more across the lot at the prison buildings and the breathtaking Blue Ridge panorama beyond. He drove slowly through the vehicle checkpoint and onto the access road, which was considerably less forbidding than it had been during construction with new landscaping and freshly seeded berms. He turned onto Mills Hollow Road, passing the drive that led to the house that Aaron Correl built, now occupied by Cecil Beckman and Jeff, and Ansel Newley's house that he himself had once occupied. That house was fully visible from the road now that the trees and brush were cleared. The gravel drive and lot had been replaced by a fully paved surface where several vehicles were parked in lined spaces. Across the road was the scarred earth where the excavators had removed Cecil's house within a few hours and graded for the surveyors who were signaling one another in the early afternoon warmth. He turned onto Two Stump Road, looking down the part of Mills Hollow Road that led to Verna Lee Capron's iconic home. A sense of resignation began to emerge within him as he descended to the highway, not so much in disappointment but in acquiescence to the reality of his existence. Entering the highway, he recalled the feeling of conflict that he had sensed when he had first arrived, realizing now that the struggle was his, that the renewal of life that he pursued was only the progression of his life as it is. The events of the past year were now part of the history that will and must endure, to be held in the distant echoes of time as each step relieves the one behind, yet the footprint remains, perhaps fading in dimension but never disappearing.

Bright's Mountain slowly dissolved in the rearview mirror as Wells County, Virginia, slid past, consumed in its richness and poverty, its sickness unseen as the parasite of drug abuse continued to snare its vulnerable populace. Mason turned onto US 23 North and looked ahead.

About the Author

Thomas A. Brigger writes from his home in Waynesville, Ohio, where he draws on his experience as a builder, traveler, entrepreneur, and observer of the variants of American life.

CPSIA information can be obtained
at www.ICGtesting.com
Printed in the USA
FSHW011639121020
74673FS